'I really enjoyed *Crow Moc*[...] mythology was fascinating, [...] honest, and McKerrow deals with mo[...] [...]sues or race and g[...] with a deceptively light touch. I am officially converted to the idea of paganism . . .' **Louise O'Neill, author of *Only Ever Yours***

'*Crow Moon* completely blew me away and I'll be recommending it to absolutely everyone this year. PHENOMENAL!'
Lucy Powrie, Queen of Contemporary blog

'A gripping tale of passion, intrigue, myth and magic.'
Sara Crowe, author of *Bone Jack*

'There's a classic, John Wyndham feel to *Crow Moon* . . . both a pacy read and something that will stand the test of time.'
Louie Stowell, author of the *Big Book of Big Monsters*

'*Crow Moon* is a wonderful mix of gripping storyline, laugh out loud humour, some great characters and a generous helping of magic . . . There's a lot of authentic pagan magic and tarot knowledge woven into the novel which adds an edge of authenticity to this amazing story.'
Lu Hersey, author of *Deep Water*

'Gripping, magical and uncompromising, this is a really fantastic debut from Anna McKerrow, and a proper page-turner – I devoured it.'
Stefan Mohamed, author of *Bitter Sixteen*

'There are lots of twists and turns within the story, of choosing which path is the right one to follow, and of consequences as a result of not always doing what is necessarily right.' **Miss Chapters Reviews**

'I loved it because it was different. I loved it because I was able to escape into this world. I could laugh, love and live an alternate life cleverly built up to leave me with mixed emotions and a feeling of wanting more . . . [...] ou forever.'

Also by Anna McKerrow

Crow Moon

RED WITCH

ANNA MCKERROW

Quercus

Quercus Children's Books

First published in Great Britain in 2016 by Hodder and Stoughton

1 3 5 7 9 10 8 6 4 2

Text copyright © Anna McKerrow, 2016

The moral right of the author has been asserted.

A CIP catalogue record for this book
is available from the British Library.

ISBN 978 1 78429 130 3

Printed and bound in Great Britain
by Clays

The paper and board used in this book are
made from wood from responsible sources.

MIX
Paper from
responsible sources
FSC® C104740

Quercus Children's Books
An imprint of
Hachette Children's Group
Part of Hodder and Stoughton
Carmelite House
50 Victoria Embankment
London EC4Y 0DZ

An Hachette UK Company
www.hachette.co.uk

www.hachettechildrens.co.uk

For Ally

*To this end he should visualize the Isle of Avalon as it
was . . . He should see the tor crowned with the circle of
standing stones of the sun-worship, below it, the Well of
the Wisdom of Merlin.*

From *Glastonbury: Avalon of the Heart*, Dion Fortune

Scrawled at the back of Demelza Hawthorne's 2046 Greenworld Journal

Writing this while I remember it. Dreamed vividly of Tom from years ago. I was nine, he was twelve. Already tall, already filling out like a man – broad-shouldered, tanned, an apprentice gardener on the weekends. His clothes always covered in mud, dirt under his fingernails. He was in our garden helping Mum with the vegetable patch. Saba flicking peas at him out of the pod, bored, until he smiled and flicked one back at her, chasing her around the garden, Saba squealing in pleasure. My fury as she raced past me, dark blonde plaits flying, cheeks flushed. They were ignoring me; I wasn't allowed in their game. It didn't occur to me to just join in. And then he stopped running, picked an orange courgette flower from the sprawling plant in the sunniest spot of the vegetable patch and came and tucked it behind my ear. 'That's what you get if you're not a bloody little heller,' he called over to Saba, but he smiled at me. 'You could learn a lot from Melz,' he shouted to her, and she shouted back something Saba-like: 'Yeah – how to be boring.' And then Mum told them both to stop running around like idiots and help her and the dream faded. He picked the flower for me and not her, and it was then that I fell in love with him. Woke up reaching for the long-dead flower against my ear. Heart breaks all over again.

Chapter One

For what we do for good or for ill, shall be returned
to us threefold.

From *Tenets and Sayings of the Greenworld*

Glastonbury, the first habitable Redworld town across
the border, is peppered with badly maintained shanty
houses: paint flaking, windows broken.

Taunton was a deserted shell; I ran through it when
I saw the rotting bodies on the roads.

That was two days ago. Since then I've been
travelling the bleak land between Redworld towns and
villages; the forests have been burned, even the peat-
rich bogs have been dug out and emptied. The Redworld
has burned everything it can for fuel.

The first night hid me, the darkness spiriting me
through the mile-deep barbed-wire Greenworld border
patrolled by dogs and soldiers.

The dark hid me from other dangers too, even on

the Greenworld side: the gangs that roam the land between our witch-run, peaceful, agrarian covensteads. The gangs that attacked my village just weeks ago.

But here, electric street lights flicker, their tired blue light unable to stay on for long. I stick to the walls and the shadows, but the town is dead at this hour: no people, only a strange indistinct rumble of voices that gets louder and quiets again. I pass things labelled CHECKPOINT at the end of some streets, but they're all deserted: thick scratched glass boxes covered in burn marks, scorches and bullet holes. Occasionally I get a flash of a face peering at me from a window, or see someone standing at a door, but they turn away, as if from contagion.

In Glastonbury litter is the most consistent feature of the ragged streets apart from the spray-painted slogans on the crumbling walls. I touch one nervously as I walk past it, feeling the anger and hopelessness in its jagged letters written quickly and in fear.

TAKE THE POWER BACK.

Why did I come here?

The street lights come on suddenly for a whole minute or so, and Glastonbury Tor looms above me. I gaze up at it, the wide softly sloping hill rising out of the shadows behind the town like a warning. It's one of the most important spiritual sites in Britain, something I thought I'd never see. A place of prayer and hermits.

Ancient priestesses once trod a processional path round it, honouring their earth goddess. Medieval devotees of our Greenworld goddess Brighid worshipped here.

And the tor keeps a secret, something that only Greenworld witches like me know. An energy portal exists here: a vast channel of power between this world and the afterlife, between life and death, where all souls must journey when they are born and die. Anticipation snags in my stomach; all of us that are witches have dreamed of entering that portal on this most holy of holy places, but none of us – at least, none of us first-generation Greenworld kids – ever thought we would see it for real.

This is why I came here when I ran away from Tintagel, my home; this is what I saw in a dream after wandering in the no man's land outside our village, numb with grief for the boy I loved, for over a week. I hid in the old sea caves down the coast from Tintagel Head, the ones witches have used for magic since the first woman threw shells and stones into the wet sand and read their portents. I drank the spring water that trickled down the mossed cliffs and ate seaweed and cockles, and one night my goddess sent me a dream of the soft green contours of the tor, lit by the full moon. It was the obvious choice. This is my pilgrimage. This is my herstory: this is my land.

If you have to leave your home, an eco-pagan community governed by witches, because you broke the rules – if you cursed the ones that killed the boy you loved; if you refused to regret it – the most forgotten holy place in the Redworld is a good place to come to. Maybe here I can be forgotten and be reborn in its natural, vital power.

The lights go out again and the tor reverts to a shadow upon a shadow, an inert power in the dark.

In the dark I hear a sudden roar of voices, and a comet of ferocious light explodes into the street.

I run towards the noise rather than away from it, drawn by the energy, as if it is sucking me and everyone else in its radius towards it: the light, the explosion, the commotion. The need for other people – faces, voices, bodies – after being on my own for so long, is sudden and intense.

The street peters out and I run on to a thick bank of grass and into a crowd. Above us, like crumbling prayers, are the ruins of a large building. People sit on the bare stone, cheering, shouting, and hundreds throng the sunken grass lawn between the old walls. I jostle my way into the crowd, curious, and see that they surround a large grey vehicle. It's the first time I've seen one of this kind, and indeed any kind of working vehicle; there are a few burnt-out old wrecks at home, but no one uses a car. There's no need for one; we stay in our covensteads, or we walk.

This vehicle is big, the size of four of the wrecks my childhood friend Ennor fiddles with at home, trying to work his mechanical magic, so they might one day roar into life. On this one there are no windows, and there are bars round the outside. Bright lights bore into the crowd from the front of it; the people shield their eyes, but stand their ground.

Out of nowhere a bottle flies past my shoulder and breaks on to the van, and there's another *whomp* of light, and this time heat hits us all. I turn my head away just in time to avoid flying glass and mutter under my breath in shock. *By Brighid*. I look at the expressions of the people around me: all ages, dressed differently to what I'm used to, but not dressed well — mends, tears, worn-out-looking trousers and thin jumpers. There is no fear in their faces; instead of turning away from the flying glass, they lean towards the van and the fire that begins to leap around its tyres and the grass.

'Take the power back!' an older woman standing next to me shouts, and the crowd cheers and takes it up as a chant — *Take the power back, take the power back* — their fists in the air.

'No more patrols!' she shouts again, her cries echoing around the shaky stone structure like an incantation. I look up at the walls. This must be Glastonbury Abbey — an attempt by the priests of a male god to stamp his presence on the Goddess's land, their ruins at the foot of Her verdant hill. Although patriarchal religions are of no interest to us in the Greenworld, we still know what they did. *Know your enemy*, Mum used to joke, but she also told us that the monks and the nuns prayed to St Bridget here. Their version of our goddess, Brighid.

The crowd pushes me further away from the van

and towards the remains of a smaller building – an old chapel perhaps. From here I see a phalanx of grey vans driving slowly across the grass and into the crowd. I watch as they herd the Redworlders away from the road.

A hand grabs mine and I turn to find myself looking at a girl about my age: dark brown skin, brown eyes, long honey-coloured hair. Her make-up far surpasses anything I've ever seen; rainbow colours explode round her eyes, and her eyelashes are unnaturally long.

'Come on. They're going to start firing,' the girl says, and she pulls me away, towards the road.

She starts to run, and I follow instinctively, though I don't understand until I hear the sudden cracks and retorts of gunfire behind me. There is a cold silence, and then screaming. Lots of people screaming. In my mind's eye I'm suddenly back at Tintagel, my village, running across a field I'll never cross in time to get to the boy I'll never kiss. Again I see the blood seep through his shirt and the confused expression on his face.

The day I lost Tom; the day I lost hope.

'Come *on*. We can't be here when they come back,' she says, and hands me a scarf hurriedly. 'Hold this over your mouth. Otherwise the gas'll choke you,' she shouts, and I hold it uselessly, standing and looking back, not really believing what I'm seeing. I watch as a grey cloud expands into the night air, but when I taste it I understand. The acid burns my throat, and the haze obscures the uniformed people climbing out of the vans.

I can only just see their plain black garments and the masks over their faces.

I turn and run, clamping the scarf over my mouth, following the girl's retreating back, because I have no one else to follow.

Take the power back.

I inhale what power tastes like here: rough and rotten. The people may want to take it back, but it's nothing I ever want to sample again.

Chapter Two

There are five things which a learned man should
  know about each day . . .
The day of the solar month, the age of the moon,
  the running of the sea,
Without folly, the day of the week, of pure festivals,
  according to right clarity.

From the *Saltair na Rann*

As I follow her away from the riot and deeper into
Glastonbury, new noises drive glassy shards into my
brain. Screaming, honking and a strange oscillating
noise I can't identify. The girl looks around warily when
she hears it.

'Police,' she says over her shoulder at me, as if I
know. 'Must be heading to the abbey. Took their time as
usual.'

Now that we're further away from the crowd, she
slows down.

'Police?' I ask. In which case, who were the people in the grey vans? 'What's that noise, by Brighid?'

She frowns at me. 'What are you, deaf? Sirens. Police sirens. From their cars.'

I only know one kind of siren. One of my favourite myths, in fact. Crows with women's faces. Once revered for their beautiful song, the sirens got too powerful and were sent to live on a desolate island. And the way that men wrote it in their his-story was that they were evil – luring poor, innocent sailors to their deaths on the rocks for sport. It's always the women's fault in the old stories. The moral of this story is supposed to be women are dangerous – resist their power.

I like to think though that the sirens were praising the beauty of the ocean. And it wasn't their fault that some sailors passed by and wouldn't take no for an answer. What were they supposed to do?

Where I'm from, in the Greenworld, we honour the goddess of the ocean and the land; we honour the songs the sirens sang. In the Greenworld, powerful women, magical women, are everywhere. In the Greenworld, powerful women – witches – are in charge.

In the Greenworld, the moral of the sirens' tale is: enjoy the company of your sisters and learn how to defend yourself.

But I don't want to be a Greenworld witch any more, always serving, always doing what I'm told. I've been wandering, hiding, on the run for two weeks now from my home – what used to be the English counties of

Devon and Cornwall. I left in disgrace, even though I'm a witch, a leader of the community: Demelza Hawthorne, daughter of Lowenna Hawthorne, head witch of the Greenworld.

We stop running when we reach a place where the pavement is thronged with young people – mostly dressed in black, but dressed well, unlike the people at the riot. Their hair is straw yellow, black or blue or pink, and is mostly short and shaved or part plaited, part coiffured or standing up in huge peaks down the middle of an otherwise shaved head. I look down at my dress – at its faded black cloth, at the ribbons I sewed on it to pull the waist in.

These kids have a kind of angular and spiky style; some of them wear hats like I've seen in his-story books: tallish, with a brim. Other kids wear heavy-looking boots, T-shirts patched with pins, baggy trousers with straps over their shoulders. I think they're called braces. Maya, my mum's friend, the village artist, liked to use his-storical dress in her pictures sometimes so we'd look at those old fashion books together. Forbidden books that Maya had stashed away in a cupboard. Saved from the burnings.

I'm not so sure about the other villages, but in Tintagel, in the early days when Saba and I were kids, there was a lot of fire. Planned fire that eradicated anti-Greenworld propaganda. Newspapers from the Redworld that some people still had stashed away; books that weren't Greenworld-approved. Most books were kept — anything deemed worthy, like mythology, literature and art and herstory and culture, and helpful books on nature or crafts or horticulture, basic manual mechanics, that kind of thing. But many were destroyed, and there were some things that burned on the book pyres that I wanted to see again: glossy clothing catalogues, books about computers, other religious books — *Disgraceful patriarchal structures designed to repress women and oppress the masses*, Mum and her cronies cried, tossing them into the flames. At the time it was a great game, hurling as many books into the fire as they could.

Maya was the one that taught me to draw, on those long rainy days when Mum was busy being head witch, and me, Saba and Maya's son, Ennor, were climbing the walls, wanting to get out, run to the beach, climb trees, do anything but be indoors. I was especially good at portraits. *You must reach inside the person. Draw their real self, their true self*, she told me, looking over my shoulder. *Yes. That's it. You understand.* And I did understand. And when I decided to curse the ones that killed Tom, the boy I loved, I knew exactly how to do it.

I poured all my grief, all my hate and resentment into those pictures, scratching the thick dry charcoal across the paper in heavy strokes as their faces material-ized among the blackness: Skye and Bali, the sister and brother who had betrayed us all. They had pretended to be our friends, but spied on us for Roach and the gangs, intent on destroying our village and taking control of our energy portal on Tintagel Head. Roach had some

13

idea about being able to make portals into usable everyday energy sources – *the idea!* That something so holy, so sacred, ephemeral, could power lamps and ovens and kettles.

When the portraits were done, after the battle, I sat at the edge of the village, at the boundary where no one ever goes, and chanted the words of death over their faces. I sat under the waxing moon, the full Crow Moon just past and the cycle dying again, lessening once more, pulling the ends of dead things into it like a wheel. I chanted words I took from an old grimoire, dusty and leather-bound, which Mum keeps hidden in her room. A book we seldom use – only in dire emergencies, when love and healing aren't enough. A book of curses, patterns, glyphs – old magic for timeless desires: fertility, wealth, happiness, but also revenge, lust, death. A remnant of folk magic from a different time, but still full of power.

And as I chanted, I rubbed Tom's blood over their likenesses, from the fragment of his shirt I tore from his lifeless body. I spat on to it to make it blood again; mixing my body with his so in some way we were together after death: together in a curse made of icy black fury and a grief that suffocated me like cold salt sand in my mouth and nose.

My hands stray to my neck, where the blood-stained cloth is folded up within a wooden locket. Tom had carved it for my twin sister, Saba, but she never wore it: a heart, hollowed out and engraved with the triskele on

14

the front. It was too rough for her, not polished enough. She complained it chafed her skin.

So when I ran away I took it. One empty heart for another.

I tore Bali and Skye's portraits into pieces, imagining their bodies and souls being torn too, in whatever way the Gods saw best. And as I tore, with my teeth, with my nails, I felt the hand of the Morrigan, my goddess, on my shoulder, like a cautioning mother. The Morrigan: ancient one of land and tides and the moon, of battle and death and sex and the cauldron of birth. *Do you really want this?* She had asked. *Because it can't bring him back, my priestess. It will condemn you more than it does them.*

But I was too angry to listen. So angry, in fact, that I didn't scatter the scraps of their torn faces to the wind, there at the boundary. I folded up the scraps and put them in my pocket, liking the feel of them, liking the way I could crush them with my fingertips as I dug my heels into the hard March earth when I walked, imagining it was Bali and Skye's fragile skulls that I ground into broken shards.

When I got home, I slid up to my room, avoiding everyone. It wasn't hard; everyone was wrapped up in their own grief and exhaustion, or tending the wounded from the battle. The battle for Tintagel, for the portal, which we won, but only just.

I took the balled-up crushed pieces of paper from my pocket and folded them inside the heart locket, keeping them with me, keeping them locked away. That

15

way my energy would continue to stream through the magic: my grieving, furious heart would power it on and on, so they would suffer as I did, by Brighid and by the great and terrible Goddess Morrigan. Bleed as I did. Burn as I did.

I don't want forgiveness. That's why I didn't stay. Even going to another Greenworld village would have been pointless. They all know Mum, Lowenna Hawthorne, head witch of the Greenworld. They'd have shipped me home or taken it upon themselves to 'help' me reverse the curse.

But I don't want it reversed. I want Skye and Bali to burn.

Gunfire snaps me back into the present, on the street, my hand on the locket, before I realize the sound is more regular than gunfire, and too loud. It has a rhythm. Is it music? It's not any kind of music I've heard before, if it is. I look around me, unsure of what to do next.

'Haven't seen you here before. New around?' the girl shouts over the thumping noise, which I realize is coming from the building next to us. She adjusts her black hat atop that long honey-blonde hair and her eyes flash curiously at me.

I try not to sound like too much of an outsider but it's hard to know how to do it, to be like them.

'Yes. I just got here. Thanks for . . . before.'

'S'all right. They do it every now and again, the proles. They just don't learn.'

16

'The proles?'

'Proletariat. The poor, you know.' She smiles at a few people as they pass. Everyone here seems very cheerful, considering there was just a full-scale riot just streets away, considering that people were shot at, maybe killed. 'They want more power, they say. But if that's what they do, just make trouble, then I'm glad they don't have any. I mean, what do they even need it for? I'm glad the security forces are there. More responsive than the police anyway.' She hugs her coat round her.

'But . . . I think those vans . . . the people inside them? They shot into the crowd,' I say.

She rolls her eyes. 'Oh God, don't tell me you're one of those bleeding-heart liberals. They know what they're doing. They don't fire at anyone; it's just warning shots into the air. And anyway, if someone's stupid enough to go to a protest, then they deserve what they get. They know what the forces do.'

'What were you doing there, then? If you didn't go there to protest?'

'It was on my way. It's fun to watch them in action, the forces. As long as you know when to get out of the way.'

I don't feel like I can argue with her, because what do I know? But I know what I felt, and I know what I heard. People screaming. People choking. Gunshots.

'Why did you help me? Pull me away?' I shout over the noise in the street.

'Dunno. You've got a weird vibe about you. Different.'

She looks me over, and I hope I don't look too dishevelled, but I know that my boots are caked in mud and I've been wearing the same dress since I left Tintagel. I washed in streams as best I could on the way, but that only goes so far. This girl is very polished-looking, with a dramatically made-up face and a glittering short dress like I've never seen before. I try not to stare at the material, but I can't work out what it is. Metal sewn into cotton? But it doesn't look like cotton even. Something stretchier.

'We get people from the Greenworld here sometimes. They have your look. Handmade. Knackered. Am I right?' the girl asks.

I clear my throat, the burning sensation still there from the gas. I have a hard time making small talk with anyone at the best of times, let alone when I haven't slept on anything except rock and moss for two weeks.

'Ummm. Yes. I'm from Tintagel. Cornwall.'

The girl looks at me. 'Cornwall?'

'Ummm . . . yes. Blessed Be.'

I give her the standard Greenworld greeting and wait for – I don't know what, maybe an insult. I think maybe she'll just walk away, but she raises her eyebrows. 'Wow.'

I look at the tips of my shoes where the scuffed brown leather becomes a dim bluish-orange every time the street light flashes on. Maybe this was a mistake. 'Wow, good, or wow . . .?' I run a hand through my henna-black hair. I look at the crowd whooping, laughing, singing. These are people my age, and I need food and water and somewhere to sleep. If I'm going to stay in the Redworld, I'll need friends.

'Wow, good. Look, d'you want to come in with me? It's cool if you do, but you might need to . . . smarten yourself up a bit,' she says not unkindly.

'OK.' I'm worried that the thumping noise inside will burst my eardrums, but I don't think I have a choice.

I reach into my red-wool-stitched bag and pull out my treasured kohl pencil. There's no make-up in the Greenworld as a rule, apart from whatever you can make yourself from plants, but Omar brought this one back across the border for me last year. It's strange, but with it I feel powerful, like it erases the uncertainties. What's more definite than a thick black line? If it was good enough for Cleopatra, then it's good enough for me.

Peering into my cracked pocket mirror I apply a dark line round my eyes. I ruffle my hair until it looks bigger and wilder, and surreptitiously pull the ribbons at my waist tighter.

Magic isn't much help with quick fix makeovers, despite all Mum's oat face masks and herbal tinctures. Sleep, good food and clean water are the basics for looking good, and I've been without all of them for the past two weeks. Maybe if I'd been less racked with grief I could have worked on visualizing myself as a beautiful, desirable witch before I got here. But I didn't, and it probably takes more self-confidence than I possess. You have to really believe, deep down, for that kind of thing to work. And I don't.

I look at the girl for approval.

'Better.' She smiles, and takes off her glittery cardigan. 'Put this on.'

She helps me with the buttons and her fingers brush my locket as she does. I pull back without meaning to. She gives me an odd look but says nothing.

Inside, it's as dark as outside, lit by round orange-red lights, their thick glass scratched and in some cases smashed, showing the raw wires inside. Huddles of people in their teens, twenties maybe, undulate to a feverish beat in the middle of what looks like a kind of warehouse. People line the walls under them, kissing, groping, grinding.

The girl shakes her head. 'Don't look, Greenworld. It's not cool,' she says, smiling, and guides me to a long makeshift bar — planks resting on top of metal crates. I stand next to her self-consciously, looking at the boys and girls, girls and girls, boys and boys kissing.

Seeing them makes me think of Tom lying on a willow raft. Buried at sea, set adrift on the waves. How much I wanted to kiss him, to feel his fingers in my hair, to touch his muscled chest. How much I wanted to be seen by him, desired, wanted. But I was never enough, never girly enough: not pretty, not confident.

The girl picks up a tall green bottle from the bar, pulls the cork out with her teeth and pours two cups of red liquid. She drops a couple of coins in a tin. I try not to peer at the coins before they fall from her fingers: money. Metal tokens you exchange for goods. I knew it existed but I've never really seen it. Handing a metal cup to me, she clinks it against hers.

'Welcome . . . I can't call you Greenworld. What's your name?'

'Demelza. Melz, really.'

She stares at me for a long moment. 'Demelza?'

'Yes. Demelza Hawthorne. Is everything OK?'

There's a long uncomfortable silence.

'Yeah . . . sure. Fine. I'm Ceridwen. Ceri.'

'Hi.'

'Yes! Hi! OK . . . well, let's toast . . . hmmm. What should we toast? Intercultural exchange? Escape? Freedom?'

I look around me. 'Freedom. That sounds good,' I shout. 'Blessed Be.'

She clinks my glass. 'Yeah, Blessed Be. Right on.'

We drink. The wine is sweet and heavy, stronger than our homemade ones. I think of Proserpine who ate six pomegranate seeds, and was imprisoned in the underworld. I think of the folk tales Mum used to tell us round the fireside, of wayfarers who stumbled into faeryland and were stuck there because they ate and drank the faery food.

I drink again. If I am lost in faeryland, here in the Redworld, I don't care.

Chapter Three

Community, family, covenstead. All one and none separate.

> From *Tenets and Sayings of the Greenworld*

'So how long have you been here?' Ceri asks as she tops up my glass.

'I just got here.'

'Tonight?'

'Yes.'

'Wow. So you came across the border? Isn't that hard?'

I take another gulp of the wine, which makes my head spin a little.

'Not great, but I managed.' It was terrifying, but I won't tell her that.

'You did pretty well. I've seen people covered in cuts, bites, everything, coming through there.'

'So there are other Greenworlders here? In Glastonbury?'

Ceri taps a blue fingernail on her cup. 'Not right now. Just now and again someone comes through. It's like the O.K. Corral here.'

I look at her blankly.

'You know. The cowboy town. Like, the first place you get to in the desert. First place you could get a hot meal.'

'Oh. Right.' I ignore the inference that the Greenworld isn't included in civilization. 'So do you know much about us?'

'A bit. Mostly what we got told at school. But me and the girls have looked into it a bit more, y'know. You could say we're Greenworld sympathizers.'

'What do you get told at school? About us?' I shout over the music.

'Basically that you're all dangerous hippies.' She smiles and shrugs. 'Sorry. I mean, I know you're not. Dangerous that is.'

I'm not surprised. I was only little when the government gave in to the early Greenworlders' pressure groups. They let the pagans and anti-capitalists have Devon and Cornwall on the condition that we shut up and stop trying to cause trouble in the Redworld. Whatever. We don't care as long as they leave us alone.

'But it's important. What we do in the Greenworld. What they do, I mean.' I correct myself. I am not of the Greenworld any more after all. 'Present an alternative to the way you live. Ecologically. Spiritually. Politically.'

Ceri holds out her hands to pacify me, eyes wide

with concern. 'Oh, I know. I mean, don't be offended. I think it's cool. I mean, the fact that you have witches in control of everything down there. That's amazing.'

She grins and beckons me closer. I lean in.

'I'm a witch too.'

I look at her, amazed. A Redworld witch? I didn't know they existed. Perhaps there is hope for the Redworld. Perhaps I do have a role here. I feel my hands start to buzz, the way they always do when I think about magic.

'Really? I didn't think there were witches here. I thought that was sort of the point of the Redworld. No magic. Just technology, science, crime, pollution, money.'

Ceri twirls around, dancing briefly to a thumping song that comes on. 'Love this song. Yeah. Well, there's only three of us. I'll introduce you; they're off snaring some poor unsuspecting lads with their wicked ways.' She points over to a heaving mass of bodies swaying and bucking to the music. 'Do you want to dance?'

I chew my lip, unsure. It looks a bit wild.

'You go. I'm fine here,' I say, not wanting to embarrass myself. I only know traditional country dancing, and I hate that. But then again, I also don't want her to abandon me. I don't want to stand here alone.

Ceri pulls my hand. 'Come on. It won't kill you.' She drags me to the dance area, where the music is louder. I hold my hands over my ears, feeling as if they're about to burst. Ceri pulls them away, and hugs me to her, swaying from side to side.

'Just feel the music,' she yells into my ear. 'Relax!'

I stand there, petrified, like one of those ancient women turned to stone by some hateful male god or another.

But as I listen to the beat the music creates a spiral pattern in my mind, leading me deeper and deeper into my unconscious. The spiral, the triskele symbol, so important in the Greenworld, representing life–death–rebirth. No one is looking at me; no one cares what I do here. It's not like the community dances at home or acting out one of Mum's mystery plays at the solstice. Saba liked all that. I endured it, but I didn't like people watching me. For me, magic is something private and personal, quiet and reflective.

The hypnotic beat pulls me deeper and deeper down. Pictures start to form in my mind's eye, and I begin to spin slowly, arms stretched out. I am a gyroscope, a windmill. The spinning generates the power for a vision. I close my eyes. I see three girls standing round a fire, holding hands and chanting. One is Ceri. One is very tall, thin and angular with vivid red hair and big blue eyes; the arm that holds on to Ceri is covered in a colourful tattoo theme of leaves, berries and flowers. The other girl has pink dreadlocked hair. Some people back in the Greenworld dread their hair; it's a practical solution when there's not that much hot water around. But this girl's dreads have none of that natural matte look; they're plump and woolly-looking, with little gold bands holding small sections together here and there. She is brown-skinned, small and curvy, dressed in an animal-print dress. Beautiful gold circlets are arranged up her arms, the metal digging slightly into her flesh.

In my vision, the three of them finish their chant — not one I'm familiar with, it just sounds like a string of nonsense sounds, and there is no magic in the space around them that I can sense. They break their hold of each other's hands and throw their arms skywards. Nothing else happens, but they look triumphant.

I stop spinning and open my eyes owlishly, back in reality. I am looking into the warm blue eyes of the tall girl from my vision, who is standing next to the small curvy girl with the pink hair. Ceri gestures that we should all go somewhere a little quieter, and we push our way back to the bar. It's busier now, three people deep, but Ceri taps a couple of boys on the shoulder and they melt away when they see her.

'So. Melz, meet Demi and Catie. Girls, meet Demelza. Just off the boat from the Greenworld.'

The tall girl takes my hand warmly, brushing back her red curls from a sweaty forehead with the other. 'Catie. Short for Hecate. Wow, Demelza? Like . . .' She glances at Ceri but the girl in the animal-print dress cuts her short.

'Shut up, Catie; it's not the place,' she snaps. She looks me up and down critically. 'I see it's true what they say about Greenworld fashion. Make that yourself, did you?'

I look down at my dress. 'I did, actually. We make most of our clothes ourselves. Sometimes we exchange.' My dressmaking isn't the best, but it isn't the worst either.

'Yeah. Well, if you're going to stay here you've got to get something better to wear. Or can Greenworld witches magic up new outfits for themselves? Cos here we earn money to live and buy stuff. You won't get shit for cauliflowers and cabbages, sweetheart.'

'Stop being such a bitch, Demi,' Ceri barks. 'We're going to look after Melz because it's our duty as witches. We've got to look out for each other. 'K?' She stares Demi out, and the other girl shrugs after a couple of moments.

'Whatever. No need to be all touchy about it.' Demi holds out a small, dimpled hand for me to shake. 'Demi. Short for Demeter. Welcome.'

I take her hand, but there's not much enthusiasm on her side. I don't need to be a witch to know that I'm not welcome. I look at Catie questioningly. 'Hecate and Demeter?' Both are goddesses from Greek mythology.

'We chose goddess names when we were initiated,' Catie explains.

Catie is staring at me intensely. It's making me feel uncomfortable.

'What?' I ask.

'Oh . . . no, nothing.' She smiles and shakes her head.

'So, who initiated you?' I look at them all.

27

I think back to my own initiation ceremony aged eight. There was a big noisy village event, which was more like a party, where Mum, Merryn and Beryan welcomed me and Saba into the covenstead in front of everyone, and we danced round the village maypole. Then there was the private, real magical initiation, where my measure was taken, where I swore oaths to the Gods and Goddesses of the Greenworld, and where I received my magical gifts: my first athame, my scrying crystal and my wand, made from a branch from the hawthorn tree in the garden. And then, four years later, the Morrigan, Celtic goddess of war, death and protector of the land, claimed me as Her priestess, Goddess be praised.

If someone initiated Ceri, Demi and Catie, then there must be other witches here too. More experienced, older witches I could get to know. Perhaps work with. But Ceri shakes her head.

'Nobody. We did it ourselves. There aren't any other witches here.'

'No other witches? Not at all?'

'Well, there might be. But we don't know them.' Catie smiles.

'Oh.'

'Yeah. I know. It sucks. It would be so amazing to be in a witch community, like in the Greenworld. How many witches do you know?' Catie asks. Unlike Demi, I can see the creative energy pouring out of her, and creation is magic after all. Maya, who taught me so much, would be a good person for her to know.

But thinking about Maya makes me think of drawing, and that isn't somewhere I want to go right now, maybe not for a long time. I haven't drawn anything since the curse. I might never draw anything again. And, though I have heard the Morrigan's voice as the shadow of my conscience, I have not talked to Her, sung to Her or worshipped Her since I left the Greenworld. I don't know if She has left me because of the curse, and I am wary of finding out. I am still a witch – I don't know how to be anything else – but I don't know if my goddess is still with me. And what is a witch without her goddess?

I look at the three of them standing there in front of me. They are witches in name only. There is no devotion in them. There is no web or weave of constant worship around them; no light threads connecting them to the moon, to the earth, to the sea and the wind. Is that what I will become if I stay here?

'So, how many do you know?' Catie's curiosity pulls me out my reverie.

'How many what?'

'Witches. How many are in the Greenworld?'

'Ummm, lots. Probably forty or more.'

'And Demelza – is that a traditional witch name or something? I mean, I couldn't decide for ages when I was choosing mine. In the end I just took Hecate because I liked the sound of it.'

'It's a traditional Cornish name rather than a witch name per se. We don't take goddess names for ourselves.

I mean, we work with the Goddess, honour Her in Her different aspects – but we don't call ourselves by Her names.' Catie looks a little crestfallen, and I really don't want to make it worse, but I can't help myself. 'I mean, we're witches, but we are people. Taking a goddess name's an intense commitment. Like, I wouldn't want to be possessed by one all the time.'

'I hadn't thought of it like that,' she says glumly.

'Oh, and you know, you're saying it wrong. It should be *heck-ah-tee*. Not *heck-kate*. If you're going to call yourself after a goddess, She's not going to be happy if you pronounce it wrong.'

Catie frowns. 'Oh. I just assumed when I read it that was how you said it.'

I feel bad for correcting her; she seems like a nice girl, so I smile in what I hope is a reassuring way. 'That's all right. How would you know unless you'd heard it said out loud?'

I don't want to be pedantic, but some things are important. If you mess up the basics, what else are you doing wrong?

Ceri smiles at Demi, who is staring at me unpleasantly. 'See? We're going to learn so much from each other. I'm making a toast.' She turns to the bar and passes us each a none-too-clean metal cup, then picks up a bottle of the same red wine as before. She sloshes some into our cups and raises hers.

'To witches everywhere, but most of all here. Good magic, good wine, good friends, good times!'

'Goddess be praised,' I reply on rote, and drink. Good friends are what I need.

Later, we stumble out of the warehouse and take a circuitous route down some unlittered roads. This part of town is different to where I came in; it has none of the graffiti, the houses crouching nervously together, the battered checkpoints. None of the anxious eyes peering from doorways as we carouse past.

Ceri's flat is one of many in a tall glossy stone building surrounded by spiked iron gates. I am reminded of the Witch's Gate back at home – the symbolic entrance to our covenstead – but whereas that is beautiful, ornate and engraved with poetry, this is stark and forbidding. No one has ever threaded flowers through these bars.

However, there is one of the large grey armoured vans parked outside it, and Ceri waves a pass at the impassive black-clothed guard inside.

'You're shtaying with ush now,' she slurs as she types a number into some buttons on a pad, and the gates swing open. We stumble towards the doors and she fumbles in her bag for a key: a flat, featureless card that makes a bleep sound when she presses it on a panel. We fall into a hallway, giggling, then climb a flight of stairs. At the top, she swipes the card on another door.

'Itsh not mush, but itsh home,' she mutters, and we follow her in.

I look around. It's small and dusty, crumpled laundry

languishes on a couple of large wooden airers, and books and half-drunk cups and glasses are everywhere. Still, it's cosy. Ceri, kicking off her shoes violently, points to a rumpled red sofa and a purple blanket.

'Thatsh you for tonight. We'll sort out something . . . out . . . better . . . tomorrow.'

Demi disappears into what must be her room without comment, slamming the door behind her.

Catie gives me a drunk hug, yawning. 'Mmmmm. Night, Melz.'

I hug her back. 'Night, *Heck-ah-tee.*'

She grins at me and touches my cheek for a little too long. 'Yesssss. *Heck-ah-tee,* thy goddesh of the cross-roads,' she slurs, and stumbles off to another door.

I lie back on the sofa, smiling, and pull the blanket over me. Hecate, Greek goddess of crossroads, witchcraft, entrances. Ways into new and secret places. On reflection, I take this as a sign that a goddess from another culture has welcomed me into this new place, an unexpected place of sorcery.

I close my eyes, expecting the room to spin, but it stays resolutely still. Perhaps, like faeryland, not everything is as it seems here.

So ends my first night in a Redworld coven.

Front page of Demelza Hawthorne's Greenworld Journal

Date – 12 November 2042
Moon phase – first quarter, waxing in Pisces
Menstruation cycle – week 1
Sun phase – Scorpio
Card drawn – The High Priestess
Dreams – see below
~~**Chosen tenet** –~~
Reflection on the chosen tenet – I am choosing not to contemplate a tenet. This is an extraordinary event.

I know I'm supposed to start a new journal on 1 November but I've been so busy I'm not catching up till now.

Just over a week ago at Samhain I received the Morrigan's witch-brand: the triskele. I am twelve and now, surely, fully a woman.

I was in the circle, the big one with all the villagers round the bonfire on the village green, holding hands with Saba on one side and Ennor on the other, staring into the fire, singing, and the next thing I knew I was in this vivid vision. I felt Her energy, big and strong and fiery, the Morrigan, filling me with incredible strength and energy, and She stepped forward and chose me, touching me on the back of the neck. That feeling is still with me, lessened, but still intense. Like I am a warrior. I feel proud to be Hers. And there was this odd vision I've been trying to interpret since: a spiral, a girl being sucked into it. A man, being harmed.

Saba is so jealous. She can't wait to get the brand now, I can tell. She whispered to me before we went to sleep last night, *It will be me next, you'll see, now we know it's not something just for Mum and the others. You must have got it first because you got your period before I did.* But I'm not so sure. That's two things Saba wanted and I got first. MAKES A CHANGE. And I keep telling her that she shouldn't wish for her period because it hurts and it's messy, no matter what Mum says about it being sacred.

After it happened, Zia Prentice came to Tintagel especially to see me. That's what I've been doing for the last week, being tutored by her in the ways of the Dark Goddess. When we met she pulled down her collar and showed me her brand, the same mark as mine, in the same place on her neck. She said, *I look forward to us working together, Demelza,* and I felt a kinship with her straight away. Then she said, *the Morrigan chooses Her priestesses wisely. Goddess be praised.*

Zia's got the best long black hair. She wears all black and a silver pendant of a crow's head, sometimes a crow feather plaited into her hair with a red ribbon. When people talk she listens with a really serious expression; when she smiles it's kind of tiredly and she's thin, like she's not getting enough to eat. But she's beautiful, so beautiful.

After she got here we did another special ceremony, just for me, for being a new priestess of the Morrigan. When I saw her draw down the moon I felt the Morrigan again, kind of radiating out from Zia, and when she walked out of the circle she still had it upon her and Saba looked at me and I knew she was thinking *I want to be like that* because I was thinking it too.

Zia is Mum's best friend. She lives in Gidleigh village; she hardly ever visits any more, what with the gangs roaming between the villages. She's got two kids, a boy and a girl, but I've never met them. She left them at home this time; didn't want to risk their safety across the moors. Gidleigh is near Scorhill circle. Mum described it to me – tall jagged spikes of rock in a wide circle on the moor.

Nobody expected me to get the brand. It doesn't hurt or anything. Mum said, *Just because you've got the brand, Demelza, don't start thinking you get more power in the covenstead. You're still a child.*

Old enough to be chosen though. And I can feel the Morrigan as if She was standing just behind me. And She is powerful.

Chapter Four

Punish the ill-educated, create the criminal.

From *Tenets and Sayings of the Greenworld*

Ceri's leather-gloved hand raps impatiently at a heavy oak door. We're outside an odd squarish grey-stone building that squats incongruously at the base of Glastonbury Tor.

'He must be up by now,' she mutters, slipping her car keys back in her pocket. The huge van-like vehicle we drove here in is parked at an angle on the cobbles. She knocks again, and her brisk raps echo across the small private road. I stare up at the huge grassy hill of the tor, ringed with sculpted levels, and in my mind's eye watch as spectres of past priestesses pace its circumference, their blue robes flowing, heads bowed reverently. In the daylight I can't take my eyes off the tor. It has a natural grandeur; it's a simple but beautiful beacon of nature worship, right here among the falling-down houses, the grit and grime.

That morning Ceri wouldn't tell me where we were going, only that there was someone I should meet. Being in a car for the first time – with a hangover – at what seemed like ridiculous speed, it took all of my attention not to be sick, so I didn't ask further.

'Ack. Why she had to drag us out so early's beyond me.' Catie bends down and angles her head to drink from a little spring pouring steadily from a small fountain built into the wall. 'Arrrrghhhh. So cold,' she gurgles, and stands up, splashing a handful on her face. 'Restorative, so they say.' She smiles at me.

'Lightweight,' Ceri snaps at Catie.

'You're point-scoring, more like.' Demi examines her nails and flashes Ceri a dirty look. 'Can't wait to show him what you found.'

'Shut up. I'm not.' Nonetheless Ceri looks guilty, and I wonder who *he* is, and whether I am the found thing.

'What is this place?' I whisper to Catie, who leans her black-sunglassed face towards me wearily. She has lent me a pair too, and they're a revelation for a hungover morning like this. My mouth feels like a strip of beef hung out to dry for winter provisions.

'The White Spring. There are two holy springs in Glastonbury – both really old, never run dry. The red and the white. The red one comes out over there in Chalice Well.' Ceri points to our right, where I can just see an overgrown garden. 'No one uses it any more. It's got a high iron content, so it turns the stones red where it comes out. Like blood.'

'Can we walk up the tor? I've always wanted to,' I ask, gazing up again at the hill rising out of the flat Somerset Levels.

Ceri smiles at me. 'Sure. We'll go up after. Walking and fresh air's what you need with a hangover.'

'What are we doing here?' I ask, holding my hand under the cold clean water and taking a sip. It's sweet and beautiful.

'We've come to see Bran,' Ceri says, knocking again. 'Lazy bugger. Answer the frigging door!' she shouts. She looks different today: her fuzzy black hair, her real hair, not the blonde wig, is braided neatly against her head in a way I haven't seen before.

'Don't see why he'd be interested in her. He's got us already.' Demi tosses her hair, which is now black and straight, in the cold spring sunlight. The pink dreads, it seems, were also a wig.

Catie sighs and slumps against the wall. 'Urgh. If nobody answers this time, can we please go home?'

I'm about to ask who Bran is when the heavy door creaks open. A boy about our age sticks his head out. 'Come back later,' he mutters when he sees who it is. The ornate door creaks shut slowly, but Ceri places her foot firmly in the crack.

'Let us in, Pete. He's going to be happy that you do, I promise.'

'Really. I doubt that. He's in bed.'

She looks at her watch with an eyebrow raised. It's ten o'clock. 'Well, get him out then. Tell him I've brought a Greenworld witch with me.'

The boy looks curiously at me; I remain impassive behind my sunglasses.

Pete sighs. 'Oh, all right. Come in, then. Wait here.'

We crowd through the door and wait inside a stone room. Even though it's morning outside, it's dark, and takes a while for my eyes to adjust to the dimness. The only natural luminescence slices in through a couple of murky skylights above, otherwise the room is lit by flickering candlelight. I can hear water trickling; the air is damp. I reach out and touch the stone wall to get my bearings.

As my eyes refocus I see that the stone floor has a cleft in it where water pools, reaching the length of the room and into a drain at the end. We are standing in a small hallway, and ahead of us in a wider vaulted room, two large black leather sofas form an L shape round an expensive-looking glass table, and a fire crackles and spits in a dark hollow at the base of the left-hand wall. On the back wall a painting of a nude woman draws attention away from the stark stone. A ledge runs round the top of the wall, where candles flicker in the murk. Despite the lack of light, the place is filled with strong positive energy; it feels warm, cosy, magical. A womb-like cave. Doors lead off to the right and left.

The girls slump down on the sofas. I go over to the painting and look at the brushwork. It's delicate but forceful; someone who knew something about conveying the spirit of the person painted this. Gently I run my finger over the paint and close my eyes, connecting with the painting like Maya taught me. Immediately the raw sexuality of it rushes through my finger and down inside me. I pull my hand away, shocked.

'So why are we here?' I ask, turning away from the painting, trying to hide my dismay at its energy.

Demi walks around the room, picking up tribal-looking ornaments from a series of small plinths and putting them down again. Masks, warriors, heads with tongues sticking out, eyes staring. They have a crude raw energy: wild earth and wood.

'We're here to see Bran, Demelza. Bran Crowley. He's our friend. He keeps the wolves from our door, and in return we do him little favours. He likes favours. He likes witches too. So he'll probably like you. Even with your terrible clothes.' Demi sneers.

Catie lowers her sunglasses and looks at me over the top of the rims. 'He likes Demi the most,' she says meaningfully. 'Demi does Bran lots of favours.'

'Shut up, *Heck-kate*,' Demi trills, deliberately pronouncing it wrong. 'You're just jealous. I can't help it if he likes my classic proportions.' She runs her hand over her rounded hip, today encased in a tight black knee-length strappy dress with a plunging neckline. She takes off her coat and I see that she also has colourful tattoos on her brown shoulders. Roses, mermaids. I think of Danny's witch-brand, and mine: tattoos that appeared magically. Mine is a triskele at the base of my neck; his is a poem, a text, a song to his god, Lugh. Briefly Danny's face floats into my mind, but I chase it away. Danny Prentice is no more a part of my life now than my stupid sister or anyone in the Greenworld.

'Why would he be interested in me, by Brighid?' I ask, leaning my elbows on the back of one of the sofas, looking at Ceri. 'I thought no one was really interested in the Greenworld out here.'

'Not at all,' purrs a voice behind me, and I jump round. 'I'm very interested. Very interested in Greenworld witches.' The young man smiles and cocks his head like an inquisitive dog. 'I take it that's what you are – why I got out of bed on a Sunday morning. To meet you?'

His voice is attractive: deep and musical but with an unfamiliar accent.

'Ummm. I suppose so,' I say, embarrassed and not knowing what to say next. *Cat got your tongue?* Mum used to say. I don't like having to perform in front of strangers, and sometimes talking counts as performing.

'What's your name?' he asks kindly, still with that beady-eyed dog look. He's a little older than us, maybe twenty or twenty-two – tall, with dark wavy hair to his shoulders and brown twinkly eyes. He's tanned, bare-chested, wearing soft black trousers with a drawstring waist, and I don't know where to look when he holds out his hand in greeting.

'Demelza Hawthorne. It means "hill fort". I prefer Melz,' I blurt out, and immediately wonder why I mentioned the hill fort. But he smiles with interest and takes my hand.

'Demelza Hawthorne. The witch's tree? Nice to meet you. I'm Bran Crowley.'

'All right,' I say, feeling awkward, shaking his hand. His hands are warm and wide – practical palms, like we say back home – but the skin is rough. Then the meaning of his name strikes me.

'Bran Crowley? Bran means "crow", do you know that? So you're Crow Crowley?' I laugh in spite of my nervousness. My goddess has a sense of humour. Crows are one of Her sacred animals. Has She sent me here to meet Bran?

He smiles. 'Aye, I knew.' He sits by Ceri on the sofa. Demi instantly follows and plumps herself next to him. He runs his hand along her leg but doesn't look at her. He's still looking at me. I sit down gingerly on the end of the other sofa.

'And you're from . . .?'

'Tintagel. It's on the coast.'

'I know where Tintagel is. King Arthur's birthplace.'

'Yes,' I reply. 'Supposedly anyway.'

'Aye. So, what've the girls told you about me?'

'Not much. They do you favours for money.'

He laughs and leans forward, opening a drawer under the large coffee table and taking out some rolling paper and tobacco.

'Ha. Demi. Don't undersell yourself.' I can't stop focusing on his voice, his strange accent: low, with an amused flick in the middle of some words. Its unusual halts and pauses are musical.

'That's not quite how we said it.' She looks annoyed, as usual.

He pats her leg again, kind of like a pet. He still hasn't looked her in the eye.

'Well, we're all friends, any road; whatever helps me get ahead in business. I'm a businessman, that's all.'

'You get them to – what? Help you choose good times for . . . deals? Make prosperity charms? That kind of thing?'

He shrugs. 'Whatever they can do. We've been looking at the possibilities.'

'Oh. So what kind of business do you do?'

The girls and Pete laugh, but Bran frowns at them, then smiles at me.

'Well, lass, I do a few different things. I've got to survive, at the end of the day. Built up my business over a long time. Buying something, selling it on, bit of protection, a few other things. I'm not lucky like this lot—' he waves his hand at Ceri and Demi – 'who can go back and live at Mum and Dad's if things get rough. I've probably got more in common with you in that way. All this . . .' He points at the painting, the leather sofas. 'It's all still a bit of a dream for me.'

'Oh. Right.'

He leans towards me, rolling the cigarette. 'So why're you here, Melz? Why leave the Greenworld?'

I look at my shoes. 'Ohhh . . . long story.'

'I'm not going anywhere.' He lights the cigarette and takes a drag, looking at me. If these are my new friends then some degree of honesty is probably in order.

'Ah . . . well, I suppose you could say I broke the rules. We . . . there was a fight. Between our village and the gangs.' The girls look blank – I'd assumed they would know what I meant. 'Oh. So, in the Greenworld, there are the villages – they're called covensteads – and they're ruled by witches. But there are some people in between the villages – living rough, tents and caravans, you know – they don't subscribe to the Greenworld ethos. They don't subscribe to anything really. We call them the gangs.'

Bran smiles. 'Aye. I know of them. Go on.'

'OK. So we had this battle. Lots of people died. Someone I loved . . . died.' Tom's face flashes in my mind's eye again, and my heart wrenches. My hand goes to the wooden heart pendant round my neck.

I see Bran look curiously at it, but he nods encouragingly at me. 'And?'

'I was angry. I shouldn't have done it, but I . . . cursed the people responsible. A brother and sister that we both knew, who had betrayed us. Betrayed Tom.'

I look at my hands – not wide and practical like Bran's, but long and thin. Psychic hands. Unreliable, floaty, otherworldly hands. Hands that act as if of their own volition. The night of the curse they flew across a page in my sketchbook, the charcoal digging so hard into the paper it almost ripped, scratching their faces

44

into being, ready to be destroyed. Afterwards I scrubbed and scrubbed, but I couldn't get the black out from under my nails.

I take a deep breath. 'We gave all the dead from the village a sea burial. I was . . . depressed. I'd lost the boy I had always loved, but he was also my sister's boyfriend. We – my sister and me – had a huge row on the way home, after the blessing. I just couldn't take it. I knew they'd all be on my case when they found out about the curse. So I ran away.'

Catie comes over to sit by me and takes my hand. 'I'm so sorry, Melz. That must have been awful for you.'

Her earnest blue eyes beam sympathy, and I squeeze her fingers. 'S'OK. I just want to put it behind me.'

'Of course.' She looks over at the rest of them. 'It's none of our business. We'll look after you now.'

Bran smiles, unreadable; Demi picks at her nails.

'I'm sorry to hear that. It's hard when you lose someone you love. The world can feel very empty, very cold,' Bran says. He stares at the wall for a few moments, then shakes his head, getting up. 'Look. I'd like to talk more with you, Melz – about the Greenworld, about you, about this battle – but now's not the time. Why don't we meet for dinner later this week? I'll make sure the lasses look after you until then. You've got a lot of catching up to do anyway.'

'Catching up?'

He smiles at my confused look. 'With everything you've missed, stuck down there in the middle of nowhere. You're in the Redworld now! Sex and drugs and rock 'n' roll. Cars, machines, literature, music, foreign food, manufactured fabrics, film, whatever you like. It's all here. Just don't blow your brains out too soon.'

I notice that he refers to the Redworld like he's familiar with how we think at home. He stands up.

'Don't feel you've got to go – Pete can make you some breakfast if you want. I've got to go though. Urgent business.' His expression clouds for a moment, and out of the blue I get a very odd vision: of Bran, in a white coat, wearing some kind of goggles, then I see the white coat being spattered with blood.

It's weird for me to get that kind of hyper-real picture in the middle of talking with someone, usually I'd have to meditate or journey or dream. As soon as it's flashed into my mind's eye it fades quickly, like the dreams that you can feel slipping away from you even when you half wake, the dreams that were never yours, which burn away with the air of lucidity.

He comes over to where I'm sitting, and looks me straight in the eye. 'Good to meet you, Melz. Hope to see a lot more of you soon.' He leans down and, completely unexpectedly, kisses me on the mouth. It's brief, and as he stands up I just stare at him. I couldn't say which I'm more unsettled by: the vision or the kiss. But whereas the kiss burns on my lips, the vision already seems like an odd imagining, something crazy I made up.

He smiles oddly and without saying goodbye to

anyone else, walks off into the next room. The door snicks closed.

Ceri clears her throat. 'Ummm . . . right. I think we'll go,' she says, standing up and wrapping her coat — long and red with a lace-up corset back — round her. Demi storms out, circling her coat round her shoulders like a cloak, shoulders thrown back.

Catie grins at me. 'You made quite an impression,' she says, as we walk out. Pete nods to us curtly and slams the door behind us, making me jump.

'See you, Igor,' Catie mutters, closing one eye and hunching her back.

'What? Who's Igor?' I think she's making fun of Pete, but I don't get it.

She laughs. 'You know. Like Dr Frankenstein's doorman. In the old films. Assistant, whatever. Pete's always rude.'

'Who's Dr Frankenstein?'

'Awwww. Greenworld. There's so much you need to catch up on,' she says.

47

Chapter Five

Knowledge comes from the earth more than any book. Listen to the songs of the trees, the beat of the soil, the caress of the wind on wheat if you would be wise.

From *Tenets and Sayings of the Greenworld*

'Where's he from? Bran?' I ask Catie. 'He speaks in this really odd way. Not like you.' Catie and the girls have similar ways of speaking to me, although they are slightly more clipped, slightly less Cornish. Their rs don't roll as much as mine do.

'Yorkshire, I think. North anyway.'

'What's he doing down here then?'

'He's allowed to move if he wants to, doll. People do it all the time.'

I suppose they do, here.

'He's got a sexy voice if you ask me.' She holds her finger to her lips. 'Shhh. Don't tell Demi I said that, mind.'

As we walk to the car I look at Demi's back a few strides in front of us. 'Are we still walking up the tor?' I look up at it towering above us. A lifetime ambition to come here, about to be met.

'Sure,' Catie coughs. 'Ugh. I shouldn't smoke.'

'She's angry with me,' I say, nodding at Demi. 'I didn't do anything though.'

Catie makes a fart noise, pursing her lips. 'Oh, whatever. Ignore her. She's jealous of you.'

I look at Demi's fur-trimmed coat and her shiny black boots, then at my own scuffed leather and hand-knitted cardigan.

'I don't see why, by Brighid.'

'You say that a lot,' Catie says, smiling at me.

'What?'

'*By Brighid*. She's the patron goddess of the Greenworld, isn't she?'

'Yes. Brighid, Irish goddess of fire, smithcraft, poetry, farming, healing.' I don't add though that She is not who I'm dedicated to. Partly because I don't want to get into having to explain the Morrigan to Catie, who is likely to be ignorant about Her, but also because I don't know where I stand with Her right now either.

'Oh. Well, you're powerful, is what I was going to say.' Catie nods at Demi ahead. 'Bran liked you. She wants to be the one everyone wants, that's all. Don't worry, she'll get used to it.'

Our feet clatter along the quiet cobbles; the town is still, as if it is breathing in.

'You're witches too.' But I know as I say it that that isn't true. I know I have more power than they do. More experience. It's not so much about natural ability – I can see the potential in Catie; it's about having put the hours in and train gradually, building up skills as time goes on. Being a witch isn't about opening a book and reading out a spell. It's feeling moon energy, sun energy, when it peaks and dips, and knowing what time is best for what – starting something, ending something. It's about training your mind to be able to visualize what you want to happen, but being open to the best solution. Leadership, compassion, faith. Doing the thing that's right, even if you don't like it. We don't always want what's best for us. I learned that the hard way.

I don't think Ceri, Demi and Catie have that mindset. I think they've cobbled together what they think it is to be a witch, and a lot of that includes what it looks like. But that's the least important element of all. In fact, it can work against you. I remember learning about how in olden times people were very secretive about being witches. I mean, *really* far back you'd get burned for it, like Joan of Arc. And then, not so far back, but still pre-Greenworld, people thought you were evil or strange if you were a witch, so you had to pass for normal.

Catie runs her fingers along the old grey stone wall. 'Sorry about your boyfriend.'

'He wasn't my boyfriend.' My response is automatic, but then it occurs to me: why did I have to tell them

Tom was Saba's boyfriend? I could say he was mine and no one would know the difference. I could enjoy the lie, make myself believe it. We were in love. We spent ages kissing on the beach. He loved me being a witch. We were going to get handfasted. It's like I want to deny myself any reality where he was mine. Penance.

I see Ceri turn left through a wooden stile, and Demi follows her, hands in pockets. Ceri points up to the tor. I nod and wave back. I can't wait to see it, to walk on it and feel its energy. The ancient place of our Celtic ancestors.

We turn the corner and start the climb.

I stop talking for a moment, stop thinking about Bran, and tune in to the energy here, expecting to feel a rush under my feet, through my chest, but it's odd. Quiet.

I turn to Catie. 'Doesn't this feel strange to you?'

She looks round. 'What?'

I point up to the top of the hill, to the tower that sits on top of it. It's dedicated to St Michael, a Christian saint who protects against bad spirits. A last-ditch attempt to control the fearsome pagans that wanted to celebrate Mother Earth, or venerate the palace of the Celtic faery king, Gwyn ap Nudd, under the hill. Looking at the tower, I shake my head, half in amusement and half irritation. Talk about a visual metaphor for the Redworld. Put a stone penis on top of the Mother's hill in a vain effort to subdue it. Good luck with that.

'This is Glastonbury Tor. One of the holiest places

in the world, certainly in England. As witches we should be almost knocked sideways by the natural energy coursing through here. It should be like entering an ocean. But there's almost nothing. Flatness. Can't you feel it?'

She shrugs. 'Not really,' she says, giving me that look again that says *I'm being polite but basically you're talking rubbish.*

All Greenworld kids have to study the mystical sites of the world. Most of them don't realize why, but we witches know it's really the study of energy portals. All these stone circles, mounds, castles. Many built around places of natural power.

Ceri has stopped ahead of us on a flat stone that marks the last ascent to the top. We catch up with her.

'Beautiful up here, isn't it?' she says. I don't say anything. It's a difficult line that I'm treading. On one hand, these girls have taken me in and I'm really, really grateful. On the other, they're pretending at something that means the world to me. Magic.

We climb the last steps to the top of the tor. The wind screams past my ears and I hold my hands protectively over them; I can feel an earache coming. I walk cautiously round the tower, not wanting to go inside, feeling the dark energy pouring from it. The girls head straight there. We have the tor to ourselves.

I sit down on the earth to try to tap into the energy deep within the hill. I don't feel the heartbeat that I should, the signature of an energy portal, or any place of power. If the hill is a womb, the Great Mother has become barren. There should be a portal here, but I can't feel it. I do a few introductory passes and symbols with my hands as we would do with the portal at home on Tintagel Head. Nothing happens. I try again. There's a very distant thread of response, but almost nothing. Whatever's there is buried and barely alive.

My gaze is pulled north, to the direction of earth and power, but something disrupts the immediate view of the Somerset Levels – flat fields reaching to other hills, as if the land was a cup, a chalice. The soft lap of the Mother.

I wave at the girls and Ceri comes over reluctantly, leaning into the wind.

'What's that, over there?' I shout. I feel I know the answer, but I've never seen one before. Tall industrial towers are silhouetted against the blue morning sky, and I can hear the steady grind of drill on rock.

She looks up briefly to where I'm pointing. 'Fracking site,' she says. 'You know. Big drill into the earth, pump water and sand in, frees the gas. Only the lights still don't stay on all the time and the hot water still packs in when I'm in the middle of running a bubble bath, so they're obviously not drilling deep enough.' She wraps her arms round herself. 'Can we go? It's so windy up here. I need to eat.'

I look at Ceri in horror. 'How is it allowed to be so close?' I point at the metal towers and the hills of sand and earth, which are only a field away – almost on the sacred land itself.

She shrugs. 'Dunno. Good fracking land?'

It's not their land. This is Her land, I think angrily, staring at the cranes moving up and down slowly, like vultures pecking at rotten meat. It's all Her flesh, Her body, the ground that sustains us.

We don't frack our land in the Greenworld, but I know what it does. The chemicals that are pumped into the earth to free the gas poison drinking water. The drilling causes earthquakes and subsidence. In the Greenworld we would no more torture the body of the Goddess than let Greenworld children starve.

Ceri stares with me for a moment. 'I know it's not ideal, but what can you do? The proles were up in arms about it polluting the water not so long ago. Mine tastes all right though,' she says dismissively, and pulls my hand. 'Look, I know you always wanted to see it up here, but we can come back whenever you want, all right? I'm starving. I need to get some food in me post haste.'

I turn round and see Catie and Demi sheltering in the tower. They beckon frantically at us.

'Where does your water come from though? On your side of town?' I ask. There are two natural springs here, and probably other water sources too – rivers, large natural water stores underground. If poisons and chemicals get into any water source that's bad news for everyone.

'Dunno. I just switch on the taps and there it is.' She wraps her scarf round her ears. 'Come on.'

The water tasted fine at the spring outside Bran's house, but what about the other spring? The Red Spring, the Goddess Spring, emblematic of natural feminine energy. She'd said no one used it any more.

'Can you drink from the Red Spring still? Do you go there?' As witches, like they say they are, it would be the obvious place apart from the tor itself to worship the Goddess.

'Nah. It doesn't taste good. That one's definitely polluted. Has been for as long as I remember,' she says.

I follow her back to the tower. I knew fracking happened here – a final and desperate effort at finding power. But seeing it in real life, feeling the drilling into the Goddess, the sacred land, feeling the vibration of that intrusion in my feet, my heart, and feeling Her pain, Her displeasure . . . and all so close to the tor, it sickens me. And as well as that – ruining a holy spring. Somehow that spring has been polluted by the fracking, I'm sure of it. It's so horribly symbolic. This town is half dead and the Goddess has been poisoned.

Chapter Six

The proles talk about freedom, but this is a truly free society. Freedom from financial regulation, ineffective government, European legislation. Men can be gods here.

From a speech given at the National Security
Services Annual Conference, 2045

We drive back into the town, even though it doesn't seem very far at all. When I ask why we hadn't walked, Ceri scoffs.

'As if I'd risk getting pickpocketed! We're better off in here. Safe.'

I try not to hold on to the seat and hope they don't realize that this is only the second time I've ever been in a car. The streets flash past at a ridiculous speed, and Ceri swings round corners without slowing, blaring a horn at anyone that gets in her way.

'Bloody proles,' she mutters as she narrowly avoids

an old woman with a walking stick. I press my lips together hard, physically suppressing the desire to tell her to *slow down, by Brighid*.

'You were walking in town last night,' I say.

She pulls into a gated car park and flashes a plastic card at a machine, which beeps and lets us through.

'Yeah, well, I was drinking. Can't drink and drive, can you? Not too much anyway. I had my knife with me, besides, if there was any trouble. Not that there would be probably. The proles had enough to do last night, with the riot. They don't usually come out at night anyway. And they know who we are.'

'Who you are?'

'Witches, and Bran's . . . friends.' She smiles and gets out of the car.

'Why don't they come out at night? The . . . proles?' I whisper to Catie. The word 'proles' sticks in my mouth. I don't know if it's bad but it feels as though it is.

'The security services. They patrol. In the grey vans,' she says quietly as Ceri and Demi stride ahead.

'They're in charge?' I ask. I remember Ceri mentioning the police. We don't have such a thing at home – a group that controls the behaviour of another group. Punishes and patrols. We don't need it. Witches counsel and protect.

'Not officially. But in effect, yes.'

'Who is officially in charge, then, by Bri——?' I stop myself saying it this time. Another habit to break.

'The police. The government in London. But they're

57

less and less effective because they're not as well funded as the security services. All the government's money's being spent on the war, and on fuel.'

The war with Russia, a continuous darkness to the east, full of the ghosts of fathers, brothers, friends. It's been raging for years, a pointless scrap for the last fossil fuels on earth. We opted out in the Greenworld – we live without any fuel we can't find ourselves sustainably. But Greenworlders still go to the war as envirowarriors. To disrupt the war, to try to make them see sense. My dad, Danny's dad, they all went. And Mum purses her lips when you ask her about it, and only says *Turning our backs wasn't enough for some people.*

'It feels like there's always been a war on,' I say as we walk through a narrow walkway, the shadows shortening as we come out into a sunny square.

'I just pretend it's not happening.' Catie smiles brightly; she's beautiful and sweet and I want not to care either, but I do.

As we get closer to the steel and glass buildings in the square I see most of them are luxurious shops, the windows arranged in elaborate designs with useless objects for sale: bags, tiny hats, metal objects I have no name for.

A stream of large vehicles negotiates its way up the road beside the square, horns blowing. I cough when I inhale the fumes they're blowing out.

'How many of those are there?' I ask Catie, who

guides me round the outstretched legs of a mother and two young children sitting in a doorway.

'What, lorries? On the street?' She counts. 'Five.'

'No. I mean, everywhere. How many in total?'

'I dunno. Just in England? Thousands, probably.'

'Thousands? Of those?' I stare at the filthy grey back of the last one as it chugs up the road. It's so many I can't imagine it.

The mother sitting on the kerb calls something out to us and Catie falls back to drop a couple of coins in the paper cup in front of her.

'You're a sap,' Ceri says over her shoulder, and Catie shrugs.

'She's got kids,' she says to me, as if I needed an explanation.

'They're probably not even hers,' Ceri mutters, and pushes open the glass door of one of the buildings along the street.

I follow them into a cafe. We have one at home that we all work in on a rota. You donate any food surplus you have, and priority goes to the sick and elderly, or pregnant women. They can go every day if they want to. That way we make sure that everyone eats, even if they can't grow food themselves.

I look around. This is not like that. The tables are full of well-dressed young and middle-aged men and women. No old people. No disabled people. No infirm people. Everyone is beautiful. Everyone looks rich. And two security guards in their black uniforms, wearing mirrored sunglasses, sit at a corner table, watching everything.

A girl in an apron takes us to a table and hands us each a menu.

Ceri scans it quickly and looks at Demi. 'What are you ordering?'

She waves her hand dismissively. 'Carry on. I'm not hungry.'

Ceri rolls her eyes at me. 'You need to eat, Demi. He loves your curves anyway.'

Demi sniffs. 'I know. It's not that, I'm just not hungry, that's all.'

Ceri shrugs. 'Suit yourself. Melz, are you vegetarian?'

I look at the list. So many choices, and so much meat. Some of it I don't recognize.

'Ummm, no. We eat meat. Just not very often.'

'OK. What d'you want, then? It's on us.'

'Oh. Ummm . . .' The list is so long that I can't remember what was at the top by the time I get to the bottom.

Catie points at the third thing on the list. 'Steak sandwich for me. It's good. You should have one.'

'OK,' I say, trying to remember the last time I ate beef. It was Beltane, last year. The first of May. A big community festival with lots of booze and food, dancing and sex. Not that I did that, of course.

Ceri hands the menus back to the girl. 'Three steak sandwiches. And a bottle of red with four glasses.'

The girl goes off, and Ceri smiles at Demi. 'You're drinking?'

Demi grins. 'Naturally,' she says, and shakes her shiny black hair. They seem to drink a lot. I start worrying about the effect it's going to have on my magical practice, but stop myself. I don't care. I don't have to have a magical practice any more if I don't want to. I mentally repeat *I don't care*, and when the wine arrives I take my glass. Wine for lunch. Kind of an early lunch too. *Why not?* I toast the girls and take a long gulp.

'So do you always come here, or . . .?' I ask Demi.

'We come here a fair bit; they know us here,' she replies, not looking at me. She's tapping a shiny black rectangle.

'What's that?' I lean over to try to see what it is, and they all look at me in disbelief.

'Oh God. Have you really never seen a phone before?' Ceri asks. I consider lying, but then I might have to prove I know how to use one, and I have no idea. She reaches into her pocket and puts an identical one in my palm.

'A phone? But they have wires, a dial. This isn't a phone.' The only phones I've ever seen were in pre-Greenworld books.

I turn it over in my hands. The whole thing is completely black. I can't see how it would work. I hand it back.

'What happens when you want to talk to someone that's not in your house?' Ceri asks me.

'I'd visit them, or wait until next time I saw them to talk.'

'But what about the other villages? What if you want to talk to them?'

'We have regular meetings with the other witches. We talk then. And if we need to, we can communicate psychically. Sometimes. Not everyone's good at that though.' I lower my voice.

Ceri grins and leans in to me conspiratorially. 'See, this is the stuff we need to know. Psychic communication. What do you mean by that?' she whispers.

I pick up Demi's phone from the table. 'You don't need to know. You've got this.' I hold it awkwardly and my thumb presses a recessed panel by accident. The front lights up, showing a picture of Demi and Bran making stupid faces at each other. Demi snatches it from my grip and puts it in her bag.

'Don't touch what's not yours, Greenworld,' she orders.

'Yeah. But we're witches, right? So maybe we want to communicate *differently*. With each other. When you say "psychic communication", what exactly do you mean?' Ceri ignores her friend and presses on.

I sigh, trying to think how to explain it, but my thoughts are interrupted by the girl — *waitress* I hear from another table — bringing us our lunch. The rich meaty smell of the beef assails my nose. It's so strong it almost makes me gag, but my stomach rumbles and reminds me that this is the best meal I've been offered in ages.

I bite into the huge sandwich – so big I can hardly get it in my mouth. The meat is tender. Much better than the tough cuts we get at home. For something like Yule or Samhain we sometimes slow-cook meat on a spit, but that's nowhere near as good as this. Goddess be praised for this sustenance, I think to myself, and make the sign of the triskele over my heart. Demi gives me a funny look but doesn't say anything.

Ceri nudges me. 'Slow down. You'll get indigestion. Christ, chew your food, girl! Anyone would think you haven't eaten in weeks.'

I haven't, I think in between chews, and certainly not like this. Perhaps never like this.

As I chew, I think about how I can get the three of them off the subject of psychic communication. I don't want to talk about it to untrained witches, and I definitely don't want to do it in a public place. Not in the Redworld anyway.

'My dad's there. In Russia, I mean. Fighting,' I say to Catie, deciding to continue our conversation from before.

'We were talking about the war just now,' Catie explains to the girls, surreptitiously inclining her head towards the guard wearing mirrored sunglasses in the corner of the cafe. I'm relieved that the other two nod. So they are wary in public too. They're transgressing by knowing about the Greenworld, by being witches, or thinking they are.

'I didn't think the Greenworld sent soldiers to the

front line. I mean, I didn't think you believed in fighting,' Demi says, her tone implying contempt for those who choose not to fight. I wonder if anyone from her family is at war. Somehow, I doubt it.

'He's not a soldier. He's an envirowarrior. An activist. They sabotage the fighting.'

I can't remember much about my dad now; he's just an old photo collaged into memory, his face cut out and stuck on to the pictures of family dinners we must have had once, before the dinner table was recarved with its central pentagram, before the covenstead took over, before I was a witch.

'Nice. Blowing up tanks. What good does that do?' Demi snaps back, and I want to slap her stupid face, but hold my temper in with great effort and don't honour her comment with a reply.

'So, earlier – you were telling me about the security services. Who owns them, then, if not your government?' I ask, changing the subject again.

Catie looks at me, surprised. 'Oh! I thought you understood. Bran owns ours. He's more or less in charge here. There's, like, a national association of security services, different people in charge in different areas. The People's Party are just figureheads now. No one really even bothers voting any more.'

'The People's Party?'

'They came into office ten years ago. It's, like, the most ironic title ever. They've done absolutely nothing for "the people" apart from reintroduce national service so that the war could continue. Luckily my parents got me out of it.' She takes a huge bite of the sandwich and chews happily. 'Mmmm. I can never, ever be a vegetarian. Fact.'

I remember Bran alluding to the fact that all three girls come from wealthy families. Wealthy and powerful, it would seem.

'What about school? Don't you go any more?' I ask. I'd just left the village school, but being a witch means constant training anyway. It's a life of school in a way.

'Nah. Optional after fourteen. The proles don't need it and we don't have to work, so there's no point staying on. Only the boffins bother with it,' Ceri explains, scowling at the memory. 'God, I hated it. The uniforms were ghastly, dahling.'

'Speak for yourself. I still have a French tutor and piano lessons,' Demi says with a superior look on her face.

'The last government I heard about must have been the ones before. The Independence Party,' I say, trying to steer the conversation back to the government.

'Oh, them. Yeah,' Ceri sneers. 'They oversaw the Greenworld split. People are still arguing about whether they should have done it, but now the PP haven't got enough money or influence to reverse the decision anyway.'

'Really?' I frown. 'But most people don't know what the Greenworld is.'

'Everyone knows it's there, but most people don't know about the witches. The propaganda was always that it was a kind of open prison for troublemakers.

Activists. Hippies. Lefties. That's why the border's there. To make sure you don't get out. No offence,' Ceri adds.

I stare at Ceri in amazement. 'No, it isn't! The border is there to protect us *from* the Redworld! So we won't be tainted by it!'

'That might be what they told you, babes. We studied it at school though. They made sure we knew the party line, you know, about you all being murderous extremists. We saw the Contract of Separation. I can show it to you. It's in my old modern history book at home. That's why it's so cool you're here. I still can't believe *the* Demelza Hawthorne's in our gang now.'

Mum must know that this is what the Redworld says about us. That the border keeps us in, not keeps us safe. That they think we're terrorists, extremists. But she negotiated Devon and Cornwall for us to live in – cleanly, reverentially. There was no talk of us being terrorists. *Was there?*

'What . . . what do you mean, *the* Demelza Hawthorne?'

'We know who Lowenna Hawthorne is. Anyone does who's studied the Contract of Separation. She's one of the originators of the Greenworld – her and Zia Prentice – and you're Lowenna's daughter. That's a big deal. To us anyway. And to the police too, to be honest. You'd better not let anyone but us find out you're here. They'd bang you up or send you home in two shakes. Luckily no one knows what you look like.'

'But I'm not dangerous.'

She shrugs and leans forward, picking imaginary lint off my clothes.

'We know you're not, obviously, but think about it. The People's Party want everyone to believe the Greenworld's full of dangerous mad activists. What would happen if ordinary people met you and found out you can actually do magic, and that you're – you know – normal? There'd be a public outcry.' She speaks in a low voice, pretending to straighten my collar, then sits back. *'Why are the powers that be lying to us, et cetera, et cetera?'*

'Is that why you talked to me, then? It wasn't an accident?'

'Yeah. Now and again we get a Greenworlder in Glastonbury; you get to be able to spot them. The way you dress. The way you do your hair. And we worked out a few years ago there was something we weren't being told about you guys. There were rumours about witches. Me and the girls started reading up, started researching. That's how Bran found us. He was into the same stuff. Conspiracy documents. Old books, old files. He's mad about magic, witches. That's why I talked to you in the first place. You don't look much like your mum but there is a little resemblance. You look more like Zia Prentice. Dark hair, pale, all intense. I didn't want to miss out on a chance to talk to a real Greenworld witch.'

Zia Prentice, my fellow priestess of the Morrigan.

'And Bran?'

'He's pretty knowledgeable about the Greenworld.

Some of his guys are ex-Greenworld or ex-gang. They told him a lot.'

I bet. I wonder just who has had Bran Crowley's ear.

'Isn't he dangerous? I mean, someone his age, with all that power . . . Connected to the gangs? Connected to the *police*?' I whisper as a well-dressed couple pass us by.

'He's a nice guy. He looks after us,' Ceri insists. 'He'll look after you too. You can trust him.'

'Can I? But you've just told me all it takes is for someone to tell the police I'm here, and I'm back home, or in prison . . . He could do that.'

'But he won't. You're too interesting. He's been looking for a Greenworld witch for a long time. Now he's got one.'

'He doesn't have me,' I snap. 'I'm not anyone's.'

'Fine with me. Bugger off back home then,' Demi hisses.

'Shut up, both of you.' Ceri glares at both of us. 'We don't mention it again in public. Right?'

'Sorry. Of course.' She's right. It's my safety that's at risk. And theirs, probably, if anyone finds out I'm staying with them, eating their food.

'Demi?' Ceri glares powerfully at her friend until she rolls her eyes heavenwards.

'Yeah, right, whatever,' she mutters. And I wonder whether I can really trust any of them.

Chapter Seven

And it was not in our name that the Redworld
burned.

From Tenets and Sayings of the Greenworld

I spend my next day in the Redworld raptly watching
television and eating food out of packets, immune to the
girls' giggles at my apparently inane questions about
family dramas, police shows and the horrifying brutality
of the news. But that evening I find myself back at the
heavily ornate oak door. As I hold up my hand to knock,
I notice the skin across my knuckles. After only two
days in Glastonbury it's soft and supple instead of
broken and painful as it usually is in the winter and
spring. The girls have a remarkable collection of beauty
products, the likes of which I have never seen before. No
homemade face masks in ceramic bowls in the fridge, to
be mistaken for cold porridge at your peril, no rosemary
wash to make your hair shiny – effective, but dark brown

and smelly. Their potions come in plastic bottles with pumps and sprays attached to the canisters, or in luxurious jars with gold lettering, smelling of foreign flowers. A sense of the alien lingers on my borrowed clothes – a pair of black leather leggings, skin-tight, from Catie, which I've had to roll up at the bottom as she's so tall, and a white silky shirt and a formal black jacket from Ceri. My hair is in plaits, pinned up neatly. A waft of perfume haloes me with a semi-hallucinogenic taint.

The promises on the bottles are conflicting. On one hand, there is the concept of being natural. AU NATUREL, one of them says, which apparently is French. However, I can attest that 'natural' smells are a lot less floral than these manufacturers seem to believe. The Greenworld is full of people that smell au naturel. I've never had a problem with it. It's the norm. But now, surrounded by all these products desperate to eliminate my natural smell, I feel, somehow, dirtier than I ever have. On the other, there is the exotic approach, with pictures of flowers I've never seen in my corner of England, and of women in costumes I have also never seen people wear. Perhaps in other areas of the world people dress this way.

Saba would love all of it. When we were kids, we'd play this game called Beauty or Truth. One of us had to ask the other what they would prefer from a choice of two difficult but related options. The other had to justify their choice. So, for instance, a beautiful diamond necklace or the ugly truth of knowing that a Redworld child had died mining the diamonds? Would it still be beautiful? Or would the truth outweigh the beauty?

Saba tended to argue for the beautiful things. She'd say, *Ah, well, the diamond necklace exists now, whatever happened to make it. It's not the necklace's fault that child died, and it's not my fault. It's still beautiful. Beautiful things inspire awe in us. There's something holy about making something so beautiful from a rock in the earth. It's a lesson about our creativity, our ability to achieve perfection. Making beauty is making magic. It's the divine in us.* Or some such deceptive crap.

And I would always argue for truth, because I would always rather know, no matter how ugly the truth. I want to have all the facts. I despise beauty on principle. Beauty is deceptive.

I knock, and wait, wobbling my heel uncomfortably in the shoes that make me taller and far less sure on my feet than I usually am. Beauty is deceptive but it's also excruciating. I couldn't walk in some of the inventions Ceri pulled out of her wardrobe. The angle my foot had to be in seemed impossible and hurt even before I'd put weight on them.

Ceri had frowned at my grimace. 'You have to just learn to take the pain,' she'd said, and looked at the shoes again. 'Granted, something like this is strictly a sitting-down shoe.'

I mean, a *sitting-down shoe*! This is a typical Redworld concept. To imbue an entirely not-fit-for-purpose thing with extreme desirability, despite its uselessness, in the

71

interests of making another thing that people want to buy, another thing to fulfil the edict of consumerism – that one is fulfilled by having *things* – and there are more *things* in heaven and earth, Horatio, than are dreamed of in your philosophy. The Greenworld skimped on a lot, I'm learning fast, but at least we had Shakespeare. Shakespeare is one of those historical people that the Greenworld likes to appropriate as its own. At school we learned about how Shakespeare, Milton, Swinburne, Byron, all these writers, were prototype neo-anarcho-pagans. And Brighid is the poets' goddess after all. Poetry is important in the Greenworld.

But a shoe is for walking, for protecting your feet against the elements; it should last a long time. These shoes fulfil none of those requirements. And they are unbelievably painful.

Pete opens the door and shows me into the lounge; I sit gingerly on the edge of the leather sofa, like before, looking around me. Pete brings me a glass of wine without asking if I want it. I find I do want it, though the dirty look he gives me as he hands it to me is less welcome. Waiting for Bran brings the tension of the past days to a sharp point in my stomach. Since I found out how wanted I am here – that I'm not the anonymous ex-Greenworlder I thought I was, but the daughter of a famous 'terrorist' – my decision to run sits heavier on my shoulders, dark as a raven. My unease is the ruffling of its feathers, and right now the Morrigan's bird has its claws in my skin, scratching the bone underneath. One word, one word is all it takes and

I'll be – what? Thrown into jail? Worse? In the Redworld I'm not an eco-pagan. I'm not an energy worker. I'm not a herbalist or the priestess of an ancient Celtic goddess. I'm a terrorist, an activist, a dangerous antisocial menace.

I chant the words of my favourite poem gently to myself while I wait for Bran. My date for the evening. *Why not go?* Ceri asked me brightly yesterday evening; I didn't have a good answer. I came because he asked me, in a formal note pushed under Ceri's flat door; I came because I don't have anything better to do.

I'm trying to remember a verse when Bran slides into the room. He makes no noise when he walks, I'm sure of it, because he catches me unawares again.

'Demelza. Thanks for coming. You look great.' He comes over and kisses me on the cheek, but I think he's going for my lips again so instinctively turn my head and we end up mashing lips after all. I pull away.

'Urgh – I mean, sorry, that didn't . . .' I start stumbling, but he laughs.

'Don't apologize. You were talking to yourself?'

'Oh. Yes. Well, when I get . . . when I'm waiting, sometimes I recite poetry to myself. You know, to pass the time,' I lie somewhat convincingly.

He looks surprised. 'Poetry?'

'Interesting language that may or may not rhyme? You know – "Season of mists and mellow fruitfulness"?' I can't help myself – if I feel embarrassed or attacked, I revert to sarcasm.

He clears his throat. 'Aye. I know what poetry is. What were you reciting?'

'"The Garden of Proserpine". Swinburne.'

'Nice.' He's giving me an odd look that I can't decipher.

'Proserpine was the Roman name for Persephone, the Greek goddess who married Hades, king of the underworld. She ate six seeds from a pomegranate without realizing that would imprison her there, but her mother Ceres, or Demeter, negotiated a deal where she could come home for six months every year. Hence the seasons. Spring comes when Proserpine returns to the world; autumn begins when she leaves,' I explain, feeling the need to fill the empty space in the room with words. 'Goddess be praised,' I add on reflexively.

'Aye. Hades. King of the underworld? Like me?' He smiles and sits down next to me, reaching for the drawer in the table by my knees. 'Sorry. I were just going to roll a cigarette. D'you want one?'

I shrug. I smoked at home sometimes. 'OK. Thanks.'

'No problem,' he says, and his thick fingers work the thin paper. He licks the edge, tamps down the tobacco and lights it, passing it to me. I breathe it in and feel the nicotine working instantly in my nervous system. It's still a drug, and normally I'd steer clear of this many stimulants, but I'm not in a normal situation. It's similar to the roll-ups we have at home, but the tobacco tastes less organic.

'So it's not just Celtic mythology you learn in the Greenworld?' he asks.

I inhale deeply. Blue smoke pools around us like mist across the Somerset Levels. I've read that sometimes mist surrounds Glastonbury Tor so deeply that it looks like an island. It was partly this that gave it its reputation as being a magical place long ago. Hidden between worlds.

'No. All cultures. Well – not all, probably. The classic ancient cultures. The matriarchal, Goddess-revering ones.'

'Aye, well, of course,' he says. I scan his expression for sarcasm but he seems sincere. His flippant comment rankles though.

'You think you're the king of the underworld? Ruler of the lower realms? I might consider that a faintly heretic statement.'

He laughs. 'No, not like that. I mean the criminal underworld. Well—' he blows smoke out of the side of his mouth – 'security. That's what they call it now. I make people feel secure.' He raises an eyebrow.

I frown at him. I can't imagine this boy being ruthless enough to intimidate anyone. 'Are you really so powerful?'

'I'm doing all right,' he says, smiling. His smile is way too nice for king of the underworld. Some stories say that Proserpine was kidnapped, but some say she came willingly.

'But you're so young.'

'Don't mean I haven't worked hard to get where I am.'

I laugh. 'So you're a real success story? True grit?'

He looks offended. 'Aye. Why not?'

'Well, because crime doesn't exactly spell success.'

'Not to you, maybe.'

'Not to anyone!'

He shrugs, rolling a cigarette for himself. 'Not where you come from, then. But I had two choices. Die of poverty or do what I do. I chose life.' He exhales the blue smoke. 'No decision, really.'

'Come on. There was nothing else you could do?'

'Not really. My parents died when I was young. I didn't have much of an education. There were two ways of making a living in our town. Crime or working in a factory day in, day out, till you die from old age or exhaustion, or a not-so-freak accident. So I did what I did, and I did it better than most. End of story.'

'But it's not like that for everyone,' I say, thinking of the bottles and jars in the girls' apartment, and the cafe, and the shoes falling out of Ceri's wardrobe.

He smiles. 'Ceri, Cate and Demi? No, they aren't suffering. There's lots like them here, you'll see. They had nice schools and nice houses that never flooded and big cars and parents that could afford fuel, then they got sick of that and moved here to be independent and live off me instead.'

'What about you though? I mean, there are other jobs here. Why don't you do one of those, now that you've got away from where you grew up? You could start again.'

76

He stands up and goes over to the painting of the woman, and points at it.

'D'you like this?'

I blush, because it's a nude, and because I remember the raw sexual energy that radiated from it when I touched it last time. But it is beautiful.

'It's lovely. The brushwork is really fine. I was looking at it last time.'

He gazes at it with me. 'Aye. Me too. The thing is, Melz, I'm really good at what I do. Somehow, I am. And I make a lot of money doing it. Why the bloody hell would I do some job that would just about pay for a dingy little shared flat, just to be *honest*, just to *know my place*, when I can be king of the underworld instead and enjoy this fine art? This fine tobacco? Sit on these soft leather sofas and sleep with curvy rich girls that never had to worry about being underweight and malnourished? Eh? Talk to you about poetry over a glass of wine that costs more than a month's food when I were a kid? Why would I do that, Melz? Why *should* I?'

'I . . . I didn't mean . . .'

'No, I know, Melz. You're a good-hearted lass and you've had the opportunity to live honestly, and I'm glad for you. But I don't want to start again. I don't see why I should. I'll tell you what I do want, shall I?'

'All right.'

He drains his glass. 'What I want is to make life as hard as humanly possible for those rich bastards that think they're so much better than me, just because their families have money, just because they had the good fortune to be born into privilege. I want to make it as hard as possible for them to get fuel. Fuel's the most prized commodity there is out here in the Redworld, Melz.'

He gets up and goes into the next room, bringing back the half-drunk bottle, and tops up both our glasses.

'A time's coming when all the lights'll go off altogether, and we'll be living like you do in the Greenworld, apart from we won't have a bloody clue how to survive. We don't have community. We don't have religion. We don't have the right kind of ethos about living on the land. And when that time comes, the people that've stockpiled whatever fuel's left will be the ones in charge. Me. I'll be in charge. And it'll be my turn to put those over-privileged bastards to work for me. My turn to pay them less than they need to live.'

I don't know what to say, so I drink. I remember Omar talking about the Redworld refugees that he thought would start arriving in our villages the longer the war went on and the worse things got in the Redworld.

'Why are you telling me all of this? Why did you want to see me?' I ask, but I feel like I know the answer. He stares at the painting and doesn't answer for a minute, and then starts, as if he was asleep and I'd woken him up.

'Ah. That's the question, isn't it? That is the question.' He smiles, and holds out a hand to help me up. 'You were sent here to help me, Demelza Hawthorne.

That's what I believe. I've known about you, all the Greenworld witches, for a long while. I know the lasses told you about how the Greenworld's represented here. How kids learn about your mum at school, how she's some kind of dangerous terrorist, how she bombed all them places in London—' He sees my shock at that and takes my other hand in his. 'Nah, I've never believed that either. That's just what they needed, some stories that bad to convince people there were a good reason for putting that border up. That it was in the public interest and all that. That the Contract of Separation was their idea and not what your mum insisted on. They tried to erase witchcraft from history, but some of us know. And I think you being here . . . it's not an accident, lass. This means something.'

'Does it? I didn't plan it. It just happened.'

'Maybe. Maybe not. Things have a way of happening when they need to is all I can say.'

'I suppose so.'

'Aye.' He squeezes my hands in his. 'But the most important question of all is: are you hungry? Have my maniacal ravings made you desperate for sustenance, or sickened you to your Greenworld core?' He's switched from passionate fury to his more customary charm, and I'm reminded that I have to be on my guard here with everyone. This is not home. People are not the same. Nothing is as it seems in faeryland.

'I'm hungry,' I admit, and he nods approvingly.

'Aye. Me too. Let's go. Never mind politics and

propaganda for now, eh? I want you to tell me all about Demelza Hawthorne for the rest of the evening.'

'All right . . . I suppose so.'

'Right you are. Let's go, then.'

We walk, or rather I stumble, through the evening streets.

'We're not going to drive?' I ask, thinking about Ceri.

'Nah. It's not far. Nicer to walk,' he says.

'Ceri seemed . . . concerned about the proles,' I reply.

'Ceri's a bloody idiot,' he says shortly.

As we walk past the bottom of the tor I'm curious to see what he feels about it, living right under it – almost in it really. And whether he's at all concerned about the fracking.

'What's it like, living here?' I try not to fall over on the cobbles with the stupid shoes, and he holds out a protective arm for me to hold. He gazes up at the tor, gauzy in a spring-evening twilight.

'It's pretty amazing,' he says quietly, even reverently. My surprise must show on my face. He notices. 'You didn't think someone like me would care about it?'

'Umm. I don't know. Maybe not.'

'It's a sacred place. No reason I can't appreciate that.'

'I suppose.'

He watches me looking up at it. 'It's special to you,' he says. A statement rather than a question.

I nod. 'Yes. I always wanted to see it. Goddess be praised.'

'Must be odd that it's not in the Greenworld. Isn't it one of the most revered places in Europe?'

I feel that strange disconnect again between my expectation of the place and the reality of it – that closed feeling, as if something is there but it's buried deep.

'Yes. It's the Heart of the World.' I stop and look up at the hill, majestic in the rapidly darkening evening. 'It's an energy centre. Supposed to be particularly heart-centred energy.' He looks blank, so I try to explain. 'It's got naturally strong energy. As a place. And that energy can be different in different places in the world because of different currents. And the particular feeling here is love. Heart-centred.' I tap my chest. 'You feel it here.' Or at least you should feel it there, I think.

He taps his chest with an amused look on his face. 'You're telling me I should be feeling love, as I stand here with you, Demelza Hawthorne?'

I look away, embarrassed. 'That's not what I meant, by Brighid.'

He smiles. 'I know, I know. I'm just joking.'

We walk on a few more paces, and the need to say something overcomes me.

'But the fracking . . .' I say, not knowing whether I should.

He looks at me quizzically. 'Fracking?'

'Yes. It's . . . sacred land out here, Bran. It would be bad anywhere, but here . . .'

'Fracking's bad for the tor?'

'Of course it is!'

'But it's not on the tor, just on the fields around it. It's affecting the tor, you think?'

'I think it is. Something is. It doesn't feel right here.'

He drapes his arm round my shoulders, and squeezes the top of my arm with his hand. 'Don't worry, lass. I wouldn't let anything happen to it.'

'Is it up to you?' I look up at him. I can't believe he is as powerful as the girls say he is. In charge of those security patrols. It seems mad.

'Let's say I can make it difficult for them, the energy companies. The power of security's rising,' he says, looking up at the tower behind us. 'They know they're fighting a losing battle with fuel any road. There's hardly any left anywhere. Without us there'd be mass panic. Revolution, maybe. We keep the people away from their door. There won't be any fracking in ten years, Demelza. Because the bastard power companies know as sure as shit that there won't be anything left to frack.'

'So what will you do instead? What fuel are you going to stockpile?'

He smiles. 'All in good time, Demelza. Let me enjoy taking you out for your dinner before we have to talk about all the boring things like science and money and corruption, eh?'

'I . . . ummm . . . OK.' I have never met anyone like

him before, and I don't know if I like him or if he scares me to death.

'Come on, then. We'll be late,' he says, and takes my hand. I don't pull it away.

We walk into the town, not really saying much. It's cool without being cold; the beginnings of spring lend a freshness to the evening. I don't mind not talking: there's plenty to look at. Everything is so new, but I don't want to bombard Bran with questions like some kind of five-year-old. We stay on what I'm learning is the richer side of town; we walk past big glass windows, more elaborate and expensive shops. A feather dress here, a glittery mask there. Strange-looking food in packages and shiny plastic. Furniture. Grey metal boxes with dials and buttons. My frown must be especially large at that, as Bran whispers 'electronics' in my ear. It doesn't help explain what they are except that they, presumably, need electricity to work. Electricity. How much of it is there, and how does it even work?

Bran takes my arm and we veer off the main high street into a shadowy alley. There's nothing down here, and I suddenly realize that no one knows where I am. The girls know I'm seeing Bran for this strange getting-to-know-you dinner, but they don't know where he's taking me. For all I know he could be planning to torture me. Or hand me in to the authorities.

We stop halfway down the alley and Bran knocks on a nondescript door, its cream paint flaking off. A shadow grows behind the smoky glass panels and the door half opens, emitting a greenish-gold light from inside.

'Eduardo. Good to see you,' Bran says, grinning, and the door opens fully. A middle-aged man with a long plaited black beard dressed in some kind of bizarre black military uniform – too many medals and spangles – laughs and beckons us in.

'Ahhh. Mr Crowley. Yes. Come in, come in. Always a pleasure. And your lady friend this evening?' He looks expectantly at me.

This evening.

'Demelza,' I reply.

He shakes my hand enthusiastically and somewhat sweatily. 'Demelza, you are most welcome. Follow me please.'

He leads us along a long palatial corridor hung with large oil paintings in ornate gold frames. A thick crimson carpet pulls at my shoes as if I were walking through raw meat. What is this place? I wonder.

We walk into a small candlelit room with one ornate gold table in the middle. There's only one table; it's a restaurant just for us. The walls are covered in drapes of thick blood-red velvet. There is another dark doorway leading out of the room. Eduardo pulls out one of the chairs for me, and the other for Bran. He brings a large dark green bottle to the table from a gold bucket on a stand in the corner.

'I think you'll enjoy this,' he says, pouring a clear bubbling liquid into two saucer-shaped glasses.

Bran sips his. 'Excellent. And what delights d'you have for us today?'

'Bluefin tuna steaks, truffles and a delightful twentieth-century Barolo to accompany it. Oh, and, of course, a delicious dessert for the lady. A confection from the finest chocolatiers in Switzerland. You won't find better anywhere.'

'Aye, sounds good.'

Bran nods, and Eduardo glides out of the room. I get the feeling I am in some kind of surreal theatre piece, where we sit in this gilded room and strange men with fixed smiles slide in and out as if on rails.

Bran sips from his glass, and smiles at me. 'Aren't you going to have owt?'

I pick up my glass. Why not?

'What is it?' I ask, twirling the glass round by its stem and watching the bubbles inside.

'Champagne. French fizzy wine,' he says, and I drink a little. The bubbles go up my nose and I snort in surprise. It's nice though.

'Hmmm. And what was that other stuff he said?'

'Bluefin tuna. A type of fish, rare these days. Truffles – they're a kind of fungus pigs dig up in the forest. What forests there are left, of course.'

I wrinkle my nose. 'Sounds horrible. Why are we having those?'

'Cos they're expensive. I wanted to give you the best of the Redworld, Melz. As a welcome. So you can see we're not all bad.' He takes another drink from his

85

glass and wipes his mouth on his sleeve. 'Well. So you can see I'm not all bad, I suppose.'

'What you eat and where you eat it doesn't tell me anything about how bad or not you are,' I say, without thinking. 'I'm a witch. I can see everything I need to without all that.'

'And what do you see about me, then?'

I look into his brown eyes. 'That you want something from me. That you believe in your own reasons for what you do. That you have been very hurt in the past and you'll protect yourself from being hurt again at all costs.' I smile at the flash of surprise in his eyes. 'That you are not all bad,' I add. A shadow memory floats just out of reach. An image that had flashed into my mind after we first met. Before that awkward kiss. But I don't remember.

He looks piercingly at me. I feel like I am the only person in the world.

'Hmm. Aye, you're right. I do want something from you. But I hope it's something you won't mind giving.'

'What?' I ask, thinking I know the answer already. He wants magic.

'Let me tell you what you think I want, first of all. You think I want to enlist you as my personal witch. You think I want you to cast spells for me. Curse my enemies. That's what the girls have told you, eh?'

'Errr . . . yes. That's what they do for you. You think as a Greenworld witch I'll be——'

'Better than them? I have no doubt. Everything about you tells me that. You're thoughtful, insightful. You have a presence that they don't. You look different, you act different. You're mindful of your environment. You're a hard worker, like me. We've both put the hours in. We haven't read a couple of books on witchcraft or crime—' he tosses a grin at me – 'and decided that was it, we were the top of our game.'

'OK – so . . .?'

'So I want more from you than a few spells.'

Eduardo comes in with the fish, which is decorated with flowers and served with an elaborate-looking salad. He places it in front of me with a set of ornate silver cutlery, then melts away. I taste the fish cautiously, which is delicious.

'What, then?'

He reaches across the table and takes my hand. 'I want your trust.'

My hand is tingling where he's grasping it; electricity is flowing between us. He may not recognize the feeling, but it's the same as when magic is going right, when there's the right balance of energy between the people doing it. Without trying, we're making something happen here. Magnetism, chemistry, something.

'My trust?'

'Aye. I want you to trust that we can work together and make something amazing. Something new, that the world has never seen. I want you to trust me enough to tell me about the portals. How to use them for energy.'

I snatch my hand away and the current between us evaporates into the corners of the room and becomes shadow. I should have guessed that we weren't just here for flirting and fine dining.

'Where did you hear about that?'

He looks unfazed and draws his hand back casually. 'I'm well connected, Melz. I told you that.'

'Connected to whom?'

He eats some fish, taking his time. Making me wait. Keeping the advantage on his side.

'It don't matter who. What matters is that I know that these things exist, and that you know how to . . . operate them. And I know that they're some kind of universal energy. Stockpiling fuel isn't enough, Melz. That'll only take me so far. What I need is a solution. Summat I can sell to the really big players.' He laughs to himself. 'At an unreasonably high price, of course. If they want salvation they're going to have to bloody pay for it.'

I can't believe that I crawled on my hands and knees under the border fences, throwing rotting bones to distract the dogs, every moment full of the possibility of being shot or mauled or worse, and I still haven't escaped the portals. I can't get away from people wanting what the Greenworld has. How dare he? How dare he think that you can ask, just like that, and I'll betray any secret of my community – not least the biggest secret; the one that I'm committed to protect? I want to say that to him, scream that at him, but even that would be a betrayal. Even to admit that they exist to an outsider is a risk.

I push my chair back from the table and stand up. 'I'm going. Thanks for the fish.'

The shoes dig into my feet but I march out proudly nonetheless, down the red and gold corridor to the back door with the frosted glass. I need to get away from here, and away from the faint reedy whisper of my subconscious that the Greenworld isn't mine any more. It isn't my responsibility to protect its secrets.

He runs after me and catches my arm, reaching round me and leaning on the door with his other hand, his arm tensed, rigid. 'Melz. Don't go. We need to talk about this.'

I pull my arm away. 'Don't touch me, by Brighid. I'm leaving.'

'I'm sorry.'

'So you should be. Let go of the door.'

'I will. But I need you to hear me out.'

'I don't need to hear you.'

'You do. You do, Melz. You came here for a reason, I know it. You didn't just come here to hang out with Ceri and get pissed and go shopping every day. You know it too. I know you do.'

He looks into my eyes earnestly. He obviously believes in what he's saying, but I know he's wrong. Wrong that I'll betray the Greenworld and show him what a portal does. Roach wanted the same thing – to use Danny's magic along with his to enact some kind of different magic with them, to be able to turn portal energy into real power, to make lights shine and machines work; he wanted to own the portals, use them to barter for power in the Redworld – and we fought him and the gangs for them. We spilt blood that day – Tom's blood, and so many others' – protecting our secret.

Bran's not going to get what he wants just by asking nicely.

'Let me go, Bran. I'm not having this conversation with you. Report me to the police if you like. Whatever. Just let me go.'

'Please, Melz. I need you.'

'Need me all you like. I'm still leaving.'

He keeps his hand on the door, biceps tensed. 'I can't let you go.' It's a statement now, not a request, and I can see his jaw set. His eyes narrow a little.

I look at him square in the eyes. 'I recommend that you take your hand off that door and let me leave, or you'll regret it,' I say slowly and clearly.

'No. I need to talk to you. I'm stronger than you, Melz, so you may as well accept that this door isn't opening till you've heard what I've got to say.'

'All right.' I smile. I have something that is much, much stronger than muscle. 'Don't say I didn't warn you.'

Chapter Eight

And Peredur stood, and compared the blackness of
the raven and the whiteness of the snow, and the
redness of the blood, to the hair of the lady that
best he loved, which was blacker than jet, and to
her skin which was whiter than the snow, and to the
two red spots upon her cheeks, which were redder
than the blood upon the snow appeared to be.

From 'Culhwch and Olwen', *The Mabinogion*

I focus my eyes on the night outside the door, at the dim
flickering street lights that glow like distant stars in the
black sky of the frosted glass, and I make the call to Her.
I don't know if She will hear me, but I have to try. I'm in
danger and I have to trust that She won't ignore me,
even though I've ignored Her since making the curse.
Even though I don't know if She wants me as Her
priestess any more. *Morrigan. Blessed Crow. Phantom Queen.*
Feathered Goddess of the Night. Help me. Lend me your wings.

Hear my battle cry. I am your priestess again, if you'll have me. Please, help me.

I look back into Bran's eyes. Only a second has passed but I feel the energy fill the narrow corridor, a surging heat, then I hear the approaching flutter of wings. *I was always with you, child,* She says in my ear. *In the darkness and the quiet, and even when you thought you walked alone, I was there. I will always be there for you.*

The first crow hits the thin glass, and Bran instinctively pulls his hand away from the door.

The second crow lands on the sill below the glass and caws loudly.

The third one cracks the glass with a headlong body blow, and the rest of them push through the weakened pane. An explosion of blue-black feathers fills the corridor. Swooping, screaming, they attack Bran. More and more fly through the broken pane; I pull the door open and perhaps a hundred more stream in, all jagged wings and sharp beaks: past me, through my shadow, towards him. They swirl around him in a funnel-like shape, a heart shape; briefly they form the face of a crow, its oversized beak opening around his head.

He backs down the corridor, trying to protect his face, and falls, crashing into a gilded table. He knocks his temple and blood trickles down his cheek. He reaches out for me and calls my name.

'You should have let me go,' I say calmly into the shrieking murder. That's the collective noun for crows.

A murder. Worse than ravens even, who are just an unkindness.

I make sure he sees me turn my back on him and walk away. I pick up a couple of fallen crow feathers from the floor and walk out of the door, back straight, head high. I feel the strength of the Morrigan coursing through me, a tingling like elation, like fury, like how the Celts felt when battle frenzy was upon them. Woman and man, they responded to Her call and fought the threat in their path.

She protects Her own. I know that now, and I know She will always be there for me.

Conscience pulls at me as I run down the alley and back out into the street, and my temper ebbs away as quickly as it came. I pull off the ridiculous shoes and stand there in my bare feet, despite the cold, holding them. I look back down the alley. It was a warning to Bran, nothing more, but the Morrigan is unpredictable. I don't think She would have killed him – there was no reason to, I just needed to get away – but I don't know that for sure.

The cold creeps up my legs and into my gut. What have I done? I've attacked the person that could make life easy for me here in the Redworld. The person that can get me imprisoned with one word to the wrong people: questioned, tortured . . . whatever they do to enemies of the Redworld. I'm not sure if that's what I am, but I don't want to find out. And yet, as I stand there, rigid with tension and adrenalin, I know that I

93

still don't want to go back to the Greenworld. I don't want to atone. I want my own life. Something new.

But my conscience whispers, *Have I done wrong? Have I hurt someone again?*

No. It's not the same. The Goddess helped you. You were in danger.

But still — what will he do if he catches up with me? I have magic on my side, but he has weapons, and people to do his dirty work.

I run in the opposite direction to Bran's house and the rich side of town; quickly the streets become the ones I first walked in Glastonbury: dirty, vandalized, broken. I know I need somewhere to hide.

I see a faded blue splintered door and look up. The building doesn't look lived in and I chance it. I push it with my shoulder, opening it just enough to slip through. If there are people here, I'll apologize. The hallway inside is dank, and the carpet is soaked, probably with urine judging by the smell. I step gingerly round the worst of it and peer into the room on the ground floor. The door is wedged open with rubbish, but it's so disgusting in there I can't go in. I scuttle up the stairs in the dark. Upstairs the room is uninviting and cold, but smells cleaner. I walk in carefully and nudge a pile of wet newspaper aside with my toe. The floor is fairly clear and the floorboards feel all right, though they creak where I walk; the window is broken, but I'm used to the cold.

I start to pace around. Like I always do in times of

stress, I split into two selves and argue it out. Strong Melz and weak Melz. Decisive Melz and waffly Melz. Melz of the definite black eyeliner and Melz of the cheeks streaked with grey tears.

I shouldn't have done that. I should have stayed and listened. He only wanted to talk.

You don't know that. He threatened you.

He's nice. He wouldn't hurt me.

You don't know that. He's a criminal, by Brighid. What would stop him attacking you, if he wanted to?

He's powerful. Now I've made trouble for myself.

So leave.

I have nowhere to go.

You had nowhere to go when you left the Greenworld, but you still left.

But I have friends here.

Not any more.

I can't do it again – leave somewhere in the middle of the night on my own.

You'll do it again, and every time you need to. You're strong.

I'm weak. I miss Mum. I miss the Hands, even Saba.

You made your choice. This is a new life. Now live it.

I can't!

You can.

'I CAN'T!' I cry out and thump my fist on the wall. I think of my cosy bedroom at home, of my drawings on the wall, of my books and my patchwork blankets. Of the cats, and Mum's teas, and meditating in the garden.

I start to cry. I knew the Redworld would be different, but I didn't know how different. I'm not made for this, I think. I don't know how to live here. As soon as anyone knows where I'm from, they want things from me. They want too much. I need help.

I kneel down on the dirty, creaking floorboards and try to clear my mind. 'Help me, Morrigan, Phantom Queen, Warrior,' I call out. 'I need your strength. I need your courage. Help me, O Goddess. Help me.'

The wind blows through the broken window and I hear someone kicking a can down the street. I look up through the dirty glass to the clouds scudding across the night sky. Suddenly the moon comes out and illuminates the room, its harsh bluish flat light reaching into the corners.

In the corner to my right there's a hump of junk covered with a faded sheet: brown with orange daisies. I stand up and poke at it gingerly. I feel like I have to know what's in there. The sheet is, at least, dry, and so I pull it away gently.

There are a couple of boxes – slightly mildewed, but not bad. I pull up the cardboard flap of the top one and pull out a candlestick, then another. Nice brass ones: heavy, with red candles still in them, half burned down. I place them on the floor and reach in again, trying to see what I'm reaching for. Something soft. I pull out a handmade fabric doll with old-fashioned petticoats and plaits. I look in to the bottom of the box; the rest looks to be plates and cups, nothing special. I heft the top box off the other, and look inside, hunkering down on my knees. Half tucked under the bottom flap is a knife, a little sharper than an eating knife, with a black wood handle. I turn it over in my hands. Every witch needs a sacred knife: an athame. I sit back on my heels, thinking.

It's as if I am being reinitiated, being given the sacred tools for the second time. And deep inside me I hear Her voice. *You may have left the Greenworld, but you can never leave me. I am the great and terrible Goddess of Death, but in death always comes rebirth. This is your second life. You are born again, Demelza. These are your tools to survive in the Redworld. Rededicate yourself to me. Remember who you are. Remember what you are.*

I stand up, holding the knife. *Honour me*, says Her voice in my head, as true and clear as the moonlight slicing through the clouds. It's a full moon and I hadn't noticed. I stand for a moment, looking up at the moon in shock. I don't think I've missed a full-moon ceremony since before I became a witch – before I was eight years old. But I was about to miss this one.

This may be a hovel, but tonight I can make it Her temple. She will guide me. I place the candlesticks on a grimy white plastic table, wiping it down with my sleeve as well as I'm able. I take the doll and unplait its black hair. I look at it critically for a moment, and then rummage in my pocket for my kohl stick. Carefully I draw a triskele, symbol of the Morrigan, on its forehead, and another on the bodice of its little dress. I lay the doll on the table. I go back to the box with the cups and

97

plates and find the nicest cup: a plain glass with a chipped silver rim. There's a small dirty sink in the corner. I turn the tap, not expecting any water to come out, but a trickle comes. I fill the glass with water and say a blessing over it. I light the candles with matches from my bag. This is basic, but it will have to do.

I hold the knife up to the moon and recite an invocation I wrote long ago: a personal prayer from me to Her.

> 'Great Queen whose laugh is the beat of crows'
>> wings,
> I honour you in this place.
> Great Mother that protects the land,
> Hold me in your embrace.
> Great Warrior that leads us into battle,
> I ask for your grace.
> Wise woman that teaches me magic,
> Show me your lined face.
> Goddess that strikes terror into the hearts of the
>> untrue,
> Enter and bless this space.
> Washer at the Ford; Banshee, Siren, Faery Queen,
> Enter and bless this space.'

The moonlight floods through the window, illuminating everything. I feel a wash of energy pass through me and feel Her presence, feel strength flowing through me. I can't stop being a witch. I can't stop my regular worship of Her and of the natural world. It's my path, wherever I live, and if I have nothing else, I still have that. I can still honour Her in the Redworld, even in this less-than-perfect space, because now She has blessed it.

I bow my head as if before Her. *What shall I do, Great Queen? Bran Crowley wants the portal, just like Roach did. The Redworld wants my magic — your magic, your mysteries. That which I am sworn to protect. Should I leave here, or stay and fight?*

I pick up the doll and trace my finger over the spiral on its chest, waiting for an answer. The Morrigan always answers. I train my attention on the moon, gazing up at Her; I try to absorb as much of Her energy as possible. To me, focusing on the moon feels like a kind of chaotic, pleasant nervousness – feeling like you don't know where to put yourself, a heady anticipation. I let it fill me.

Listen to him, says a voice in my ear. *Listen, even though you won't like his message. He has a part to play as much as you, my priestess, and he is part of your journey. You must stay, and do as your instincts tell you. He will not hurt you as long as I protect you.*

'But he could betray me. To the police. He has the power here.' I speak into the moonlight-filled room.

Her voice resounds in my head again. *No. You have the power. You are mine, and I am Mistress of Magic over all. I am the sea and the earth and the sky. Don't fear this boy, priestess. Only fear the enemy.*

I stare into the flames of the candles, feeling the energy in the room and staying centred, feeling the new strength flow through me, warm and steady. I let go of worrying, and have faith that the right thing will happen. I know that wherever I am, my goddess is always with me.

Don't neglect your journal, She says, and I remember I brought it with me. I haven't written in it much in the past month. Longer. Grief stills the pen and dulls the mind. But now, feeling the bright moon soaking into my spine, I put the Goddess doll down and turn to a new page in the leather-bound book. I pull out my pack of tarot cards, always with me, and pull out one card at random. Looking at it, I chew the old blue pencil attached to the book with a strip of plaited wool for a minute, and begin writing.

Excerpt from Demelza Hawthorne's Greenworld Journal

Date – 10 April 2047
Moon phase – full in Libra
Menstruation cycle – week 2
Sun phase – Aries
Card drawn – The King of Swords
Dreams – I don't have dreams any more.
Chosen tenet – *We are called the Greenworld as green is the colour of life, regeneration and purity.*

The moon is in Libra – a time for emotional balance, or a definite imbalance. Partnerships, romance, yin and yang. That's what a Libra full moon is all about, and in the month of Aries – passion and adventure too. I feel only disdain for romance and the attraction of opposites. Romance isn't for me.

I suppose Bran is the King of Swords. He has power and cleverness, but he might be sneaky. Underhand. He may have a flexible approach to morality. Is he a liar? But his words are enticing; he is attractive. Can I trust him to keep me safe?

Reflection on the chosen tenet – If the Greenworld is green because green is purity and regeneration, what is the Redworld? The inference has always been that the Redworld is red because it burns everything. It consumes; its streets run with the blood of the innocent, shed by the corrupt. But now I'm here I can feel its power. Red power, passion and fire. Blood isn't always bad. Blood is of the Mother. The Morrigan, Brighid – sometimes they ask for blood sacrifices from their priestesses.

Monthly blood, like the Procession of the Maidens ritual at Yule, the blood of their people in battle. That too, and recently.

Red and green are simplistic divisions. Nothing is completely good. Nothing completely bad. In a sense, then, is that the realization about balance from the Libra full moon tonight? See the dark spot in the yang, the light spot in the yin. No light without a shadow. No shadow without light.

Chapter Nine

> Mistress of Magic, hear my call:
> You who are one, who are many, who are all –
> Give me wisdom, give me sight,
> Lend me your vision in the sharp moonlight.

> Scrying chant, from *The Book of the Morrigan,*
> *Greenworld Prayers and Songs*

I dream of Daniel Prentice.

He is facing away from me, hunched over something, and I can tell from the way that his back convulses that he is crying. I go over to him and touch him gently on the shoulder, surprised at the compassion I feel for him – at best he usually irritates me, and at worst I hate him. He was the reason Tom died. The gangs wanted Danny, and in the fight for Tintagel, when they attacked us, Tom died defending him. If it wasn't for Danny, Tom would still be here, and maybe I'd still be back home. Maybe we'd even be together.

He looks up at me, eyes red and watery. I look down at his hands and see that he is holding a dog-eared set of tarot cards spattered in blood. I can't tell whether it's his blood or not. The card on top is the Queen of Swords.

'This is a woman that guards her heart with a blade,' he says, looking sadly at it, and hands it to me. I take it, and notice that my hand is smeared with blood too.

I sit down next to him. We are in the middle of a stone circle – a wide circumference with tall spiked sentinels. Intuitively I understand that this is Scorhill circle, although I have never been there before. It is night-time and the moon is full and low above us; charcoal clouds sail across it like pirate ships.

'Her power rests in the circle,' I reply, not having any idea of what that means, but at the same time feeling that there is a truth in what we are saying somewhere underneath, somewhere in the gauzy astral web of symbolic interconnectedness that is the world of dreams. I hold Danny's hand and feel that surge of pity for him again.

'There is one more, then the formula can be written,' he says, and a series of symbols – none that I recognize – flash around us within the circle, lighting up the grass and the stones. The lights stop, and the night darkens. I feel Danny's hand slip from mine.

I wake up, holding the doll, and it's morning.

Chapter Ten

Study me then, you who shall lovers be,
At the next world, that is, at the next spring;
For I am every dead thing,
In whom Love wrought new alchemy.

From 'A Nocturnal upon St Lucy's Day'
by John Donne

I get up and perform a salute to the sun. The yoga stretch fills me with light and positivity. I am a witch, and witches maintain their bodies' natural energies. They also take notice of their dreams. Last night's dream about Danny was odd. I am enough of a witch to know that vivid dreams are magical dreams, where two souls can connect in the dream-space, the astral plane.

I woke up hating him a little less. That annoys me. But I have to concentrate on the material realm, not dreams. I need somewhere better to stay, and to pay rent I need a job. I don't know much, but I know that's how money works here.

I consider going to see Ceri and Catie, but put it off. I'm not sure what to tell them about last night yet, and I don't want them to try to persuade me that working for Bran is my best option while I'm here. There must be other things I can do. I lie on the blanket on the rough floorboards, watching the sun move up and through the glass. Bran and the girls knew my name, and when they knew I was from the Greenworld they put it together. Who I was, who Mum is. But no one else has to know that. No one else knows I'm from the Greenworld, and if I make up another name, just to be on the safe side — then no one's the wiser, right?

I neaten myself up as well as I can with the trickle of cold water in the sink and reapply a little make-up. Then I go down on to the street, resolved to find a job. I don't believe that on the rough side of town anyone's going to need to see any papers proving I am who I say I am. I'm more worried about my complete lack of Redworld skills, but maybe some of the things I did at home might be useful here. I look down the street filled with litter, at the graffitied walls, the flaking paint, the broken windows. It's hard to imagine what need there might be for rune-casting, incense-making or psychic defence, unless it's my own.

I go into the first shop I come across, a little down the street; the sign says OFF-LICENCE, which turns out to be a shop that sells alcohol. The shopkeeper looks at me suspiciously as I walk in, rattling a string of brass bells on a faded red string that ring shrilly. I run a hand through my fringe self-consciously.

'Can I help you?' he asks in a tone that says he really isn't interested in helping me at all.

'Oh. Yes. Well, I'm looking for a job,' I say, trying to look friendly and hard-working.

He snorts. 'You and everyone else,' he says, looking me up and down. 'I don't need anyone.'

I look around at the dusty shelves and the dirty lino floor. 'Maybe a cleaner?' I ask.

He looks embarrassed and angry; I regret saying it as soon as the words are out.

'What are you saying? That my shop's dirty? Get out of here, you cheeky bitch!'

I hold up my hands in a conciliatory way.

'I'm sorry, that came out wrong. I didn't mean your shop was dirty. Just that all shops need cleaners, I imagine? It shouldn't be something that a manager does?'

He snorts again. 'Shows how much you know. I can't afford to employ anyone, OK? Whether I need them or not. There's too much booze on the black market. I get robbed every week, more or less. I barely make enough to feed myself,' he says, then points at my clothes. 'And anyway, if you want a job, you need to look smarter. Who in hell's going to employ you? You look like you slept rough last night.'

I catch my reflection in an age-spotted mirror

overhanging the counter: I look pale, with dark circles under my eyes. Unkempt.

I back out of the shop. 'I'm sorry,' I mutter.

I hear him shout after me as I pull the door closed. 'Try having a bath next time! Filthy kids.' I look down at myself. The borrowed outfit is creased from being slept in, and my hair needs a wash.

I walk further down the road. This would appear to be the roughest area of town; I walk past a tatty-looking cafe and look in hungrily, but I don't have any money. I sit down on the kerb outside a budget shoe shop, next to a middle-aged woman in a long threadbare skirt and cardigan.

She looks at me out of the corner of her eye. 'First time, is it?' she asks wheezily.

I smile politely. 'First time doing what?'

'Begging. Haven't seen you before. I know most of them,' she says and points up the street. I notice that there are men and women, some children, on pretty much every kerb, every step. As I watch, a man comes out of a shop a few doors down and shoos a young kid away with a broom. The kid walks up the street, finds another space, and sits down again.

'Oh. No. I'm not a beggar. I just needed to sit down,' I say, the cold kerb seeping through my leggings.

'Ah. I just thought, because of your . . .' She waves her finger up and down. 'You know. You look a bit scruffy,' she says.

'I slept in my clothes last night. I've been staying

somewhere without a bathroom. Or heating. I just got here.'

'Squatting, is it? You need to be careful of that. The security forces do sweeps of all the unoccupied houses. They catch you, they'll put you in prison.'

'What, even if no one's living there?'

'Yep. They don't take kindly to it.' She coughs a deep hollow cough and pulls her cardigan round her. 'Spring. If you can call it that. Still freezing.'

We watch the street for a while, the people passing by. An anxious-looking well-dressed man tosses a couple of coins at the woman next to me, hardly stopping, and not looking either of us in the eye. He doesn't want to be walking on this street, on the wrong side of town.

'Bless you, my love,' she calls out nonetheless, and pockets the coins.

'Do you know anywhere that I can find a job?' I ask her bluntly. If she's local she might know of something, but she laughs, though it turns into a cough again.

'Ha! Yeah, there's lots of jobs here. I just choose to beg because I object to the principle of working for a living. Is that what you think?' She laughs again. 'Christ almighty. What boat did you get off?'

'So there aren't many jobs?'

She looks at me like I'm being some kind of idiot, which I suppose I am.

'No. No jobs, dear.' I look up the street at all the beggars. 'They aren't scared of work. They don't object to it. They'd all love a job and a room to call their own if they could get it, but they can't. This is all they can do. Hope that those rich bastards toss us their spare change every now and again, and ignore us while they do it.' She spits on the pavement.

'I'm sorry,' I say, not knowing what else to say. The wind whips down the street. I shiver.

She shakes her head, like she's a mother duck and I'm a runaway duckling.

'No point being sorry, is there? Sorry won't keep you warm.'

I hug my jacket round me.

'What about the rich people? How do they get jobs?' I ask, thinking of Ceri and the girls.

She laughs. 'They're born in the right place to the right people, and when they grow up they get handed the money and the power.' She catches my eye and smiles ruefully. 'Old socialist, me. You probably don't even remember what that is.' I shake my head. 'Lot of inherited wealth round here. Lot of kids your age don't have to work. Don't even have to go to school if they don't fancy it. Why bother, with all that money?'

'There really isn't anything at all I could do?'

'Well, there's the criminal life, if you want it. Sell drugs, do security, that kind of thing. Not a good life though. Other than that there's the factories, but there's fewer and fewer jobs for people there. Mostly mechanized now. You get some positions come up but not much. Suppose if you smartened yourself you might get a bit of waitressing or something.'

'I don't really have any experience.'

'Oh. Well, that doesn't help. What can you do?'

How to explain what my skills are? Leading mystery plays and festivals. Spellcasting. Meditation. Divination. Herbal lore.

'It's hard to explain.'

'Hmmm.' She looks at me critically. 'You got any friends here?'

'Kind of.'

'Do they have room for you to stay?'

I sigh. 'Yes. But I don't—'

She interrupts me. 'Then go there. Ask if you can stay for a while – maybe you can find some work in one of the big houses. They take in servants sometimes, though I'm not sure what you'd get without experience. I'm serious, girl. If you can avoid sleeping in a doorway, avoid it. At the very least, go and get a bath and something to eat.'

I shake my head. 'It's complicated,' I say.

She coughs, and dabs her mouth with her cardigan. 'Life is complicated, my lover. Tell you what's a right pain though. Emphysema on cold nights. Trying to make sure your kids get at least one small meal a day. Chilblains. Frostbite. Whatever it is, love, sort it out. You don't want to be next to me tomorrow. I can guarantee you that.'

I look at my stupid borrowed shoes, ashamed of myself.

'I'm sorry,' I say again.

'Don't be. Come and see me when you get some

money,' she says, coughing again. I get up. The cold is starting to seep through my bones.

'OK,' I say, not knowing what else to add. *Hope you don't die? Hope you don't freeze to death?* 'I'll come back.'

She smiles.

'You might, you might not. I won't hope.'

Chapter Eleven

Pale, beyond porch and portal,
 Crowned with calm leaves, she stands
Who gathers all things mortal
 With cold immortal hands;
Her languid lips are sweeter
Than love's who fears to greet her
To men that mix and meet her
 From many times and lands.

From 'The Garden of Proserpine' by Algernon Swinburne

It takes a day of being ignored, spat on, looked down on and sneered at for me to give in. Only a day, and I'm ashamed to admit that it's hunger that takes me back to Ceri's apartment. Is this all it takes to weaken my resolve? One day on my feet, painful shoes crippling me, a growling stomach, thirst? The need for a friendly face, for someone to tell me something other than I'm worthless, valueless, an intrusion, an irritation?

The last place I tried was the worst. It was close to Ceri's apartment block: a huge gated mansion that I buzzed just because the woman on the street mentioned servants, and it was the biggest house I'd seen. They might need servants, and by this point I was getting desperate and faint from hunger. As a uniformed man with mirrored glasses and a gun at his belt opened the gates, I felt the Goddess pulling me away, *This isn't for you, you are my priestess, not a servant*, but I stood firm and looked up into my own reflection, trying to level my stare up at this mountain of a man in combat gear. For a moment I wondered if it was Roach come back to find me, and then he barked something and the illusion broke.

'No beggars.' He pointed to a shining golden sign bolted on to the brick wall by the gate.

NO BEGGARS, TRAMPS, POOR

WE GIVE TO STATE FUNDS

TRESPASSERS WILL BE SHOT

'But I'm not begging. I'm looking for a job.' I tried to make my voice strong and commanding as if I were back on Tintagel Head summoning the quarters, but it came out as a croak; I was parched, I hadn't drunk anything for hours.

'Not hiring.'

'Nothing at all? I'll do anything.'

'Not hiring.'

He reached to his belt that held a silver bottle and

took a swallow, watching my eyes follow the bottle as he drank, following the water dribbling down his thick chin.

He held it out to me. 'Thirsty?'

'Yes,' I gasped.

He poured the rest of the water on the black concrete between our feet where it glittered, reflecting the sky.

'Not hiring,' he repeated, and shut the gate in my face.

I sat down on the pavement and cried.

I rap on Ceri's door after buzzing the gate and she answers, towelling her hair, holding a half-eaten bread roll.

'Melz! I was wondering what happened to you. You didn't come home.' She stands aside and I walk in, easy as that, to warmth and shelter.

'I stayed out,' I say cagily, sitting down in relief on the sofa, kicking off the torturous shoes. 'Have you got any food? I'm starving.'

'Sure.' She goes into the kitchen and comes out with a banana and a couple of pastries. I tear into them hungrily. She watches, one eyebrow raised.

'I thought he took you out for dinner. Or didn't you make it that far? Had you locked up in his sex dungeon all day and all night, has he?'

'No, we did, I just . . . left, before we ate, really. And I didn't eat today.'

'I can see that,' she says drily as I devour the pastries. 'What happened?'

'Today? I was looking for a job.'

115

She snorts. 'Where? *Why*, more importantly? You don't need a job, babes.'

'I do.' She hands me a glass of water and I gulp it thankfully. The Goddess's own life in my veins. I look around. 'Is Demi in?'

Ceri shakes her head. 'Nah. She's gone to her folks. What was the row about? With Bran?'

I sigh. 'Complicated. Greenworld stuff. He . . . wants something from me that I can't give him. I thought, after we . . . disagreed—' I remember the plummeting crows, the broken glass, Bran lying on the floor, calling out for me – 'I thought he'd hate me. Report me to the police.' I peel the banana and look around for somewhere to put the skin; Ceri takes it from me and throws it carelessly towards the wastebasket. It lands on the carpet but she doesn't bother to pick it up.

'Well, without knowing what that issue is, it's kind of hard for me to comment,' she says, raising an eyebrow and sitting down on the sofa, one leg curled under her. 'But he's not going to report you to the police. I can almost guarantee you that.'

'Well, that's good to know,' I say, sitting down beside her. I hope she's right. 'But I need work. I need not to be in his power. I need to be independent if I'm going to stay here, Ceri.'

'But what would you do? You can't get a job. With the proles? No.'

'I need money to live here, and I don't want to live off you. Off him.' As I talk I realize I'm trying to manipulate her into helping me. 'And, you know, I do want to help you with your training. All of you. I can help you be better witches. But if there's no way that I can earn a real living, then I won't be able to stay here in Glastonbury. And I have to be able to trust all of you. Really trust that you won't give me away.'

Ceri plays with her earring: a diamond stud that twinkles against her brown skin. She has six, going up the side of the cartilage. I think of Saba and the diamond necklace. *What would you prefer? Beauty or Truth?*

'Hmmm. Well, you know we won't tell anyone you're here.'

I smile, but that's just it – I don't know that at all. What if we have a minor argument, what if I do something – anything – they don't like? They've got that power over me, always. All of them. And I might trust Catie OK, and maybe Ceri – Ceri wants something from me, like Bran. But Demi? Demi would march me up to the next police person we see without so much as a second breath if it wasn't for the fact that the others would be really angry.

'What about a job?'

'I can't think of anywhere you can work – I mean, it'd just be weird. What, like, we go to the cafe and you're the waitress? It just wouldn't work. You're worth more than that.'

'I feel uncomfortable not paying my own way. Or doing something really useful. At least at home I was useful. I was needed.'

She takes my hands in hers awkwardly. 'We need you, Melz. We want you to stay. You know that.'

'I know. I just don't want to keep taking your money – his money, that's all.'

'It's not all his money, you know. I do have some of my own—' she looks at her nails – 'but if he wants to pay our rent, who am I to argue?'

'But doesn't that feel funny to you? Like he's buying you?'

She looks up, and there's a combative note in her voice when she speaks.

'No, not really. This is the real world, Melz. Everything's for sale. Everyone. If he wants to pay for his own little coven, I'm not going to say no.'

He's paying for faulty goods though, I think to myself. And he knows it. But I won't argue. It won't help me now. 'I guess.'

She tears an edge off her roll and chews it. 'Look. Go and have a bath. Wherever you stayed last night, I'm thinking that it didn't have hot water?'

I shake my head.

'Right. So get washed, get dressed, put a bit of lippy on and you'll feel better. Then we'll go for a drink and talk about it.'

I smile. A drink solves everything. 'OK.'

I go into the bathroom and run the taps, thinking about the woman on the street. *Life is complicated.* For her it is, but for Ceri everything is simple. A bath, fresh clothes, a glass of wine. I sink into the bath gratefully.

Hot water when you want it – most of the time anyway – is an amazing thing. I wish everything was simple. I close my eyes and drift, half floating in the hot sudsy water. Perhaps it can be.

When we stumble home from the bar, much later, Ceri slips on a note pushed under the door.

'Shit. I almost went flying.' She picks it up and peers at it. 'For you, Mishtresh Magic,' she says, shoving it into my hand. 'I'm gonna get the shotsh ready. 'K, babes?'

I lean on the wall and slide down to the floor, legs bent, and try to focus on the writing.

Demelza,

I'm sorry that our evening together ended so abruptly. I apologize for making you uncomfortable; I should never have prevented you from leaving dinner. Please don't think badly of me.

It occurs to me that you haven't seen much of the Redworld yet, and if this is to be your home, you should see how the rest of the country is, and how much it needs your magic. I'm going to York next week for business and I'd like it if you came with me. I can show you the Redworld and – perhaps – you can show me the magic of a stone circle. There's one nearby I've always wanted to see. I'll pick you up on Monday at nine a.m.

Please trust that I am your friend.

Yours,

Bran

I fold it up and slot it under my bra strap.

'Bran wants me to go to York with him,' I call weakly to Ceri in the other room, as the hallway spins.

'Sex dungeon,' she shouts back, and I hear glass breaking. 'Oh bugger it. Melz, c'mere. I broke Demi's shot glass. She's gonna be pissed off.'

I stumble blearily into the lounge where Ceri is ineffectually brushing up broken glass with a cushion.

'What's a sex dungeon?'

'I'm joking, I'm joking. He'sh probably a very sensitive lover,' she slurs, and slumps on the sofa. 'Arse to it. I'll do it tomorrow.'

'But what . . .'

She closes her eyes. 'I'm teashing, babes, I'm . . . teasing. He's all right when you get past the crime-boss stuff. Give him a chance, Melz. Give us all a chance.' Her voice slows, and in a minute or so she's snoring softly on the couch. I pull the blanket over her and go and lie on her bed, waiting for the room to stop spinning.

Maybe I should give it all a chance. I've dreamed of seeing the country I was annexed from all my life. The forbidden land; Bran's offering me the chance to see a sacred site in the Redworld. There's nothing stopping me now. What harm could it do?

Chapter Twelve

Have you not heard that our hearts are old,
That you call in birds, in wind on the hill,
In shaken boughs, in tide on the shore?
O sweet everlasting Voices, be still.

From 'The Everlasting Voices' by W. B. Yeats

The shop is lit with blue and green lights, which give it a kind of underwater effect. Racks of glinting jewellery twinkle with an enchanted glow. Mermaids adorn the walls, their tiny waists and huge breasts tapering away into impossibly proportioned tails. The music is loud and screeching; a woman is singing, but her voice drops and soars so unexpectedly that I find it pretty off-putting.

'I've never been anywhere like this before,' I whisper to Ceri, who, as part of my getting-to-know-the-Redworld initiation, has taken me shopping for some new clothes.

'I know,' she drawls faux-dramatically. 'It's terribly

passé, darling. But if you ignore the décor, they carry a decent selection. I mean, it's not London, but what is out here?'

She pulls me to a rack of dresses and starts flipping expertly through them.

'That's not what I . . .' I whisper back, but a tall green-haired girl comes over to me.

'Can I help you?' she purrs in a low voice. She has a mannish face, like the Pre-Raphaelite models I remember from an old book. Her hair is obviously a wig, a bit like the pink one Demi was wearing the first night I met her. This one is piled high in an elaborate chignon and studded with jewels.

'Oh. Ummm, no. Well, possibly,' I say, looking around me.

'She needs a new wardrobe,' Ceri says, fixing the girl with a flat stare.

The girl looks at my black cotton Greenworld dress – the one I was wearing when I got here, which I insisted to Ceri was fine now it's been washed – and then back at me.

'She does,' she agrees. 'What in particular?'

'Everything.' Ceri waves a thick wad of cash at the girl. 'Mr Crowley's treat.' She makes a face at me. 'Oh, don't worry about it. He's got more money than God. And that thing's practically a potato sack. This is a fashion intervention, babes.'

The tall girl's smile gets noticeably brighter.

'Oh, I see! Well . . . an evening dress first, for

entertaining, and some day outfits, a coat, shoes?' She looks at Ceri for confirmation, not me, who gives her a curt nod. 'Hmmm . . . something in red, I think, with your lovely colouring,' the green-haired girl says, and starts flipping through a rail. It's the first time I've been described as having *lovely colouring*. She holds out something long and silky. 'This looks like your size. You're a ten, right?' I touch it gently. It seems so flimsy that I can't imagine it being clothes at all.

'Oh, I don't know. I just make everything to fit me usually,' I say.

'You have someone make all your clothes?' she asks, like that's impressive.

'No – I make them. When I need them,' I say.

'Oh.' She exchanges glances with Ceri.

'There aren't many decent fabrics where she's from,' Ceri says airily, holding a short shimmery orange dress against herself. I shoot her a look. We shouldn't be talking about where I'm from. She catches my eye and mouths 'sorry'.

The shop girl smiles uncertainly at Ceri and collects a few more things from the rails without asking me what I like – ripped-on-purpose jeans, a few more dresses, some silky blouses. They're like the clothes Ceri and the girls wear, kind of semi-punky but well-cut luxurious materials.

'All right! Let's go and try these on!' She takes me by the arm and propels me into a little room with a mirror and a curtain, hangs the clothes up on a hook and pulls the curtain shut. 'I'm outside if you need to try anything in another size.'

'Oh . . . OK.' I don't feel like me, but maybe the old Melz has to be peeled off just like this old dress, and the new one worn like a mask for a while until she becomes me.

'Where *are* you from, if you don't mind me asking?' the girl calls through the curtain.

'Oh, errr . . . not far.' I bite my lip. I have no idea what to say, what lie is best.

'Where? I can't place your accent – it's broader than here, kind of . . .'

Shit, shit, shit. I'm panicking. I have a dress halfway over my head when thankfully I hear Ceri's voice outside the changing room, asking if the girl can show her something. Their voices ebb away and merge with the music.

I zip the dress up the side and look at myself in the mirror, amazed. I have never looked like this before. The dress is long and red, with a split up one side to the hip. The silky material hugs my middle and breasts and straps with red jewels go over my shoulders. It's beautiful. I have never seen anything like it before, or felt the luxury of fabric like this against my skin.

I open the curtain shyly and peek out. Ceri is lounging in a turquoise and gold chair outside the curtain. Her eyes widen when she sees me, and she gets up, one eyebrow raised.

'What do you think?'

'Well, look at you, Miss Thing!' She spins me round by the shoulder. 'Not bad. Not bad at all! Shave those legs and pits and you'll be one of us yet.'

I blush, clamping my arms down by my sides. No one at home gets rid of their body hair, but they've got some kind of obsession with it here.

The shop girl comes over and adjusts one of the shoulder straps.

She smiles kindly at me. 'Do you like it?'

'I love it,' I say honestly, twirling round gently so that the skirt spins, and stopping abruptly when I realize Ceri will see my hairy legs, but she turns away to answer her phone. 'No, we're shopping now,' I hear her say. 'We'll be there later.'

'Good.' The shop girl riffles through some necklaces hanging on a stand near to the changing rooms. 'I'm looking for something that will set that dress off. I know I saw something perfect.' She has her back to me. 'You know, my gran used to live in Cornwall. Your accent's a bit like hers. Pre-Greenworld, obviously. She moved when all that started. Wouldn't want my gran down there with all those weirdos.'

'Weirdos?' I start to feel power coursing through me; maybe it's the red dress, the colour of anger and passion, but I don't know if I can stand here and listen to a stranger talk shit about my home. My family. And at the same time I realize this is exactly what I will have to listen to for as long as I'm here. Ignorance. Propaganda. Hate. Fear.

125

'You know. Terrorists.'

'They're not terrorists.' It slips out before I can stop myself.

She looks at me, surprised.

'Of course they are! Everyone knows about it. They send their envirowarriors to sabotage military operations. Just last week they bombed a military hospital. A hospital, for Chrissake.' She tuts.

'But . . . no, that's not what envirowarriors do.' My shock at the lie blows any caution away. 'They're trying to stop the war. Protest as peacefully as they can.'

'You make them sound like heroes.'

'Well, they are! My dad—' I stop myself. My dad wouldn't hurt anyone. My dad wouldn't bomb a hospital, I think angrily. That's what the Redworld does. Kill the innocent. Rape the land. How dare she?

'Your dad? He one of them, is he? You poor cow.'

I lean in close to her, angry now, not caring what I say.

'You don't know anything about the Greenworld. Everything you know is a lie. The women that run the Greenworld, they're not dangerous extremists. Not terrorists. They're witches.'

'Witches?' The girl steps back in confusion. 'Girl, I don't know what you're on, but I don't want any. Turning people into frogs and whatnot, are they?'

'That's not what witches do.'

'Oh, really? What do they do, then? I s'pose you're going to tell me you're one, are you? Turn me into a newt?'

'Goddess. What's your obsession with being turned into an amphibian?' Ceri is on the other side of the shop now, on the phone. 'Look, witches run the Greenworld. But they're women with power, women that know the old teachings. The old natural ways. That's the truth of it. Not this terrorist thing. That's a Redworld lie to distract people from the real truth. That people – women – can make their own realities. Have power. Heal. Be independent.'

'Oh, come on. Witches. It's like me standing here all serious and saying I'm a real mermaid.' She points to the murals and then at her chest. 'Smaller tits, I'll grant you.'

'It's not anything like that. Mermaids are mythical creatures. Witches are real,' I spit at her, furious.

'Yeah. And I've got a tail under here. It just *looks* like a willy.' She taps her long tight blue skirt.

'What?' Is this a boy dressed as a girl? I didn't know that even existed.

Ceri returns, putting her phone away in her bag. 'Everything all right, babes?' She frowns at my dismayed expression. 'What?'

'I'll be at the till if you want me. Bloody psycho,' the shop girl says before she flounces off.

'What was all that about?'

I'm annoyed at myself for getting drawn into an argument about the Greenworld.

I frown. 'I thought he was a girl.'

Ceri laughs in disbelief. 'Really? Couldn't you tell?'

I wriggle out of the red dress.

'No! How could I? I've never seen . . . that . . . before.'

'*She*, Melz. Not "that". Christ. What, no one ever steps out of the traditional in the Greenworld? Hetero Skirts 'n' Trousers R Us?'

'Not like that. Not . . . dressing like that. I mean, yes, lots of people are in same-sex relationships. Mostly women. But—'

'Really? So you're all lesbians, but—'

'Not all lesbians. About fifty-fifty.'

'OK, but there isn't anything else?'

'Anything . . .? I don't . . .'

'Other interpretations of gender identity. How you identify.'

I don't really understand what she's saying.

'I don't think so.'

'Why not?'

'I don't know why not. That's just the way it is.' I've never felt that the Greenworld oppressed anyone's choices before, and I don't like the thought now. What if there are people at home – my friends, even – who want to be perceived differently? Does my childhood friend Ennor want to dress like a girl? Be a girl? Does Bert the grocer want to be a woman? Am I somehow part of not letting him or someone else be themselves? Without knowing?

I'm sweating now. The changing room feels oppressive.

'Let's just go,' I plead. 'We can leave all this.' The dress pools on the floor like blood.

'No! We're taking all this. If you really want, you can try it on at home and bring back anything that doesn't look right.' She hands my dress back to me. 'Are you sure you weren't talking to her about witches in the Greenworld? I heard something.'

'Yes. She didn't believe in witches. She had some pretty offensive views actually.'

Ceri sighs. 'Come on, babes. What did we say? We can't tell anyone about you,' she whispers.

'I didn't say that was where I was from! I just . . . argued the Greenworld side of things, that's all.'

Ceri looks over at the girl by the till. 'She's ignorant of the facts, Melz. Like a lot of people here. And just like you are about her.'

'Should you call her "her"?' I look at the girl – boy – now watching music films on the TV. 'I mean, I don't know if the Goddess—'

'You can stop right there,' Ceri hisses, holding up her hand in my face. 'She has chosen to look like a girl today, so we'll call her "she". She knows her gender better than us, Melz. And don't even bring the Goddess into it. You might have some outdated Greenworld ideas about what's "natural" and shit but let me tell you you're wrong on that one. Gods evolve, faiths evolve, people evolve. It's the presence of the sacred masculine and the feminine in all of us that's important. Having a fanny doesn't give you a hotline to the Goddess.' Ceri's usual

129

cool is replaced with a focused passion; for the first time I feel her magic. Maybe I was wrong about her.

'No, I—'

'Come to that, I doubt there's many black faces in the Greenworld either, is there? Many like me back home?'

I shake my head. 'Not many.'

In Tintagel a visit from Danny or Omar pretty much represents the only non-white faces we see.

'And are you going to tell me the Goddess doesn't love me as much as anyone else? As much as you, girl?' Her hands are on her hips, her brown eyes boring into my skull.

'Of course not.' I lower my gaze. Brighid loves us all equally. But the Morrigan loves me more than Ceri. This I know. I am Her branded one.

'Right, then.' Ceri touches my arm awkwardly and we stand in silence for a minute.

I finish getting dressed and we go to the till together.

The shop girl holds up a gold necklace to show me as Ceri hands over a roll of notes.

'I thought this would go really well with the red dress,' she says flatly, and I nod, not even looking at it.

'That's fine,' I say. 'Thank you.'

'My pleasure,' the girl says, her tone suggesting it definitely wasn't.

'Look, I'm . . . I'm sorry I reacted strangely to you.' I try to apologize.

The girl shrugs. 'Whatever, sweetie. Whatever.'

Ceri pulls my arm. 'Come on. Don't make it worse. Anyway, at the end of the day, she's a prole, and we're not.' She doesn't bother to lower her voice as we walk out. 'Don't worry too much about it.'

'But you were defending her, and then . . .' And then you attacked her to her face and didn't even care. You defended her against one kind of prejudice but not another. To suit yourself. But I can't say any of that, because Ceri and the girls, and Bran, are my compass here. And they hold power over me as much as the red wool that Mum keeps in a box along with all the other witches' measures. Our loyalty, our blood.

Chapter Thirteen

If yet I have not all thy love,
Dear, I shall never have it all;
I cannot breathe one other sigh, to move,
Nor can intreat one other tear to fall;
And all my treasure, which should purchase thee –
Sighs, tears, and oaths, and letters – I have spent.

From 'Lovers' Infiniteness' by John Donne

A week later I am on my way to York – northern, dark, broken and polluted – far into the Redworld. At least, that's how I imagine it as Bran holds out his hand to help me up into the black metal monstrosity that is his car; dimly I see Pete's still outline behind the dark glass windows at the front.

'You didn't reply to my letter,' he says as I lean on his arm and step up on the high chrome ledge under the doorway. The car is half a person taller than me and at least as long as three cows nose to tail.

'I didn't know if I was going to come until this morning.' I look down at him from the step, his face turned up to me like a supplicant to the Goddess.

I wavered all week, but in the end curiosity got the better of me. Why not see how the rest of the country lives, if I'm part of the Redworld now? I'm not going to tell ordinary people about the portals, about where they are and what they can do, but he already knows some of it. He knows they exist. He even says he cares about them, wants to preserve them. But, like Roach, I know that his version of caring for them involves this pseudo-scientific, pseudo-mythical, pseudo-bordering-on-crazy idea that they can be harvested for usable energy somehow. And I have to protect them from that.

Every time I rolled over in bed last night, still on the sofa at the girls' flat, the sheets rucked uncomfortably between my legs. Desire tugged at me. Bran. The way he looks at me, the way I feel seen for the first time, ever. Would it really be so bad to go? And would it really be so bad to stay here too, with the girls? They've promised to keep me safe. I don't want to live in a deserted broken building that smells of urine. I don't want to be someone's servant. I *am* more than that.

I sink into a deep brown-leather seat; he gets in after me and shuts the door. He can stand up in this . . . thing. I gaze around me at the shining silver details, the buttons with their secrets, their clean, mechanical magic. This is way fancier than Ceri's car, and that was different enough for someone who has never done any travelling apart from on foot or riding the occasional fat Cornish horse.

'Drink?' He doesn't wait for me to answer but rips the gold foil from a large green bottle – I remember it from our dinner, the strange solo dining room, the wine with the bubbles – and pours two tall crystal glasses he selects from a leather box on the wall, handing me one. As I take it he glances at his hand and wipes something dark from the back of it with a napkin.

'Sorry. Been working this morning. The science stuff gets messy sometimes.'

I frown, confused. 'You work with science?'

'Aye, you know. Defence systems. It's all oil and mechanics,' he says, and something flashes in his eyes briefly. Then it's gone, but just for a second I know he's lying.

I take a sip of champagne and as I do a deep growl explodes under me and I let out a cry, spilling my glass.

'By Brighid. What was that?'

Bran looks amused. 'That's the motor. Turbocharged.' He cocks an eyebrow. 'Like it?'

'It's . . . err . . .' I feel the car start moving, gliding steadily over the ground, speeding up and the houses start to move then flash past the windows. I feel a bit sick. 'Great,' I murmur, holding on to the door handle tightly.

However, the sound of strings ripples through the moodily lit interior of the car, and as I sip the champagne it transports me to a different land of magic: one free of

Greenworld dirt and cold and concentration. This is a magic of beauty, flow, colour and softness.

'Like the music? I chose it especially for you. Thought it would remind you of home,' he murmess. I lay my head back cautiously on the soft leather and watch as the town and then the fields flow past at unnatural speed, my stomach settling slightly. Bran leans back next to me.

'How far is it to York?'

'Two hundred and fifty miles or so. About five hours, four maybe, if Pete puts his foot down.'

I sit up and look at him in amazement. 'By Brighid! Two hundred and fifty miles? That's like . . . a week and a half, two weeks walking. More maybe.'

'And with all your booze and music needs catered for. Not bad, eh, lass?' He grins at my discomfited expression, but it just seems wrong. People shouldn't be able to travel this far this fast, not even noticing what goes past, not seeing it, in a blur. A journey should involve noticing nature around you, watching the wildlife and their habitats, how the season is changing. A meditation.

'So, what spells can you do for me, Greenworld witch?' Bran changes the subject, moving in closer; I feel his breath on my face and lean back again cautiously.

'I didn't think you wanted me to do magic for you. I thought you just wanted my *trust*.' I mimic the earnest tone he used when we had dinner and raise an eyebrow.

135

'I know, but it seems like too good a chance to pass up, having you here. All that magic in your fingertips. You can't blame me for asking.' He smiles and his warm brown eyes twinkle at me.

I look up to the ceiling of the car where tiny lights flicker like stars.

'It's not in my fingertips. I don't live in a children's book.'

'I know, I know.' He smiles and closes his eyes, humming to the music.

There's a silence. I make him wait.

'What do you need?' I ask, looking disinterestedly out of the window.

'What can you do?'

'Depends.'

'Vast wealth?'

'No. It doesn't work like that.'

'Bloody typical. All right, protection from my enemies, then.'

'How many enemies have you got?'

'Happen there's a fair few.'

I look back at him to see if he's joking, but he looks serious.

'A fair few people all wanting bad things to happen to you?'

'All part of being a "crime boss".' It's hard to know when he's being serious and when he's not.

'I'd recommend you be nicer to people, then.'

'Nah.'

I laugh, despite myself. 'All right, well . . . make a witch bottle.'

'What's that?'

'You have to pee on some rusty nails in a jar.'

He sits up. 'Bloody hell. That's disgusting! What would you do that for?'

'It's a deterrent. You make something unpleasant and hide it in your house. It repels negative energy. Like, really negative stuff. Out-nasty the nasty.'

'Ugh. No thanks.'

I laugh. 'You're a crime boss and you think peeing in a bottle is disgusting? Your enemies must be shaking in their boots.'

'Crime's one thing. That's just horrible.' He grimaces exaggeratedly.

'Count yourself lucky. In the old days witches in Cornwall would make them with far worse than pee and nails. There's some old ones at the Archive that are still too noxious to be opened.'

He shivers and leans back next to me. 'Think I'll give that one a miss, thanks.'

I shrug. 'Your loss. It works.'

'Aye, well, I'll take my chances.'

He leans into me a little and I don't pull away; he smells good, of spice and cedar. I shut my eyes and remember Tom's smell: honest sweat and earth. I try not to think of him, but he's always there, just beyond my grasp. I wanted so much for Tom to know I loved him. I wanted him so badly, wanted to feel his strong wide hands on me, look into his kind blue eyes one more time, see his warm smile, feel his fire under my skin.

The loss of Tom is physical. I crave him: crave his solidity, like food. I sometimes feel that he is almost real, almost present, and that if I could only dissolve a little, we could meet somewhere between real and not-real.

I smooth the rough edges of the heart locket round my neck, appreciating the way that the wood scratches my fingers. I don't want it to feel good. I wear my grief round my neck; I wear the memory of the boy I loved and lost, so I can't forget. And I wear the curse of the people that killed him there, folded inside. I bear that curse, feel it and fuel it every day.

I open my eyes again and a tear rolls down my cheek. Bran leans forward and wipes it away gently without a word. His isn't the body I want, he isn't the presence that's missing, but he's here and I lean into him, resting my head on his shoulder.

Chapter Fourteen

Respect Nature, for She has no respect for you.

From *Tenets and Sayings of the Greenworld*

When we get to York I'm hungry and restless.

The car slows to a stop. Pete opens the doors for us and I step out on to the pavement of a busy city. It's so much busier than Glastonbury: so many more people, taller buildings, more dirty brick. Horns blare and the smog is terrible – the air thick and poisonous. I hold my hand in front of my face, coughing. By Brighid, this is horrible.

Bran smiles and points up at a grand stone building in front of us. 'This is where we're staying.' Along the street are glass-fronted high-ceilinged shops, glittering with commercial purpose amid the smog and bustle and noise. 'I'll come and get you for dinner from your room later, around seven. OK?'

I look at the building doubtfully.

'OK. But how do I get into my room? In there?'

'Just go inside and ask at the desk. It's booked under my name. You're Demelza Crowley while we're here, aye? Just to be on the safe side. They'll show you where it is. I've got to show my face at a demonstration, then I'll be back.'

'All right.' *Just to be on the safe side.* Is the Hawthorne name really so incendiary in the Redworld?

Pete hands me my bag, scowling as usual. I try to thank him but he mutters and gets back into the driver's seat. If Bran notices Pete's rudeness, he doesn't show it. He kisses my cheek, and they drive away, leaving me on the street. In the city. Alone. I look at my feet and try to connect with the earth to feel more grounded, but there's too much noise, too much distraction. I have to get out of this air and away from these people. They jostle me as they go past, but don't meet my eyes. I think of the way people always say hello or 'Blessed Be' as they pass each other in the street in Tintagel. I think of how, even in Glastonbury, there is room to move. But this is . . . this is something else again.

I must stand there for five minutes, just letting the crowd part and re-form as they go round me, enduring the knocks and the muttered swear words, before I come to my senses and think *Enough is enough.* Shoulders hunched, I walk into the building, and I feel it swallow me up, like a stone python.

There's a man at the front desk and I go up to him, painfully aware of how I must look – scruffy, crumpled and agitated.

'Can I help you, miss?' he asks politely.

'Yes. There's a room for me here, I think.'

'All right. May I take your name, please?'

'Demelza Haw— Demelza Crowley.' I look around me, wondering what I'll do if there's not a room for me. I'll have to hitch-hike back to Glastonbury. 'Ah, yes. Miss Crowley. Welcome. I'll ask Cherie to take you to your room.' He signals to a girl about my age in a smart blue and gold uniform.

'Cherie, please take Miss Crowley to her suite and see she has everything she needs,' he says, and gives her an ornate key.

Cherie guides me to a door in a wall and presses a button just next to it. I feel weird being Miss Crowley. Like I've been married without my consent.

We stand for a moment and nothing happens, and I wonder whether she's waiting for me to open the door. I look at her but she just smiles back at me. What am I supposed to do?

Then a bell sounds and the doors open automatically to a small room.

Cherie steps in and beckons me. 'This way, Miss Crowley,' she says, and I walk into the box. It has a sofa along the back wall under a large mirror.

'Is this my room?' I ask, thinking I can probably fit on the sofa to sleep, but she laughs as if I've made a joke and pushes a button on the wall. The doors close and the room glides upward. I hold on to the wall in surprise, and she looks at me again but doesn't laugh this time.

The bell dings again and the doors open into the hugest room I have ever seen.

Cherie walks ahead of me and opens a door at the far end.

'This is the bathroom, Miss Crowley, and that's the interconnecting door to Mr Crowley's apartment,' she says, pointing at a grand wooden door with black iron fastenings in the wall. *Miss Crowley.* I wonder who she thinks I am. His sister? His cousin? We look nothing alike. She opens a glass cabinet. 'Drinks and snacks in here, coffee maker's in here too, menu for room service and entertainment – all in here. If you need anything at all, please let hotel reception know. Is there anything else I can help you with?'

I try to stop staring at everything and sound like this is all normal to me.

'No, no . . . that's fine, thank you, Cherie.' My voice is somewhere between querulous and awestruck.

'All right, enjoy your stay at the Grand Hotel,' she says, giving me a look I can't decipher, and goes back into the moving box. I sit down cautiously on the gold-embroidered sofa and look around me. The opulence stares back at me with an arrogant sheen. I walk cautiously over to a huge glossy black bed with four long posts, one at each corner, with velvety emerald-green covers edged with gold and an artful pile of green and gold pillows, and sit down on the corner, smoothing the softness with my fingers. I keep expecting Cherie to run into the room, saying that this has all been a terrible mistake and, in fact, my room is somewhere else, or that I shouldn't be at the hotel at all, but she doesn't. I sit in the warm, soft silence and listen to my heartbeat slow. At least it's quiet up here, Goddess be praised.

Curiosity gets the better of me and I get up, trailing my fingers up the shiny black bedposts and then on to the matching black cabinet beside the bed. There are all sorts of switches above it, but I leave them alone.

I remember I'm hungry. Even though there will be dinner later, I look around and find a large cupboard that opens out into a mini kitchen. There's a shiny silver sink, and when I turn on the tap, instant hot water. This is still an amazing thing to me. I open a silver door and find a fridge stacked with ready-to-eat food. Sandwiches, salad, wine, chocolate, all wrapped in plastic. I look at it for a moment, remembering our larder at home. A cold room off the kitchen where we kept food, nothing like as efficient as the harsh blue light of this machine. I think of the homeless woman in Glastonbury, and guilt threatens to choke me. I shut the fridge door and stare at it for a few minutes, fighting my hunger, but it's too tempting. I open it again, take all the food out and eat it as fast as I can, standing there in front of the gleaming sink and the hot water, stuffing it into my mouth like an animal. If I eat it quickly, no one will know. I'll feel less guilty about being here, even though my rational brain knows no one cares. But I feel the Morrigan cares, and disapproves.

Chapter Fifteen

> I don't go around breaking windows for no reason,
> and neither should a demonstrator. We have to be
> the peacekeepers, the gatekeepers. We cannot let
> mob rule take over.
>
> From a speech given by Bran Crowley at the
> South-west Region Security Officers annual
> dinner, Bristol, December 2046

I go to the palatial bathroom, run hot water into the giant claw-footed bath and pour in a glug of spicy-smelling stuff from one of the many bottles by the sink. I wait for the hot water to steam up the mirror before I take my clothes off so that I can't see myself. It's a habit; I've always done it that way, though the steam is much more plentiful here than at home, what with needing to heat water up in one of Mum's stained cooking pans and having to carry it upstairs, trying not to slosh the dim brown water all over the stairs over and over again until the water reaches the line Mum's painted in black on the inside of the tub — ten centimetres. *Perfectly deep enough to get you clean, doesn't ravage the environment, girls*, she'd say. I've perfected the art of closing my eyes as I step into the bath at home, to avoid the big cracked mirror. The Greenworld celebrates the female body every way it comes. But I don't really like the way I look naked. I'm pale and skinny and hairy, and my hair's too dark and my feet are too big and my tits are too small.

I step into the scented bubbles and submerge myself in the gallons of hot water. I watch the water drip off the brown hairs on my arm and think about Tom. He didn't want me. Now he never will. Bran wants me, I can tell, and he sees me for what I am: darkness as well as light.

He isn't perfect. An understatement. But at the same time, he has power, his own kind of power, and I can feel that enflame the darkness in me. I feel it rushing through me like a bush fire. Out of control. Deliciously, delightfully wild.

When I'm clean, I step out of the tub and the dirty water spirals down the plug. I imagine it taking the hurt and pain and anger and loss of Tom with it. I imagine myself cleansed, new.

I go back out to the lounge and pull the red dress I bought with Ceri out of the bag. I lay it out on the bed and it lies there like a starved girl, wanting a shape. I look at it, touching my witch-brand thoughtfully. At home the brand meant I was special; here, it means nothing.

But the Redworld needs me. They need something

to believe in. The shop in Glastonbury where I got this dress was like a sea cave: a place where women could buy dresses that would make them feel like mermaids, like sirens. Because maybe, in the Redworld, people are crying out for something they don't have: magic, mystery. Unconsciously they're trying to reconnect with the natural world. I can give them what they need: the skills, the belief. I could, if I wasn't a suspicious associate of a notorious terrorist.

I hold the dress against myself. They need a faery come alive, a priestess from a strange land. Perhaps this is a chance to become a new Melz. Someone who has power among those that have none, someone that brings them magic. Someone beautiful and wise and . . . *seen*.

I sit down in front of the ornate dressing table and uncurl the towel from my wet hair. I comb it carefully, and braid it in a style I used to do for Saba sometimes. I make up my face, making my eyes blacker and more shadowy than usual. I turn over some of the capsules and boxes on the table and find a red lipstick.

Now I get the dress and slip it on gingerly, as if it might rip. I'm not used to such flimsy fabrics. Too late I realize I didn't bring any shoes to go with it. None at all apart from my old comfy boots. My posture slumps, and the dress clutches dumbly at me like a wet sail. *Who are you trying to kid?* that voice in my ear says – that familiar dismal voice. Not the Morrigan. The voice that came before Her. The sly, introspective voice of my insecurity.

What were you trying to do exactly? I haven't done this

right, because I don't know how to be in the Redworld. And, really, maybe because I've never been enough of a girl. Not pretty enough. Not the girl who understands about dresses and jewellery and beauty tips and how to get boys to like me.

I sit down on the edge of the bed and feel tears coming. I've failed before I've begun. And I look out of the window, past the heavy green draping curtains to the evening sky. *Help me, Great Goddess*, I ask quietly in my head. *Help me*. But nothing comes. I push the window open and lean out, looking for crows, looking for some sign of Her, but there are none.

'Goddess! Morrigan, Great Queen! Be with me!' I scream out of the window and wait, but nothing happens.

I slam the window, suddenly angry. Angry at feeling lost, ignored, deserted, angry at always feeling like the freak.

I pull on my boots, not even bothering to wipe them clean. I pin my long braids up so that the witch-brand at the base of my neck is visible. So what if people can see it? I *want* them to see it. I am me, with or without the Goddess. I *am* powerful. Powerful enough to resist whatever the powers that be want to throw my way.

I look at myself in the mirror for a moment and suddenly remember that there was a necklace that went with this dress. I go back to my bag and find it at the bottom wrapped in blue tissue paper. I pull it out and laugh. A crow in flight, silhouetted against a golden moon. My goddess has a sense of humour. *You can't outrun me; you can't evade me. You're mine and I am yours*, She whispers in my mind, and as I hang the necklace round my neck I feel Her around me again. Her dark, warm presence fills me with strength.

The chain hangs at the perfect length for the dress's neckline, well below the wooden heart locket that sits just above my heart. It would look better if I took the locket off, but I'm not ready to do that yet.

The dress would look better – prettier, more conventional – without the heavy boots too, but suddenly I don't care. I don't care about pretty. Pretty doesn't fill people with awe. Pretty doesn't make the ground shake or the clouds roll.

That's what She does, what I do.

I am Melz the Red Witch, the Morrigan embodied. I don't care what people think I am.

I don't care that Lowenna Hawthorne features in their messed-up version of his-story. I don't care that here I'm the daughter of a terrorist. My power will protect me. My goddess will protect me.

They're going to see me.

They're going to see that magic is real.

Chapter Sixteen

There go the loves that wither,
    The old loves with wearier wings;
And all dead years draw thither,
    And all disastrous things;
Dead dreams of days forsaken,
Blind buds that snows have shaken,
Wild leaves that winds have taken,
    Red strays of ruined springs.

From 'The Garden of Proserpine' by Algernon Swinburne

I feel his hand on my shoulder as I stand looking out of the window at the city below, the people clustering and swarming like insects on a corpse.

'Beautiful, isn't it?' I feel his words hot on my neck, but don't turn round.

'No,' I reply.

'Not even from up here? Away from the detail,

149

the mundane, all the particular tragedies of their little lives?'

'No.'

'Because it's not the Greenworld?'

'No. Because they never look up.' I watch the stream of bodies slowly going down one side of the street and the other – all looking ahead or down, charging ahead, intent on their own route, their own story, following their own path. 'They don't look at each other. It's like they're sleepwalking. Shut down.'

'Only way you can cope in a city like this. It's too big, too busy. London's worse.'

'Then I never want to go there.'

'Never say never, lass. It's a beautiful city.'

'A contradiction in terms.'

'Cities are beautiful. It's just people that mess them up.' He shrugs. 'Any road, you look beautiful, and not from a distance either. Where's the girl that I drove up with? You transformed into . . . I dunno. A goddess.'

'Thank you.' I'm on my guard; I'm in control here. I am Melz the Red Witch.

He nods, taking me in, looking, not saying anything. The silence spreads like a red rose blooming in the room, and the strange electricity starts flowing between us again, slowly spiralling from him to me and me to him again. Neither of us drops our gaze. He looks different too – he's wearing black jeans, a white shirt and a straight-cut black coat, his shoulder-length tousled dark hair under a hat with a brim, which he tips to me.

'How was the demonstration?' I ask.

He looks out of the window again. 'The wha—? Oh, aye, fine.'

He tries to hide it but there's hesitation in his voice.

'Why did you have to come up to see it?'

'Just maintaining a presence, that's all. Making sure the rich bastards know who's protecting them.'

'And?'

'They know. And I'll tell you what, the people are getting close to it up here. They're ripe for revolution. There were a few hairy moments.'

'Were there injuries?'

'Of course. But nothing too bad. Pride, mostly.' He smiles at me like I'm a curious child, which is annoying. He places his finger on my lips. 'Anyway. I don't want to talk about that now.' A smile crinkles round his deep brown eyes. '*Goddess*, I'm at your disposal for the evening.'

He's not going to tell me anything else about it, I can tell. I remember the riot in Glastonbury when I first arrived. *Take the power back*, the people had shouted, and they'd surged towards the grey vans. Are the people here even more determined?

'Damn right you are,' I say eventually, and I raise my eyebrow and smile. We get into the lift in silence and I try to act like the sinking motion doesn't fill me with unease as the floor falls away beneath us and we descend towards the street.

We walk away from the hotel down small winding alleys, avoiding the main streets, saying nothing.

151

'I grew up here,' he says, his expression unreadable.

'Oh. This street?' I look around as we walk through an arched doorway in a tall old stone wall on to the banks of a wide river, a stone bridge to our left, another one a way off to the right.

'Nah. The city. That side though.' He points to the far riverbank, which is a mixture of small unimpressive houses and scrubland. Distantly, across the water, I hear sharp cracks that could be gunfire, breaking glass, shouting. 'Most people live that side. Only the super-rich can afford it over here. Lot of those people work this side though,' he adds, talking over the noise.

'Why the wall?' I say, gazing back at it. From the other side the wall was quaint; from this side it's ugly – industrial grey peppered with warning signs and graffiti.

'Flooding. The council had to build a barrier round the riverbank.'

'But it's only on one side of the river.'

'Aye.'

'Doesn't it flood on the other side?'

'Every year.'

'Then why isn't there a barrier?'

'Not a priority.' There's a catch in his voice.

'But those people must get flooded . . .'

'Every year,' he repeats, and holds up a hand, beckoning at something. 'I don't miss it.'

I watch as a boat, all silver and glass and curved whiteness, emerges from the evening twilight, the setting sun gleaming gold on the river. It's powered by a motor: no oars, no sails. It chugs to a halt in front of us and a young woman in a bright white uniform hops on to the riverbank.

'Good evening, Mr Crowley,' she says, and her accent isn't like his; hers is clipped, quick, angular.

'Evening, Jane. To the jetty, please.'

'Of course.' She holds out her hand to help me aboard.

'Where are we going?' I ask, trying not to catch my red dress as I climb on to the boat.

'I hope you don't mind, but I thought as we're here I'd show you where I grew up. Get some dinner too. I'm starving. It's been a long day.'

'That's fine.'

He hops on board without any help and Jane heads to the front of the boat. There is a deep rumble as the engine starts but this time I know better than to look surprised, although I still don't like it. Boats should have oars. Bran takes off his coat and drapes it over my shoulders as we pull away, zipping through the cool night.

I pull the soft, heavy black material round me. It smells of him, warm and spicy. 'Thank you.'

He takes off his hat and puts it under a seat. 'I'm glad you're here,' he says, and takes my hand. The wind blows our hair as we gaze at the far banks of the river, watching distant fires burn.

We stop at a small wooden jetty overgrown with river weeds. Out of habit I name them in my mind: pennyroyal, dandelion, herb robert. The pungent minty, oily smell of the pennyroyal mixes with a more familiar composty smell as I step off the boat. I look down at the water and almost retch at the sewage floating in the water.

'By Brighid! Is that . . .?'

Bran glances down as he jumps off the boat and holds out a hand for me.

'This side of the river the plumbing hasn't been upgraded for a long time.' A look of disgust mixed with sadness passes over his features. 'You get used to it.'

I hold his coat sleeve over my nose but say nothing. Don't these people have the good sense to use it on the farms? At the very least, don't poison your own water. That's a basic. But as I look around, I don't see any sign of farming. Only falling-down houses – shacks, little more than sheds. Bran holds my hand and we walk along a dirt track into the middle of the city. Into a York that is unrecognizable from the gleaming streets outside our hotel.

'You grew up here?' I ask as I step carefully on the street, holding my dress to my knees to avoid getting the beautiful fabric dirty. A pot-bellied man sitting in a tatty metal-and-fabric chair watches us walk past, unshaven, ragged clothes, dirty. Bran nods, but the man just watches us unmoving, his tired eyes looking through us, the faded orange-and-brown pattern of the chair's fabric straining under him.

'Aye,' Bran eventually replies.

'Was it always . . . like this?'

We pass a group of kids about my age standing round a fire that leaps crazily out of a metal container of some kind; they're feeding it pieces of plastic, whatever rubbish they can find. The acrid air wreathes them in a dull light as they whoop and caper about, trying to find bigger and worse things to burn.

'Aye.' He sees me watching the kids. 'It's not their fault. They dunno any better. Don't have any skills. Nowt to do.' He rubs his thumb gently over the back of my hand, and prickles go up my back. 'Not everyone's as lucky as you, Demelza Hawthorne.'

'You got out though. So why don't they?'

'Not everyone's as gifted as me,' he says grimly.

We walk up a hill of faded terraced houses, some with broken windows, missing tiles from the roofs, peeling paintwork. Two women sit on their front steps, talking to each other across a short gap. When we get close, one touches the other on the arm to make her stop talking. She smiles up at Bran, an unexpectedly bright smile breaking across her worry-lined face.

''Ow do, love,' she shouts, her voice warm and sincere, accented like his. The other woman nods and smiles at him, but looks suspiciously at me.

He smiles down at them both. 'Can't keep away, Reet. Evenin', Dot,' he says to the other woman.

''Ow do,' she echoes, and they both look expectantly at me.

'This is my friend, Demelza.'

I smile as nicely as I can.

''Ow do, flower. Goin' up the big 'ouse?' Reet shields her eyes against a sudden shard of the red setting sun that lights up her face and the house behind her.

'Aye. Not been for a while.' He's apologetic, and I wonder who these women are to him to make him so contrite.

'We know you try.'

He scuffs his shoe absentmindedly on the dusty ground. 'Well, we should be getting on.'

'Nice to meet you,' I say as he leads me away.

'Ta-ra, lass. Nice ta meet thee.'

After we've walked on a decent way I whisper to Bran. 'Who were they?'

'Just some people I've known a long time.'

'Since you were a child?'

'This were my neighbourhood. They've been sitting on their front steps since forever, watching everything turn to shit around 'em.'

'You talk like them. I mean, more so now you're here.' His soft accent has deepened and it sounds strange again.

He shrugs. 'Can't help it. You lose the Yorkshire down there in t'south. You forget, lass. You'll lose yours when you've been away long enough.'

'But I don't have an accent!'

He grins. 'Ye do, Melz. Ye do.'

We turn a corner at the top of the street and I look up at a squat brown building with a large green double door propped open to the street. Pushed back behind the doors are black cast-iron gates. The building is ugly but well kept: no broken windows, no peeling paint.

'Here you are,' he says, and leads me through the front door. Just inside, a boy and a girl of roughly five or six are playing with a bouncy ball in a wide terracotta-tiled hallway, giggling as it pings across the slippery tiles and ricochets off the white-painted stair barrier.

'Jenny. Be careful,' Bran says and rests his hand on the girl's black curls.

She turns her sweet face up to him. 'You're back!' she shouts, and he kneels down to hug her.

The little boy runs up and hugs Bran's leg as he's trying to stand up.

'Hi, Bobby.' Bran reaches into his pocket and pulls out two chocolate bars. 'Not before dinner.' He wags his finger at them playfully and they grin conspiratorially. 'Any road, not where Jeannie can see you.'

They laugh, take the chocolate bars and run away, obviously intent on hiding away and eating them as soon as possible.

'What is this place?' I look down the hall at the colourful children's paintings and displays, the box of boots in a huge variety of colours and sizes by the doorway and a long rack of coats above them.

'It's an orphanage,' he says quietly, as we walk along the long hallway. Children's voices, laughing, shouting, and the thumping of feet echo down to us from a long stairwell. 'I'm showing you my roots, what little they are. What do you think of me now?'

He doesn't give me a chance to reply but pulls me through an open doorway into a busy hall with long rows of tables set for dinner. Several adults are setting large tureens and dishes out at intervals on the tables covered with bright wipe-clean tablecloths and mismatched knives and forks.

One of the women sees Bran and cries out in surprise. 'Bran! We didn't know you were coming!' She comes over and gives him a hug, and smiles warmly at me. 'And you brought a guest. Here's me in my rags. I'd have put my face on if I knew you were bringing someone so lovely.'

I feel overdressed; the red dress was for Melz the Red Witch doing magic, being otherworldly and powerful. Not visiting an orphanage.

'This is Demelza,' he says, and she hugs me.

'You always were a dark horse. Don't be shy, lass. I'm Jeannie. I run this place, with all my happy helpers. You're staying for dinner?' She looks expectantly at us and my stomach growls.

'I think that's a yes.' Bran grins at her. 'Is that all right?'

'Of course, flower. This is your home.'

I watch Bran's face as a softness takes it over, smoothing out the lines that Goddess knows what put there in the first place. I wonder who this boy is now — no king of the underworld. Just one orphan among many. A son come home.

The kids explode into the hall like excitable locusts as we stand there awkwardly.

158

'Best take a pew,' Jeannie calls over. 'I'll come and find you in a bit. Got the babies to feed.' She turns back to two other women who are placing chubby toddlers into high chairs along a table.

'My lady.' Bran bows deeply at the waist, grinning, and holds a seat out at the long table for me. A girl, perhaps ten, snatches his hat from his head and puts it on, the rim coming over her eyes and resting on her brown nose.

'Does it suit me?' she asks, and slides into the seat next to me.

'Not bad,' I say, and tip the hat back a little. 'You need to be able to see your food though.'

'Nah. She inhales it.' Bran sits down on my other side. 'What's on the menu today, Debs?'

'None of your business, poo face,' the girl snaps back in her prim little voice and I burst out laughing.

'She told you.'

He raises his eyebrow at me mock-sternly. 'Don't encourage her.' Bran makes a face at Debs, who sticks her tongue out at him.

I help myself to a plate. 'I won't, poo face,' I say.

He snorts with surprised laughter. 'Really?'

'Really.'

He grabs his hat off the young girl and puts it on me. 'Queen of Comedy or summat, are you?' he says but he's smiling, a good smile that uses his eyes. There's something good about breaking him out of his usual control – and knowing that I can do it. Me, cold,

159

sarcastic Demelza Hawthorne. There's someone in the world that thinks I'm funny.

Dinner reminds me of community feasts at home: good basic food, people laughing, plates spilling, kids playing between the chairs. But despite the chaos, everyone clears their plate – and there's enough for everyone, but no waste.

When we're halfway through our dinner – a hearty vegetable chilli with plain rice and bread on the side – Jeannie slides into the seat opposite me and reaches out for the large stained cooking pot in the middle of the table.

'Ah. Still some left,' she says, and ladles out the last of the vegetable chilli on to a scrubbed plastic plate, once white but now stained a dim orange by hundreds of meals. 'So. How did you two meet?' She points at Bran across the table and grins at me. 'He's never brought a girl home before. He must like you.'

'Melz is . . . different.' Bran's eyes are on mine, full of that intense look that makes my stomach flip.

'She's something, all right. You're like a faery girl. So delicate and beautiful,' Jeannie says.

'There's no faeries, Jeannie.' He smiles at me. 'She used to tell me that when I were a kid. I hope you don't tell the rest of them your tall tales.'

'Not so tall,' I murmur.

'Aye, well, you know. To her it's tales,' he murmurs back, touching the back of my hand again, and the electricity stabs me with a new intensity.

'I do at that. These kids need stories. They don't

have much else, bless 'em,' Jeannie says. She spoons up her dinner fast.

I look around at the children and the other adults, some with the smaller children on their laps, eating together like a big family. 'How do children get here? I mean, why aren't they with their own families?'

Jeannie wipes the sauce-covered face of the kid next to her, a girl of eight or nine who spoons her chilli into her mouth mechanically while watching me studiously through thick glasses.

'They don't have families, most of them. Parents are soldiers, some of them, and left them here when they both got drafted. Or one parent goes to war, the other one can't cope, or gets ill. Some parents are junkies, drunks or too poor to feed the kids, so they end up here.' Jeannie reaches across the table and squeezes Bran's hand. 'Bran was one of my first. He came when I'd only been working here a month. He was six but he was so little, so skinny. Always bright though. Grew like a monster once we fed him up.'

'What happened to your parents?' I ask and Bran's hand tightens on Jeannie's.

He looks away. 'Died in a factory fire. The building were unsafe. Ceiling collapsed on 'em.'

'I'm so sorry,' I say, and touch his leg awkwardly.

'S'all right. I were lucky. The orphanage took me in.'

'We didn't have as much capacity then. There were only about ten children and we didn't have enough money to keep them as it was. The kids slept two to a

161

bed and we slept on the floor, but they had three meals a day and we taught lessons and games in the daytime. Read to them at night. Stories kept them going.' Jeannie looks around her proudly. 'And look at us now.' Her voice is full of love.

I look at the long tables in the hall – five rows along the length of the hall with kids on both sides. There's maybe two hundred kids or more.

'So what changed? Does the government give you money now?'

She laughs drily. 'Demelza, bless your innocent heart. No. They don't give us shit. Nobody cares about orphans.'

'Then how do you manage?'

'Bran pays for everything,' she says, and her face, already full of light, glows when she says his name. 'My boy. He's always been my angel.'

'Jeannie, I'm not a kid any more, you know.' He looks pleased but uncomfortable.

Jeannie goes back to eating with a smile on her face. 'You'll always be that tiny little six-year-old to me, flower,' she says, then turns to me. 'He had these huge dark eyes. Like a little field mouse or something. He didn't talk for the first six months, just used to follow me around wherever I went. Even to the loo.'

'Jeannie!' He blushes properly now and she laughs loudly.

'Ah, bless you. Am I embarrassing you in front of your girlfriend?' She twinkles at me. 'I've been looking forward to this day for a long time. It's a rite of passage, being able to embarrass your son in front of a girl.'

'Does anyone else know about this?' I look at Bran and hand my now empty bowl to a serious-looking young boy who is clearing away the dinner things with a wide tray. He smiles at me shyly.

'No.' He's unreadable again. This is his secret, and he let me see it. Does he think it makes him vulnerable, me knowing?

Jeannie catches the look between us and gets up, her chair squeaking on the worn lino floor.

'Well, anyway, I'll leave you lovebirds to it. You staying long?'

'Just for dinner and to look around.'

'OK. Let me know when you leave.' She touches him lightly on the shoulder. 'It's always good to see you, flower. Don't leave it so long next time.'

He presses her hand on his shoulder and she nods at me. 'It was lovely to meet you, Demelza. Next time, make him bring you for longer so I can get to know you.' Two small boys run up to her and start tugging at her dress. 'As you see, evenings are always a bit busy.'

She chivvies the boys away from the table like ducklings and Bran gets up. 'Walk?' He holds out his hand for mine.

'OK.'

We go back into the long hall where a group of kids

163

are playing Off Ground Touch, balancing crazily on boxes and hanging off the banister like monkeys.

'When did you leave?' I ask as we dodge past the door to the kitchen; inside, a row of older girls and boys are drying up the dishes from dinner with worn striped dishtowels, talking and laughing.

'I were sixteen. I could've stayed longer but I wanted to get out on my own.'

We get to the end of the hall and Bran pushes open a door to a wide garden, half taken up with vegetable beds and fruit trees, the other half a scrubby lawn covered with toys. Bats, balls and headless dolls punctuate faded white chalk lines, the winners and losers of a forgotten game. He drapes his jacket round my shoulders again. The night is coming and the moon is rising over the jagged lines of the city roofs.

'Where did you go?' I ask.

'Jeannie had a friend. I stayed there for a while, trying to get work, but there were nowt happening. The only place that were hiring were the factory, and I wouldn't go there.'

'The factory where your parents died?'

He points past the trees at the bottom of the garden and across the tatty roofs to two tall chimneys belching out smoke in the near distance.

'Still operating. Still dangerous. I've tried to get it closed down, but the owners are too rich. Too powerful. There's no regulation, no safety measures. People still die there. A lot of these kids'll work there when they're older. Maybe die there, or lose a leg, an arm, an eye. It's that or go to fight against an army they know nowt about in a war they don't understand.'

'These children? That's what will happen to them?'

'Probably. Jeannie can only look after them for so long.'

I feel the Morrigan at my back, then, sudden and angry, black wings outspread. *All children are my children,* She whispers in the wind, *and all wrongs to them are wrongs done to me. I will strike down the ones that hurt the future leaders, the future thinkers, artists, carers, the ones that will shape the world in light and not darkness. The ones that can see beyond the shadows that lie upon them now.*

He looks behind me suddenly.

'What?'

'Nothing, I . . .' He narrows his eyes at me. 'I thought . . . you looked different for a minute. I felt . . . heard summat.'

He sensed the Goddess around me; I feel Her diminish but stay close. She wanted me to see the orphanage. She wanted me to come here. To know, to see. To feel the outrage for these children. To help them somehow.

'So what did you do instead?' I say to bring him back to the conversation to distract him, and She flutters into the back of my consciousness, still there but waiting.

He does a *ta-da* gesture, palms open. 'You know what I did.'

'Not really. How did you get to be so powerful?'

He blows out his cheeks. 'OK, OK,' he says. 'I were doing security jobs in York here and there. Started off in a shop looking out for lifters. You know, thieves. I were good at it. Had a good eye.' He laughs humourlessly. 'Probably cos I grew up with most of the people doing the thieving. I caught the attention of the top brass at the time.' He catches my blank expression. 'Top brass. The boss, like. I reminded him of his son who'd died. He trained me. I were driving an armoured van at seventeen. He made sure I knew everything about the business. Wanted me to take over eventually. Turned out a bit sooner than anyone expected.'

'Why? What happened?'

'He had a heart attack,' he says. 'Well. That's the public explanation.'

'What really happened?'

'Electrocuted in his swimming pool. Another security firm wanted his territory. They thought he were getting weak.'

'Was he?'

'Maybe. I weren't though.'

'What does that mean?'

'It means I did what I had to do. Sold up in York, kept the West Country part of the business. I didn't fancy being another dead body. I made a tidy profit and kept the local competition sweet; I made myself scarce round here for a few years. Still don't come back much, but just recently they've asked me up. Tide's turning, they need all the boots on the ground they can get.'

'Does Jeannie know?'

He shakes his head. 'Nah. I mean, I think she's got an idea, but I make sure she don't know the details. Glastonbury's a long way from here. She don't have to know owt.' He looks at me meaningfully. 'Aye?'

'All right.'

He takes my hand and we walk past the vegetable patches; it reminds me of home, and my heart tugs a little.

'I didn't think anyone in the Redworld did things like that,' I say, and point at the peas growing up an A-frame trellis.

'There are good people here too,' he says quietly. There's a stream at the bottom of the garden and we sit beside it. Under the willows I can't see the factory and the other houses; it's quiet, private, like its own little world. Almost like being in the Greenworld again.

I touch his cheek softly. 'You're a good person. You could be so much more than you are, you know. If you tried,' I say.

'I have tried. I've done all I can on my own. I need someone to help me.' His hand catches mine and he brings my fingers to his lips. 'You could help me. I could be good with you,' he murmurs, his words teasing my fingertips.

'What makes you think I want to be good? That I'm not damaged, like you?'

He strokes my hair. 'No one as beautiful as you could ever be damaged,' he says.

What would you prefer? Beauty or Truth?

'That's not true. A pretty face doesn't mean anything,' I say, and even as I say it I feel the disbelief of even talking about myself as pretty.

'I don't just mean that. You're beautiful inside and out,' he says, his eyes never leaving mine. 'I see you, Demelza Hawthorne. You can't hide from me.'

The air stills around us; the leaves hush on the trees. In the distance I hear a crow cawing.

'Help me. Help me make my world more like yours. Help me . . . be good,' he breathes, and leans in and kisses me surprisingly sweetly; his lips are gentle on mine and his hand strokes my hair and the side of my face. The smell of hyacinths wraps us up in their dreamy air, and the distant crow caws twice more. I feel my heart open to this lost boy, this abandoned boy who did what he had to, who lost everything and still found it in himself to fight. The boy whose dark secret is the orphanage cupboards he stocks with warm blankets, the larder full of food and the love on Jeannie's lined face. This is his secret life, and he invited me in.

Without saying anything else we lie back on the soft grass, under the protective reach of the whispering willows. His eyes are the dark blaze of banked-down coals, and as the kiss grows deeper I journey into the depths of him. Together we dance on the astral, hearts blazing, and the sad children inside us both cling to each other's warmth, no longer alone.

Chapter Seventeen

Morrigan, Ancient One; Morrigan, Dark Mother,
  Wise Mother
Morrigan, Shining One; Morrigan, Shape-shifter,
  Soul Healer
Morrigan, Sovereign One; Morrigan, Goddess of
  Rebirth

> Devotional chant, from *The Book of the
> Morrigan, Greenworld Prayers and Songs*

'How will he know where to go?'

I climb into the car and gesture to Pete beyond the partition, who has brought the car round to the orphanage.

'The navigation system'll take us there. The Twelve Apostles, aye? Should take about an hour and a half.'

Although I've never been to this particular stone circle, I remember from my time with my Aunt Tressa that there's a portal there. Tressa and her circle of witches keep the Archive, our witch herstory, and are in charge of monitoring the energy portals across the world. As far as I can remember, it should be operating fine. It's in the middle of the Yorkshire moors, which means it's still relatively unaffected by pollution and hardly anyone goes there. So hopefully no one has messed with it.

We pull away from the street, waving to the children that follow us out of the orphanage.

'They should be in bed,' Bran says mock-fatherly.

'You didn't say goodbye to Jeannie.' I see her come out and join the waving.

'S'all right. It's bedtime; she's busy. She won't mind.'

'You should have.' I watch the love in her face and all around her in her aura as we move away until she grows smaller and smaller. A mother of many. A goddess of sorts.

He sits back in his seat and smiles. 'So. Tell me about the Greenworld. What don't I know?'

'I don't know. What *do* you know?' I reply.

'Just the usual. Separate community, live off the land, ruled by witches, of which your mother is the leader.' I look away at the mention of Mum, but he smiles and carries on. 'She has the witch-brand, like you do.' His fingers reach up and stroke the back of my neck sensuously, and this time it's not sweetness and flower-scented air but lightning that shoots through my body. 'But not the same as this one. You have the triskele. She has something else . . .'

My hand follows his to the base of my neck and I clasp his fingers there, holding his gaze.

'The triple moon,' I say, and I feel the energy build between us again.

'Do you know what the triskele represents?' I ask him. I want to see if he knows how important it is to me in particular. The sign of my goddess, the Morrigan: mistress of birth, death and rebirth.

'The symbol of your Greenworld. It's about progress, aye?'

I frown. 'Not as such. More like evolution. A spiral relates to time, but differently to the way you think about it. The months repeat every year – the same points on a wheel – and every year you're at the same point but a year forward in time. So you're on a spiral of life, going forward, developing, but still visiting those same points of reference. The past coexists with the present.'

'Isn't that what I said?'

'No. You said "progress" like it was a straight line, a quick answer.'

'Nothing's a simple straight line in the Greenworld, eh?' He smiles.

I point to my eyes, lined in black. 'There's a place for it. I like a straight black line as much as the next person. More, probably.'

He looks at me. 'Straight-ish,' he jokes.

I push him playfully. 'Whatever. But, you know, the triskele represents lots of things. Past, present, future. Creation, preservation, destruction. All in infinite cycles.'

'Aye. But you being here. To me, it's a sign. A different kind o' sign. From your goddess, maybe. That it's time for us all to move on. Make some leap or another.'

I think about this stone circle we're visiting, and the portal it contains. They're supposed to be secret. But they're my secret as much as any witch; the secret belongs to me as much as them. I trace my fingers across the soft leather of the car seat, rationalizing.

The Redworld is a new frontier. If I choose to share the secret, if I choose to demonstrate my power as a witch here, who's going to stop me? A corrupt government that's devolved all its power to a collective of private security firms – one of which is run by the young man whose girlfriend I might be? A government that's spent all its money on a pointless foreign war? Whose population might be on the edge of revolution? I don't think I'm very high up their priority list right now. The Morrigan stirs in my heart and my mind again. I'll take my chances, thanks.

And who says that what I'm about to do isn't fate? Magic is real, whether they choose to believe it here in the Redworld or not. I am real. I exist.

I feel Her again, nearby, leading my thoughts. *Do you want me to show Bran the portal?* I ask Her inside myself, and close my eyes. Immediately the image of a crow flying over a full moon appears behind my eyes, and I see myself surrounded by a blue portal, arms outstretched. I take that as a yes.

I reach over and take his hand. 'Look. The energy portals. You have to understand they're very sacred. Only witches know how they work. Only witches understand how to enter them.' I look at him, at his serious eyes.

'I know that,' he says. 'So you're going to show me one? There's one at this Twelve Apostles place?'

I look out of the window at the receding city lights as we speed along; we're going so fast that their on—off flashing thins into a streak of artificial light through the dark.

'Yes.'

'Is that a magical coincidence?'

'There's no such thing as coincidence. This is fate.'

'I didn't think you'd show me one. What changed your mind?'

I look down at my dress. 'I don't know. You. Tonight. Her. The Morrigan.'

'I'm honoured. How so?'

'You showed me something secret for you. You trusted me. So I'll trust you with this. And She . . . She wants me to. I don't know why, but She does.'

My fingers stray back to my witch-brand.

'I got this when I was twelve years old. I'd already been a witch four years, but the Morrigan hadn't chosen me yet. Then, one day in circle, I had a vision. I was in this garden, and there was a spiral laid out — stones on sand. Big. I mean, you could walk round it in thirty paces. I looked up at the sky and there was this black circle against the blue, and very quickly there flashed these magical formulae. Symbols. And the ground under the spiral started moving.'

In my mind I am back in the vision; I feel myself stepping on to the sand from the cool grass.

'It was scary, moving fast. There was a little girl on it already. She got sucked into it, into its centre. Like a vortex, like water spiralling down a plughole. And she disappeared. And then this guy kind of flung himself into it, but he didn't disappear. It just stripped him of his feet.'

I shiver at the memory of the exposed bone at the bottom of the screaming man's legs.

'I knew that meant that the spiral was dangerous for people who weren't witches; literally that people could lose their footing there if they weren't careful. If they weren't properly prepared. And I knew that the little girl was a sacrifice. This power, my new power, demanded sacrifice. I think that it was telling me I had already sacrificed my childhood to magic. But then I stepped in and I saw Her.'

'But you were already a witch. You already had power.'

'I had some. But after that I had a lot more. I walked into the vortex of my own free will, and She was there. The Morrigan. I'd met Her before, at initiation, with the other gods. But She touched me on the back of the neck, and I came to with this.'

'Aye. You're special,' he says, touching the brand

again with his fingertips, like its magic might transfer to him. 'Do any of your other friends have them?'

I look at him warily for a moment, but there's no harm in him knowing.

'Daniel Prentice. He's another witch. His mum's the witch in Gidleigh. He has one.'

'Like this?' He touches the triskele again.

'No. Different.' I hold his gaze for a moment, then drop it, watching the fields spread out under the moon as we speed out of the city.

'Go on. Why have you changed your mind? About showing me the portal?' He gives me another one of his penetrating looks.

I sigh. 'I've lived with magic most of my life. I've given up a lot of standard kid experiences for it: studying when I could have been playing; fasting and going on psychic journeys when the other kids were making dens in the trees; leading the ceremonies and not enjoying the dancing afterwards. Magic is real.'

'So?'

I try to bring my thoughts into line.

'Those kids at your orphanage. I want them to know that magic is real. They could be the generation that changes all this. The Redworld, the Greenworld. Poverty, destruction. Us hiding away in seclusion. It isn't right. Children shouldn't be losing their parents to this war. This stupid war that no one will ever win. If they knew, then . . .'

'Then?'

'Then they could make life better for themselves. Change things. Know that it isn't the only way.' I think of the hovels and the dirt, and the orphanage like an oasis inside it. 'The factory. Disease. Death. It's not good enough.'

'No, it isn't.'

'We can help them, Bran. I know we can. And . . .'

'What?'

The memory of that vision comes back to me again.

'If I sacrificed my childhood then I want it to mean something. I want it to be worth something. And I don't want those children to have to sacrifice theirs. Or for their lives to mean nothing.'

His eyes blaze at me and he grips my hand. 'I knew you'd understand once you saw it for yourself. Why I'm doing what I'm doing. There's a higher purpose here. We have to help those children if we can. We have to try. By any means necessary.'

It all seems so clear now and I wonder why I didn't see it before. There's a reason I'm here, that we are here together.

'The Redworld needs to see magic to believe it. Because until you all know in your hearts that there is an alternative to the way you live now, then nothing will change and more and more people will die. And that will be on my hands unless I . . . unless I try to help. Unless I share the secret of the Greenworld with you. It might put me in danger. But I don't care.'

He kisses me again. I see the man leaping into the

spiralling earth, and I see his face as it strips the flesh from his ankles, his calves. But now it's Bran's face, and the Morrigan stands behind him, smiling. *If you don't believe in me now, you will. One way or the other*, She says, and my eyes snap open.

I pull away from the kiss, horrified.

'What is it?' he says, startled.

'Nothing . . . nothing.'

The kiss lingers on my lips, and I wipe it away. Suddenly my elation fades, and all I can hear is Bran saying *by any means necessary* and the Morrigan's *one way or the other* and I grip the shiny metal door handle inside the car for some kind of anchor, but it can't stop the feeling of being pulled apart.

Chapter Eighteen

War is not for the Greenworld. We leave war to
those that have not found peace.

From *Tenets and Sayings of the Greenworld*

We pull up in wide moorland. It's totally dark and quiet,
but as Bran helps me out of the car he hands me a storm
lamp with a tall white candle inside.

Pete gets out of the car and lights a cigarette. 'Should
be just over there,' he says, pointing off into the darkness
and turning his back on us.

Bran and I set off across the tussocky moor, the dim
light of the flickering lamps like faery orbs in the dark.
The smell reminds me of Dartmoor – damp heather and
stone and the sharp twist of wind. I try to suppress my
vision. His kiss lingers on my mouth, not altogether
pleasantly now. What is the Morrigan trying to tell me?

Then I see them: the Twelve Apostles. Twelve tall
standing stones. They rise haughtily from the ground as if

they have been pushed up from below, and the closer I get the stronger I feel their power throb through the ground and air. There won't be any problem with the portal here. The feeling of this circle is completely different to the stopped-up blankness of Glastonbury Tor; this, like the portal on Tintagel Head, is a wild place, pure and bursting with a virile blood-rushing power.

I take Bran's hand and he follows me into the centre of the circle.

I take his other hand so I have them both; palm to palm we stand under the moon.

'Can you feel it? The power here?' I breathe, and let the circle take me over. I stop worrying, stop thinking, and just feel. I feel the polarity between Bran and me, between us and the circle, like we are the circuit. Our hands get hotter and hotter.

He draws in a breath in shock; I know he feels it.

'Wow . . . that's . . .' He doesn't finish.

I watch him as the natural energy of this place surges through him. For an experienced witch like me this is still a very strong feeling; to Bran it must feel like the top of his head just blew off.

'Just breathe and relax. Let the power go through you. Don't resist it,' I say, and I feel the tension in his hands loosen, and he closes his eyes to be able to focus on how it feels. After a few moments he opens his eyes again.

'OK?' I check in with him, but he looks all right.

'OK. Wow. That were a rush.'

'I know.'

His eyes are wide from the power of the place, but there's calculation there too.

I laugh, and see his hurt expression. 'Magical sites, they all feel different – like people, they have different energies. But they're all kind of intense, like that. All the ceremonies that have taken place here over the years get built up. They increase the power of the place. And they're naturally powerful places to begin with, that's why our ancestors built these places. Stone circles. Burial mounds. Sacred hills, castles, fortresses. They knew the power of the land, the lines where the power was most concentrated.'

I take his hand and we walk to the stone on our right, the westernmost. I trace his fingertips lightly on the stone; it speaks to me immediately, of the rain and wind that whittled it slowly over the years, of the ancient power of the granite it was hewn from, of the compressed wisdom of the world, long before humans evolved to chip it away and place it upended in the earth. And lastly it tells me that it is one of the guardians of the portal. Here there are no witches to protect it. The stones look on, and cast their magic.

'It's here. This stone – all of them – they protect it.'

He places his palm flat on the rock instinctively and smiles.

'There's a sort of grandfatherliness about this one. Like it's old and wise. And watchful,' he says.

'Yes. Exactly. Now I'll open the portal.'

I raise my arms to start the process, but hear voices and turn round.

Pete is running towards us, following a group of shadows. Our lamps throw light across the stones and their faces as they approach, and I see two girls about my age and two young men, a little older than the girls, maybe twenty or twenty-two. Worn-looking somehow. I realize the taller boy only has one arm. The other blinks, surprised by the light on his face, and holds up a protective hand in front of his eyes. The light caresses deep scars on his wrists, face and neck.

'Hey!' one of the girls shouts, and points at me. 'Hey! What're you doing?'

'Nothing. Go away,' I call.

Pete gets to us, panting. 'I tried to stop them,' he says to Bran.

'What are you wearing that dress for out here? It's freezing!'

The other girl laughs, and I'm angry again. I feel rage slip up my spine like a familiar eel.

I flatten my tone. 'Go away. Now,' I say, and they stop laughing.

'Christ. No need to be rude,' the scarred man says, and steps through into the circle. 'Room for everyone.' I feel his energy disrupt the circle immediately.

'No, I don't think you understand. We're doing something . . . important,' I say, but they all sit down in the middle of the circle and begin passing around a bottle of wine.

'Whatever, red girl. Why don't you and your boyfriend find somewhere else? There's more of us,' says the other girl, lighting a cigarette. Its tip glows in the darkness like an eye.

I look at Bran for help, but he shrugs. 'Can't do much about it if they won't move,' he says, uncharacteristically submissive.

You could do a lot about it if you wanted to, I think, and wonder why he doesn't muscle them out with Pete, or bribe them.

'Maybe they can watch,' he says.

They laugh.

'No offence, but I don't think we're into that,' the man with one arm says, dragging on his cigarette and narrowing his eyes at us in the lantern glow. He holds my stare.

I'm the first to look away. This isn't my turf. I am off-centre here in the Redworld. I don't know how to be.

I was looking forward to seeing what this portal was like. How it was different to the one in Tintagel. How it felt. And, yes, I wanted to show off a little. I wanted to be seen by Bran: really *seen*.

Bran touches my arm, and electricity jolts through it again.

'Think about it,' he murmurs so they don't hear. 'This is your chance to show someone else, not just me,

that magic is real. I believe it already. But they don't.'
He looks me in the eyes, his dark irises the same depth
as the night. 'Don't you think, maybe, your goddess sent
them? I mean, don't you think it's a bit weird that
someone else should appear just when you were going to
open the portal?' He traces his finger over my braids.
'Just when you look exactly as you should – Priestess of
Magic, Queen of the Night?'

I look back at them laughing and talking between
themselves, oblivious to the magic that throbs through
the ground under them, through the air above them.
Can I show them that magic is real? Can I make them
believe? I want to. I want to be seen.

'Go and stand over there,' I order them, and they
laugh again, not moving. My anger slides further up my
spine and starts writhing round my neck eel-like. Eels
are one of the Morrigan's sacred animals.

'You don't know who I am,' I say, and the girl
smoking a cigarette looks up at me.

'No, lass, we don't, and we're not bothered about
knowing either. So why don't you take your boyfriend,
and his mate, and your ego, and sod off and have your
own party somewhere else?'

'No. You're going to know who I am. He knows.' I
point at Bran.

They laugh, all together.

'What are you on about? God. Some special ones
out tonight,' the other girl says to her friend, rolling her
eyes. 'Look. The boys just came back from the war,

OK? They need some R & R, 'specially after the demo today. So chill out or bugger off.'

Bran and Pete exchange glances at the mention of the demonstration, but don't comment.

'The war? You were there?' I've never known anyone that came back from the war.

'Nalchik,' the boy with one arm says, and the candlelight catches the raw expression on his face.

'Is that in Russia?' I ask, thinking of my dad.

'Course it's bloody Russia. Near the border with Georgia. We were there for two years, but there's worse places. Nalchik's like a tactical centre, they have to keep it cos of Elbrus nearby, but the worst fighting's up near Tunguska. Bloody freezing. Men losing legs to gangrene and frostbite all the time.'

I look at the space where the boy's arm should be. Not just legs by the look of it. I remember my dream again and the man that lost his feet. Sacrifice.

'Why Tunguska?'

'It's the last coalfield on the planet. Whoever gets it gets fuel for another ten, twenty years maybe.'

'I heard it were less than that,' Bran interjects laconically. 'Think about it. The war's been going for, what, twelve years now? That's twelve years' use gone already, powering Russia. I'd be surprised if it had a year left.'

'That's bloody rubbish. The commanders told us it was at least ten.'

'They would. They wouldn't want you knowing you

184

lost an arm for less than a year's worth of coal, would they?' Bran nods to the boy's empty sleeve, pinned to his chest.

'Bugger off. You don't know what you're on about, soft lad.' The boy draws on his cigarette and narrows his eyes. 'You been out there?'

'Nah. Protected profession.'

The boy nods slowly, looking at Bran's expensive clothes.

'I bet. Government paper-shuffler. Got soft hands, has he, lass?' he asks me, but I ignore him.

Bran smiles. 'Something like that.'

The scarred man stands up, comes over to me and points back at his friend's arm or lack of it.

'See that? See this?' He pulls back his collar and I see his raised scars criss-crossing his collarbone and down on to his chest. 'I were trapped in a burning building. Neither of you look like you've seen much action recently. We know the war's a bloody lie. It's just a war to distract everyone from what they're doing here. Killing the poor by sending us off to fight or starving us to death.' He waves his hand at the stones. 'So I dunno what you think you're doing up here, drifting around in your long dress, but why don't you just sod off and let us have whatever fun we can, while we're still young enough to enjoy it?'

I exchange glances with Bran. He shrugs. 'You'll get no argument from me. He's right. That's why we have to find summat else. Summat better. Here, at home.'

The first girl snorts. 'Fat chance. There isn't

185

anything left. Let's enjoy ourselves while we can.' She stubs out her cigarette on the ground, which makes me angry – mistreating sacred earth.

They all look expectantly at us, their faces lit by lamplight. Waiting for us to leave.

I take a step backwards, knowing I'm going to go through with this, and that gives me a sense of calm. I'm going to show them what magic is. Whatever the consequences.

'They're lying to you about the war for the same reason they're lying to you about me. I'm Demelza Hawthorne. Does that name sound familiar?'

Bran's gaze snaps to me; I'm taking a huge risk by saying my name but this is too important. I have to show them that magic is real.

'No. Should it?' the girl says, finishing her cigarette and frowning at me.

'Lowenna Hawthorne, then. The Contract of Separation.'

She pulls on her cigarette, narrowing her eyes. 'Oh yeah. Greenworld. She's in charge. Terrorists and all that.'

'I'm her daughter, Demelza Hawthorne. But I'm not a terrorist. None of us are. I'm a witch. She is, and so is my sister. We're in charge in the Greenworld. A peaceful, beautiful, self-sufficient community.'

There's a pause, and then they all laugh uproariously. The one-armed man smiles, but his eyes are dead and flat.

'The Greenworld's full of nutjobs.' The girl with the cigarette lights another one and frowns at me.

'No. That's wrong. I live there. Lived there.' I can feel the fury mixed with sadness that they don't believe me. But fury wins, and starts spiralling up my spine like sage smoke.

'It's, like, full of murderers and shit,' the scarred boy says, upending his beer bottle to finish the dregs. 'I read about it.'

Bran smiles thinly. 'Aye. We all know how trustworthy the media is,' he says. 'But the Greenworld isn't what you think it is. Devon and Cornwall – it's a witch-led community. Agrarian, pagan, harmonious. For the most part anyway. Because the government, the media, they don't want you to know that people can live in peace and not be fighting a war for fuel. That people live well off the land, aren't obsessed with shopping and possessions, that they have spirituality in their lives. That there's thousands of people that're motivated by a genuine sense of community and a love of the land. They don't want you to know owt, so they manufactured the lies about Separation you get taught at school. Wake up. You know they're capable of lying to you about the war. So why not summat else?'

The guy with one arm looks up, peering at Bran in the darkness. 'Who the bloody hell are you, the Prince of Darkness?'

'Don't matter who I am,' he replies crisply. 'The point is, I know she's telling the truth. She's not a terrorist. She's a witch.'

187

The girl with the cigarette stands up. 'Then she better get lost. I'm not going to call the police but there'd be plenty that would.'

The rest of them get up, and it's a stand-off between us and them. The stones seem to tower over us in the darkness, and they cry out at me. I can feel their frustration at not being seen, at being ignored; I can feel their hunger for acknowledgement.

I close my eyes and step forward. It's time.

The others move away, letting me through, perhaps instinctively. I feel out for the portal with my mind, and see it before me like a blue keyhole floating in the night air.

It's here.

I open my eyes and look back at all of them. They stare at me blankly, only Bran's gaze is charged and glowing. I drink in his expectation for a moment, then focus on the portal.

I make the opening symbols and feel the different energy; the portal is like a heavy door that needs grease on the hinges. I can't push too hard, only encourage it gently and feed power from my hands into it slowly, slowly. And it opens, pulsing blue light, unlike the orange of the Tintagel portal, and twice as large. It blooms around all of us like a nightmarish flower. It swirls in a spiral of light, with an underlying noise in my ears like blood and singing at the same time.

I look back and register their faces. Even those completely unused to magic, like these kids, can see an open portal this close up, especially one this powerful. They look pretty terrified.

'What . . . what the . . . I mean, what is that? What did you do?' whispers the cigarette girl, and she holds on to the scarred man like he's a raft.

'My name is Demelza Hawthorne, witch of the Greenworld, priestess of the Morrigan,' I intone into the darkness, and the portal swells again, as if burgeoning with my pronouncement. It is much harder to control than the one at home – bigger, harsher, wilder. Yet I know I can do this.

'This is an energy portal. This is the way from life to death,' I say, and I raise my hands above my head, widening the circumference until it is all around us. The stones light up blue in the darkness, and I hear them singing like struck chimes, like the hum of a finger traced round a crystal glass.

'This is what we protect, as witches of the Greenworld. Magic is real. These places of magic are real.' I turn round slowly, pointing to the stone crags in the circle one by one. 'And you should honour them. Protect them. The land can give you everything you need – good food, clean water, fuel, clothing, protection – but only if you respect it. Only if you don't take too much. And it's these natural places – these places of power – that hold portals. Passageways between life and death. We need these to survive as humans. We need the way to be able to pass into the next life. These are a part of our spiritual ecology as much as keeping our streams clean, keeping our food pure. The more you corrupt and pollute the land, the more you destroy these natural energy centres, the more troubled this world becomes.'

'What happens if they get polluted?' one girl asks, the blue light of the portal reflected in her eyes.

'Then souls can't cross over. It would become a world populated with the dead, with no way of leaving,' I reply.

'What would that mean?' Bran asks quietly. I look at him, and Glastonbury Tor flashes into my mind.

'The end of days,' I say softly. 'And you are closer to it than you know.'

I look back at the pulsing lights and into Bran's eyes. He still needs me to show him the final part of this. He more or less believes, but he's a pragmatist, and his eyes still don't give anything away. I can't see the awe and desire I'm looking for there. I can't see the unquestioning faith. He hasn't lost control. He's watching me intently, but he doesn't really see me. Yet.

The night kisses my skin, but I'm not cold. I feel the moonlight on me like a lover's hands, and I feel power rush from my feet, up my spine, and into a sphere around myself.

I turn away from all of them and walk into the portal.

To be seen, I have to disappear.

Chapter Nineteen

God and Goddess, sun and moon,
Rising sap and witches' rune,
Join as lovers, dark and bright,
Celebrate this Beltane night.

Chant for Beltane, from *Greenworld Prayers and Songs*

You have to know how to enter a portal; you can't just wander into it. Only witches know how to open and enter them at will.

To open a portal you channel your energy into a concentrated cone directly at the portal location, and trace a particular set of symbols into the space. Then, when the portal opens, like a huge flower made of light, you concentrate on walking into it and making yourself . . . dissolve. That's the best way I can describe it.

So I walk forward and imagine myself getting blurry at the edges. Less defined.

The world goes blue for a moment, and I find myself inside the portal, just like at home, but also different.

It's the same sense of being in a long tunnel that reaches out into the far distance, but this is taller and wider, and more like being in a temple than a corridor. There are ornamental pillars along the length of this one, and arched doorways. As I watch, two open and close, letting two souls into the walkway – they float serenely to the end and disappear. The end of the tunnel is death. The tunnel is a walkway everyone must pass down, getting lighter and lighter, less and less defined. Leaving the body and the physical world behind them.

Once inside, I feel the magnetic pull of death from the far end of the tunnel on my blurry, lighter, less defined body. Death has such an attraction for the soul, as if it knows that's where it will find peace. And it is also the desire to see my goddess, the Morrigan, the crow of the battlefield and the raven of death. In this in-between place it's easier to connect with the Gods; it's an in-between place where the rules of both realms are relaxed.

I look under my feet and see that the pathway is softly lined with crow feathers. I smile, and reach down to pick one up; its fibres are silky and gleam blue-black and I stand there turning it in the soft light of the space, feeling its peace. It's Her message to me – *I have seen you; I am with you.* But I know I have to turn round and go back. I've achieved what I wanted to: I've proved magic is real to these non-believers, but most of all to Bran. I have shown him that I am powerful. He saw me disappearing temporarily from the normal world. But he *saw* me.

I murmur a prayer of thanks to the Morrigan and walk out of the portal, gradually imagining my body becoming more definite as I leave it: retaking my outline, my solidity.

I've only been gone a few moments. I concentrate on feeling my body whole and heavy and real. I look up, and I know how I look in Bran's eyes. It's as if I see myself for a half-second: pale, wild, a little hazy, but magical, appearing from the blue light like a faery.

I walk up to him and kiss him, hard and full of passion, knowing that he feels the magic burning me up, feels the fire in my kiss. I am Melz the Red Witch.

He pulls away at first, looking a little flustered. I've broken his cool. Even the attack with the crows at the restaurant didn't make him look like this: a little awestruck, a little scared. I take his hand, and hold out my hand to the girls, who move as if enchanted. We all form a circle, hands interlinked. I close my eyes and call the Goddess. They have come this far; they can go a little further, these non-believers. Their disbelief is like bricks around them, like strengthened glass. I need to crack it thoroughly to allow air inside – to their hearts, to their minds.

I start to sing an invocation to Her in a low voice.

Morrigan, Ancient One; Morrigan, Dark Mother,
  Wise Mother
Morrigan, Shining One; Morrigan, Shape-shifter,
  Soul Healer
Morrigan, Sovereign One; Goddess of Rebirth.

They sway with me, Bran's voice joining mine haltingly. The chant gets louder, and I feel Her coming to us. I open my eyes and see Her stand before me.

'You have to let them see me,' She says, and holds out her hands. I see Her white flesh under Her red dress like mine, and the blue-woad spirals that ring Her arms under a heavy tartan shawl. I have only done this a couple of times before – channelled the Goddess – and I know it takes a lot of energy. I recoil slightly. But I also know it has to be done.

I open myself to Her, and feel Her take over. I am still there, but I give up control. I feel Her fill me with an awesome power and dynamism, as if I am one of a vast flock of horses in full gallop across a red desert. I don't know where we are going, and I don't care; I race with them. I feel Her speak through me like a hot wind and I am not aware of what it is exactly She says; I feel Her move my arm and She points at each one of them in turn. They all ask a question and She answers, but I don't know what the questions or answers are. I am running, running, free in the desert.

The pack surges towards a cliff; I feel anticipation in me and prepare to stop, but the wave of rippling horse flesh propels me on, on, and we flow over the edge of the cliff and down into the ocean as smoothly as if it were long grass. This is Morrigan as Macha, in Her guise as Horse Goddess of the Celts, riding sovereign on Her land. And when we meet the ocean we become horses of water, shape-shifting again, our backs forming and breaking waves, our manes drawing lines of foam. When the horses' hoofs become the power of the water, I feel Her leave me and open my eyes. They are all staring at me.

There is a long silence.

'How did you do that?' The cigarette girl drops my hand, and the circle breaks. 'I closed my eyes, and I saw this village circled with barbed wire, and this big iron gate . . . It had birds' heads on the spikes. There were bodies everywhere. On the ground. Blood.'

'It was Her. The Goddess. She showed you.'

'It was . . . so real. I was there, breathing the air. I could hear birds cawing.'

'Crows.'

'Maybe. I don't know.'

'It was Tintagel. My village. In the Greenworld.'

She looks at me, eyes wide.

'There was a battle there. Those people died defending your village.'

'That's right.'

'How do I know that?'

'She gave the knowledge to you. She wants you to know that the Greenworld is real. Magic is real. These are the things worth fighting for.'

The boy with the scars looks at his friend. 'I saw . . . this is crazy. I saw you . . . On the banks of a black river. This old woman was next to you – tall, hooded. She was in these black robes, but her arms were covered in blue tattoos. Spirals, lines, going round and round. She took you in this wooden boat. A barge, painted black. Carved symbols on it. And when you stepped in . . . your arm – it was there again.'

The other boy frowns, looking at his friend and then at me. 'What was that, then? My arm can't magically grow back.'

'No,' I agree. Not in life. I choose not to elaborate on what I know is the truth: that this boy will die when he is still young, still recognizable to his friend anyway. We all die. She takes us all in the barge eventually.

'It was the Goddess,' I say simply, stamping my feet on the earth. I need to eat something, to ground myself. It's cold now.

'You looked different. Held yourself differently.' The boy with the scars peers at my bare arms. 'I could have sworn you had tattoos just now. Blue spirals round your arms.'

'It was Her. The Morrigan. My goddess. I channelled Her. She was here. You saw what She gave you, and you must believe in the truth of what you saw. You've seen the portal. You know what the Greenworld is now. I'm real. It's up to you now if you want to know more.'

The scarred man points at the spinning blue portal, still open. 'You went inside that?'

I nod. 'Where did you think I went?'

He frowns, trying to understand. This must be hard for them.

'It was a trick. You're . . . like an illusionist or something.'

I gesture at the portal. 'How am I doing it, then, by Brighid?'

He shakes his head. 'Dunno. It has to be a trick though.'

'Why?' Bran asks, taking my hand. 'I told you. She's a witch. There's a lot more like her back in Cornwall. They can do this kind of magic. The government tells you summat else because they're scared of what they can do. Scared of their power.'

I step forward and trace the closing symbols into the portal; the blue vortex shuts, leaving us in the night air among the sentinel stones.

There is another silence. They don't want to believe, but the truth got in. It changed them, even though they might not know that yet. *What would you prefer? Beauty or Truth?* Sometimes the real truth is too beautiful to look at directly.

Bran looks at me, drinking me in again. His prize.

The group exchange glances.

'If this is true, I mean, people should know about it. Shouldn't they? Shouldn't they know about – her? About . . . the Goddesses, and all that?' The girl with the cigarette grinds the discarded butt under her heel, looking cautiously at me and the portal. She points at it.

'So if you really went inside it just now – what's stopping any of us from wandering in? Having a look around?' She walks forward, holding my gaze.

I step aside. 'Only witches know how to open and close them. You can only get in when they're open, and only if you know how,' I say. 'But you should know they're there. Respect this circle. It's a magical place.' I look at all of them. 'Respect the land, and not just here. Care for it. Do everything you can to protect it.' I reach down and pick up a handful of black soil, and stand, letting it crumble between my fingers.

The other girl, the non-smoker, watches me intently. I know from her eyes that she believes me. She may not really understand what she just saw, but she knows I am telling the truth. She knows I'm real.

'Magic is real,' I say, and go to her, taking her hand. My energy is still high, and she feels it; her eyes widen as I touch her.

'I . . . I . . . I don't understand,' she says, but she doesn't pull away.

'You don't need to right now. Just believe that there is an alternative. To poverty, fear, war. Darkness. I'm from that alternative. The Greenworld.'

The one-armed man snatches her hand from mine. 'Leave her alone, witch. Whatever you are. Whoever you are. Just leave us all alone.'

I feel the deep fear in him and I understand it. Maybe he understood his friend's vision for him: the black river and the barge. And maybe he's already lost a part of himself to a lie and he can't risk believing in another.

I wonder what She showed him, but I can see in his eyes he won't tell anyone.

Making people believe in the real Greenworld, what we really are, and all the implications that has, will be a rocky path. Not everyone will want to hear what I have to say. Not everyone in the Redworld will believe, even if I take every single one of them by the hand and show them the portal, show them the Goddess, their future, and enable them to feel their connection to life, real, true, terrible and beautiful life. But I have to try, because of the children in that orphanage. For them and for every other child who has no future otherwise. I feel the Morrigan close and hear Her words again. *All children are my children, and all wrongs to them are wrongs done to me.*

Bran's arm snakes round my waist, possessive and hot.

'Come on,' he says to me, and we turn away. I walk to the edge of the circle, and loosing his arm from me say a blessing and thanks to the circle, feeling its resonance in me. It doesn't feel wrong what I've done. I feel free, powerful, as if I am the mistress of this place.

Then I turn away, take his hand and lead him back to the car.

I look back and call out. 'Just remember me. Tell your friends. Bring them here. Talk about the war. Find out more about the Greenworld. Find out what else your leaders are lying to you about. You're already protesting about the way they would have you live. Educate yourselves. There is an alternative. But you need to learn how to live in a different way, and that'll take time.'

They stand in the circle, staring after me.

'I think you just started a revolution,' Bran murmurs hotly in my ear.

'Goddess be praised,' I reply and mean it.

The car is idling and Pete pulls away smoothly as we get in. I roll down the window and let the cool night air caress my skin. As we drive down the dirt track, three crows caw and fly past, a sign. I stretch out my arm to them, releasing the crow feather in my hand, which rises up into the blackness, and I know I have done what She wanted.

We ride back in silence holding hands. My power and his desire thicken the space between us like flesh, and when we reach the hotel we go straight up to my room without talking.

As soon as the lift gets to our floor, I lead him to the bed. The lights are low and someone has made a fire in the ornate fireplace; I recognize the sweet incense of apple wood. He pulls me to him and undoes the fastenings on my dress; it falls to the ground in a red puddle. I kick off my boots, and he takes off his shirt and trousers. I watch his long limbs, his taut muscles. He has no tattoos, but scars. We still don't talk.

He takes my chin in his hand and raises my lips to his, kissing me deeply, and I feel passion flowing through me again, the same as magic, only redder, hotter, full of the desire for another body, the way he feels, the touch of his skin on mine. We fall on to the bed, and I let go of the old Melz, the fearful, shy, ignored Melz. I leave her standing alone and friendless at the border of the Greenworld, because that's where she belongs.

Here in the Redworld I am fearless, desired, respected. I am seen. I am Melz the Red Witch now, and I know deep in myself I have nothing to be afraid of. The Goddess still lingers from the channelling, not entirely gone. Shreds of Her flesh stay under my nails and black wings spread over our bed. She has been with me a long time, but never so deeply; She will never be totally gone from me ever again.

Chapter Twenty

The populace will periodically demand peace by
holding demonstrations or rioting. You are the
peacekeepers. Give the people what they want.
[Laughter.]

From a speech given by Bran Crowley at the
South-west Region Security Officers annual
dinner, Bristol, December 2046

On the way back to Glastonbury the next day he's
subdued. I roll the window down and smell the green,
fresh, hot, fertile land.

'Happy Beltane,' I say, leaning over and kissing his
cheek shyly.

In the Redworld they call it May Day, and, like
everything, they don't know what it means. It's the
high point of the agricultural year, the big party.
Specifically it's the day when we dance round a maypole
and celebrate sex. The life force of the world is at its

peak: conception, consummation, raw energy pulses through the earth. Free and uninhibited.

'What? Oh, right,' he says, looking out of the window. 'That's some kind of big deal where you're from, eh?'

'You could say that.'

Usually it's my least favourite of the eight seasonal festivals. To me, the mysteries of death and regeneration in the winter are the most interesting times, even though I honour them all as part of the whole. I also grudgingly accept that my goddess, the Morrigan, has a sexy side and isn't just about war and death. But I always hated Beltane, because no boy ever wanted to take me off into the woods for a kiss and maybe more after the main ceremony. I'd see Tom leading Saba off to the boundary to be alone, and I'd try so hard not to care, but I *did*. And I hated how everyone got drunk and stupid and you couldn't turn a corner in the village in the evening without running into a couple snogging against a wall, or worse. Beltane is the day of the year when everyone goes wild, women and women, men and women, men and men, together. In public, unashamed, drunk and . . . disorderly.

Mum would just laugh when I said I didn't want to be part of the festival, and say something like *Oh, Demelza, lighten up, we're allowed to have some fun sometimes. We're celebrating the fertility of the land, the union of the sun and the moon. Can't you feel the life energy pounding through the world at this time?* And she always made me go. And I always hated it.

Until today. Last night I celebrated Beltane in the way it should be celebrated; we honoured the Gods with our pleasure.

'What's on your mind?' I want to kiss him, but he seems distant.

Still, he smiles and catches my hand. 'Oh, you know. World domination.'

'I know that when *you* say that, you're serious,' I reply, looking carefully at his face. His mask is back on and he's not giving anything away. Last night was amazing, but today he's all business again. Wings of unease flutter in my stomach.

He releases my hand and reaches for the heart pendant round my neck, but I pull away. I'm still wearing the gold moon necklace too. Both together: old and new Melz.

'What is that? You don't take it off.'

'Just something from home.'

He peers closer. 'What is it, a locket?'

I curl my fingers protectively round the wooden heart and feel the dark energy of the curse leaking through my fingers.

'Something like that,' I say, clipped and flat. I look past his curious eyes and out of the window. I can tell he's watching my face.

'From that old boyfriend, is it?' He doesn't take the hint to shut up.

'None of your business,' I mutter.

'What?'

'None of your business!' I snap at him, the energy from the pendant infesting my heart suddenly. He keeps staring at me, those eyes boring into me like drills, but he doesn't seem fazed by me shouting. 'Anyway. What about Demi? Isn't she your girlfriend? What would she think about what happened last night?' I snap, the anger and the negativity of the curse seeping into me.

'It's over with Demi. She knows we were only ever casual.'

'Does she know that?'

'Are you calling me a liar?'

I look away from him angrily. 'No.'

'I see,' he says coolly.

There's a silence, and I feel stupid for having shouted. The locket is an open wound, a sore I won't let myself forget, but it's mine. I don't want anyone else touching it, knowing it, feeling it. Except Bali and Skye, of course.

'It'll be interesting to see what happens in York now.' He changes the subject as simply as if we were discussing what to have for dinner, and I pull my heart, my real heart, back under control with some effort.

'Interesting how?'

'How quickly word gets out about you, and the portal.'

I study his face: calculating, brooding, closed. This is the Bran Crowley that runs security in the south-west. Last night's Bran . . . I don't know him so well. But I prefer him.

'How will I know I'll be safe? Once word gets out about me being a Greenworld witch?'

He waves my concern away like a spiderweb. An insubstantial irritation. 'You're safe with me. They wouldn't dare try anything.'

'The police?'

'The police haven't got any power. They don't do nowt unless security services say it's OK.'

'And the government? What are they going to do when they find out I'm here? Unravelling their propaganda?' Again I imagine the spiderweb: lies woven together, only words, but strong enough to trap and kill. *Oh, what a tangled web we weave, When first we practise to deceive.*

He smiles then, and gives me all of his attention. 'By the time they realize what's going on it'll be too late. The revolution will have started.'

'The revolution?'

'They're at breaking point already, the proles. Once they find out they've been lied to about the Greenworld, about all of you, about the way they could live in harmony with the earth, that'll be the turning point. They're sick of poverty and war. If it's you or the government, I'm betting Westminster gets burned before you do.'

'I'm . . . I'm not sure that's what I want. I just want to inspire people. Not be responsible for them . . . burning anyone. Anything. I just want to be sure they understand. What the Greenworld can offer the people here is a way of living, a way of being. A new future. Not just a new way to power a television.'

He pours a coffee from the built-in maker in the car and hands it to me.

'They'll understand. They're ready for this. And if owt's burned, it's not your fault; it's theirs, the government, for making the messed-up decisions they have for so long.'

'But you're part of their power. It's your foundations that will shake when this revolution starts, by Brighid.'

'You know I don't care about that. The rich. My wealth, my power, the armoured vans, whatever – it's all a means to an end. I always knew that, but I never knew how it would happen. I know now. Last night you showed me.'

'Showed you what?'

'Magic is real. A vast untapped power. I want those kids fighting on my side when the time comes, because they want to save the world. And I'll be there out in front, telling them I know how to do it. I know how to give the world all the power it will ever need. Stop the war. Stop poverty.'

'Close the factories?' I ask gently, putting down my coffee and taking his hand.

He grasps it for a moment, then smiles and releases it, tracing a circle on my palm. But he doesn't answer.

'Together, we'll be unstoppable,' he murmurs, and unease settles on my shoulder, ruffling its feathers.

'Unstoppable how?' I watch the streets of

Glastonbury pass by and glimpse the tor through the black-tinted windows. Almost back. What happens now?

'My networks and your power. You'll help me access the portals. We'll make them produce energy, and I'll be the only person that knows how. I'll own them all in effect. Own the energy. I'll be able to control and distribute it. We're going to be very, very rich, and very, very powerful, Demelza.'

I look at him carefully. 'That's not what I agreed to. I can educate the Redworld, teach them about energy and how to live. I didn't say I was going to show you *inside* the portals. I can't show you how they work, and I'm not going to help you with this stupid plan of yours. You know that, don't you?'

He smiles indulgently, as if talking to a child. 'Oh, I know you think that, Melz. But you'll come round to my point of view, I promise you.'

I shake my head. 'No. It's my power, not yours. I'll use it as I see fit.'

He laughs, as if we're having some kind of trivial disagreement, and that annoys me.

'I'm serious, Bran. The portals don't belong to anyone, but witches protect them. I'm a witch. That's my job.' I look out of the window and notice we've gone past the turning to Ceri's flat. 'Hey. Aren't you taking me home?'

He smiles quietly. 'Not yet. I've got a proposal for you.'

We stop outside Bran's stone lair at the bottom of

the tor and he steps out, extending his hand to help me out of the car.

'If you want it, you can have a new home and a job,' he says, as Pete parks the car and we go inside. He covers my eyes with his hands and I feel him leading me through the lounge.

'What job?' I ask.

'Queen of the Night, Melz. Saviour of the Redworld. Woman of Magic. You're not just another Greenworld witch any more. You're more than that. I'm going to make you famous. Melz the Red Witch,' he says, reading my mind and the name that came to me yesterday, and takes his hands away from my eyes. 'Only if it's what you want though. I can't make you do what you don't want to do.' He chuckles darkly. 'I learned that the hard way.'

We are in a large room with a vaulted ceiling, which has been hollowed out of the rock and lit by candles and firelight from a huge fireplace at one end, the chimney snaking up mysteriously into the foundations of the tor. On the ground is a red velvet rug with a magic circle painted on it in gold, the elemental symbols at the cardinal points. There are two large bookcases filled with leather-bound volumes of all sizes. I look at the titles and see poetry, art and literature alongside antique herbals and grimoires – magical books published before the Greenworld.

An altar is set up at the far end of the circle, with gold cups, exotic-coloured crystals, tall candles and bowls of fragrant incense. It's beautiful, if not quite how I would have done it. But my gaze is drawn to the trickle of water that flows over a whitened stone in one corner of the room.

I look at Bran, who smiles enigmatically.

'What's that?' I ask.

'The White Spring. Holy water. Dedicated to Brighid, who just so happens to be . . . oh, right, the Goddess of the Greenworld.'

I walk over slowly, and run my fingers in the cold, clear water.

'It's calcium in the water that makes the stone white,' I say, looking up at him. 'I read about it.'

'Aye, I know,' he replies, and kneels down next to me. 'There's more too.'

'More?'

He points to another shadowy vaulted room next to this one. 'Get a candle. Go and see.'

I take one from next to the spring and peer into the gloom. The candlelight bounces back at me from a surface of water several metres wide. I step in further and crouch down, looking into the water.

'A pool?' I ask, and he brings in another candle to light the room. It is a round pool, perhaps a metre or so deep, which has been naturally hollowed out of the rock.

'A healing pool, apparently. Or whatever you want to use it for. The spring water collects here. It's all yours now, if you'll take it.'

I look sharply at him. 'What do you mean? What do you want me to do with all this?'

He sits back on his heels. 'Whatever you want. You're the witch. You've got the power. I just happen to be able to provide a setting and some . . . staging, let's say.'

'For what?' I ask, trailing my hand in the water. It's cold but pure, and the energy in it sets my nerve endings tingling and the magic in my blood on fire. 'Witch of the Redworld?'

'Why not? You'll live here. Do magic. Be magic. Be the priestess of the Redworld, of this magical place. You'll have Glastonbury Tor as your temple. You can bring magic to this place, to these people. You can bring the best of the Greenworld here, to them. We can do it together.'

'Glastonbury Tor is blocked.'

'Then unblock it. I know you can.'

He takes the candle from my hand and places it in a sconce next to the pool; the gleam of fire ripples across the water.

'I don't know if I can,' I say, entranced, feeling the pull of the underworld, of Bran, of what he's offering me, just as strongly as the pull of death at the end of the tunnel inside the portal. 'And I don't have to be a part of this . . . energy plan you've got?'

He shrugs. 'I'd like you to be. But it's just as important to teach the people here about magic, about how to live sustainably. If you decide that's all you want to do, that's more than enough.'

His expression is earnest, his brown eyes alight. I don't think he's lying.

I look back at the pool. This place of magic, all for me. I've known about the White Spring and the Red Spring all my life, but nobody had ever seen the White. It was hidden away, lost forever, in the rock – only a myth. The spring of the moon, of magic, of mystery; the sister of the Red Spring of Chalice Well – the blood of the Mother. A sudden sadness takes me over – that the Red Spring is polluted, and also that Mum and Saba can't see this, can't bathe here in the caves under Glastonbury Tor. And then, an equally sudden fierce joy: that I can. That I can be mistress of this place. Mistress of the underworld. Proserpine, finally home where she belongs, Goddess be praised.

And when I take the candle from the wall sconce and walk round the pool I see it: the far back of the cave, the closest you can get to the underneath of the tor. The door to the underworld, the realm of magic, the kingdom of the faeries, ruled by Gwyn ap Nudd. That's what the old stories say.

I think of Mum's house and Ceri's flat, and how neither is mine. I look up into the dark stone ceiling that fades away into blackness. This can be mine. Even though, technically, I will be living in Bran's house and eating his food – this magic place will be mine. And I believe I can do good things for the Redworld. I believe I can be the person to do that.

'Where would I sleep?' I ask.

'With me,' he replies bluntly, looking away, and I remember his tight muscles, his scars; I remember the way his expression softened when we kissed. That in bed he was boyish and silly and kind. Not so tough. Not taking over the world. Not desperate for revenge. Just . . . nice. That sweet boy Jeannie loved, who kissed me so softly under the willow trees.

And as I hunker down and put my palms to the stone floor and feel the ancient power in the earth, I also know I have nowhere else to go.

'OK. I'll stay. On my terms,' I say, looking into his dark eyes.

He grins, but seems unsurprised. 'Excellent.' He gets up and dusts himself off. 'Stay and look at everything. There are some new clothes in the cupboard in there, and towels if you're going to bathe. I'll get Pete to get some food and drink together for us.'

He disappears, and leaves me there to look at my shadowy reflection in the pool.

Chapter Twenty-one

The moment is all we have and the one thing we cannot keep.

From *Tenets and Sayings of the Greenworld*

The weeks pass in a strangely pleasant fugue, as if my mind is filled with the fragrant smoke the witches use back home to help them gain visions. Not thinking too hard about anything, my usual analytical instinct is lulled by luxury, by my feelings for Bran. For once I chose Beauty.

When he's home, we eat and drink and kiss in the caves of the White Spring, the magic soaking into everything we do: the curvature of his muscles by candlelight, the flashes of red and gold in the burgundy wine, the poetry of our voices as they murmur together in the night. But by day I am alone to explore and discover.

It's late May and the days are bright, and the steady heartbeat of fertility thrums through the earth under my feet. I often walk to Wearyall Hill, another large sloping hill facing the tor; it sits behind a gatehouse to which Bran gives me a rusty key. *And lo, the treasures of the city were hers.* He bows and smiles when he gives it to me. *But the Queen must be careful to take her faithful knight Pete with her for protection, should she roam too far into the barren wastes.* I ignore that advice. Pete doesn't want to come with me any more than I want him there, I can tell, and I don't want his stubborn utterances and defensive, disinterested body language anywhere near me if I'm trying to meditate or make magic. I can look after myself.

From the windy top of Wearyall I look across the valley, back at the tor, like a mirror. Alone with the sheep and the sacred thorn tree I think about Bran. Already I feel lost without him, like a divining rod quivering for water. And he's away a lot, sometimes with strange explanations or no explanation at all. I wake up on two different occasions in the night, in his bed, to find him gone; when he slides back into bed later I whisper 'Where were you?', but he refuses to answer. *Nowhere. Go back to sleep.* But he smells different – of chemicals, a charred smell, and I re-enter my dreams with unease.

Sometimes the girls visit me. Today, Catie, cross-legged on a thick red cushion, flips through the pages of a pre-Greenworld paperback from the shelf, a rainbow and a pentagram on its cover.

'I still can't believe there was so much witchcraft

before Separation. I mean, people were doing it everywhere, according to this. The girls and me have got a few old books – there're some you can get from specialist suppliers, if you know what you're looking for – but there's not many. And the stuff we've got's a bit obscure.'

'We've got as many books as Mum could save, but there must have been so many more. All lost,' I say, thinking of the books and papers in the Archive, and all the others we don't have.

'Where *did* they all go, d'you think?' she muses, looking over at the shelf.

'Don't know. In the Greenworld we burned books that weren't part of our ethos. Me and Saba – my sister – we were really little, but we remember throwing books into the pyres. Maybe they did the same here. Or maybe there's other collections somewhere.' I put down the grimoire I'm leafing through. 'Bran might know.'

'Since you brought it up: Bran. How's life with the south-west's most eligible sexpot?' Catie gives me a mischievous grin. 'Bet you don't have a lot of time for reading right now!'

'Sex-what?'

'You know what I mean. Half the girls in Glastonbury want to eat the fruit of the underworld, to be sucked into its delicious depths.'

'That's disgusting.'

'Yeah, well?'

I blush, and I'm glad the other girls aren't here. I'm

not comfortable with them knowing my personal life. Though Catie will probably tell them.

'It's all right,' I mutter, looking down at the thick leather cover of the grimoire. Animal skin, binding a book. I think of Bran's smooth skin and the way it feels electric against mine.

'Come *on*. I want the details.'

'No! It's private.'

'Demelza Hawthorne. You're going to spill, this minute, or I'll cast a truth-telling spell on you.' She waggles her fingers dramatically.

'Yeah, right.' I grin at her. 'If only it was that easy.'

'Oh, fine. Don't tell me, then. You look happy though. Are you?'

'Yes.' I look up at her seriously. 'I can't believe I'm here. I live under Glastonbury Tor. Every day I get up at sunrise and watch dawn break from the summit, then I walk back down the ceremonial way with bare feet. It's beautiful.'

'Well, that's lovely, but it's not really what I asked,' she says, laughing, and I smile gently, but it's what really matters to me, being here. Bran is . . . attentive, and passionate, but it's the magic that draws me in closest. Sometimes at night, when he's asleep, I make magic outside under the moon, feeling Her in me, the thrill of her energy at my back like bees, like a chill excitement in my hands, my feet, my mind.

'It's not perfect though,' I say, lighting some candles.

'Why not? Does he want to do weird stuff? You can

tell me, you know.' Catie looks at me half wary but half curious, and I know that she'd love nothing more than for me to tell her all the gory details of some strange sex cult that Bran wants to revive or something.

'No! I don't mean that. That side of things is . . . all fine.'

She groans. 'Throw me a bone, Melz.'

'What?'

'Never mind. What were you going to say?' she asks hopefully.

'The fracking site. I mean, when I go up on the tor it's beautiful, but then I see those bloody cranes and drills, and it just makes me want to cry, you know?'

'Err . . . I guess so.'

Catie doesn't understand. She has never experienced a portal so she doesn't know how wrong it feels here, how every morning I fail to rally the heartbeat of the hill. And when I ask the Morrigan all She says is, *It is coming, it is coming, but this is not the time.* So I wait, feeling the energies around me – the land, the spring, the air and the unconscious realm, the place of magic and dreams – peak at the full moon and fade away afterwards, knowing She will help me waken this ancient, slumbering earth power when the time is right.

But waiting is hard.

'You're such a case, Melz. Anyone else would be all over Bran Crowley like a rash. Demi was.' Catie clucks her tongue. 'She couldn't keep him interested for long enough though.'

Guilt murmurs at the back of my mind for a moment. Much as I dislike Demi, I never wanted to split her and Bran up.

'When I asked him about Demi he said it was already over.'

Catie raises an eyebrow. 'For him, maybe.'

'Oh. That's not the impression I got.' I sit on my cushion, obscuring the circle with the elemental quarters painted in gold.

'I can't believe you're not going to give me something. Come on. Anything.'

I sigh. There's nothing I want to tell her.

'He doesn't dream. Well, that is, he doesn't remember his dreams.' There. That's intimate information.

She groans. 'Oh, Melz. That's really not the kind of thing I was looking for,' she sighs, and goes back to flicking through her book.

But it is important. It shows how repressed Bran is, how determined he is not to connect to his instincts, his unconscious, his conscience. Because he may not remember them, but I know he dreams, because I'm there every night and I hear him talking in his sleep, muttering and rolling from side to side. He might refuse to acknowledge his demons, but they're there, every night, wrapped round him and refusing to let go.

My dreams here are beautiful but also sad. I dream of birds – crows and ravens but also eagles and falcons; I fly as one of them and see the land, the whole land of

219

Britain and even further. I fly over the water, over the cold, dark seas to other warmer countries, France, Spain, Italy, Greece, and watch in sadness as their people suffer too, as their people starve. One night I fly over Russia, and see the thousands fighting for the few dim seams of coal that thread the darkness of the land, like snakes of candlelight, flickering out, one by one.

'You know, doll, girls gab properly about their boyfriends here. Not this vague privacy shit,' she says huffily, wandering over to the healing pool and trailing her fingers in the water and then pulling them out shivering. 'Mind you, I'm surprised you're seeing as much of him as you are. After the riot in York I thought he'd have to go back and sort it all out.'

'What riot?'

'You should know. You were there when it happened.'

'I wasn't! I mean, there was a demonstration, but I didn't go.'

'I bet you didn't. He wouldn't have wanted you there.' She looks around the room, as if checking Bran isn't lurking in a dark corner. 'I heard it got out of hand,' she whispers.

'How out of hand?' I feel anxiety cross me like a cloud.

'Bad. Usually his vans shoot blanks into the crowd, maybe use a bit of gas if they get rowdy. But this time the proles firebombed the control room. So the security services had to use live rounds. Flamethrowers too, I heard.' She shivers. 'Glad I'm not poor.'

'He didn't mention it.' All he'd said that evening when we visited the orphanage was that there had been a few 'hairy moments'. Not a full-scale riot. 'Do you think you might be wrong?'

She shrugs. 'It's only what I heard.'

'There hasn't been anything in the newspaper,' I say, knowing how stupid that sounds.

'Not overly surprising. Gossip's more trustworthy than the media,' she says, raising an eyebrow at me, and the cloud of anxiety that passed over me settles in the room, growing darker, preparing for rain. What if it's true? How would I feel about Bran then? Is he really a misunderstood boy from the wrong side of town – or something else completely?

'Look, I'm sorry I said anything. I'm sure it's not true. He wouldn't do that.' Catie squeezes my hand, but there's no conviction in her voice. 'How deep is it anyway – this pool?'

My hand in hers, she leads me to the water, obviously trying to distract me: a kind girl, red hair over one shoulder, her twining tattoo pattern of leaves and berries like a garland of harvest treasure. But can I trust her? Can I trust any of them?

'It gets deeper the further in you go. Up to my neck at the back,' I say slowly, gazing there, where the magic of Annwn, the Celtic underworld, thrums through the earth of the tor and makes ripples on the water.

'You should be careful, then,' she says, blinking in the candlelight. 'It'd be easy to slip on this wet rock.'

I sit down beside her and plunge my hand into the icy water, the shock of it numbing everything. I keep my hand immersed and slowly it begins to acclimatize, but the heaviness of the cold water slows my fingers; I can feel my blood retreating from the top layers of my skin. Sometimes it's good to be numb.

'I won't slip,' I whisper, and the room whispers the sibilant word back at me like an echo of snakes.

Chapter Twenty-two

No growth of moor or coppice,
     No heather-flower or vine,
But bloomless buds of poppies,
     Green grapes of Proserpine,
Pale beds of blowing rushes
Where no leaf blooms or blushes
Save this whereout she crushes
     For dead men deadly wine.

From 'The Garden of Proserpine'
by Algernon Swinburne

'You should invite Catie over again soon. All three girls probably. Do some magic with all of them,' Bran says to me a week or so later as we sit drinking wine in the lounge.

I look at him over the rim of my glass.

'Why?'

I don't really want to do that. You choose a coven wisely. I wouldn't choose to expose myself to Ceri or

Demi at a vulnerable psychic moment. Catie, perhaps, with training. But I don't say any of that.

Over the past week there's more and more I haven't said. Bran's growing increasingly distant, leaving me alone more. He's only come home at a reasonable time once; every other night he slides into bed in the early hours. And Catie's words won't leave me. *I heard it got out of hand.* When we were together in York he lied to me. People were seriously hurt; they might even have died that day at the demonstration. The vans shot into the crowd and it wasn't rubber bullets. I didn't know, I didn't know, I keep thinking. But then comes a deeper and guiltier knowledge: You should have known. And, What else don't you know, Melz?

Bran is still talking. 'Why not? Start consolidating your power. Start doing things people can talk about, Melz. You want your message to get out after all,' he says, smiling smoothly at me. As ever, his eyes are masked.

'I suppose,' I say. Some company would be nice at least. I'm getting lonely and I don't like it. And the message – about how I can help the Redworld – doesn't seem as high on Bran's list of priorities as I thought it was, whatever he might say.

We don't have to be a coven. Just a group for an evening.

'Well, then?' He looks at me again with that flat smile, those analytical eyes.

'I don't know what I'd do with the girls. They're not

very . . . experienced,' I try to explain, but he waves at the magic room vaguely.

'You've got all those books in there. Loads of ideas. Go up on the tor.'

There's no way I'm doing magic up there, I think, shuddering at the wrong feeling of it all over again. I haven't been up there in the mornings all week; in fact, I've stopped waking up just before dawn. My usual disciplines are slipping and I don't like it, but at the same time a kind of lassitude is in my veins – that fragrant smoke still filling me up, making it harder to see. It's odd living in this old bathhouse under the tor. The door might open on to the street but the back of it reaches right under the hill, right into the old places of faery. To all intents and purposes I live in the underworld; I sleep here, I eat here, I take my pleasure here with the King of Hades. And yet, though I feel the power of the otherworld calling me through the thick walls every night, I can't feel the thundering power of the earth, the goodness of the land, and I should. It is a place without balance, out of sync, and no good magic can come without balance. I didn't mind at first. But now I've started doing less magic altogether. The irony nags me – living in a place of power, but being less of a witch. The energy of the White Spring is strong. But without the balance of the tor, it is overwhelming and dark – not evil, but of the otherworld. The land of the dead, no matter how beautiful and full of vision, is no place for the living to stay long.

He looks at my expression and raises an eyebrow. 'Come on. You must be able to think of something.'

I sigh. There are things I'd love to do if I had the Hands with me now — the witches I've worked with all my life. But they're not here.

'All right. I'll ask them to come and do a blessing ceremony for the spring,' I say grudgingly. The moon is waxing. It's as good a time as any, and I doubt the spring has been consecrated recently.

'Good,' he says, taking the glass out of my hand and putting it on the table. 'Melz the Red Witch needs a coven. A coterie of admirers. Not just me.'

He takes my hand in his and leads me into the bedroom.

'Now?'

'*The moment is all we have and the one thing we cannot keep,*' he says, quoting the Greenworld tenet back at me, and it feels wrong. It feels wrong for him to say it. But I still follow him, hoping for the sweetness of those first few times we were together. Hoping for his true face, for his vulnerability, although I am beginning to suspect that may have been a mask too.

Chapter Twenty-three

> Build a fire of juniper, cedar and sandalwood. After
> the flames die down, it produces a clear, glowing
> ash, which can be used in clairvoyance to induce
> a vision in the same way as looking into moonlit
> water.
>
> From *Greenworld Covenstead Magic: A Practical Guide*

A few days later Ceri, Demi and Catie crowd excitedly
into the pool room. I have decorated it with candles and
flowers. A fire crackles in the grate and its fragrant
smoke fills the room – a Fire of Azrael, a traditional
Greenworld burning of juniper, cedar and sandalwood.
When the fire burns down staring into the coals induces
vision. The woods are one of the few things I know
Mum gets on the black market from Zia's boyfriend,
Omar, though she hates going outside the Greenworld
for anything. It's hard to grow cedar or sandalwood in
Cornwall; we have some saplings growing slowly in a

special protected horticultural garden, but until they're big enough to be harvested she has to get them from elsewhere. Needless to say, when I asked Bran for what I needed it was no problem for him to find.

I have dressed for the occasion in a long red robe with a hood, a long white cotton dress underneath. Colours of the Goddess: white for the Virgin Huntress, red for the Mother.

'Wow, it looks beautiful in here, Melz!' Catie grins and shrugs off her coat. 'Where d'you want us?'

Demi sniffs the fragrant air and coughs exaggeratedly. 'Ugh! What's that smell? It's choking me.'

'It's a ritual fire. Come in. Take your shoes off.' I close the door behind them, ignoring her. I point to the pool. 'Get in.'

They look at the pool and then at me.

'Are you sure? It looks a bit cold,' Catie ventures.

'It's not too bad once you're in. We're going to bless the spring. Connect with the water. Best way to do that is by getting in it,' I say, taking my red robe off. They exchange glances.

'OK . . .' Ceri says as I climb in, steeling myself against the bite of the freezing water.

They strip down to the white garments I've asked them to wear – nighties, pyjamas. I went round to their flat a couple of nights ago with a list of instructions. *It's like we're being summoned*, Ceri had said, only half joking. *Bran suggested it*, I replied without thinking, and felt immediately guilty as her face fell. It's been weird with

Ceri and Demi since I moved in with Bran; Demi never liked me, but Ceri was the one who took me under her wing when I arrived, and now I can sense she feels abandoned.

The candlelight glows on their cheeks. They climb in and we join hands round the pool: north, south, east, west. Our breathing sets a gentle tide in motion in the black water.

I lean my head back and breathe in the scented air, feeling the water soak my hairline.

'Did you learn your parts of the blessing?' I address the darkness of the ceiling, the high vaults where spirits gather.

'Yeah,' Demi says, pretending to be bored — but I can feel her tension.

'Yes.' Ceri's voice is halting.

'Me too.' Catie's voice is full of wonder.

'Let's begin.' I shut my eyes and feel the water around me, feel the energy of the girls, of us together in the pool. Four poles, four cardinal points, joined in a circle. 'We are here to bless this spring and the holy waters of life. We acknowledge the power of Brighid and the power of Lugh, but we know that this place is of the Fae, the old folk. This is the river of the underworld. Here the Morrigan guides Her barge; this water fills Her cauldron with new life, new inspiration. But beyond these walls are the halls of Annwn. Stay too long in these waters and you will be lost. We recognize the power of this place, and respect it.' My voice threads the words through the chamber; I feel the spirits around me, assembling, being called. Elemental forces flow around us, through the water, around the candle flames, in the air and of the stone.

'I honour the energy of the East: of Air, of the wind that pushes the ripples on the face of the water. Spirits of the East, welcome.' I start the calling the elements, the four quarters.

'I honour the energy of the South: of Fire, of the sun that warms this water on its journey from rain down into the rock. Spirits of the South, welcome.' Ceri's voice is steady, and she speaks smoothly.

Catie follows. 'I honour the energy of the West: of Water, of the drop— droplets that make the rush of water, ever-renewing, in this spring. Spirits of the West, welcome.' She makes a face at me as she stumbles over a word and I smile reassuringly.

'I honour the energy of the North: of Earth, of the grass and mud and rock that filters this water; of the brick and stone that shapes this holy pool. The earth that holds us all. Spirits of the North, welcome.' Demi's voice is flat, but she says what she's supposed to.

'We call upon the magic made here throughout the ages. Of priests and priestesses, new and old magic. The nameless, forgotten ones that bathed here before us. We taste the water that was yours, and are blessed with its power,' I call, and nod at the girls. They cup their hands in the water and taste it.

'Magic of water now within me and without, join

my body to Brighid, my blood to Gwyn ap Nudd,' we all chant.

'We call upon Brighid and Morrigan, Arianrhod and Ceridwen, Lugh and Gwyn ap Nudd. Bless this sacred spring with your fierce brightness and the depth of the dark; we consecrate this holy space in Your Names,' I call out, my arms reaching up to the dark cave vault above me.

We rejoin hands and I start to sing, hoping they'll remember what I taught them a few days ago.

Brighid, Morrigan, Powers of the Earth,
Magic of the waters and the secret of rebirth,
Elemental fire and water,
Air and earth, we are your daughters.
Brighid, Morrigan, Powers of the Earth,
Magic of the waters and the secret of rebirth,
Streams and rivers and springs into the sea,
In my blood your blessing, and my body Blessed Be.

Our song lifts like a wave, like a tide, and washes over us. We start to sing in a round, so that our words and melodies mesh. I can feel the energy building in the room, filling the space with beauty, taking us back to timelessness within this space. Joining our song to all the other songs that were sung here once in this most holy of places. Weaving and plaiting, sewing and patching. *A quilt is a web of time, stitching memory to eternity*. I remember the Greenworld tenet as my voice quietens, and the echoes ebb around us like spirits themselves.

'Take a moment and look into the water. See what messages, what visions are there for you,' I say, and let go of Ceri and Demi's hands, placing my hands gently on the black surface of the water, channelling the energy we have raised into it, so it is a cauldron of vision itself, a liminal place of magic where time has no meaning.

I gaze down into the water, letting my mind stray and my eyes defocus. The candlelight plays on the surface: fire on water, held by stone, surrounded by air. As I watch, the light makes patterns and pictures, like a dream.

The picture expands and fire takes over. It's only fire I see, explosive and roiling inside a room – rippling and curling across a ceiling like a perverse waterfall. I feel no fear, only marvel at its natural beauty, the unpredictability and relentlessness of it. The image changes to hands linked in a circle. Three people, six hands; there is fire here too, around us, within us, between us: fire that burns and gives off a fragrant smoke, but passion in our bodies and in our fingertips too, in our lips. We are channelling our passion into something greater than us. Symbols that I don't know or understand flash in front of my eyes, faster and faster, and I start to feel dizzy. A song unfurls dimly at the edge of my perception:

Three to bind, to open, to see,
The power in them as within thee,
From life to death and death to life,
You bring the moon, and she, the knife,
He brings the sun and the song, the key –
The power in them as within thee.

I start to hum the song's melody, but it's interrupted by a sudden scream and a frenzied splashing in the water.

'I've got to get out. Out!' Demi is already half out of the pool as I look up, confused, still half in vision.

I grab her arm. 'You can't go. We haven't finished. The ritual . . .!' But she pulls her wet skin through my grasp and climbs out, banging her knee on the side of the pool.

'What's up?' Ceri stands up, and the vision energy – the cup so full of magic – upturns. I feel the magic dissipate into the corners of the room and the best I can do is mutter a quick blessing after it, thanking the quarters for helping us. The pool should be a charged space after this: consecrated and made new. Without bringing the power down properly at the end of the ritual, all this will be wasted.

I've got one hell of a clean-up job to do, is all I can think as I climb out reluctantly after Demi, who is sitting on the hard stone floor half wrapped in a pink fluffy robe holding her knee, which is pumping blood.

Catie climbs out after me. 'What was that all about?'

she says, complaining. 'I was right in the middle of this amazing dream. I was looking at the water and—'

Ceri cuts her off with a glare. 'Come on. We've got to get Demi's knee seen to,' she says, hurriedly towelling herself off and dressing, her clothes snagging on her still-wet skin.

Catie just stares at Demi's knee, like me, still half in a meditative state.

'What?' she asks dumbly, dripping on to the floor.

'Bloody get dressed, Cate! Wake up! We're leaving!' Ceri yells, and her voice bounces off the dark stone walls.

I cringe at the sudden change in energy and kneel down next to Demi, holding out my hands for her cut.

'Here. Hold still. I can help,' I say, my hands buzzing with healing. I can make it stop bleeding and start to knit the skin. 'Once I've made it stop bleeding I've got herbs to clean it. It's OK, don't worry.' But she screams and kicks at me with her good leg and Ceri pushes me away.

'I'm getting her to a doctor. That's enough for one day, Melz, all right? That's enough.'

I look up and see the distaste in her eyes.

'Don't shout at me. I was just trying to help,' I snap.

'You've helped enough. I'm bloody freezing and I don't know what all that was about but she's really freaked out. Just leave her alone.' Ceri picks up one of the towels I'd laid out for us for after the ritual and holds it over Demi's knee, placing Demi's hand on it. 'Press down on it if you can. Have you got an on-call doctor?'

Demi shakes her head. 'Dad only pays for office hours. Says the cost for on-call's gone through the roof. Tight bastard. What're we supposed to do, just get ill Monday to Friday?' She winces as she presses down on her knee.

Ceri frowns. 'You can use mine, then. You just have to pretend to be me. We're not going to the hospital. You'll bleed to death before you get seen. And I'm not sharing a room with mental outpatients and screaming babies. God knows what I might catch.'

'But I can help her! Don't be stupid,' I bite back, feeling my anger. I made the effort to have them here in this sacred space at Bran's request, even though I knew they didn't know what they were doing. Even though all my instincts told me not to.

'We're not stupid. She's going to a doctor. We don't need hocus-pocus, Melz; we need stitches and drugs,' Ceri says. She stands over Demi protectively, like I'm going to attack her or something. And I see it then: how, for them, magic isn't in everything. Magic isn't in healing and eating and growing and walking. They want magic to be exciting, sexy; they only want the fireworks.

'Fine. Go. I'm not working with amateurs. You don't know the first thing about being witches. Any of you. So don't ever pretend that you do. Ever!' I throw their remaining clothes and towels at them. 'Go on! Go!'

'You need to watch yourself, Demelza. Cos when

Bran gets tired of you, you don't have anyone except us,' Ceri warns, as she helps Demi up and picks up the rest of her stuff. 'And we can't protect you like he does. Come on, Cate,' she says, and Catie looks wide-eyed at me, like a wounded deer.

'I'm sorry, Melz,' she says, easy tears pricking her eyes.

I reach out and touch her arm. 'It's OK, Catie. You didn't do anything wrong.' I know she would have finished what we started.

'Touching. Come *on*, Cate. Let's go.'

They leave, banging the door after them.

Excerpt from Demelza Hawthorne's Greenworld Journal

Date – 10 June 2047
Moon phase – waxing second quarter in Sagittarius
Menstruation cycle – disrupted
Sun phase – Taurus
Card drawn – The Devil
Dreams – I'm trapped in a tall transparent tank of water while people come to look at me. I am a mermaid, but I'm drowning. I'm banging on the glass but no one seems to notice. Bran is selling tickets in a booth next to the tank. I wake up coughing.
Chosen tenet – There are none appropriate.

The Devil. Temptation, sex, attachment to material things. Handfasting. Contracts. Commitment. None of these things have to be bad. Handfasting isn't bad, if you're in love. Commitment isn't bad if you're ready for it. Contracts help everyone know what's expected. Sex is . . . sex is good.

But the dream was unsettling. Am I Melz the Red Witch, Queen of the Night, or a freak exhibit? A mermaid is a symbol of magical feminine power, goddess energy, water energy, moon, emotion, but I was trapped, stared at, something to look at for entertainment. And I was drowning. I wasn't comfortable in my element. I couldn't breathe.

Reflection on the chosen tenet – I'm not in the Greenworld any more.

Chapter Twenty-four

Brighid, bless the corn,
Brighid, bless the grain,
Blessed Brighid bless our food,
And make us whole again.

Chant for food preparation, from
Greenworld Prayers and Songs

A week later Bran organizes a party – Ceri, Demi and Cate, me, Bran and Pete. I haven't seen the girls since the night of the blessing ceremony and I don't want him to invite them all over, but he ignores me. *They're my friends, too*, he says, getting dressed one morning as I lie in bed. I haven't been out for a walk since the ceremony. I haven't done anything but stay in, bathing in the pool and communing with the underworld. *Are you going out today?* he asks, but I roll over and face the wall. I miss Tintagel.

As I walk into the lounge Ceri stops talking and

looks at me; they all look. It took a lot of courage to walk in here at all. Ceri and Demi hate me.

I'm wearing a long-sleeved white velvet gown, cut from the neck down to the waist in a V, with my locket, gold moon necklace and gold sandals. I have painted my lips the same fiery red as the night with Bran at the Twelve Apostles, and I do as Saba would. Stand tall. Shoulders back. Chin up. Look like you own the world.

'Wow, Melz! You look amazing!' Catie cries, and comes over to kiss me on the cheek. I'm forgiven, then, by her at least – though Demi and Ceri are reserved, and stay where they are with thin-lipped smiles.

'Thank you, Catie,' I say, and Bran puts a possessive arm round my shoulders. I avoid Demi's stare, which I can feel cutting through me like a hook. But I remind myself who has power here, and who doesn't, and force myself to give her a warm smile. Like a goddess. Like a queen. After a few seconds, she is the one that looks away.

'To Demelza, first witch of the Redworld! To the Red Witch!' Bran cries, raising his glass, and they all clink dutifully. I take a sip of champagne to avoid saying anything, because I know what the girls are thinking. That I'm some trumped-up foreigner that's slept her way into Bran's affections. But they aren't witches, and I am. I am Melz the Red Witch. I hang on to it like a mantra to drown my nerves.

My dream flashes back to me. Trapped behind thick glass, drowning.

Pete carries in two large plates with exotic finger food and puts them on the table. I follow him out, wanting to get away from the girls' eyes.

He looks startled as I walk in behind him.

'I just wondered whether you wanted any help,' I say, an excuse to stay out of the room a bit longer, away from the girls' gazes.

He looks at me scornfully. 'No thanks. Wouldn't want you getting a stain on that nice white dress, would we?' he mutters.

'No, really, I don't mind. I did a lot of cooking at home,' I offer, but he scowls and turns away.

'Pete? Have I done something to offend you?'

'No,' he mutters again and starts clanging pots around.

I catch his hand. 'Pete. Come on. Can't we be friends?'

He must have a crush on Bran, I realize. He's jealous of me.

'Were you and Bran ever . . . close?' I ask carefully, but he laughs suddenly.

'What, like you are? Ha. No,' he snorts.

'What, then? Why don't you like me?'

He turns round and looks at my dress, at my braided hair.

'I don't know you. But I know every other girl he's done this with. Flavour of the month. You won't last long.'

'Demi?' I hear her laughing in the next room, and

Bran's rumbling voice laughing along with her. I feel my insides turn.

'Her, and others. He's always looking for the next big thing. Someone who's got something he wants. She lived here for a while. He uses people.'

'Has he used you? I thought he paid you. Gave you a job.'

'In a sense.'

'What do you mean?'

He sighs. 'I work for him so he'll protect my family. They're poor. That's what he does. He provides protection, if you pay him – but even that's a lie, because there's no one worse that you need protection from. If you don't pay, or do what he wants, one of his heavies comes and breaks something of yours. Your legs or your arms. Maybe a finger if you don't owe him that much.'

'I don't believe that,' I say, but I'm unsure.

Pete looks at me flatly for a moment, then rolls up his sleeve. The top of his forearm is a wide red raised burn: rivulets of red flesh.

'Believe this?' he says quietly.

I reach out instinctively to touch it, but he pulls away.

'He did this?' I whisper, my mouth suddenly sour with the wine that was so sweet just seconds ago.

'I was going to leave. Being poor is better than working here. He disagreed.' He runs one index finger lightly over the scarred arm. 'I was ironing that day.'

'Oh Goddess. Pete, I'm so sorry, I . . .'

'Be sorry all you like, it makes no difference to me. But tell me one thing. You care about this place, right? The tor, the spring?'

'Of course. Yes. They're sacred places.'

'Yeah. Well, ask him what he does up there on the tor at nights sometimes. In that makeshift lab he's got up there. Ask him about the people that go up there and don't come back. Ask him about the bodies, Demelza Hawthorne, and tell me if he's lying when he says there are none.'

I stare at him, mute, and remember the blocked energy on the tor. As if something bad was stopping this place of huge power feeling as it should. Bodies? Bran is murdering people and burying them up there somewhere? It seems utterly ridiculous. Why?

'A lab? What for?'

An image of Bran as a bald-headed mad professor in a long white coat swims into my mind. Ridiculous.

'I don't know. But they go up there sometimes when . . .'

He breaks off as Demi wanders into the kitchen.

'More wine,' she says, and bumps the door to the wine cellar expertly with her hip. She has a thick bandage on her knee, but it doesn't seem to be affecting her mobility as she strides inside. Pete shakes his head at me as if to say *Don't say anything*, and I nod. He rolls his sleeve back down quickly and buttons it.

She emerges from the darkness, smoothing her shimmering pink dress down over her hips with one gold-fingernailed hand and holding a dusty bottle with the other. She looks at both of us suspiciously.

'What's going on here? You inducting poor Pete into the mysteries of the Greenworld? Don't worry, Pete – there aren't as many as she makes out.' She smiles overly brightly at me. 'Or are there still more supernatural delights in store, Melz? More flashy lighty treats?'

'Maybe. Why don't you have a vision about it? Oh, right. You'll just freak out,' I snap back at her.

Something changes in her face for a second, and her fear at whatever it was she saw drowns her pretty face. Then she reverts to composure again and looks me up and down. 'Whatever. You've impressed him, for now. I would tell you that he's not what he seems, but then neither are you, are you?' She leans in and strokes the velvet of my dress, close to my breast, and smiles when I flinch. 'Ah. I bet he loves all that coyness, all that little-Greenworld-girl-lost act. Maybe you do have more power than us. Maybe you do know what to do with all those dusty books, all those crystals. That bloody freezing pool out there.' She gestures in the direction of the healing pool. 'But I'll tell you one thing. You don't have these—' she points to her rounded breasts and bottom – 'and you don't have these either—' she traces her finger round her full lips – 'and believe me, he's going to get tired of your scrawny little arse pretty quick. And what're you going to do then, Greenworld? Cos you can't move back in with us,' she hisses, and walks away.

I look at Pete, but he picks up another tray of finger food and pushes past me into the lounge.

'I warned you,' he murmurs as he passes me.

'Melz! Where are you? Come and taste this incredibly expensive wine!' Bran shouts, and everyone laughs. Perhaps a little too readily. Perhaps a little too loudly. My fingers go to my witch-brand.

'Coming,' I call, and join them, unease unfurling in my belly.

That night, after the party, I wait until Bran is asleep and slither out from under the thick cream-silk sheets. Bran's bedroom is another hollowed-out cavern room next to the lounge; a fireplace burns low still, the smoke disappearing mysteriously into a shaft in the rock. I tiptoe across the blood-red rug and find my warmest clothes – my old boots, an indigo wool dress, soft black leather leggings and a floor-length black cape coat with a hood. I carry them into the lounge and get dressed there, quick and quiet. I pick up my old bag and fill it with my tarot cards, some candles, a few snacks and a couple of the books from the shelves in the magic room. I look around longingly at all the crystals and books and goddess statuettes, but I have to travel light. Because, depending on what I find on the tor, I might not be coming back.

As I stand there, bag in hand, it's hard not to put everything away again and climb back into bed. It's really hard. Because it's one thing to abhor beautiful things when you know you'll never have them, but when you're given more than you even thought possible it's tough to walk away. To walk away from someone – even someone that you know is bad – who treats you like a goddess: someone that desires you, wants you, *sees* you, when you've walked in someone else's shadow all your life. *What would you prefer, Melz? Beauty or Truth?*

I tiptoe over to the pool and trail my fingers in the stream, and feel the deep call of the water on my soul. I feel the mystery of the underworld vibrating through my blood. It's hard to choose truth when magic is this beautiful.

But I have to see if what Pete told me is right. If there are bodies up on Glastonbury Tor. Because if that is true, then there's no beauty in the world that can make that OK.

I take a torch from beside the door and pull the front door closed as quietly as I can behind me, cringing at its dull thud, hoping neither Pete or Bran wake up. Pete hates Bran, that's clear, but I don't know how far he'd go to protect himself. If he saw me, would he tell Bran? Go in and wake him up, right now? I think he would.

I walk swiftly along the dark street, keeping in the shadows. The street lights aren't working tonight and I'm glad of it. I find the bottom of the steps leading up the tor.

As I climb I cast the light of the torch around me, looking for wherever this place of Bran's might be – a lab, a building of some kind, and – if they really exist – the graves. I don't remember seeing anything before, but I wasn't looking then. And I don't want to see now, but I know I have to.

My breath gets short on the steep climb and my lungs feel hot and raspy – the result of too much wine and rich food and not enough exercise. But there's also a heavy dread mixed with something else – that flat feeling of a suppressed nothingness, a buried power, a paved-over, forgotten maligned force. Instead of a joyous thumping energy coming up through the earth, it's a weak whisper.

It's very, very quiet. I reach the tower on top of the tor and look around me. Nothing. I remember learning at school that once, thousands of years ago, there was an astronomical observatory on top of the tor, where ancient wizard-priests mapped the movements of the planets and stars and made magic under the moon. I look up; it's hardly there – a dark moon, a day off new, a sliver in the black sky. A time for destruction, of old things falling away.

I centre myself and try to feel part of the sloping green-grass hill, try to feel out any particularly dark spots of energy. The dark-moon energy will help me tune in to the quiet frequencies I need – the drifting traces of the dead, the places of delay and entropy, things that could be missed on a different night with different energies.

Wait for the right time, She'd said, and She was right.

Because as soon as I close my eyes I see them, but they aren't energetic traces.

246

They're people.

I snap my eyes back open, and there's nothing there apart from me and the wind and the grass. Cautiously I close my eyes again and there they are. Souls. The dead that haven't passed over, but are – what? Wandering, lost? They are clustering around me, drawn to my warmth, my energy, my aliveness. I step back as they get closer and hold up my hand in protection.

'Stop, by Brighid!' I call out, but that doesn't make any difference. More and more materialize in the dark space behind my closed eyes. They don't speak, but I can feel them. I can feel what they want.

'You can't move on,' I say, translating the rush of urgency I get from them. Instantly I feel them draining energy from me and realize I should be protecting myself. Quickly I draw energy up through the earth by imagining roots growing out of my feet, out of my centre and down deep into the ground; I imagine a silver cord linking my heart and the stars, and mentally I draw a black cloak round myself.

'Where are your bodies?' I ask, not wanting to know, but knowing I have to. 'Show me,' I command, and some of them point to the other side of the tor, away from the steps. I open my eyes and follow where they pointed, knowing they are with me as I tread carefully down the tussocky hill in the darkness.

I get to the bottom of the tor, where fields stretch over to distant hills; in the distance the towers of the fracking mine loom like shadow monsters in a child's room at night. No one comes here. I close my eyes. *Here?* I ask, and I feel them answer *yes*. The souls surround me anxiously. Some of them are wronged ones, killed and buried here, while some died naturally, but they still can't move on because of the portal being blocked. But I pull back from feeling everything they feel before it starts to take me over.

I open my eyes and crouch down, looking across the flat of the land for something I still don't want to see.

I shine the torch to my left, but see nothing. The dark moon watches, shadowed, hiding.

But I feel the light touch of a spirit hand on my right wrist, and turn that way reluctantly. I don't want to believe.

What would you prefer? Beauty or Truth? Saba's voice says in my head. Then, the whisper of the Morrigan: *You know it's always truth, no matter how ugly. You know, Melz. Open your eyes.*

There are three rows of graves, the mounds barely grown over, curving up from the flat grass. Buried bodies where there should be no bodies, here on sacred ground.

'Oh Goddess. Oh, no, no, no.' I stand, my hand on my mouth, as if to keep the horror inside. And it's not the bodies themselves that are horrific, but how they got there. Pete was right. And I've been wrong. So, so wrong.

The graves are unmarked. There's no respect, no acknowledgement of a life lived. The grave is a place of peace, returning the body back to the earth. But here there's a terrible sense of force and unrest and fear, that these bodies were not laid here with care, but abandoned, murdered, cut down. And no one comes here. An ideal place to hide the dead. Despite my psychic protection I feel sick and dizzy, and crumple on to the grass.

I look up and see a crow alight on one of the graves, then another. A third joins them. I know this is Her sign, the Morrigan, and I reach out my arms to them, head bowed. I feel one land on my right hand, and one on my shoulder. The third looks at me beadily from the earth, as if to say *We are with you, Melz. What will you do?*

I close my eyes and pray for help. 'Help me, Morrigan, Queen of the Night, Warrior of Death!' I call out. 'I need your courage and magic. Help me, O Goddess. Help me!'

The crows caw and fly up from my hands, then the third joins them and they circle over my head, above the graves, above the souls that cluster around me. I crawl over to the graves and place a hand on the two closest to me.

I call out to Her again. 'Great Morrigan, Queen of the Shadows, take back these souls so they may rise anew to serve you. Bless these bodies as faithful vehicles that are no longer needed. Take the souls to the next world where they may heal and find their own ways to happiness. You are the wound and the death, the crone that guides us to the otherworld. Great Morrigan, hear my cry.'

The crows caw again, but no Goddess appears. *That's not enough, Demelza*, a voice says inside me. *There's something you have to let go of. I will only come if you do this for me. The time is right. I require it as a sacrifice.*

I wrap my fist round the wooden locket by my heart. No, not this. I can't. Not Tom. He's dead, but my revenge on Bali and Skye, on the ones that killed him, is all I have left.

'I can't. I can't let him go!' I shout into the night.

You must.

'I won't!' I cry, and the wind takes my words away and leaves my throat dry. I gasp for air.

Then you cannot do this work, Demelza. Your curse is your broken heart. If you refuse to be healed, I cannot help you. When you let these souls pass into death, you must let him go too.

'I can't let him go, Great Morrigan.' I feel the sadness in my throat; that familiar ache. 'I love him too much.'

You must. Love him enough to let him go. Love yourself enough, Demelza. And trust me.

I let the tears come, then, finally, and sink to the ground among the graves. I throw back my head and scream, grief ripping my throat apart and exploding into the quiet air of the tor. I sob the grief out into the land. It absorbs the pain, taking it down into the earth, into the Great Mother, grounding me, calming me, until the tears stop and the Morrigan stands before me smiling, and my heart empties out and is refilled with a new, quieter sadness.

Her black robes blow in the night air, and Her long thin white arms are covered in blue spirals, words, spells. Her face is old and lined, but Her eyes are bright and sharp. Her white hair is plaited and wound round Her head. A blue-woad triskele is painted on Her forehead.

I bow my head reverently. 'Great Queen,' I say.

'Priestess. You have sacrificed your grief to the land and been made pure again.'

She reaches out a hand and I take it. She pulls me up and traces a spiral on my forehead. 'Now you know the true nature of sacrifice. Your energy, back to earth, back to me. Without the blocked energy of your grief you can heal yourself, and heal the portal. Now take off the necklace.'

I unclasp the wooden heart and hold it out to Her.

'No. It must burn.'

I pick up the golden moon necklace. 'And this?'

'Let go of the temptations you have been offered. You know in your heart they are wrong,' She intones.

I know that those temptations are what Bran has given me. Being Melz the Red Witch – living with him at the White Spring, in the cave, at the entrance to Annwn, the Celtic underworld. Being a kind of witch celebrity for the Redworld. Because in the weeks I've been there, he and I have not talked once about how we will help the people of the Redworld. How we'll share my wisdom with them, the wisdom of the Greenworld.

'But why? Why would that be so bad?' I challenge

Her. 'You are the goddess of the underworld. You are the hag of death. I am your priestess after all.'

The wind whips me across the cheek like a slap and I reel backwards from it.

'I am the Goddess. Not you. Yours is the path of service. Service to mankind is service to me. It is your job to help them in this life. Help them find me, help them know the sanctity of my land, the sovereignty of themselves, the comfort of me when they feel pain. And help them reach for my hand when they draw their last breath.'

'That's what I thought I was going to do,' I protest. That was what Bran and I talked about.

'Evil is fed with good intentions,' She says severely, and I flinch but I know She's right. I may have wanted to help the people, but I haven't, not yet. 'You will do it. But not with him. There is something that must be destroyed before we can make this portal what it was again,' She says, looking up at the tor. 'And quickly. Time is not on our side.'

'The lab?'

'A place of evil. It must be cleansed. Its energies are blocking the portal.'

'But I don't know where it is.'

She approaches and puts Her hands over my eyes. 'See,' She commands, and I close my eyes, feeling Her energy ring through me like bells, like choirs singing.

Instead of a gradual psychic feeling-out, I see the tor like a geological map in cross-section from above, from below — I see everything mathematical yet real, and clear as daylight. I see the internal route of both springs running through the tor and out at the Chalice Well and Bran's cave; I see the ancient entrance to the tor — the old entrance to Annwn, the Celtic underworld.

And I see it, not far from where we are, hidden in a small group of trees: a mineshaft with steps leading down into a concrete bunker.

Chapter Twenty-five

There shall be a black darkness,
There shall be a shaking of the mountain,
There shall be a purifying furnace,
There shall first be a great wave.

From *Cad Goddeu (The Battle of the Trees)*
from the *Book of Taliesin*

A path lights up under my feet for me to follow, illuminating the grass. As I approach the bunker I can see how it's been camouflaged with thorns and briars, hidden by low hawthorn branches. My trees. I lift them aside, wrapping my hands in my cloak but still getting cut. I pull the door open and look for a light, but there isn't one. The torch will have to do.

I descend the steep steps carefully, dread filling me as I go deeper. This is a bad place. Stale air gradually overtakes the sweet clean air of the tor, and blackness overcomes me.

My torch goes out. I click the switch back and forth but nothing happens. Sweat beads my upper lip and a wash of cold that has nothing to do with the external temperature crashes over me.

I feel in my bag and pull out a candle and a match. I scrape the match on the rough concrete wall and carefully I light the candle and let its flickering warmth focus me for a moment.

The candlelight fills the room with shadows – I'm in a large concrete-walled room full of equipment. I look around for a light switch and see a panel of switches by the door. I turn them all on, and a harsh, clinical blue light thrums on long strip lights.

The walls are covered with odd diagrams and posters of human anatomy, the parts of the body stripped of skin, the ligament and muscle like meat, and there are reams of paper on a table covered in wavering thin blue lines.

Less recognizable are the numbers and formulae scrawled on boards and poster-sized paper that is stuck on the walls. There are also symbols I recognize, but they're all wrong, used wrongly in the wrong context: pentagrams and spirals and magical glyphs, but combined with all this other weird stuff as if whoever worked here – Bran? Someone else? – was trying to collage their own language. And then there are photos, a whole wall of photos of things I would never, ever want to see. Bodies and faces burned horribly. Heads with the hair a black sticky mess sculpted round the blackened skin like human candles.

I hold on to a dented filing cabinet and retch, the sudden horror filling me with acid. Is this what he has done to people? This orphan, the sweet boy I thought I knew? Why would he do this? What is it? Why burn these people alive . . . because that's what it looks like.

In the centre of the room is a long metal table with leather straps and buckles attached to it at the top and the bottom, a metal mask at the top. I want to look at it but the Morrigan reappears in the room.

'Time is against us. You know what you have to do here.'

She points at the candle flame.

If there's one thing the Greenworld teaches you, apart from forest craft and community folk tales, it's how to make a fire. If you want to make something burn hot and make it devour everything in its wake, you need an accelerant. In Tintagel we make turpentine from steaming pine wood. We use it to make soap to varnish outdoor furniture and maintain fences. It also burns like Brighid's holy fire.

I look around, moving bottles and cans. No turpentine, but I find a large metal canister labelled ETHANOL. I splash it about liberally, coating everything, including the walls and the metal table.

I pick up my bag. 'Whatever you've been doing here, Bran, it's over.' I speak into the dead space. The fumes are dizzying and cloy my brain. I place my wooden heart locket on the table, my fingers tracing its rough harshness one last time. *Goodbye, Tom. I will always love you.*

I open the locket. The tightly folded paper falls out on to the surface. *I release you, Bali and Skye, wherever you are. Dead or alive, I release you from this curse, this dark bond of my heart.* Like an unnamed black-tentacled being from the deepest ocean, I watch as the curse energy crawls over the paper, and feel suddenly disgusted that I held something like this next to my skin for so long. I take off the gold moon pendant too and place it next to the wooden one. I am still Melz the Red Witch. I can't be bought.

I run up the concrete steps and throw the candle back down into the basement room. The *whump* of ignition blows past my legs, and the force and heat of the explosion pushes me up the last few steps. I land on the soft green grass outside, gasping for breath. As I lie there, I remember my vision from the pool-blessing ceremony. Fire unfurling across walls and floors; fire leaping beautifully, destroying, burning. This must be what that was – a vision of cleansing fire. But I have no idea what the other part was, with the song whose words I've forgotten, and the hands held in a circle. Fiery passion. Making and not destroying.

I lie on the grass and suck in the clean air of the tor. I feel the Morrigan tug at my hand. *You are not finished, Demelza Hawthorne*, She says, and I look up at the tower on top of the tor.

You must work quickly now.

I drag myself up from the grass – I'm tired and aching and stink of smoke. The souls gather around me like fussy hens. They know what's coming.

I stumble up to the top of the tor, wheezing at the long, steep climb. My head pounds from lack of sleep, lack of food and adrenalin. The tor is hard on your lungs, like an initiatory challenge – *climb me, and sacrifice your breath*. The wheezing brings light-headedness, and my stomach grumbles. I ignore both.

I look back to where smoke is pouring out of the hole in the ground that is the entrance to the bunker. I hope the fire burns hard enough. It has to. Burning the lab, or whatever it is, won't stop Bran doing whatever twisted experiments he was doing. But at least, for now, it means I can reopen the portal. It means that these souls can go home. And I can move on.

I centre myself and concentrate on what I need to do to open the portal, just like at home; just like in York with the Twelve Apostles. The souls can sense the power coming up from below the earth; they can feel the deep boom of stored-up energy from under us – the repressed, suppressed, banked-down fire that knows it's about to be unleashed.

I start the opening sequence, and as soon as I trace the first symbol into the night air I feel a hot stream of deep pink energy come roaring up through the ground and up my legs, twisting around my body. Volcano-like, it consumes me in a deep earthy fire, racing up my body and over my head into the sky as if I am the conductor, a small filament for a light that has suddenly been switched on. As I trace the following symbols the energy gets more and more intense until the whole tor seems to be shaking at an atomic level; as if the whole hill is swirling, regrouping, coming apart at its core. I push the final symbol out, shuddering with the effort, and the portal rips through the air into reality.

It is by far the biggest of the three I've seen – Tintagel, York and here. As it unfolds, I see immediately why it was called the Heart of the World in the old book we bent over as children in the firelight, why Mum's voice got so reverent when she described it. It's a deep cerise and roughly heart-shaped, in the same way that real human hearts don't have a neat point and two arches. *I fear we will never see it, girls*, Mum had said, *but this is one of the most important energy centres in the world. We couldn't get Somerset to be part of the Greenworld, and so we had to leave the tor. Leave the wells, the portal, the Isle of Apples. Leave it to be ruined. It was that or give up the Greenworld entirely.*

I remember asking whether it wouldn't have been better to stay part of the Redworld, to try to change it from the inside. *We tried that*, she said. *We tried for a long time. But there came a time when Separation was the only thing left.*

I step back, forced back from the power streaming out of the earth, out of the heart shape all around me, which stretches as wide as the top of the tor and as high as the tower. And as I look at the tower it starts to shake.

A lasso of dark pink energy like fire uncurls from the heart of the portal, like the stamen in a lily, and lashes out at the tower. I blink and stand back, staring, and at the same time feel the rush of souls pass me into the portal like a warm wind. Like butterflies hatching on a summer's day, their murmured thanks are like wings fluttering on my cheek. I watch the Morrigan following them into the portal like a shepherd, herding the lost into safety. Her black robes billow in the updraught and Her head is bowed reverentially. Her three crows land gently on my still upstretched hands, but I know She has left, gone where She is Queen. Goddess be praised.

I hear a voice and look down to see a torch flickering at the bottom of the hill – it's Bran, I know it. I feel the goodness and joy of the portal radiating through me, but I know I can't stay any longer. I have to go. Now.

I make myself stand and start to make the symbols for closing the portal, now that it's alive and well again, but as I push the first one into the air there's a cracking sound and a thud.

A stone falls from the top of the tower, dislodged by the energy current.

Then another.

Then another large stone falls a few centimetres from my feet and I step back, hurrying to close the portal, but my hands can't move as fast as they need to. I can see Bran's face now, pale and livid in the torchlight as he runs up the steps. He's at the far end of the last zigzag turn, where the steps are farthest away from the summit before they lead in. I look at him, and then at the portal. It's dimmer, but still vast and pulsing with such vital energy that trying to close it feels like trying to stuff a tent into a medicine bottle.

He pauses for a brief second to catch his breath, and that's when I feel the earth shift under my feet: a rumble of disquiet.

I look at the tower warily. Another deeper rumble moves the ground and I have to hop to regain my balance. On one of the far surrounding hills, just beyond the fracking site, a cloud of crows fly up from the trees, a deeper stain of black against the indigo sky. They soar towards the tor and circle me, cawing loudly.

Then the tower collapses.

But it doesn't collapse. The whole thing separates into individual stones like peas being shelled, yet keeps its tower shape. Then it spins faster and faster and the stones start to separate, spreading wider and wider. The stream of energy from the portal wraps round the whole thing like a ribbon of fire, raising it up and up – and then lets it go.

I hear the stones thud around me but I know they won't hit me. I am doing Her work, and Hers is the power of the earth. I make the final symbol and the portal closes somewhat reluctantly. I know I don't have any time left.

The stones land on the soft grass, forming the three joined spirals of the triskele on top of this holy hill. A sign that it is Hers again.

As the last stone from the tower hits the cold earth of the tor, the ground buckles under me and I fall, rolling down the hill until I hit Bran, who is outstretched on the grass, as still as the medieval stone lying next to him. He's been hit, but he's alive.

He opens an eye slowly and grabs my wrist.

I pull my wrist away and roll over, away from him, and feel another tremor shake the tor.

'Run!'

Bran is trying to sit up, but the voice isn't his. Instead I see Pete running up the hill, and as he reaches Bran he picks up the stone next to Bran's head and drops it on him.

'Run!' he screams at me as Bran's body convulses from the impact.

I run.

Halfway down the tor, the earth shifts under my feet again. My lungs heave and I taste blood in my mouth. I feel panic wash over me; I can feel the power coming up from the ground as if all the spirits of nature were galloping to the surface of the earth from below, shouting their war cries, screaming their curses and banging their drums – a rebellion, long asleep, and now awake.

I stand and look to the horizon where dawn is slicing through the night; shards of red light stripe the sky like blood in a cut. I know what the crows knew, and what the Redworld should always have known once it started drilling into the earth, pumping cancerous chemicals into the water. *Respect Nature, for She has no respect for you.*

I feel the earth heave under me and I drop to my

knees. The tor thrums and wavers, but keeps its shape —
and I watch the horizon as the hills round the fracking
site waver and collapse, covering it in earth.

The earth flows like water over the grey towers, the
trucks and the roads and the hulled-out land round
the mine; it fills the ditches and covers the machinery.
The lights flicker out one by one.

In a few minutes it's as if the drills had never been
there.

The Goddess has taken back what was Hers.

Chapter Twenty-six

When you cut Mother Earth, you bleed.

From Tenets and Sayings of the Greenworld

On my way out of Glastonbury I steal a rusty bike from outside one of the tattered houses. I feel guilty, but I need to get home and I can't do it on foot. Even worse, I ride past the window of the cafe I've eaten at many times with the girls, smash it and clamber in, the broken glass pulling at my clothes and the shop alarm blaring into the dawn. I stuff food from the huge fridge in the cafe kitchen into my bag and into my mouth: cold chicken, cheese, bread. A bottle of water I can refill once I get over the Greenworld border. I can't trust the streams and springs here.

I ride out towards the levels, heading for Compton Dundon before the security trucks can arrive, putting quick miles between me and Bran's slumped body. Between me and the ruined mine, the landslide.

Past Taunton, a ruined town, full of drunks and lost people staying in the shadows, through the barbed-wire border just outside Tiverton, avoiding the Redworld border soldiers. Then into the Greenworld again thankfully, skirting Dartmoor and heading west for the coast.

The sun has risen and is well into the afternoon when I reach Tintagel. The journey by bike was much quicker than scrambling to Glastonbury on foot was, pushed on by panic and grief, but the lack of clean roads in the Greenworld still made it difficult. By the time I reach the barbed-wire village boundary I'm faint with exhaustion and aching with hunger.

I manage to open the energy circle round the village and see the defences have been renewed: fresh planks, new barbed wire curling round the high fence. I knock at one of the thick wood-and-steel gates: old but still effective. The gangs didn't break them all when they attacked.

The view hole on the door cracks open and a gruff voice asks me my business.

'It's Demelza. Melz. Demelza Hawthorne. I've come home.' I lean the bike against the village boundary wall and slump against the door for support. I'm so tired.

'By Brighid.' The door creaks open and I fall into Ennor's arms. Ennor, my little brother – if I had a brother. Even in the few months I've been away he's got taller, filled out in the shoulders. The dark stubble on his chin looks like it's halfway to becoming a beard.

He catches me and sets me back on my feet. 'It's really you. Thank the Gods. Your mum's been beside herself. We all have.' He looks at me with concern. 'Can you walk? Like, can you make it to your house?'

'I'm OK. Just give me your arm to lean on,' I say.

We leave the bike and walk slowly through the village, all the familiar faces going about their business. It's slow progress because I'm exhausted, and people keep stopping us. *How are you? We're so glad you're home. Where have you been, Melz?* But I can't begin to tell them. *Where have I been? I've been to the underworld.* Ennor holds me up and I shuffle down the familiar streets like a crone. If not a crone, then a woman, and not a girl.

When Mum opens the door I collapse into the hall, the last scraps of energy leaving me. Running on empty, on adrenalin, for long periods is damaging; I learned about the endocrine system when I was ten. Part of witch training is understanding how the body works.

But at no point in those lessons in Mum's kitchen, with Saba staring out of the window and twisting her hair round her finger, humming under her breath – at no point did Mum ever talk about battles and escaping through barbed-wire borders and being afraid to breathe too loudly in case your betrayed lover was still chasing you, still wanting to enslave you, to make you his totem, his witch. At no point did she ever use any of these events as an excuse for how your adrenalin might get exhausted, overworked, how your internal organs might go into shock from prolonged exposure to the flight response.

I suppose when I was ten she didn't foresee anything but love and light for the Greenworld and her girls. She had built a new world for us. She had every reason to be optimistic.

As I black out I feel Mum's strong arms lifting me like she did when I was a child. *But I'm not a child any more*, I try to tell her; *I'm Melz the Red Witch*. The words won't form on my lips.

In my dreams Bran is bleeding, searching for me in the cave of the White Spring. As I move cautiously around the room, away from him, my fingers navigate the rock wall to the very back of the cave: the entrance to the faery underworld. I feel the power of the rock; it moves under my hand like a door. I push it and step into the darkness beyond.

Only it isn't dark. The Morrigan, in Her wise-crone aspect, sits with a large cauldron in a cave lined with books, medicine bottles and glass jars – like Mum's, some with browned curled labels, some newer. But instead of herbs and roots and resins like Mum's, these have words like 'strength' and 'compassion' and 'endurance' and 'bravery' on them. She smiles at me with jagged yellowed teeth, Her long grey hair hanging in plaits against the lined, sagging skin of Her chest.

Though Her body is old, the blue woad of Her spiral tattoos stands out as clearly as always; they ring Her arms and swirl across Her chest to Her throat and neck.

'My Queen,' I say, and incline my head to Her. In my dream I am no longer tired.

She stirs the cauldron and nods. 'My priestess. This is a place of power. How do you honour me?'

'I . . . I honour you with my truth.'

'And what is that?'

'That I will not corrupt your sacred places. That I will not be bribed. That I will not help him.'

She cocks her head to one side, and we both listen to Bran calling out in the cave. Stumbling, looking for me. Calling for help.

'He will not see,' She says. 'He cannot, now.'

'I know,' I reply, but still my heart constricts. I feel guilty about leaving him. I could have helped him. Maybe I could have changed him. Maybe we could have done good things together. It isn't his fault he is what he is.

And I know he isn't all bad. There is a good Bran, but he's hidden too far away. Perhaps he hardly exists any more. But he saw me and loved me once. I know he did.

She reaches out for my hand, and I kneel before Her.

'Blessed child. Truly you have fought hard, and walked the path of conscience past temptation. You do yourself credit. I am proud of you, my priestess. Mine is not an easy path, but it brings great rewards. Drink this and restore your resolve.'

She hands me a cracked earthenware cup glazed blue inside. She reaches for the bottle marked ENDURANCE, and pours a green liquid into the cup.

'Yours is a steep hill to climb, full of rocks,' She says, as I drink. 'And yet it has always been so. Know that I am always with you, and I will provide what you need to do great service to me.'

'Thank you, Great Queen,' I murmur and drink. I feel it fill me with strength and resolve. I ignore Bran's cries for help in the next room. *Demelza. Help me. Don't leave me. Demelza. Melz. Melz.*

I sit up, feeling a hand on my shoulder.

'Melz. It's OK, it's OK.' Saba rubs my back calmly and I peer around me at my old room. She hands me a glass of water. 'You were dreaming.'

I gulp the water gratefully. 'What time is it?' I peer at the weak light coming in from the window.

'About eight.'

'I dreamed of Her.' I smile, and swing my legs round to get up. Saba holds out a protective arm, but I pat it and pull on my dressing gown. 'I'm OK. Really. Just hungry. Come on, let's go down.'

As I walk downstairs I hear crows cawing in the dusk, finding their way home.

I sit across the table from Mum and Saba and watch their faces in the firelight. My portraits stare down at us from the walls, mocking me. I haven't drawn anything since cursing Bali and Skye.

In legend, crows were white and it was a curse that

singed them black. When I collapsed into the hallway here, I didn't have anything left but confusion. But now I am renewed. I have drunk the Goddess's potion, and Her strength and endurance flow in my veins.

The crow wasn't singed black as punishment; the Goddess made it that way. The sirens didn't lure men on to the rocks; the sailors were lustful and deserved their fate. I am not bad. I may have made mistakes, but I am still a witch. I am still a priestess of the Morrigan.

I am a black crow, and it isn't a punishment. It is my power.

'So tell us about the Redworld,' Mum says, pouring me a cup of tea. I crave the rich red wine I drank in Glastonbury, but wine is reserved for special occasions here. Celebrations and rituals. Me coming home isn't a celebration apparently.

'What do you mean?'

'I mean, you've been there now. Met people. Interacted. Observed. You must have a lot of useful information for us.'

'I suppose so.' I feel a strange protectiveness about my Redworld time. In a way I don't want to betray it. 'They're not all bad people, you know. It's not all bad there. Not everyone's unhappy. Some things are quite . . . nice.'

I think of my wardrobe of new clothes and shoes, Ceri's bathroom of bottles and potions and pots of beautifying products, Bran's car, the hotel. How can I explain any of those things and not make them sound horrifyingly wrong, exploitative, wasteful? Because they are all of those things, especially to Greenworld sensibilities.

'I'm sure everyone's just lovely and the sun shines all the year round, Melz. That's why you've come back exhausted, beaten up, hungry – I mean, you've put some weight on, I'll give you that – but don't sit there and tell me the Redworld's wonderful. I know it's not. So what can you tell me?' Mum asks tersely.

I look at the table, at the pentagram carved in its centre. It has room for thirteen witches, one from every covenstead in the Greenworld. Witches, ruling thousands of people, witches using magic, supporting the community, holding the seasonal celebrations, living in peace.

'They think we're criminals. Terrorists. Religious extremists,' I say, watching Mum's face as I trace my finger along the lines of the five-pointed star. How will she react? She must know. But she watches me coldly.

She tries to cut me off. 'Demelza, I—'

'What?' Saba looks amused.

'Mum's a celebrity in the Redworld. Didn't you know? An infamous terrorist. Her signature's in every modern his-story book. There's a Contract of Separation that Mum signed on our behalf. Stipulates that any Greenworlder setting foot on the Redworld side of the border's committing a crime. Accepts responsibility for a number of supposed terrorist attacks on London. Apparently. Strange how we never got taught about that, isn't it?'

Saba looks intently at Mum. 'What's she talking about?'

'That's not quite right, Demelza. You—'

I interrupt her. 'What? I'm lying? I don't think so. You're the liar.'

'I am not a liar! How dare you!' Mum glowers at me. 'There were things . . . back then . . . it was too difficult to explain. We agreed it was better to tell things our own way.'

Saba frowns at Mum. 'How is that difficult? Sounds like it's pretty straightforward to me. We're not allowed in the Redworld. Whatever. Fine. We'd never go anyway.'

'What about the bombs?' I look Mum squarely in the eye, but I know the truth. I've always known how far she would go for the Greenworld. All the way. Just like Bran. *Whatever it takes.*

'Surely not. There's no way. We're peaceful,' Saba says.

I know Saba won't want to believe it, but I reach for her hand. 'We're peaceful now. Or we were until we fought the gangs. Don't you remember the book burning, Sab? Don't you think there was some ruthlessness in setting up the Greenworld? To change it from what it was to what it is now?'

Saba's tawny eyes search Mum's for reassurance, but I know there won't be any. 'Mum?'

'I did what I had to do. For you. I saw what was

coming, and I was right,' Mum says curtly and purses her lips together as if to say *That's it, no more.*

'But . . .'

'But nothing. I know what they say about us there. Propaganda and what have you. That's the price we paid for Separation. We became the bogeyman. Whatever. I don't care. It got us what we wanted.'

'But at what cost?! You let them make us out to be evil. You . . .'

'I kept us safe. What they believe about us is up to them.'

'But they . . . the people, they don't know what we know. They could be living like us, safe, fed, happy. Isn't that . . . wrong? To have our knowledge, our ways, and not share them when people need them so badly?'

'I can't be responsible for the whole world, Demelza. I made my choice.'

'But you made it for us as well!' I scream at her. 'Why don't you understand? You're supposed to trust us! You're not supposed to lie to us! This is the Greenworld!'

'I won't be held to account by my own daughters!' Mum shouts back, and the glass jars on her dresser shake as she pushes back her chair and walks out of the kitchen.

'That's that, then,' I mutter as the door slams.

Saba gets up and starts pacing the kitchen. 'As usual. I can't believe she never told us any of this. Makes me wonder what else I don't know,' she mutters, hugging her arms to herself.

273

'I'm sorry,' I say. She looks dejected, not something I'm used to seeing on Saba – but I haven't seen her in a long while. 'Are you OK?'

'I'll be all right. Just tired. The Archive's hard work.'

She's been with Aunt Tressa in Boscastle. Tressa likes the witches that stay with her to do a little remote viewing if they can – to check in on other energy centres around the world and see if they're OK. Taxing work, psychically.

Saba keeps pacing. 'Where did you go, then? North?'

'Glastonbury first. For most of the time. Then York. That's north. I met this group of girls – about our age – and they thought they were witches. They were acting as if they were, and other people—' I still don't want to mention Bran, but I know I have to somewhere in this conversation – 'other people were treating them as if they were using magic.'

'But they weren't? Aren't?'

'No, not really. They've got hold of a few books and got a bit from them but not much. It's all about looking the part – the part they think anyway, and acting . . . mysterious, sexy. I don't know.' I think of Catie, who I could sense actually had some natural ability. 'They don't know anything about training. Rigour. Proper development. And I . . .'

'What?' Saba knows me better than anyone. 'You met someone!' She comes back to the table and looks in my eyes. 'Oh, Melz. You fell for someone in the Redworld.'

I try to tell her about Bran, try to explain, but the words won't come.

He buried the bodies on the tor.

I set his lab on fire.

He manipulated me.

He loved me.

'I can't. I can't tell you. Not yet.' A tear slips down my cheek. 'I'm sorry.' And I am sorry. For him, for myself; for all of us, in that second. Despite the Goddess's gift of endurance.

Saba sighs. 'I'm sorry too. About Tom. When he . . . when he passed, I behaved badly, that day at the funeral. I said things I didn't mean,' she says, and sits down next to me. We'd had a huge fight on the way back from Tom's sea burial. It was partly that that made me leave in the first place.

'I know,' I say.

'By Brighid, what a mess,' Saba breathes. There's a silence.

'She's still furious you ran away, you know. We've still got a lot of work to do on that curse you set,' she says softly.

I say nothing. The legacy of the curse is mine to bear, even though I dissolved it in true fire. What's done is done.

'You broke her heart,' Saba sighs.

'I broke mine too,' I say, but she doesn't respond, just lays her head on my shoulder.

'I missed you,' she says into the darkening room.

Chapter Twenty-seven

A mother's love, the strongest bond
Of earth and rock, stone and pond,
Teach the mysteries of fire and water,
The lore of wind and air and storm.
Teach them to your son and your daughter.
A mother's love, wisdom reborn.

Verse from 'A Mother's Love',
from *Prayers and Songs of the Greenworld*

Later that night, I walk through the village and up the familiar tree-lined road that leads to Ennor and Maya's house. The cosy white stone cottage with the black trim was a second home for me when I was a kid – so many days and nights were spent there when Mum was doing secret witch things, when the Greenworld was setting itself up, and there were tons of committees and debates and rituals all running late into the night. We'd get farmed off to Maya, who'd feed us vegetable bakes, stuffed apples and occasional sips of homemade cider, and tell us stories around the fire in her old beamed sitting room surrounded by her pictures. Later, she taught me how to draw, how to paint, even though charcoal became my favourite after a while. I loved its broad strokes, its definiteness. I even loved the way it stained my fingers and tasted of bonfires when I licked it off. I'd come home from Maya's covered in its coal-black dust, magic flowing through my fingers. Even before she taught me how I knew I was making magic with my pictures. Making my own reality.

When Maya opens the door I'm shocked to see how much smaller she looks: more stooped and there's more grey in her curly black hair. But she holds out her arms to me and I hug her as hard as she squeezes me, smelling the warm comfort of her lined skin, feeling the roughness of her calico scarf against my cheek.

'I'm so glad you're home, Melza,' she whispers into my hair, and I feel the tears coming. The tears I couldn't cry at home.

She pats my back solidly but kindly.

'Tears are good, sweet girl. Tears make us whole again,' she murmurs, as they come in a storm. We stand there in the doorway, me weeping against her, her rubbing my back in the way that Mum never did.

Tears make us whole again. Maya is the only one to see that I'm broken.

When the heaves ebb away we sit in the kitchen drinking warm milk. The moonlight slices through the window.

'You must be exhausted.' She gets up and takes a bottle of brown liquid out of a cupboard and pours a little of it into my milk. 'There. That'll help.'

I sip it, and she smiles at me over the rim of her mug. 'Don't tell your mum. Finest Redworld brandy that is. For homecomings and tears and romantic trysts only.'

I laugh, despite myself, and feel its warmth filling me up from my toes.

'Romantic trysts?'

'Passion isn't just for the young, you know,' she scolds. 'Now. Where have you been? You had us all worried to death.'

I tell her; all of it, this time. Of being seen, of being powerful. Of Glastonbury, the tor, the graves, the Morrigan. Of the crows storming the restaurant. Of rededicating myself to Her in that shitty room in a deserted street in Glastonbury. Of the portals, the protest, the poor. And Bran. I find the words to talk about him with Maya.

'Goodness' is all she says, sipping her drink.

'I did a lot wrong,' I confess. I can say it here because there's no judgement. The space is free for me to judge myself.

'So? We all do things wrong,' she says, stretching her arm out slowly with pain in her face. 'I made the mistake of letting some thug break my arm. I won't be doing that again in a hurry.'

'Oh Goddess. Have you been getting healing?' I can

already feel my hands buzzing, which is what usually happens when someone needs it.

'Yes, where I can. But they're all so pressed for time at the moment,' she says. 'So many people got injured after the battle. It's hard pulling everything back to where it was. Bodies and minds, houses and boundaries,' she says.

'Houses? I didn't think the battle got in that far.'

'Most of it, no. But there were a few gangs that got into the village. Looted some of the shops, stole food, broke windows, that kind of thing. I suppose they're as short on food as we can be sometimes.'

I think of the poor I've seen in the Redworld, and instead of being angry like the old Melz would, feel only a kind of inevitable sadness for the gangs too. I feel sad that there are hungry people everywhere, while the precious few at the top revel in the luxury of extreme wealth. We should save our fury for them, not each other.

She looks into my eyes. 'You've made mistakes, but you've grown because of them, Melza. Never think that you should be perfect. Even as a witch, even as the protector of people,' she says, taking my hand and squeezing it tight. 'You're still so young. Don't be so hard on yourself, sweet girl. We're all here to help each other and make this world a better place.'

I smile wanly. Maya always has a way of putting things right.

'You know your own power now, but you also know that you don't need a young man to give it to you. He might have made you feel seen, Melza, but you were always visible. All you did was let yourself believe it for the first time.'

I look at my hands. 'Maybe. But boys . . . they never liked me as much as Saba. I could never compete with her.'

She laughs. 'Oh, sweet girl, if only you knew how beautiful you were.' She reaches over and brushes my hair out of my eyes. 'The only difference between you and Saba is that she knows what she's got and makes the most of it. She believes she's beautiful – too much, in my opinion, but there you are – and so others believe it. It's the simplest magic in the world. I can't believe you've never realized that. You, the witch.'

'I guess. I just . . .' I'm on the brink of telling her about Tom, and cursing Bali and Skye, when Ennor comes in and gives me a hug.

'Hey. You're here.'

'I am.' I smile at him, and his brown eyes twinkle back at me. 'Thanks for taking me home earlier.'

'Welcome.'

I look him up and down. 'You've got taller,' I say. 'You're not going to look like my little brother much longer. You're too big.'

He sits down at the table with us. 'Finally,' he says, looking at the bottle of brandy between us. 'You both been at the booze, then?' He picks it up and peers at the label. 'I didn't know we had this.'

Maya takes the bottle and puts it away in the

cupboard. 'There's a lot you don't know, nosy,' she says, then she turns to me. 'It's late. Are you staying over, Melza?'

I look out at the moon. I'm too tired to walk home.

'Do you mind?' I ask, knowing she doesn't, and that I've slept here almost as many nights as in my own bed.

'Course not. I'll just go and put some sheets on,' she says, and a minute later we hear her fussing in the hall cupboard, pulling out bedclothes.

Ennor and I smile at each other.

'I'm glad you're back,' he says, and touches my arm briefly.

'I wish everyone felt the same,' I say, thinking of Mum storming out earlier.

'Lowenna? She was so worried though.'

'Can't see it myself.' I drain the last of my brandy-laced milk. 'Why didn't she send someone after me, then?'

'They did, I thought. Danny was all fired up to go looking for you, I heard.'

'Well, if he did, he didn't find me,' I snap back, and Ennor gives me that look he always does when I'm being a bitch. 'Sorry,' I mutter. 'It's been a long week.'

'Anyway, look. I've got something for you,' he says, putting a school workbook down on the table.

'What's this?' I pick it up. 'A Guide to Reflective Greenworld Journalling? I didn't think you bothered with it.'

'No. Open it.'

I turn the cover over and flick through the pages.

281

There are reams of numbers, calculations and diagrams, all in pencil, in Ennor's handwriting.

'I don't get it. What is it?'

'Well, I was talking to Saba and she told me all about how Roach thought there was some kind of way of making the portals into a fuel source.'

I stop looking at the book. 'You know what a portal is?'

'Yeah. She showed me.'

'Why? That's supposed to be a secret.'

I can't believe Saba showed him. Not that we can't trust Ennor. I'm just about to tell him off when I think of myself in my flowing red dress at the Twelve Apostles, opening the portal for Bran as well as the cigarette-smoking girls and the boys back from war. I snap my mouth shut. *That ship has sailed, my lover*, Maya would say.

'She needed someone to talk to when she came home from the Archive. She was missing Tom, she was worried about you, worried about Roach and the gangs. That they'd come back and attack again. She told me why they'd attacked in the first place.'

'Oh,' I sigh. I'm too tired to be angry about it. 'OK, whatever, En. So what's this book all about?'

He opens it and starts pointing to the pages but I can't really follow what he's saying. My brain is fried.

'. . . solutions. I thought it might be photovoltaic energy. Then I started thinking about radon and uranium, you know, radioactive elements; they're unstable. Maybe that's what gives you that kind of hallucinogenic experience when you're inside it . . .'

'Wait, wait, wait. What? What're you on about, En?' The milk-and-brandy has had the intended effect and all the tiredness in me has now coalesced into one lump, starting in my aching legs and feet and working all the way up to my eyes. 'I can hardly keep my eyes open, and you're not helping. Photovoltaic energy? What's that, by Brighid?'

'It's all theoretical, Melz, but what I'm saying is Roach might have been right. There might be a way to use the portal for fuel, if we can understand what it actually is – in scientific terms.'

I pull a face at him. 'In scientific terms? Why? We know what it is.'

'Yes, but your magical philosophy . . . well, it doesn't explain what it is on a molecular level. What the nuts and bolts of it are. It has to have nuts and bolts in some way. It just depends if science can name those bolts yet.'

'But, Ennor, we live in the Greenworld. We don't use science. We don't learn it. Science gave us war – weapons, electricity, bombs. How have you even been learning all this anyway?' I look at the book again, at the numbers and slashes and dots and strange signs and symbols. 'I mean, this is a whole other language. This isn't what we're about.'

'Don't be stupid. We brew cider. That's a chemical process. We make dyes and fabrics. We use science all the time, Melz. It's not evil. It's the basic building blocks of life.'

I look at him, aghast. 'No. The Goddess, the God,

life and death, nature. They are the building blocks of life. The elements.'

'It's just language, Melz. A different language for the same thing. You want to describe the seasons with a myth about a dying god and a goddess that gets pregnant and then old and then young again, that's fine. Science says the same thing but in measurements – the temperature of the land caused by weather, caused by the distance the Earth is from the sun and at what angle, where your home sits on that angle and therefore how much daylight you get, how much heat, what the plants do in that time. No one can deny that you have magical experiences as a witch, but I think they're just experiences no one knows how to explain in any other language yet.'

'I don't agree, Ennor, and I think this path you're going down is very dangerous. Keep it as a hobby, by all means, but—'

'No, Melz. This is important. Come on. Listen, please. For me.'

His deep brown eyes look imploringly at me and I sigh.

'All right. But just quickly, OK? I'm shattered. I need sleep.'

'OK. So, there's this effect called biomass.' I roll my eyes but let him continue. 'What it means is a tree captures this gas, carbon dioxide, all its life. It filters it out from the air. That's why having trees around is good for you,' he explains.

'OK. We love trees.'

'Yeah. So, when you burn a tree – burn wood – that carbon dioxide is released back into the air. That's biomass, when living things – usually plants – store energy and release them.'

'Right, OK, but what does this have to do with the portals?'

'Well. It – they – are ways from life into death, right? Souls pass through them?'

'Yes.'

'So what if souls – the dead – give off some kind of energy when they pass through the portal? A stored-up energy in us when we're alive, which then dissipates after death?'

'Ummm . . .'

'It's kind of an out-there theory, but . . .' Ennor sits forward and pushes his book towards me.

I push it back. 'It's more than out there. It's crazy.'

'But . . .'

'No, En. It's strange, and I'm tired. I'm going to bed.' I stand up and kiss him on the forehead. When I'm at the kitchen door his voice stops me; it's lower and stranger, full of edges and fear.

'Did you hear about them? About Bali and . . . Skye?' he asks, and I stop dead. I can't tell from his tone whether he's accusing me or whether it's grief that's cracked his voice.

Skye was Ennor's girlfriend until the battle, until we realized she and her brother had betrayed us. But

Ennor doesn't know about the curse. He doesn't know about the biting, burning revenge I pounded into their bodies, their spirits. Does he?

'No,' I say neutrally.

'They . . . their bodies. They washed up on the beach.'

'When?'

'Couple of weeks ago.'

'They drowned?'

'Maybe. Saba said they couldn't tell. No other wounds they could see.'

'Oh. I'm sorry.' I turn round to look at him, but he avoids my gaze.

'Looks like they were up on Tintagel Head and fell. Gets pretty windy up there.' His voice is guarded and I can't read him. Has Saba told him about the curse? If she has, does he think that this was my doing? *Was* it my doing, or was it an accident? There are no accidents or coincidences, Mum taught Saba and me. There is only intention and energy.

'It does,' I say quietly. 'I'm sorry, Ennor. I know you loved her.' And I am sorry, sorry for him.

'She betrayed us. I hate her,' he snaps. 'She used me.'

'I'm still sorry,' I say softly.

He nods.

'Goodnight, little brother.'

'Goodnight,' he mutters.

I look back and he's staring blankly at his journal.

Chapter Twenty-eight

All loves are great, but the greatest loves are
motherhood and sisterhood, whether a sister from
the womb or a sister of the soul, a blood mother or
the Great Mother of us all.

From *Tenets and Sayings of the Greenworld*

The midsummer fire in the middle of the village green
is so hot that I throw off my brown knitted cardigan,
aiming it at a big pile of boots and jackets outside the
circle of dancing villagers. The day has been spent in
worship, in meditation and making midsummer crafts:
good-luck charms, flower crowns, herb blends. All
week it's been strange between me and Mum. Functional
but strained. The curse hangs between us. *I have to
reconsider your place in the covenstead, Demelza*, she said last
night after we'd finished preparing for the festival. *You
can't just pretend nothing happened.*

But tonight, for the village, we're all holding hands,

circling and singing, looking happy. I'm sweating; the blue woad of the triple-moon symbol painted on my forehead is smudging and drops of blue-tinged sweat drip into my eyes. I need water, but the ceremony isn't done until we finish raising the energy in the circle, until we stop dancing and the Goddess, Brighid – which is always Saba – jumps over the fire with the sun god, Lugh. It was often Tom before . . . before he died. Mum always liked to have a witch and a non-witch doing the symbolic purification for the village. Lugh and Brighid, protectors of the people, renewing their strength in the midsummer fire. Demonstrating why the village needs us, and how well integrated we are.

Whether you believe that or not is another thing.

But tonight the God isn't being played by Tom, although in my mind, it'll always be him self-consciously brandishing Lugh's spear. Tonight it's Ennor.

I can't actually believe my eyes as he prances after Saba, the villagers all shouting their encouragement at them. As he passes me he avoids my eyes; he's ashamed.

It's incestuous; he's like a brother to us both. I can't believe that he's stepped in where Tom left off, like Saba needs constant round-the-clock adoration or she'll die. Ennor should know better; he saw what she did with Tom and Danny, two-timing them, keeping them both on the hook for her. Ennor knows Saba as well as I do. Or he should.

But if Ennor is with Saba, then he must know I cursed Bali and Skye, because Saba can't keep secrets.

He knows, by Brighid. And I know that he isn't sure how he feels about it, not yet. Because despite his bitterness that Skye betrayed him, betrayed us all, he loved her. And she might not have loved him, but that rarely matters. Love is like a curse; it clutches at you whether you want it or not.

I keep dancing, keep following the movement of the circle round the green, round the fire. Later, couples that want to be handfasted will leap over the fire when it's burning low to represent their commitment to each other for the next year. Mum will bind their hands together with green and white ribbons and say some nice words. Couples 'tie the knot' Greenworld style, like this, at quite a few of the festivals. The ones about love and fertility. Not the ones about death and decay.

Tonight Merryn is being handfasted with her new lover Rhiannon. We have far fewer men than women in the Greenworld, and witches, in particular, tend to pair with other women. Perhaps it's the wisdom that the Goddess gives us, perhaps it's just that boys are trouble.

Merryn clasps Rhiannon's hand and they run up to the fire, leaping over it and laughing. The God and the Goddess, symbolically at least. There is masculine and feminine in all of us. I think back to the boy dressed as a mermaid in York and feel shame. I've been taught that we all contain duality all my life and I still acted like an idiot when faced with something just a tiny bit different to my norm. I wonder what Maya would have said.

Brighid guides us all to true selfhood, she would say to us when we came to her with the problems Mum was too busy to hear.

The crowd hoots and cheers, and the circle disbands. This is the signal for people to get drunk and dance under the moon for the rest of the night. I want no part of it. When Mum's not looking I sneak away from the green, from the raucous singing, right out to the boundary. I don't want to be here any more. There are too many odd looks. People won't meet my eyes. I've been away, into forbidden territory, and returned under a cloud. Perhaps they can see it on me, the Redworld: in my skin, in my hair, in my aura.

You can get to the boundary without seeing anyone if you're careful and you know what you're doing. I follow the cracked path round the houses at the far end of the village and walk until the trees thin out. This is my private place, where I sometimes come to think, to meditate, to make magic.

I climb up on the throne-like rock that I use, one of the strange Bronze Age sacred stones that are dotted around the landscape here and there. This one, the only one in the village as far as I'm aware, has a faint ancient spiral carving on it. As I sit in the hollow of the rock, looking through the boundary fences and out to sea, I always feel like I connect to our ancestors, those pagans that came way before the Greenworld and lived on the land, honoured their dead, and knew the power of the earth and the sky.

I lie back in the hollow of the rock and close my eyes, listening to the music thumping in the centre of the village, knowing that midsummer fires burn all over the Greenworld tonight.

My eyes close and I dream of Danny Prentice. Danny Prentice, the liar. The chosen one. A branded witch, like me. Danny Prentice, my sister's lover. My enemy.

I'm in a forest, watching Danny as if I were a tree or a tree spirit. I watch as he skirts the trees cautiously, putting out a hand for his dog Gowdie. Somehow I know he's looking for someone. He's looking for me. I recognize the surroundings; this forest is in Chagford. We're still on the Greenworld side of the border, near Danny's village in Gidleigh. For some reason he's come out looking for me.

I feel the sour dislike I've always had when I see him. Annoyance at his offhandedness about the Greenworld, as if it didn't really matter at all what we were doing. Dislike for the way he was so good at everything without even trying – just like Saba. And, yes, I'll admit it – jealousy of the way his eyes slid right over me and back to her when we first met.

It's then that I catch a second's glance of a man, maybe ten metres away. It's Bran. He's bleeding and walking carefully, holding his side, but it's him. He survived, and he followed me. Only he didn't find me. In the dream I know I'm lying on an uncomfortable rock in Tintagel. Sudden dread twists my stomach. Is Danny the reason Bran didn't find me? Why am I seeing this?

Run, I want to shout at Danny. *Run away from him as fast as you can. Don't look back.* But he can't hear me.

Danny has seen Bran and ducks behind a tree. I watch as he forms an energy bubble around himself, making himself invisible to the casual observer. Saba and I taught him how to do it, projecting energy around yourself, making you like a mirror. A witch will still be able to see you if they try. But a casual observer's eyes will slide over you.

A crow swoops overhead, followed by another, and another. The Morrigan is here, and that knowledge fills me with foreboding. Because the Morrigan often comes when someone needs protection.

Danny suddenly peers into the distance, then recoils. 'Oh shit. Shit, shit, shit,' he mutters to himself.

I look up, and there he is. Roach, the leader of the gangs, walking towards the trees, large as life. I've forgotten how big he is – tall, thick-necked, bullish, dressed in combat clothes, holding a gun at his side and a serrated hunting knife tucked in his belt. But where he used to have a shaved head his hair has grown long, patchy and white. As he gets closer I see the burn marks on his face. What is he doing here?

In my dream I murmur a prayer to the Morrigan. *Phantom Queen, Mistress of Magic, protect him, please protect him. Protect Danny Prentice.*

Roach strides towards Danny. If he concentrates, he can stay hidden. But I can feel Danny wavering. He hasn't had the training I have – the years and years of

292

practice, of meditation, concentration. His abilities are still mostly instinctive, and the problem with instinct is that it's unreliable. Prone to hesitation if you're excited. Or if you're scared.

I can feel the fear sliding off Danny. I feel his concentration wavering. I feel his fear getting the better of him. The crows caw above his head, and he glances up. He overbalances and hits his knee on a stone on the ground, crying out.

Then Gowdie barks. That stupid dog barks.

Danny runs, but not fast enough. Roach catches up with him quickly.

Gowdie's going mad, barking and launching herself at Roach but he kicks her hard and she whines and stumbles.

Neither Bran or Roach will give in. I remember Bran saying he had contacts in the gangs, but it never occurred to me it might be Roach. How blind I've been. They want a witch for something – the memory of the burning lab flashes into my dream. No, no, not that! I burned it. I remember the pictures on the walls. The flayed bodies. The diagrams. And the table with the straps and the mask. It's gone; they can't hurt him with that. I destroyed it. I burned it. But they still take Danny. Instead of me.

They still want him, and they won't give up.

But the crows, the crows won't give up either.

In the shape of a vast triangle, they arrow towards Bran, cawing loudly. They surround him, and he reaches up to bat them away, shielding his eyes, remembering what they did last time. But this time they're not letting him get away.

I watch, in the dream, feeling as though I'm being turned into salt.

Roach has Danny, holding both his hands behind his back, smiling and saying something to him. Danny's face is pale, his eyes full of pain.

The crows are whirling around Bran, a miasma of black and beaks and sharp eyes, darting in to peck at him. He falls to the ground, his hand over his eyes, legs thrashing in panic, but he can't guard against them. They're too many, too fast.

His cry rings out sharply and I see the blood run down his cheek.

Legend says that crows were white once. The god Apollo scorched them black with fury when one failed to peck out the eyes of his lover's new paramour.

My crows have not failed me.

Chapter Twenty-nine

Crows call: I feel the storm coming,
You who are one who are many who are all.
Who hears my longing; those who heed the call;
Those who call themselves mine.
You who are one who are many who are all.
You who are blood who are blade,
You who are grass where the bones are laid,
You who are one who are many who are all.

Chant for the Morrigan, from *The Book of the
Morrigan, Greenworld Prayers and Songs*

I sit up, disoriented, and wince at the crick in my neck;
Bronze Age stones are no feather beds. *Danny.* The
images dissolve, but I know it happened for real.

There's a movement outside the boundary fence.
Instinctively my hand goes to my bag; I always keep it
next to me, and in it is a knife.

I swallow back the acidic taste of cider from my

mouth. 'Who is it?' I call out as confidently as I can, wishing for my shotgun.

The figure steps up to the fence. 'It's me. Omar,' he whispers, and I let out an indrawn breath.

'Goddess, Omar. You frightened me.'

'Sorry. What're you doing out here on that rock?'

'Avoiding everyone. What're you doing, skulking round the boundary?'

'Looking for you. I need you to come with me. To the Redworld. Danny's gone missing.'

'I know,' I say, sitting up painfully.

Omar frowns at me.

'Don't look at me like that. I didn't know until just now. I dreamed . . . I saw him.'

'Zia said you need to come. She told me where you'd be.'

Zia Prentice, my fellow priestess of the Morrigan. Danny's mum.

'What if I don't want to come?' The sense of dread from the dream is still all around me in my aura, churning in my stomach.

'Look, it wasn't my idea,' he mumbles. 'I'm just following orders. She says you're meant to go. You're the priestess of the Morrigan. Only the Morrigan can rescue Danny, she says.'

I stand on the other side of the fence to him and whisper through the wire, although Goddess knows if anyone happened to come this way they'd be too drunk to notice us. 'Zia's a priestess of the Morrigan. She's his mum. Why doesn't she go?'

'She can't leave the village unguarded. Anyway, she said you, and that you were meant to go. When she says things are meant to happen I find it's best not to argue,' he rumbles back.

'But I can't go back! A Greenworld witch in the Redworld – I just got back. I don't want to go!'

And I'm afraid, is what I don't say. Afraid of what he'll do to me if he catches me. Bran Crowley. And I'm afraid of what I'll feel if I see him again. I'm afraid I might still love him.

'I'll make sure nothing bad happens to you. Don't worry.'

I know I would probably be safe with Omar, but I still don't want to go.

'I—' I start to make up an excuse but he interrupts me.

'I dreamed about him, you know,' he says, his bull shoulders silhouetted against the fence in the moonlight. 'Danny. He was in terrible pain. Strapped on to some table.' He looks at me, and I look down guiltily. 'People doing horrible things to him. Torturing him. I'm going to get him, Melz. On my own or with you.'

'But I can't!'

He gives me a long appraising look. 'I can't make you. I wouldn't make you. Because you're a witch and I respect you. But you've got a responsibility to each other, as witches, haven't you? Or does all that initiation loyalty crap really mean nothing?'

I look at my hands. He's right and we both know it.

'Do you really hate him that much?'

Omar is the only dad Danny ever really knew: an intermittent here-and-gone boyfriend of his mum's. But he loves Danny. He would die for him.

'I don't hate him.'

'So?'

I can't tell him about Bran. I'll have to. But not yet.

'All right. I'll come.'

The thought of having to go back fills me with dread, but it's the right thing to do. I might have hated Danny Prentice once, but I won't let him suffer.

'I was hoping you'd say that,' he replies, and throws a rope ladder over the top of the boundary. It puddles at my feet like betrayal. But I hoist my bag over my shoulder and put my foot on the bottom rung anyway. There are so many betrayals woven together that I can't separate them any more. All I can do is rise above them.

Chapter Thirty

> It is customary to leave offerings in the wild for
> the spirits that live there. For instance, flowers and
> feathers or small amounts of food or wine may be
> left at a sacred tree or rock or as an offering for the
> sea itself.
>
> From *Greenworld Covenstead Magic: A Practical Guide*

We are a couple of hours outside Tintagel when they
find us.

Omar has just ducked behind a tree for a pee and
I'm discreetly looking the other way when I sense
movement in the trees to our right. It's not as open here
as many spots on the way to the border, which are flat
moorland with the occasional stone outcropping; here
we are in the wild wood. The pines whisper avarice
above our heads, and though trees are always our friends
it feels too old, this forest, too old for friendliness or

299

alliances either way. This is a forest that rightly, in this day and age, only cares about itself.

I make a crow call, our agreed sign if needed, and rest the shotgun on my shoulder, narrowing my gaze through the old manual viewfinder. Omar brought it for me: thankfully it's as similar to mine as it could be. I learned to shoot my dad's old hunting gun when I was ten. Seems like Omar wasn't expecting me to have time to say my goodbyes.

He appears soundlessly at my side; he has soldier training, so he's able to move without making a noise, despite being so big.

'What can you see?' he whispers, taking his pistol out of his belt.

I shake my head. 'Not sure yet. Movement. There was definitely something . . .' I pause and we both hear the snap of a foot on a fallen branch, then another. I nestle my chin down and make sure I'm standing evenly. Two people, at least. I feel in my pocket for additional rounds, and hope there aren't too many gang members. Shotguns are cumbersome to reload, even if you're used to them.

Omar checks his aim and squints into the shadows under the trees. It's early morning still, just past dawn, but the forest keeps a lot of the early-morning light out.

When they stumble into the clearing we're ready for them.

The man holds his hands in the air. 'Don't shoot! Don't shoot!' he cries, and we lower our guns in dismay.

It's obvious that they are not from the gangs, both because of the way they're dressed – I recognize the Redworld clothes – but also because they have children with them, and they look terrified.

'Who are you? What are you doing here?' I shout, but I know. And, in a way, I'm surprised it hasn't happened sooner. I look at the pinched face of the little girl – maybe four or five, but small for her age. Undernourished and pale, with a faded blue dress completely unsuitable for hiking through the moors. Her mother holds her hand, gaunt and tired. Redworld refugees, looking for something better in the Greenworld.

'We left. We can't afford food any more, can't afford anything. We can't face another winter there,' the father says, looking at his daughter. The anguish in his eyes cuts into me. 'Please don't kill us. We don't have anything you can take. We just want to leave.'

'We're not going to kill you, by Brighid.' I put the shotgun down and reach into my bag. Omar also packed provisions – apples, sandwiches, a bottle of water. I hold a sandwich out to the little girl. 'Here. Take it.'

She looks longingly at it but hides behind her mother's stick-thin legs.

I give the package to the mother instead. 'You give it to her, then,' I say, and hold out an apple to the father as well. He looks at me cautiously, but takes it and bites into it.

'Bless you,' he says, and the woman kneels down

and unwraps the sandwich with her daughter. The girl eats slowly, chewing the bread and watching me.

'Where are you headed?' Omar asks, his gravelly tone neutral.

The woman sits down on the forest floor and I hand her my bottle of water.

'Oh, it's glass,' she says weakly as she puts it to her mouth. 'I thought it was plastic. How old-fashioned.' She takes a long drink and turns to Omar. 'We heard there were villages here that might take us in. We heard they have food and you don't need money there. We don't care if they're extremists. We're desperate.'

Omar hunkers down next to them and smiles at the little girl, who hides behind her mother again.

'She doesn't like strangers,' the father explains, 'and she's afraid of men like you.'

'Men like me?' Omar raises a bushy eyebrow.

'Shaved head, tattoos. You're some kind of . . . criminal, right?' the mother asks fearfully. 'You've got guns,' she adds, looking at me too.

I interrupt because I see Omar's smile falter – it's not their fault that's what they think. What else do they know? Poverty and crime. Quite possibly they're from Glastonbury.

'We're not criminals,' I say, but don't say what we are. 'Look. By all means go to the next village – Tintagel, that's where I'm from. It's a good few hours' walk, but you'll make it as long as you head west.' The man and woman exchange glances. I rein in my impatience that

302

adults don't know the simplest of things and point to the sky. 'West, OK? Keep the sun behind you until midday and then follow the sun until it gets dark. You'll get there before then. When you get there, tell them you need food and shelter. That you've nowhere else to go. They'll take you in. But you have to realize that people are different down this way. Life's different. You have to contribute, share; I mean, d'you have any useful skills?'

'I trained as a bricklayer back when there was work,' the man says, finishing the apple.

'Good. Anything else?'

'I'm a decent cook,' says the woman.

Talk about gendered jobs, I think. The Redworld likes to put everyone in their traditional boxes and wrap them up nice and tight.

'OK. Well, tell them that too when you get there,' I say, and get up.

'Should we say anything else? To get in?' the mother asks, taking the girl's hand. She studies me with her fierce, serious expression but doesn't smile. She's been silent the entire time.

'Not that I can think of,' I say.

Omar shoulders his rucksack and checks the barrel in his pistol. 'Tell them Omar and Demelza sent you,' he says, looking at me. 'And tell them that there's more of you on the way. And you – all of you – be prepared. Tintagel – the Greenworld, that's where you are now – it's a religious place. You're going to have to get used to the way they do things there. Believe me. It's hard for an

303

outsider to understand the world the way they see it. Even if you hate what you left behind.'

They nod, and we walk one way through the trees and they walk another. Soon they're out of earshot and we plod along silently again.

'They've got a real wake-up call coming their way,' Omar grumbles as our feet fall into a familiar march.

'Well, it's still better than starving and freezing to death in the Redworld, Goddess be praised,' I say, sympathizing. I'm glad that little girl will grow up in Tintagel, safe in its walls.

'I didn't mean them. I meant the village,' he says, and takes a swig of his water. 'This is just the start. There'll be more and more like that family – refugees – and they're not going to stop coming until something changes in the Redworld. I don't see that happening anytime soon. There's going to come a time when the Greenworld just can't take any more.'

I study his face as he stares off into the distance. He has always been our one link to the outside world, navigating the border, bringing supplies and information.

'D'you really think it will come to that?'

'Yes.'

'What happens then?'

He sighs. 'I don't know. But you can bet that for every nice little family that joins one of the villages, the gangs will recruit one or two young kids or older guys without families – people who are looking for a community but who don't like the look of the Greenworld and all its rules, all its religious observances. Or, worse, people who've already started their criminal careers. They'll fit right in.'

'The gangs will get bigger,' I say, thinking about it. 'And that will mean more of a threat to the villages.'

'Yup. And even within the villages it's going to be hard to maintain the Greenworld culture, with that many Redworlders coming in, however receptive they might be to Celtic mythology and wool and organic vegetables, you know? Cos with the best will in the world, that's all new to them. They grew up where they grew up. They internalized all that, just like you ate up magic and cycles of life and death for breakfast every day. So, inevitably, Greenworld culture will change.'

I think about it, think about the good things I experienced in the Redworld. Music and fashion and food and drink. Other knowledge. The things I saw. Other books, other architecture, people from other cultures, even from other countries.

'But that's not necessarily bad,' I say.

He raises his eyebrows at me. 'No, it's not, though I'm surprised to hear you say it. Your time away must have had quite an impact.'

I look at my boots. I don't know Omar that well but I feel like he'd understand about Bran, about how not everything is as straightforward as Greenworld and Redworld, good and bad.

'I suppose,' I mumble.

'Hmmm. I suppose now's a good time to ask you

what you know about Danny. About who's got him, where he is. Why Zia was so definite that you had to come with me.'

'All right.' I try not to blush awkwardly – I mean, how much do I need to tell him?

He frowns at me. 'Who do you think has him, then? Let's start with that.'

Like that is the easiest thing in the world. To say his name again. To explain.

'Roach. And the other one . . .' I sigh, not wanting to have to say his name again but knowing that I have to. 'He's called Bran. Bran Crowley.'

Omar takes his gun out of his belt. He looks at it and looks at me. 'Bran Crowley?'

'Yes.'

'May I ask how you know Bran Crowley?'

'Is it important? I just do.'

'I think it could be pretty important, yeah.' He holds my eyes, not letting my glare cow him.

'Fine. We . . . we were lovers.' I try to say it confidently. Not because I don't have mixed feelings about it, but because I am a woman, and a witch, and witches take responsibility for their actions.

'Ah,' he says. 'Anything else you want to tell me?'

'Like what?'

'Like why Zia told me you had to come on this rescue mission. Why it's so important that I have to look after some scrawny seventeen-year-old girl instead of just going myself. What else Bran Crowley knows about you. Why he's kidnapped Danny. Where Danny is now. Danny Prentice. The boy I've known since he . . .' He stops talking and takes in a deep breath. I realize how upset he is. 'Whatever. Just tell me, Demelza. Everything you know.'

'Do you know him?' I ask.

'You might say that. You might say I know Bran Crowley pretty well,' he says darkly.

'How? Who is he to you?' I can sense a weight behind his thoughts: worry, guilt, wrapped up in years of secrecy and solitude.

He walks ahead of me, bear-like, clearing a path through the trees with a steel machete and doesn't answer.

'Omar?'

'It's not how it sounds. You won't understand.' He cuts a branch from a pine with unnecessary vigour, making me wince on behalf of the tree.

'Just tell me.'

He stops, resting his palm on the trunk of the tree as if asking for forgiveness, back still turned to me.

'He's my boss. Back in the Redworld. I work for him.'

Chapter Thirty-one

They sang, but had nor human tunes nor words,
Though all was done in common as before;
They had changed their throats and had the throats
of birds.

From 'Cuchulain Comforted' by W. B. Yeats

'What?'

I stop walking; the forest goes quiet momentarily at my outburst and then comes back to life. I hear a crow caw in the distance.

Omar turns back to face me. 'I work for Bran Crowley. Have done for a few years now.'

'But he's half your age!' I splutter, like that matters. I've seen the extent of Bran's power. And the Greenworld accepts that Saba and me and Danny are witches, and that gives us authority over other people, even though we're teenagers. Still, it seems strange. Maybe because

Omar's such a big man, obviously a fighter, a soldier, a man seasoned in combat and survival.

'He's in charge in the south-west outside the Greenworld. He pays. I need to work,' he grunts, and starts walking forward again, swishing the machete from side to side softly.

'Does Zia know?'

'She knows I work for someone there. She doesn't ask questions.'

'Did you know about . . . what he was doing?' I think of the bodies on the tor.

He shrugs. 'I knew what I was doing for him.'

'Which was?'

He glares at me. 'Nosy, aren't you? You're Lowenna's daughter all right.' He walks along a few paces. 'Driving, sometimes. The armoured vans. Repairs. Mechanics on them aren't easy. And sometimes . . . other things.'

'What other things?'

'None of your business.'

'It is my business. I would have found out anyway, if I'd stayed.'

'As his lover. And his sorceress, no doubt. He's been after one of those for a while. A real Greenworlder. He's tried the home-grown witches but they're not up to scratch.'

'Yes. He offered me . . . a lot, to stay and do that. To . . . I don't know. Convince people that him taking control of a new power from the portals would be a good idea. Like the Goddess's power was on his side, maybe convince them he had a divine right to control this new energy source. This fictional energy source.' I look away from his gaze, embarrassed.

'He seems to believe in it enough to bother seducing you, and now kidnapping Danny. There must be something in it.' Omar's voice rumbles in the branches of the trees. Hurt cracks my heart; the thought, though it's most likely true, that everything Bran did to get to know me, to get me on his side, was manipulation. But I grit my teeth and walk on. I'm not going to cry in front of a man I hardly know.

'It's Roach's paranoid delusion. Bran likes the idea because he wants power. He sees it as a kind of class reversal. He wants revenge on the super-rich and powerful. He wants to break them. Induce mass riot and hysteria and then have a total monopoly on fuel. He wants to believe it.'

'I don't know. He's a pretty rational guy,' Omar replies, but I think of Bran at the Twelve Apostles: his shining eyes, his hot arm round my waist as he guided me away from the portal, away from the stone circle where he *saw* me for the first time. That wasn't rationality. It was a deep, fiery passion: possession.

'So . . . if you work for him, this means . . .' I think ahead of us. Somewhere in Glastonbury Danny is being held by Bran and Roach. Tortured, even. Omar is relinquishing his job by doing this, by rescuing Danny.

'It means I won't be safe in the Redworld for a while

after this. If ever,' he says, his voice clipped of emotion. 'But it's not a choice. Danny's like a son to me. I've done worse for him and I'd do it again.'

I remember Omar following Danny into the portal, to death and beyond. I still don't know how they got out alive. Somehow Omar brought him back, and that fills me with hope he can get us all back safe.

'I know,' I say, and we walk on.

Glastonbury is wreathed in deep mist when we get there; the layers shift like a blue-grey sea, keeping the tor separate from the rest of the land like a mysterious island – secret, woven with old tales and legends. It's so different to the way it was before, when it was closed up, secret and repressed. Now it's bursting with energy, with vitality, glowing in the moonlight like a beacon. Even from streets away, Omar's eyes widen. He'll have been here before if he knows Bran but he can feel something's different.

'It's like the tor's . . . alive somehow,' he says, as we stand in the dark misted street and gaze up at it. Around us are the echoes of coracles and barges from long ago, poling their way through the marshes that used to lie here, seekers, monks and nuns, all searching for the Isle of Glass, the Isle of Apples. I shiver, feeling their light touch as herstory passes by and through us, and we stand breathing in the same mists as the priests and priestesses of the moon all those thousands of years ago.

Omar frowns at me. 'Where's Danny?'

I look up at the tor. 'I don't know, but I will,' I say.

I don't really have a plan as such. The only thing I know is that I can connect to Danny, and that he's somewhere nearby. I just have to find him. And if I'm going to be able to connect to him anywhere, it's on the tor. The natural power of that place makes it stand out, even to Omar, a non-witch; if I go to the top and commune with its energy again I can find him. I know I can.

'We have to climb it. I have to get to the top,' I tell him, and he nods without asking why. We continue along the dirty streets full of beggars sleeping in doorways, their possessions in faded plastic bags. There are more than when I left. We pass the Chalice Well Gardens, the home of the Red Spring. I hope that now the fracking site has been destroyed, the water will be able to return to cleanliness.

Omar follows me as I walk the processional way up the tor, not straight up the side, but circling it in a spiral shape, slowly ascending. As I climb I centre myself, align my energy with the tor and with the portal, even though it remains closed. I open all my chakras, my energy centres, and see their colours flash behind my eyelids one by one: red at the base, orange in the stomach, yellow in the solar plexus, green for the heart, blue for the throat, indigo for the third eye, and white for the crown. My third-eye vision reaches out for Danny as I walk, round and round, through the long grass and taking care on the uneven ground, slowly up and up, my feet treading the old ceremonial path the druids, perhaps even the Christian hermits, trod thousands of years ago and more.

A cloud of crows thins out into a line across the sky, hovering over the town. As I watch, they move into a V shape like migrating geese. This isn't usual crow behaviour. I follow them with my eyes as the V moves down into the town. I squint, following the layout of the streets. They're showing me where Danny is. It's the street Ceri took me on that first night in Glastonbury; in my mind's eye I see the warehouse doors, the oddly dressed kids clustered outside, talking, laughing, kissing; I remember the primal heartbeat of the music. I know where he is.

I murmur a blessing to the Morrigan, thanking Her for Her help, and point across to the crows.

'He's there. A few streets away. It's a warehouse where they have parties. I went there once.'

Omar just nods and follows me down, not asking anything, not remarking. He is well versed in the odd ways of witches.

Chapter Thirty-two

Much care must be taken when invoking the Gods within yourself and should only be tried by a senior witch with the full permission and support of her high priestess and the covenstead at large. It is vital to prepare mindfully and carefully beforehand, be rested and strong, and to ground instantly afterwards by eating, drinking and, ideally, receiving energy from another witch.

From *Greenworld Covenstead Magic: A Practical Guide*

We stand outside the heavy wooden doors.

'Have you been here before?' I ask Omar — it's conceivable he might have, but he shakes his head.

'Didn't get involved in this side of the business. I was mostly repairs.'

'This side of the business? He owns this, then?' I didn't know.

'Yeah. Moneymaker, this place. Keeps the rich kids on side.'

The rich kids, like Ceri, Catie and Demi. The ones that spotted me and brought me to him.

Omar peers at the lock and shakes the door.

'They don't want visitors,' he grunts, looking at the heavy locks.

'Can you open it?' I ask.

He grins a cocky grin at me and reaches into his pocket, bringing out a dark blue folded-up cloth. 'Yep,' he says, and extracts a thin sharp implement and a small pair of bolt cutters. 'Should be in in a few minutes. What's the plan when we get in?'

'I didn't think we had one.'

'Oh. I s'pose I just thought you were thinking the same as me – get in, grab Danny, I'll fight anyone that needs fighting, and you'll do something magical as distraction if needed.'

'That's pretty vague. What if there's more of them than us? You can't fight them all,' I say.

He screws his face up in concentration, holding his ear to the lock as he twists the sharp thing inside it. 'You'd be surprised,' he says, talking out of one side of his mouth. 'You need to think of some magic to use,' he adds.

'It's not like that. I can't decide before we get in there. I don't know what I'm dealing with,' I explain.

He sits back on his heels, makes a last twist with his

wrist and the padlock pops open. I look at the bolt cutters in his meaty hand.

'Wouldn't it just have been easier to use those?' I hiss, but he points to a flashing light on the side of the padlock.

'Alarm trigger. If I cut it a siren would go off,' he hisses back, and takes an automatic pistol out of the bag. 'All right. Ready?'

'Stay to the side when you get in. It's an open space, a warehouse. But it should be dark,' I say, remembering dancing and drinking there with Ceri. It feels like a life ago.

He pushes the door open gently and we sneak in. There's no one here; we pace our way carefully to the bar area and Omar checks round and behind it.

'No one here,' he says in a low voice. 'Now where?'

I point to the door behind the bar. 'Try that way.'

He pushes it softly before putting his ear to the crack. He frowns and gestures to me to stand behind him. Then he puts his finger to his lips. 'Sshhh. I can hear something.'

He pushes the door open a little more and leans into the dim light beyond.

I peer past him and strain to hear a low murmur coming from down what looks like a corridor.

'Let's go,' he whispers, checking his pistol again. He holds the door open for me. I shoulder the shotgun and follow him in.

It's a surprisingly long corridor – there's far more

space behind the main bar than I had expected. Doors lead off to the right and left, but only one has light leaking under it into the hallway. We stand outside it against the wall. There are voices, but I can't make them out. Omar looks at me and I shake my head, not sure.

But then someone walks past the inside of the door, and his voice gets louder.

'Turn up the wattage. We have to keep trying at different frequencies.'

The footsteps stop on the other side of the wall, and there's a kind of zapping noise, and a grunt, followed by a thump, like a body falling on to something hard. This is it.

Omar holds up three fingers and counts them down. I watch as the darker skin at his knuckles bends into his brown fist.

Three.

I plant my feet squarely on the floor and settle the viewfinder of the gun to just the right level.

Two.

I whisper a short prayer to the Morrigan, Queen of Battle. *Great Goddess, lend us your strength and speed. Lend us your forbearance. Keen and wail so that our enemies may be filled with fear. Great Crow, be with us.*

One.

I feel the spread of blue-black feathered wings on my back; I feel them span the width of the hall. She is with me, with us.

Omar kisses his fist, his fingers closed inside.

There is a long scream from beyond the door.

Danny.

Omar punches the door open, and it swings back to reveal a makeshift lab. A woman in a lab coat looks up in surprise from a workstation at the back of the room.

I feel my eyes roll back in my head; the Morrigan is taking me over, more intensely than She ever has before.

I see, but through a crow's shiny black eye.

Omar charges in. The door hits Bran in the face, and Omar punches him hard in the stomach. He hits the floor, doubled up in pain.

Roach stands, surprised, on the other side of a stainless-steel table. Danny is strapped to it, his face covered by a metal mask; he is held down by thick leather restraints just like the ones I saw at the lab on the tor. Next to the table and by Roach's hand is a control panel. I know as soon as I see it that I have to get Roach away from it immediately. He's quick though; he grabs the first thing to hand and throws it at Omar, ducking down beside the table as he does so. The scientist cowers at the back of the room, her hands over her head.

The glass measuring jug hits Omar on the forehead and shatters, shards flying everywhere.

But I am the Phantom Queen; I am untroubled by such things.

I feel the rage of a thousand battles fill my chest and open my throat. I feel the ancient Morrigan as Battle Queen rise up inside me, avenging protector of men, women and children. And I feel my own familiar grief fill me and take me over: the tide of grey hopelessness that comes of knowing I will never see Tom again, not in this life, of knowing that I will never get to tell him or show him how much I loved him. The tide fills me up and spills out of my mouth; it spews out into the air, every last thought and word — *you left me, you left me, I loved you. I loved you.* And I am suddenly heartsick and full, as full of pain as I could ever possibly be, my grief magnified by the grief and rage of the Morrigan, even though I let it go, even though I am slowly coming to terms with it. But grief never really lets go its chokehold, and in that minute I feel my own broken heart amplified with Her archive of all the suffering of loss, humanity's unending book of sadness and anger and implacable horror.

The wail fills the room like a wave. My head is thrown back; the screech coming from me is inhuman, animal. It is not me; it comes through me from Her, from the Morrigan.

They all cover their ears: Bran, Roach, Omar, the scientist. But no hands can protect them from this.

All the glass in the room explodes. Vials, measuring jugs, bottles, jars. Clear glass, brown glass, blue glass — it all makes a jumbled mosaic of chaos on the floor.

Cracks appear in the glass screens of the computers around the room and the monitors that are attached to Danny blow out from the inside like black glass bombs, giving up their graphs and jagged lines to the electrically charged atmosphere in the room.

The taps in the deep steel sinks turn on, obeying this call for release; nothing is immune from this pressure. Nothing is deaf to the screech of the Morrigan — flesh, steel, water, glass.

The Morrigan comes to liberate. She comes to make Her enemies quake in fear.

The scream stops, although it feels like it echoes inside me, and I realize that it reverberates eternally within the Goddess: the ledger of atrocity, the unending record of human injustice that grows daily, cataloguing names and places in a continual epitaph. It's something She holds for us and with us; She protects us from it, but makes sure we never forget.

The noise has served its purpose for now. The sudden quiet is just as disturbing as the ear-shattering screech. But She is still with me.

I reach forward and, filled with the immense strength of the Goddess, rip the metal mask from Danny's face. Under it, a mass of wires are attached to his head. I rip those away too. He stares in terror up at me, at Her. I don't know what he is seeing, but I know it isn't just me. I can feel the wings at my back reach out across the room.

I undo the heavy metal fastenings on the leather restraints; I feel like my own hands would falter, but She lends me Her strength and skill. I reach out my hand and pull him into a sitting position.

'Take him,' I say, nodding at Omar, who carries Danny off the table as if he were a small child and settles him on a broad-backed chair, sweeping the broken glass off it with one wide hand. Danny's dog, Gowdie, appears from nowhere – she must have been hiding in the hall and followed us inside, looking for Danny.

Roach grabs my arm. 'You're not taking him anywhere,' he says, pulling himself up from the glass-covered floor.

I shake his arm off. 'Don't touch me,' I say.

My voice is louder and steadier than usual but I can see him fight to resist the command. He is a witch too. He will be harder to subdue.

'By the one and true God Lugh, I command you to surrender His priest to Him,' Roach orders, but his voice shakes. He stoops and his eyes are dull. He might have made it back from Death, but only just, and being that close to Death takes its toll.

'Let us go, Roach, or face the Morrigan.'

'You can't hurt me. The God is with me.' He tries to square up to me, but Lugh is not around him like She is with me. I catch sight of his forearm. His witch-brand has gone, and has been replaced with a scar, perhaps a burn. Did he remove it, or did the God himself take it away?

'I haven't tried yet,' I reply tersely.

The Morrigan feels impatient around me, like an itchy wool cloak. She wants us to leave and take Danny. Roach looks like he's going to reply, but I see Bran behind me reflected in broken glass. I see him get up from the floor slowly holding his side and I turn round. He walks towards me gradually, his hands outstretched. And I have to be careful here. Very careful. Because I still have feelings for him.

And She knows this, like She knows everything about me, because I hear Her in my head, saying, *Come further into me, child. Let me deal with him.*

And so I turn away, inside myself, and go far into Her, into the dark forest of yew trees where it is always winter and snow blankets all the sound. And I take my love with me far away from him. Far away from any of them. And so it is as an observer only that I watch what happens next.

He reaches out for my hand, not knowing I am not really there. She lets him take it, eyeing him beadily from Her crow's eye.

'Demelza. It's so good to see you,' he says, and he leans in for a kiss. He wears a patch over one eye, and he can't stand as straight as he did, but amazingly here he is still. Despite being crushed by stones from the tower on the tor and attacked by crows. Goddess knows what magic Roach has done to keep him here in this world.

She returns his kiss, long and sweet, and even from deep back here in the forest I can feel some of the heat from it. He stands back afterwards, still not knowing that I'm not really me right now, and that makes me sad. That perhaps he never could see me. Never could see who I really was, my deep self.

'We need to talk. There's so much you don't understand,' he says, stroking my arm, Her arm.

'I understand there were bodies buried on the tor. Bodies you put there. People you murdered.' I hear my voice saying the words, me and not-me.

'Every great advancement needs sacrifice.' He continues to stroke my arm, gazing into my eyes. Her eyes.

'Murder is not sacrifice. Sacrifice is a sacred transference of energy, a gift to your goddess. Sacrifice is your faith in Her, giving Her your heart,' She says.

'You always speak so beautifully of your goddess, Melz. Everyone should have what you have – that faith, that connection to summat outside of you.' He smiles, but his eyes stay cold.

'Who were they? The ones you killed?'

He drops my arm and his gaze flickers at Roach.

'Does it matter?' Roach interjects. 'Homeless, lost, whatever. They'd have died anyway, of the cold, disease, hunger. At least we gave them a purpose.'

'It is not for you to decide the life purpose of another human,' She intones. We intone.

They killed them together, Bran and Roach. Experimenting. Doing whatever they were about to do to Danny.

Bran picks up the metal mask. We look at it together, me inside and Her outside. It's a mess of wiring and sharp edges.

'A toy,' She says, taking it.

'A great advancement,' Bran says doggedly, taking it back from Her. 'With this, anyone can have the sight. Anyone can heal. Anyone can be a witch. Anyone can connect to the Goddess, have that richness in their lives, like you. With this the powerless could have power.'

I feel emotion rise in Her, like the air getting thicker before a storm.

'Anyone *can* be a witch,' She replies, putting the stress elsewhere in the sentence. 'With commitment and reverence. With hard work. And giving power back to your people — the poor, the orphans — won't be achieved with a machine.'

His expression clouds for a minute at the mention of orphans. 'But this little invention — this means we can copy the powers of one of you in a matter of hours, and give them to someone else. Like me, for instance.'

'You don't know what power is. Work. Commitment. Balance. Love.'

'But I love you, Demelza. And you have power. And I will too now. Will that make you love me?' He touches my face, and She lets him, holding his gaze levelly. I'm glad I'm inside, away, because hearing him say he loves me is difficult. Because I want to believe him. And I know I shouldn't.

'No,' She says.

Roach, who has been standing watching, holds out his hand. 'Give it to me, Bran. You can see the transfer in action, if you want. Both of you.' He looks at Omar, who is supporting the weight of Danny's slumped body in the chair, a protective arm round Danny's shoulders, watching us carefully. He wipes blood away from a cut on his forehead; it drips on to the white tiled floor.

'Now I can meet you on your terms, Melz. We can both be witches. Together. Think what we could do.

Just think about it for a minute.' Bran takes both of my hands, staring into my eyes in that intense way he has, making me feel like I'm the only person in the world – even though I am far away with the Morrigan in the yew forest. Yews: the trees of death and resurrection.

Omar breaks in. 'That monstrosity, it's designed to do what exactly? Take a witch's power away and give it to someone else?'

'Not take it away, Omar. That would be reductive. There should be more power in the world, not less. It'll replicate their power. This scans the energy field of the witch and records the heightened alpha waves in the aura, the higher brain function, the increased visualization ability.'

'It . . . it can't work,' Danny mutters. 'You can't measure magic. Those things aren't what it is. It's . . . dedication, study, practice. Everyone's different, got different skills. Connects to the Gods differently. It's not something you can dissect in a lab. It's in here.' He holds his hands over his heart.

'I disagree,' Roach says. 'Bran believes in the future. We can liberate the Redworld. We can sell them a new energy source. But to do that, if you won't help us, Bran has to become a witch.'

Deep inside the forest, under the snow-capped trees, I feel my own rage building. How dare they assume that being a witch is something you can switch on in any person in a matter of hours? It makes a mockery of my whole life. Years of study, of prayer, of dedication, of meditation, of attuning to the natural ebb and flow of the world. And I can feel the same rage, amplified, in the Morrigan.

She taps the cold metal of the mask with my finger. 'Show us, then. This work of great magic. Show us.'

Roach stares into my eyes, and I can't tell if he knows or not that it is the Morrigan he is speaking to rather than me.

As he picks up the mask an unusual-feeling energy passes from the Goddess into it. Something of Her. And, deep in my forest, I feel anxious. But She sends calm winds into the trees and says, *Have no fear, child. I am Mistress of Magic above all. He might bend the steel in fire, but I can tear it apart at the atom.*

Bran lies down on the table and Roach gestures to the scientist who is still cowering in the background to come and attach the mask to his face.

Roach fastens the straps. 'As a precaution,' he says, but there is something in his eyes. Just a glimmer. Unease. He suspects something. But he's too close to his goal to stop.

The scientist runs through some initial checks and then hands the control panel to Roach. 'It's ready,' she says, and backs off, staring at me. I doubt she can see the signs of the Morrigan — I'm guessing she doesn't have psychic abilities, so she can't perceive the dream-like shadows of feathers on my body, or the beak on my face. But she heard the wailing, the screeching.

Roach presses a green button. The mask lights up and a whirring noise starts.

'Are you ready?' he asks Bran, and Bran nods. I can feel apprehension coming from him, but a sense of conviction too. He genuinely thinks he's doing the right thing.

I want to come back, I say in the forest.

I will protect you, She says, *but you cannot feel pity for him. He has made his choice.* And just like that I am back in full consciousness. I exchange a glance with Danny and Omar. I don't know if they see the difference in me from a moment before, but a message passes between all of us.

Be ready to run.

Roach presses the red button, and Bran's body convulses.

He lets out a high-pitched scream, not unlike the Morrigan's wail. Then, suddenly, Bran's hair catches fire.

Roach gasps and presses the green button, but it doesn't do anything. The sharp savoury smell of burnt hair fills the room. The scientist unplugs the system from the wall, but it doesn't stop. Gowdie barks in panic.

I push out of the door with Omar and Danny behind us. 'Don't look back,' Omar orders. 'Melz. Run!' And just like that day at the battle I run, leaving a dying boy behind me.

Dying or dead, the Morrigan will help him through the portal to the next world. She takes everyone along the path – good or bad, Greenworld or Redworld. But She protects Her own in this life.

Roach has had his own experience of holy fire. He should know better than anyone.

Magic is real, and you can't tame it with machines.

Chapter Thirty-three

Though one were strong as seven,
    He too with death shall dwell,
Nor wake with wings in heaven,
    Nor weep for pains in hell;
Though one were fair as roses,
    His beauty clouds and closes;
And well though love reposes,
    In the end it is not well.

From 'The Garden of Proserpine'
by Algernon Swinburne

Omar hefts Danny over his shoulder – he can't walk, let alone run – and we jog down the corridor, into the bar and out on to the street, Gowdie following. The sun is only a couple of hours away. Thankfully the street is deserted.

'We're going to have to hurry if we want to make it through the border before it's light. Even with my connections. You need to make some effort at secrecy otherwise the border guards get pissed off. They need an excuse to look the other way,' he puffs. I stride off, but he calls me back. 'No, Melz. We're not going to make it fast enough on foot. Not with Danny like this.' He points down the street at a sand-and-green-coloured military-style vehicle, with an open top. 'That jeep. Help me get Danny in it.'

He beckons me over with his head and we lower Danny into the back seat through its open side. Omar vaults over the driver's-side door and leans over to open the passenger door for me. He whistles for Gowdie who jumps in on my lap; I push her into the back with Danny.

'Don't you need a key?' I look behind us in the mirror and see two soldiers coming round the end of the street. I'm guessing this is theirs.

Omar's eyes flicker to the mirror. 'Nope,' he says, and sticks a screwdriver into a hole under the steering wheel, turning it. The jeep engine roars under us and Omar pulls the steering wheel hard to the right on to the road.

I twist round in my seat as the soldiers start running down the street towards us, shouting.

'Here.' Omar hands me his pistol. It's only then I realize that I lost the shotgun in the lab. 'Shoot if they get too close.'

The jeep revs hard and we swing round the far end of the street and on to the main road. A shot echoes in my right ear, stamping a hole in the side of the vehicle. I fire back, not aiming specifically at them, but as cover.

'Shit,' I mutter as more shots crack into the pre-dawn darkness.

'Should be clear of them in a bit.' Omar swings us round another corner and then fast down a wide road.

Danny's body slumps against the back of my seat; he's unconscious now. Omar catches my eye and half smiles. 'He'll be all right, Melz. He's made of stronger stuff than you give him credit for.'

But I can sense Danny moving away from us, across the astral. His body might be here but he is far away, drifting. I need to pull him back. Omar brought him back from death before and I know he won't give up now. Because he loves Danny. And Mum always taught me that love is the strongest magic there is. I don't believe in love right now, but I have to believe in Omar. And I have to believe in myself.

We drive straight through the border without being stopped. Omar has enough contacts to make our progress fairly smooth. I hide in the footwell of the passenger seat, a blanket over me, and we cover Danny with a tarpaulin in the back.

Omar sings the same song under his breath all the way through the border:

I love the White Rose in its splendour
I love the White Rose in its bloom
I love the White Rose so far as she grows.
It's the rose that reminds me of you.

His husky voice blends with the deep thrum of the jeep's engine in a hypnotic song. I don't realize I've fallen asleep from sheer exhaustion until he pulls the cover off me and daylight floods in.

'We're through,' he says, and smiles down at me.

By the time night comes on the second day we are on Dartmoor, still a good day's walk away from Gidleigh, Danny's home village – further still from Tintagel. We stop by a small coppice of trees on the moor and Omar taps something on the display panel of the jeep.

'Empty. We'll have to walk tomorrow,' Omar says, grunting as he gets out of the driver's seat and stretches. 'We'll stop here tonight. If he can't walk tomorrow I'll have to carry him.'

He carries Danny out of the jeep and lays him on the ground. 'We can't make a fire – the gangs might see. Melz, if you can keep us hidden, we'll be OK.'

I sigh and crawl over to Danny who is flat on his back on the grass. 'OK. Let's see what's going on with you,' I say, and place one hand on his chest and one on his forehead.

The healing starts pulsing out through my hands and into his body. I close my eyes and feel Danny's body, his aura, pulling the energy from me. Flashes of red parade before my eyes like flags; his physical energy is depleted. I feel him filling up slowly, but it's going to take a while.

Omar takes off his jacket and folds it up like a pillow. He nods at me and lies back, resting his head on his backpack. 'Wake me up when you've finished and I'll take the second watch,' he mumbles, and closes his eyes.

I sit there in the dark, the energy spooling through my aura into Danny's from the vast reserves of the universe, watching as the last traces of the dusk fade away from the sky and the stars come out, feeling the Morrigan guard us, Her wings stretched across our camp.

I'm not aware of falling asleep but I know I am, because suddenly I am walking across the moor in an in-between light, towards Scorhill stone circle again. The portal there is open already; its colour is red, though more orangey-red than the hot pink of Glastonbury. The same red as I was channelling into Danny's inert body, the red of blood and fire and flesh. I look up and see the moon, which is also red, reflecting the portal.

There's something wrong but I don't know what it is. I see a figure at the other end of the moor, approaching the circle from the other side. As I get closer I see it's Danny. I wave to get his attention but he doesn't see me. I start running. I don't know why, but a sense of urgency fills me. He starts running too. As I'm running I'm thinking how glad I am that he is alive, that he is conscious and seems to be well.

We meet in the centre of the circle and look down at the grass. There is a crow and a snake fighting in the grass. The crow hops away from the snake, but the snake draws itself up and lashes out at the crow's neck, and as we watch it rams its fangs into the bird's soft feathers. The crow caws loudly, flapping its wings wildly, but the snake won't let go. The light goes out of the crow's eyes, and the snake slithers off on to the moor.

Danny reaches down and picks up the crow gently in both hands, cradling it. He starts to cry.

As I watch, the crow starts to crumble. Its feathers flutter away from its body and make a little pile on the grass, and that pile spirals up, as if in a breeze, and floats into the portal. As it does so, a voice in the wind starts to sing softly:

Queen of the Shadows, take back your priestess,
Take back her soul to the wild and the wind;
Take her to guide the lost and the fallen,
Take her to tread where others have been;
You are the wound, you are the death-crow,
Take her to tread where others will go;
Take her to tread where others have been.

When the last of the feathers have been swallowed by the portal, it closes itself, and we are alone in the circle, the wind whistling between the jagged stones. The song fades away until there is silence again.

'She's dead,' I say, feeling his tears in my own eyes, the ache in my own throat, and the surety in my heart that a witch has passed between the worlds.

I open my eyes and Danny is sitting up, holding my hands, tears streaming down his face. We are under the trees in the coppice; Omar lies sleeping on the grass, and the moon is high above us.

'She's dead,' he says, and I pull him to me, holding him tight, because I can feel his heart breaking. I can feel his disbelief that he will never see his mother again.

Because someone has killed her.

Someone has murdered Zia Prentice.

Chapter Thirty-four

There is pleasure in the pathless woods,
There is rapture on the lonely shore,
There is society where none intrudes,
By the deep Sea, and music in its roar;
I love not Man the less, but Nature more.

From *Childe Harold's Pilgrimage* by Lord Byron

It is a fine summer day when we bury her in the circle, but there is a chill in the village that has everyone on edge. I can't stop shivering.

No one has ever been buried in Scorhill circle before, not to anyone's knowledge, but no one argues with Danny when he says that's what he wants to do. The villagers are mostly kind but distant to both Danny and his young sister Biba; they feel for two kids that have lost their mum, but they're witch kids – they don't quite know how to handle them. And things haven't been

335

happy between witches and non-witches in Gidleigh for quite some time now.

Omar and Danny carry Zia's body in a woven wicker casket to the hole dug in the middle of the stones, and the people of the village stand round the outside. I hold Biba's hand tightly among them, watching. She's about twelve, a small, skinny, intense girl, with completely straight black hair, unlike Danny's black curls, and earnest brown eyes for his cat-green stare. I only met her once and briefly that I remember: last year when she visited Tintagel with Zia. Even so, when Danny and I arrived with Omar, it seemed natural for me to take care of her while they arranged everything, and she's stuck to me like a limpet ever since.

Mum and Saba stand a metre or so away from us, among others from the covensteads – Tressa, Merryn and Rhiannon, witches from Treligga, Port Isaac and Zennor, but they can't all leave their covensteads unprotected, especially after the battle with Roach. Not even to mourn one of the original Five Hands, from when it was Mum, Zia, Roach, Omar and Linda. How times change. Witches are very cautious now, and today isn't going to help. Gowdie has been left at home, howling. She knows.

'I am the end of things. I am the hag on the battlefield. I am the sweet release of death. I will take you to the forever lands,' we all chant as we watch from the sidelines.

I offered to do the ceremony, but Danny refused. He wanted to do it himself, and after he and Omar lay the casket in the grave he calls down the Goddess Brighid, and then the Morrigan, as She is the one that governs death.

Then he sings the lament we heard in our dream, which is different from the usual chants, and I join my voice with his. Our two voices carry the song into the air above the moor like a ribbon fluttering the air, unfurling into the elements.

Queen of the Shadows, take back your priestess,
Take back her soul to the wild and the wind;
Take her to guide the lost and the fallen,
Take her to tread where others have been;
You are the wound, you are the death-crow,
Take her to tread where others will go;
Take her to tread where others have been.

Danny traces the holy symbols over her grave – the triskele, the pentagram, the triple moon, the spear of Lugh – and throws in a handful of earth.

Body to earth, blood to earth,
Back to element, back to birth.
Soul to fire, mind to air,
Love to water, life laid bare.

One by one, others come and throw a handful of earth on Zia's woven coffin. No burial at sea here, like at home, but this is a special burial after all. The village witch. The first one. The first of the founding members of the Greenworld has died. Mum is the next to throw earth after Danny, then Saba, then me. Biba clutches hold of my hand as she throws in her small handful of black earth from the moor; she stares down into the pit, her soft brown eyes dry, her expression blank – shock is all that registers on her small face. I know that the tears will come later. Some other villagers come and pay their respects, but many don't.

Omar is the last to add his large handful of earth to the grave. He kneels down by the edge and we all move away respectfully. I watch as his lips move, but the wind steals his words; perhaps She steals them to blow into Zia's ears, in the next world. But even though I can't hear him we all see his mouth form round the familiar last three words. *I love you.* And as we watch those words detach heavily from Omar's muscular shoulders, from his thick bull's neck, and pull away from his heart, two fat tears running down his weathered black cheeks thick with stubble and hardship. He bows his head and his shoulders heave: once, twice.

Danny goes over to him and puts his hand between Omar's shoulders. I signal to Mum that she should take the villagers away from the circle and leave the family to their grief. She nods, and she and Saba murmur to the crowd, then lead them away, black wool cloaks flowing behind them, silver moon circlets glinting in the summer sun. I turn to follow the last of the surrounding circle, but Biba won't let me go.

'You need to be with your brother,' I say to her, but she just hangs on my hand and says nothing, lip jutting out. I look over at Danny and Omar. 'You want me to stay?' I ask her, and she nods. She has stopped talking. She was in the house when her mum was murdered: stabbed in the heart. But she can't tell us what happened or who did it. I asked Mum about it when she arrived. *Temporary amnesia. She'll remember when she's ready*, she'd said.

'All right, then.' I hunker down and put my arms round her, kneeling on the grass. She doesn't cry, just stands there, thin as a reed in the strange summer chill, but I can sense the hard knot of bilge-coloured grief deep inside her, twisting tighter and tighter, the knot growing harder and harder. It will break, but not now. I hold her tight, thinking of Tom, and we watch the man and the boy stare into the ground.

Excerpt from Demelza Hawthorne's Greenworld Journal

Date – 30 June 2047
Moon phase – waxing, first quarter
Menstruation cycle – menstruating
Sun phase – Cancer
~~Card drawn~~
Dreams –
~~Reflection on the chosen tenet~~

Recording my dream last night.

It is neither sun or moonlight as I stand in the middle of the stone circle. The funeral flowers are gone, and the burial mound is flattened. The circle stands as it did much longer ago: the stones straighter, cleaner, newer. Their natural bluestone glows with an internal luminescence rather than an external light.

A girl walks across the circle to me. She has long red hair plaited in one long braid across her shoulder and blue eyes. Her arms carry the blue-woad tattoos of Brighid, spirals and crescent moons. She is dressed in a blue tartan, which is pinned on one shoulder with a silver moon brooch studded with pieces of raw amber. She holds out her arms to me and I go to her. She embraces me with great love.

I pull away and see that this girl is both the Goddess and a girl like me, but she is a priestess of Brighid not the Morrigan. She smiles at me and walks away.

*

Two weeks later I'm doing the washing up in Zia's kitchen — no one else is fit for housework — when there's a knock on the door. Wiping my hands on my beetroot-pink hemp dress, I answer it. A red-headed girl looks quizzically at me.

'Hello?' I haven't seen her around in the village.

She looks past me into the hall. 'Is Danny here?' she asks.

Her wide cornflower-blue eyes have dark rings round them — she hasn't slept for a while by the look of it. Her eyes come back to me and I'm slightly unsettled, though I can't say why, and I feel a frown forming on my face.

'Yes. But he's not really seeing anyone at the moment. Can I help? I'm a witch, if it's healing or anything herbal you're after,' I answer.

'Oh.' She looks at her feet. 'No, nothing like that. I wanted to see him. To . . . give him my regards, you know. About Zia.' She looks up at me and smiles suddenly: a small, sweet smile I can't help returning.

'You're a witch?' she asks.

'Yes. From Tintagel.'

'I saw you at the funeral, but I assumed you'd gone after that,' she says. She looks uncomfortable. 'I shouldn't have come.'

'I don't remember you from the funeral.' I'm sure I would have.

'I was at the back of the crowd,' she says, looking down.

'Oh.' I look at her again. Then I realize. The red-headed girl from my dream. 'The dream . . .'

341

'I guess with you being a witch, and . . . I guess we were both having dreams about Scorhill. Maybe we just ended up there together.'

'Maybe. I have a lot of vivid dreams. Witches can pick up on strong energies from other people.'

It's unusual to connect astrally that way unless it's with another witch. At home, the Five Hands, the witches of Tintagel, would dream about each other all the time, vivid dreams that are different from the norm.

'I'll tell him you came. He's really not up to seeing anyone,' I repeat.

Last time I looked in on Danny, he was lying on his bed, back to the door, with Gowdie next to him. He hasn't moved, as far as I can tell, for three days, and the dog has only come down for food then gone right back up again. She won't leave him. Danny hasn't eaten anything I've taken up there, and only drunk a little water. He must have got up to pee but I haven't noticed. Maybe he feels like if he gets thinner and thinner, eventually he'll slip away in the wind and be with his mum. Food is life after all – if you want to die, you don't eat.

I know how it feels. I know that feeling of wishing you could just walk into another room where everything was calm and pull the door shut behind you, leaving the world to carry on somewhere else. If you could leave the horror and the hurt behind, pull the blanket over your head and hide away from everything. I felt like that just after Tom died.

Biba comes up the corridor behind me; her eyes are red from crying, but at least she's up and about and eating. She doesn't leave me alone for longer than five minutes, unlike Danny, who doesn't want anyone. I've hugged her to sleep every night. She slips her hand into mine and looks over my shoulder.

'Hi, Biba,' the red-haired girl says, smiling uncertainly, and I feel Biba's grasp on my hand tighten. I look down in surprise at the pressure on my palm.

Biba leans past me and spits at the girl, her little body suddenly rigid as stone.

'Go away. Go AWAY!' she hisses, her voice croaky from silence, and spits again. 'You're not welcome here, Sadie.'

Biba's solemn face is contorted with a sudden rage. I'm startled to hear her speak. I've already grown accustomed to her being silent.

'Sadie?' It sounds familiar.

I look down at Biba. 'What are you—?'

But she doesn't let me finish. 'Linda's daughter. They hate us. Hate magic. Hate witches.'

I remember now. Linda Morgan. The woman that burned Zia's tarot cards; that was why Danny came to us in the first place, to Tintagel. He'd handed them over to Sadie – no doubt in an attempt to impress her – and her mum got hold of them and threw them in the hearth fire. She caused no end of trouble for Zia after that too apparently. I remember the covenstead meeting last Yule when I saw Zia. Pale and drawn, she'd tried not to

343

make it seem so bad, what was happening back in Gidleigh. But we all knew. She was trying to manage a growing tide of resentment, of trouble; dissent was being whispered by Linda to the other villagers. And, as the only witch, she was failing.

'That's not true, Biba, if you'd let me speak, I—'

But before Sadie can finish Biba wrenches her hand free from mine and tackles Sadie to the ground. There's a crack as Sadie's head hits the front step. Biba sits on her chest and starts pounding at her with her fists – ribs, neck, head, anywhere she can reach. Sadie, dazed by the fall, holds her arms over her face but Biba rains slaps and punches down on her still, like an avenging whirlwind.

'Biba! *Biba!* Get off!' I shout, pulling her upright and making her look at me. 'Come on. Look at me. Leave her alone.' She looks back at Sadie, still on the ground, groaning, and snarls – a real feral snarl, like a dog. I guide her chin gently so she looks back at me. 'Come on. What's wrong?'

'I remember. She did it. She was there. With Mum. And Lin— Linda . . .' Biba's eyes widen as if she's seeing it happen again. 'Linda. Came with the knife. Stabbed Mum. My mummy.' Her voice pitches high and she starts sobbing. I hold her to me as a flood of memory engulfs the poor girl. Her grief and shock had blocked it out until now. I can feel it flooding back through her like a spring tide.

'Is this true?' I ask Sadie, and see tears in her eyes.

'No. I mean, yes, I was there, but I was just with Zia

'. . . I didn't do anything. It was Mum. I didn't know she—'

'Shut up!' Biba lets go of my skirt and screams at Sadie. 'SHUT UP! LIAR!'

She pulls away from me and bends down so that she's staring into Sadie's bewildered face. 'Listen to me. If you're not gone by the end of the day, I'm going to come and find you. And I'll lock the doors, and I'll burn down your house with you inside it.'

Sadie sits up painfully. 'Biba. I didn't kill Zia. I came to see if you were both all right,' the girl says, and wipes her bloody mouth with her sleeve. 'I was worried about you. I care about you.'

'You care about me? Why do I not believe that?'

'It wasn't anything to do with me,' Sadie pleads. 'You've got to believe me, Biba.' Tears flush her eyes and she bites her lip, looking away.

'Why should I believe you? Linda's your mum.'

I crouch down and pull Sadie up gently. I don't know what to think – if Biba's right, this girl should be punished, but it's hard to get a sense of who's telling the truth.

'I'd normally suggest you come in and I'd take a look at those cuts, but it's probably not the best idea today,' I say apologetically, and she nods, but her eyes are full of fear, and I don't think it's just fear of Biba. This girl is terrified of something.

'Thanks. It's OK,' she says and turns to go.

'Yeah, go home, bitch!' Biba calls after her.

'Remember what I said! I'm going to burn your house down if you don't leave!'

I shush her, shocked, but she stands there in the doorway, glowering at Sadie like a small beacon of hate, lit and flaming with no sign of going out anytime soon.

'Biba. Come inside!' I pull her hand, and she follows me reproachfully back into the house. I shut the door and look in her eyes.

'You're not serious now, are you? I know you're angry, but this isn't the solution. Threatening to kill that girl.'

'She was in on it. I know she was. They planned it together. They must have. Why else was she here in the first place? They were in the garden. Sadie was there already and Linda just came in and . . .' Her eyes fill with tears again.

'Come on,' I say gently and hold her to me, feeling sobs shake her body. 'I know. I know. It's horrible. We'll find out the truth, I promise.'

'I know the truth!' Biba wails into my shoulder and I hug her tighter, that physical instinct to contain the body of someone in distress, to hold them to you, as if your heartbeat was medicine enough. But nothing is enough for Biba right now. 'She was stabbed to death. Linda Morgan stabbed my mum . . . to . . .'

I hold her, thinking about Tom. How I sat on Danny's bed after it happened and said *It should have been you, it should have been you*, desperate for someone to blame. Knowing, deep in my bones, that it was wrong, that it wasn't his time to go, and that knife through his heart – another knife, another cut, another death – that knife wasn't meant for him.

But Tom did die, and I can't change that. He died defending his village, like so many did. Maybe it wasn't anyone's fault, really. If Tom had been less heroic, if he had been less kind, then maybe he'd still be alive. If he'd thought more about himself in the fight, maybe he'd still be here. But if he had, he wouldn't have been Tom. He wouldn't have been the Tom I loved.

Death can't be beaten. Not with magic, not with bargains, not with pleading. Death is deaf to your pain. Death is the only absolute. The only non-negotiable thing in the universe.

I want to tell Biba all of this, but I can't. I can't say the words yet. Tom's death is a story I repeat over and over to myself. I am a silent audience of one: his smile, the feeling of his body up close when he hugged me, the moments when it was just us alone – all preserved and perfect in my mind. I can't talk about him dying yet and I can't share this with Biba, much as it might help her.

'Look. We'll do what we can to find out what really happened, OK? But with Danny . . . the way he is, it's too soon to have a proper enquiry. He wouldn't be able to cope with it right now.'

I'm in an uncomfortable position in Gidleigh. I came here with Danny and Biba and Omar, and I'm happy to be here and help, but Danny and Biba are housebound. Omar's off in the wilderness, only coming back to rummage in the cupboards and then disappear again like a wolf cut off from the pack. So I can tell when I do go out for food or for a walk to clear my head that the villagers are wondering who I am and what's going on. They're uneasy. Their witch is dead, and there's no formal government.

As bereft as he is, Danny needs to take charge soon, otherwise there'll be trouble. More trouble than there already has been. They won't listen to me. They don't know me. But they know Danny. They'll listen to him.

'OK.' Biba snuffles into my shoulder.

I sigh. She's a sweet kid, but it's hard being a surrogate mother to someone you're only a few years older than – someone you didn't even know until a few days ago. How long is this going to last? I wonder, then feel guilty for thinking it.

I'm a witch, and Danny and Biba need me. Mum taught us that being a witch can bring unexpected events and responsibilities. I suppose this is what she was talking about.

'Come on. Let's have a cup of tea and a biscuit. We can take one up to Danny too. Just promise me you're not going to do anything stupid,' I say, looking imploringly at her, but she refuses to meet my eyes.

'OK,' she says.

'Promise me,' I insist.

'I won't do anything stupid,' she says.

Chapter Thirty-five

Lament for the life cut short,
Lament for vitality waned;
Keen for the spirit taken away,
Cry for the loss of the world.

Suggested lament for the dead (short version),
from *Greenworld Prayers and Songs*

Later, I take a walk out to Scorhill circle. For the first time since we got to Gidleigh Biba has reluctantly agreed to sleep without me, and I've given her a herbal tea that helps relaxation. I looked in on Danny before I left, but he ignored me, his back to the door still. His tea and biscuit were untouched on the bedside table.

Why did Linda do it? I don't think Biba was lying. She saw the stabbing. But it's less clear what Sadie's involvement was. And I don't know her, but coming to the house of your victim, if she did help – the horror in her eyes, the shock – I don't think she would have done that if she'd wanted Zia dead. I think about it as I walk along. All I really know about Linda is that her and Roach were together once, and Sadie is their daughter. How must that have been, to have Roach for a father? Or for Linda, to have loved him once, and watch him change from the young man she fell for into a thug, selfish, violent and lost in bitterness? How old was Sadie when he left to lead the gangs? Does she have any of his natural ability for magic?

I breathe in the summer air as I walk past the boundary in the waning sunlight. The evening warmth settles on my bare shoulders like a cloak. When you live most of your life in varying layers of wool, it's good to cast them off and feel the sun on your skin. There's a slight prickle of evening cool, but it's worth it to go without a wrap. I'm wearing a simple strappy shift dress of Zia's, not having brought any clothes with me. I twist my hair into a knot as I walk along, letting the sun pierce the witch-brand at the base of my neck. I'm watchful for signs of the gangs, but I've also constructed an energy bubble around myself. For anyone not used to perceiving it, their eyes will glide over me as if I am a feature of the landscape: a mossy boulder, a tree, long summer grasses swaying in the breeze.

The fact that I dreamed of Sadie inside Scorhill stone circle must mean something. Does it mean she has power? But she spent all her life in Gidleigh, with Zia, and never became a witch. Surely if she had potential, Zia would have seen and nurtured it?

Unless Linda went out of her way to forbid it. She burned Zia's tarot cards after all. That was why Danny came to us originally, to get a new set, only Mum says that wasn't really why he came. His instincts took him to Tintagel when he knew it was time for him to become a witch. Because Zia hadn't trained him. She let us do that.

The circle is on the common outside the main part of the village. The stones stab the sky like jagged teeth. As I come to the edge of it, my eyes are immediately drawn to the mound in the centre: Zia's grave, marked with a new stone that Omar has engraved.

GONE BUT NEVER LOST: PRIESTESS, WITCH,
MOTHER, LOVED ONE.
ZIA PRENTICE, 2000–2047. TAKEN BACK
BY THE GODS.

I trace my fingers over the letters. *Taken back by the Gods.* She was of the Morrigan, like me. The wind stirs my fringe and traces its hand across my neck. I look around me and up to the clouds drifting across the evening sun. The day is ending; the sun is setting in the west, the direction of the dead.

I've come to talk to her, if she is still here.

I walk round the circle, calling the elements and the four quarters to be with me: spirits of the north, south, east and west; ancestors; the spirits of the circle; the guardians of the moor. I feel them stirring and welcoming me. The land of the Greenworld – Devon and Cornwall – is deep with magic, and imbued with ancient powers and spirits that demand to be honoured.

I've brought offerings to the spirits of the circle and the land here: a little wine and honey, a few cakes, some flowers from Zia's garden. I lay them round her grave.

Next, I take a deep breath and open the portal.

I'm not sure what to expect. I don't know what happens to a portal when a witch is buried in the ground around it — portals aren't of the earth, but they're attached to the earth around them in the same way that a stream runs through its stony bed. I saw what happened to the portal at Glastonbury Tor when bodies were buried on it.

But this must be different, because the circle doesn't feel odd or blocked or wrong, and when I open the portal I know it's OK. It opens easily, the symbols as easy to push as a well-oiled grass cutter. This one glows red, just like in my dream, and I feel my body radiate to it. Red for the base chakra, for physical vitality and strength, for blood and mothers.

I was intending to enter the portal to see if I could find Zia, in case she hadn't passed on fully yet, but I don't even get that far. As soon as it's open I see her in front of me, smiling, dressed in a silver gown with a pair of shadowy black crow wings, surrounded by the red light.

She holds out her hand. 'Demelza. Priestess of the Morrigan. I knew you would come,' she says, her voice low and musical like I remember, burring with Cornish softness.

I take her hand cautiously and find it still makes an impression on mine, not as a flesh one would, but a definite pressure.

'Are you all right?' I ask, a stupid question, and she laughs.

'Quite all right, thanks. Just dead. There are worse things.'

I smile. 'You knew I'd come?'

'Yes. How are my children?'

'They're grieving for you.'

'Did you tell them you were coming?'

'No. Should I have?'

'No.'

There's a silence.

'Biba misses you,' I say, remembering her small hand in mine.

'I know. I miss her. My baby.'

'She's very angry. She says Linda killed you. Did she? You were stabbed.'

'I know. I was there.'

'Did she do it?'

She smiles sadly. 'That girl has the gift. Sadie. She has the brand. Did you know that?'

'Sadie has a witch-brand?'

'Yes. The triple moon, same as Lowenna. It only just happened for her.'

'Goddess be praised. How? Only initiated witches can be branded,' I say, my hands straying to my own tattoo, thinking *that makes three*. The same three brands

353

repeated. Roach, Zia, my mother. Danny, me, Sadie. Why?

'She initiated herself, here in the circle. A month ago.'

'Initiated herself? Is that even possible?'

'Perfectly possible, it seems.'

'And she told you . . . . afterwards?'

'She came to see me. She'd long been nagging me to train her, and I'd always turned her away. I knew she had the gift but I was angry with her and Linda. They'd been stirring up trouble in the village, turning people against me. Linda had burned my cards and she made sure everyone knew about it. People started avoiding the full moon ritual, then the festivals. And then some of my equipment went missing. I knew it was them. Probably it was Sadie, trying to learn on her own. I should have helped her earlier.'

'But you did help her?'

'Yes. When I saw the brand. I couldn't ignore that. Brighid had claimed her.'

'So . . . what? You trained her?'

'A little. I didn't have a lot of time, as it turned out.' She looks up at the moon, rising in the darkening sky.

'So . . . it was Linda?'

'Yes,' she says. 'We were very close, once. But she came to hate me, because of what I represented. Magic. The Greenworld. All the things that she thought turned Roach from her lover to who he is now. But she still stayed here, because her and Sadie weren't safe from him anywhere else. And even here he could threaten her. She was afraid of what he would do with Sadie. Make her a witch too, like him. Tread that dark path.'

'So . . . he told her to do it? Why?'

'No. I don't think so. He was blackmailing her, certainly. He'd told her that if she made trouble for me in the village, enough so that the people didn't support me any more, he'd leave her and Sadie alone forever. He knew if I lost the support of the village he could take the portal from me. I'm only the witch here if people believe in me, and only the witch protects the portal. I'd need the village to fight for it if he decided to attack with the gangs. He learned that at Tintagel.'

'Now you've gone the village isn't protected at all any more,' I say, confirming what I've been worrying about.

'No, it isn't. But he doesn't want the village. Roach doesn't care about the people; he just wants the power. This plan he's got for an energy source or what have you. But that wasn't why she did it.'

'What was it, then?'

'Linda came to the house looking for Sadie. She'd been getting more and more suspicious about where she was disappearing to at night. She interrupted Sadie and I holding a circle in my garden. She barged in. She didn't even stop. Just picked up the athame and stabbed me with it.'

'Oh Goddess. No!' In the circle. A profaning of a sacred space as well as a murder. I feel dizzy, and it's not just the open portal's influence.

355

'I know. I don't think she planned to do it. I think . . . I don't know. It was the last straw for her. Thinking that Sadie would become like her father. That's how she sees it, I think. That I was inducting Sadie to become something evil and twisted.'

'What should I do?'

'Protect Sadie. She's a chosen one, like you.'

'Chosen for what?'

'It will become clear.'

'Biba thinks she was in on it. Danny probably does too, or he will. They won't welcome her with open arms.'

'Maybe not. But you have a responsibility to make sure Sadie doesn't end up like Roach. She has his raw talent. But she has to have training.'

'You want me to train her?'

'No. Lowenna will. You have to get her there, Demelza. You have to make Danny and Biba let her go. And you have to persuade Lowenna to take her. For the sake of the Greenworld. Maybe for more. Your whole future is at stake. Danny's too.'

I look up at the moon. 'I don't know if that's possible.'

'Anything is possible.' Zia smiles, but doubt unfolds like a black flower in my heart. I don't believe that. Some things *are* impossible. Bringing Tom back from the dead was impossible. Expecting revenge to make my heart full again was impossible. Being with Bran was impossible.

'But why? Why is she so important?' I ask.

'Because she's the last branded one. You, Danny, Sadie, you have a destiny together.'

'What are we supposed to do?'

The light of the portal dims.

'I can't stay much longer,' Zia sighs, and her outline blurs. 'I know more now I'm on this side. Before, I just thought that you were all following in our footsteps. Powerful witches for the new era of the Greenworld.' She smiles wryly.

'Aren't we?'

'Yes, you are. But it's not just that. We were three, and we had the first task: to set up the Greenworld. And we did that. We sacrificed everything to do it. Only Roach left, so it was unbalanced. There was no High Priest for the mysteries, no figurehead for the male energy. He's right about that. I know that now. So we couldn't complete the next task. That's why you have the brands. Why you have the power.'

'For the next task?'

'Yes. I don't know the details. She will let you know in Her own time. But remember the Morrigan is a goddess that protects the land, Demelza. She has sovereign rule of it; She *is* it, and this task . . . it's something to do with the portals. The energy. You have to defend them from being exploited. Not just here. All over the world. But it's something else too.' She screws up her face. 'I can't quite get a sense of it. Balance, between all three of you. Male and female, god and goddess, but not just that. It's like you're a key to something. You have to do something with the portals that hasn't been done before. There are ways that the Greenworld can help the Redworld, but it means change. Lots of change for everyone, and the people won't all like it.' She meets my eyes. 'The witches won't all like it, Demelza. Do you understand what I'm saying? I don't know exactly what this change is, or what you have to do, but I know that the three of you . . . you might be on your own. At least for a while.'

She lets go of my hands. I'd forgotten she was holding them; the light pressure disappears and she turns away. 'I have to go.'

'Should I bring Danny and Biba back here to see you?' I call out to her, and she stops, her back to me.

'No,' she says in a choked voice. 'I can only come back once.'

'Why? Danny would be able to see you, if not Biba. He has the ability.'

'Because death is death, Demelza. I was allowed to stay outside death, in between, this once to talk to you, and only you. Danny . . . Danny must make his own way. Without me.'

'And Biba?'

Even with her back to me, I feel Zia's grief slide through the evening air, reaching out its greedy hands for my heart.

'Biba too. They have to mourn and let me go. Their grief . . . They need to follow where their grief will lead. Even to the darkest places. They won't do that by calling me back.'

'But if they could speak to you one last time . . .' I plead, thinking of Biba's small warm body cuddling against mine under the patched quilt at night. So desperate for comfort, so full of sadness.

'No!' she shouts, turning to face me, and though she is fading – being drawn back into the portal – I can see the tears on her cheeks and the despair in her eyes. 'No,' she repeats softly. 'It has to be this way. I can speak to you this one time as a priestess of the Morrigan, but there are laws that cannot be broken. You know that. Danny and Biba have to look death in the eye just like everyone has to. They have to grieve. They have to face the wall and beat their fists on it until they accept the silence.'

'What about Omar? He's grieving for you too. He's like a lost dog. He doesn't know what to do with himself.'

She smiles sadly. 'I've always been in his dreams, and he in mine. He'll dream of me for as long as he needs to,' she says, walking into the portal.

That might be forever, I think. I've seen Omar's eyes when he looked at her across the room. I've heard his voice caress her name. I remember him singing about the white rose.

'Then it's forever,' she calls back, her voice light on the wind. 'I always knew that. He knows it. We were lucky to have that kind of love for as long as we did.'

The portal closes, and I bow my head. She is gone, gone to cross the river.

'Bless you, sister. Bless you, Daughter of the Crow. The birds fly you home,' I whisper, and walk round the circle, touching each stone, acknowledging their power and feeling their presence, their guardianship of this place. I know they mourn her: their priestess. A good warden, a good witch. Yet the circle remains, and will stand tall for many more thousands of years, with or without another caretaker, with or without anyone hearing their song, feeling their power.

I close the portal and lie down in the middle of the circle, keeping watch in the circle as, unseen, Zia passes over where no one else can go. I sing the lament for the dead quietly – 'Lament for the life cut short, lament for vitality waned; keen for the spirit taken away, cry for the loss of the world' – the simple dirge weaving round the stones and through the long grass.

I imagine her rowing across the River of Death in the barge with the Morrigan and say a silent goodbye to my fellow priestess. I listen to the song of the stones and feel the steady thrum of energy through the earth until the stars fade into the dawn. I let the earth fill me with the energy I need for the days ahead and feel thankful for it. The rising sun casts shadows from the stones on to me like sentinels, like guardians.

Excerpt from Demelza Hawthorne's Greenworld Journal

Date – 16 July 2047
Moon phase – waning in Taurus
Menstruation cycle – preparing for ovulation
Sun phase – Cancer
Card drawn – The Moon
Dreams – Skye and Bali holding hands and jumping off Tintagel Head into the sea. I see their faces before they jump. They don't want to, but something is making them. As I watch, Skye holds out her hand and catches mine. She pulls me under, and seaweed wraps round the three of us, tangling us together. I feel the salt water filling my lungs. I wake choking.
Chosen tenet – *For what we do for good or for ill, shall be returned to us threefold.*

I don't know who I am any more. I don't know who I love or what love is. Sometimes my body craves Bran. Craves the way he looked at me that night at the Twelve Apostles: his goddess, Melz the Red Witch. And when we made love I felt Her wings cover us. We took our pleasure in the shadow of Her dark heart. Bran saw me, but everything he showed me in the mirror of myself was an illusion. Yet I still can't get him out of my head.

Tom was everything Saba had and I couldn't. I loved Tom. I loved him so much that I killed Bali and Skye in revenge for his death. They jumped off Tintagel Head. They didn't fall. I know that. Saba, Mum, Ennor – they all know I murdered those kids. Would I take it back? Maybe. But some days I'd just as happily follow them down under the waves and never come back up.

Reflection on the chosen tenet – Has the curse been fully returned to me yet? I don't know. I don't know if I want to know.

Chapter Thirty-six

> It is unusual, but possible, that the Gods will speak
> to you in your dreams. Dreams dictated by the
> divine can take many forms. Write down as much
> as you can remember, as always, and seek the advice
> of a covenstead witch.
>
> From *A Guide to Reflective Greenworld Journalling*
> (schools edition)

I wake up confused, sitting on the edge of my bed. I rub
my eyes and look at the sky: barely dawn. The light is
murky and thin, and the birds are just stirring. My eyes
burn, and I rub them again, then catch sight of my hand.
It's black, covered in charcoal dust. I stand up unsteadily
and a pad of paper thuds on to the wood floor in
Zia's bedroom, where I'm sleeping. I kneel down and
pick it up, and a charcoal cylinder rolls towards my bare
foot.

What on earth? I pick up the top sheet and angle it

towards the window. It's covered with strange diagrams, letters, numbers and shapes. I flick through the pad. There are three pages of it altogether: an unrecognizable series of symbols scrawled across the pulpy paper. I must have done this in my sleep, but I don't remember at all.

I light an almost-burnt-down candle and peer at the pages. As well as the diagrams, there are some words. They're in my handwriting, but I don't understand what they mean. There's an odd drawing of a spiral, and underneath that numbers, formulae.

I have channelled the Morrigan and heard Her speak through me. She can inhabit me when She needs to, like when we rescued Danny, like at the Twelve Apostles. And I have used art before to cast spells – and curses – but that is always something I make and put out into the world. But this has never happened before. I can't even tell, looking at the symbols, whether this is a communication from Her, or something else. A receiving, a channelling of information, translated into the smudgy charcoal on the page. I don't know what to think of it, and I have no one to talk to about it either. Danny will be no help right now.

I get up, knowing I won't go back to sleep. I wash the black dust from my hands in the cold yellowish spring water that sputters from the bathroom taps and watch the grey water spiral away down the drain after I pull the plug out. I wipe the black smudges from my face and change into a faded blue cotton dress of Zia's.

Later, Danny comes down the stairs, dressed and looking like he's combed his hair for once. I look up in surprise from kneading bread dough, the odd diagrams and formulae from the paper upstairs flashing in front of my eyes. Kneading bread is a meditation, but it hasn't given me any solution to what on earth those symbols are so far. I try to remember what it was that Ennor showed me in his school notebook, but I can't see the specifics in my mind. It's possible that I absorbed it unconsciously and wrote it out in my sleep – but why?

'You look better,' I say, surprised, looking him over and continuing to work the dough. Biba likes my bread and there's not much else she'll eat at the moment.

'Thanks,' he says, looking in the cupboard. 'I feel a bit better. I slept.'

'Great.' I watch him without appearing to. He's even thinner than usual, gaunt, with deep-etched black shadows round his startling green eyes. His long black curly hair – too beautiful for a boy – is lank, and his warm brown skin looks dry and tired. He might have slept, but not enough.

'Anything to eat?' he mumbles, pulling the doors of all the cabinets open and rummaging around, but there's precious little.

'Not much. Apples. The bread'll be done in a couple of hours. It needs to rise.'

I consider telling him about the automatic drawing, but decide against it. He's too frail, too unfocused. He wouldn't take it in.

'Thanks,' he says, and takes a small apple from a bowl on the counter.

The kitchen's nothing like Mum's. Hers is carved wood with stained glass and funny little figurines everywhere, goddesses and animals. Shelves and shelves of different coloured glass jars and potions and bottles, some with spidery writing in Latin. Plants that bask in the moonlight through the big windows, easy chairs and cats.

Zia's kitchen is much smaller – the whole house is small. Somewhat dirty too; stuff everywhere. The units have stains and some of the doors are hanging off; nothing matches, like it's all been thrown together in a hurry. But she was the sole witch in charge of the village and the portal. I suppose she didn't have time to make everything pretty.

'So are you up to going out? We need more food.'

He sighs and sits down on a rickety stool. 'I suppose. I don't really want to.'

'I know. But you have to sometime.'

He raises his eyebrows together and nods.

'Biba should go too,' I continue. 'She needs to see her friends, see ordinary village life going on as normal. She needs a distraction. Did she tell you about . . .?' I leave the sentence unfinished but his expression darkens. Biba must have sneaked up and told him last night.

'Yeah.'

'It wasn't Sadie's fault. Biba thinks it was, but it really wasn't.'

'How do you know? You weren't there. Sadie lies.'

'I . . . I talked to your mum. In spirit, last night.'

He looks up at me, dazed. 'What?'

'I spoke to her. In the circle at Scorhill.'

'She's still here?' He looks alarmed and hopeful all at once. 'Can I see her?' He gets up, pushing the stool back. 'Come on, let's go!'

I place my palm on his chest to stop him. 'No . . . she's passed now. She was allowed to stay back. To talk to me, as priestess of the Morrigan. Just once.'

His shoulders slump; he pulls away from my touch. 'She's gone? Really, really gone?'

'Yes. I'm sorry.'

He looks at his hands and sits back down again. My heart breaks for him.

He takes in a ragged breath. 'And?'

'And what?'

'What did she tell you, then?'

'She and Sadie were in the middle of a ritual. In the garden.' I point out at the apple trees and the straggly uncut grass. 'Linda discovered them. She lost it. Attacked your mum with the athame.' I don't say *in the heart* – it's too raw, too unnecessary. He knows, anyway.

'Linda. Biba's right, then.'

'Yes. But not about Sadie. She didn't have anything to do with it.'

'I don't believe that. And what do you mean, they were in the middle of a ritual?'

'Sadie has the witch-brand. The triple moon. Same as Mum.'

'What? No, she doesn't. I'd have seen it.'

'It's very recent. She's been trying to train herself; your mum kept refusing. But then she did some kind of self-initiation ceremony at Scorhill and got the brand. Zia couldn't refuse, then.'

He frowns. 'Self-initiation? Can you even do that?'

'Apparently. I haven't heard of anyone else doing it, but . . .'

'I don't believe it.'

'Well, it's true. Your mum told me.'

He stares furiously at a kitchen cupboard, away from me, and I know he's trying not to cry. 'She came to you and not me. Or Biba.'

'I know. I'm sorry.'

'This is really shitty. All of it,' he says, and his voice cracks. He kicks the cupboard door by his knees.

'I know.'

I don't know what else to say, so say nothing.

He half smiles sadly. 'I thought I loved her once: Sadie.' He says it to his folded hands.

I place my floury hand on top of his. 'I know,' I say quietly.

'I never thought it would come to this,' he says, looking up at me. 'All those years. I was in Linda's house maybe every week. Seeing Sadie. Reading her books. I . . .'

'I know.'

It's all I can say but it's a lie. I have no idea how he must feel.

'She's a witch, then? How does that work with you and me and the rest of the Hands?'

'I don't know,' I lie. I don't want to tell him what Zia has asked me to do, because it means leaving him.

There's another silence.

'You've been really great with her. Biba. Thanks. I . . . I would never have thought . . .'

'What?'

'No, just that . . . I wouldn't ever have thought that we'd be here together, like this. That you'd be looking after us both. You don't have to.'

'I know,' I say, going back to kneading the dough. 'But I'm a witch. We look after each other. That means Sadie too, now.'

'I can't think about that right now,' he snaps. He bites into the apple, frowns, then pulls out a little worm and carries on eating. 'I don't see Saba coming to help,' he adds.

'She came to the funeral,' I offer weakly, but we both know she and Mum left as soon as they could afterwards. Like they didn't want to be tainted by the aura of a dead witch, like they might catch something. In Saba's case, also, I could tell that Danny looked like too much hard work. Like he wasn't really in the right headspace to do too much Saba-worship right now, and that's all she really wanted him for.

I know her. Danny was different. Striking. That brown skin, those big green eyes so like a cat's, piercing but often irreverent. She wanted to say she'd had someone different. The only boy witch. Just because Danny always irritated me doesn't mean I couldn't see what Saba saw in him. I could. I'm not made of iron.

He shrugs. 'She's not here now though, is she?'

'No.' I pound the bread a bit harder.

'No,' he repeats and looks at me. 'You're different since you came back from the Redworld. I feel like I'm seeing you in a whole new way.'

I look away, embarrassed, then make myself meet his eyes. I wanted to be seen after all. I came back as Melz the Red Witch. Is that what Danny's seeing?

'Different how?'

I want to hear him say it. Beautiful. Powerful. Desirable. That's how I want everyone to see me.

But he squints at me in the golden light coming through the grimy kitchen windows and smiles. 'Dunno. Softer. Nicer. More colour in your cheeks. Bit more human, I s'pose.'

'Oh,' I say. It isn't the image of the all-powerful, desirable goddess I want to be. What I created for myself, out there beyond the border. What Bran helped me to be. *He is part of your journey*, the Morrigan said. Maybe part of that journey – part of the experience of knowing Bran – was letting me see myself in a different way. As someone who is powerful. Someone who can inspire others. It didn't happen the way he made me believe it could, but I'll still never be the same again. And maybe that's a good thing.

He gazes out at the garden for a moment, away from

me. 'There's so much out there that needs doing. Weeding. I need to pick the strawberries. Mum made jam every year. There's loads of windfalls to preserve. And the potatoes, carrots, onions, greens. It all needs doing.'

I wipe my hands on my apron and go over to him, looking out of the window too. 'You'll do it. Just take one thing at a time,' I reply quietly.

'I don't know if I can. There's loads of things I don't know how to do.'

'You'll do it,' I repeat.

'I don't know how. I never paid attention,' he says, and reaches into his pocket. 'And here's another thing I don't know how to do. I wrote to Dad, to let him know Mum . . . Mum—' he can't say 'died' yet; it's too hard a word – 'passed over. But I don't know where to send it. Or how.'

I take the letter gently from his open hand, the lightness of the thick handmade paper at odds with the heavy words inside. Words I know it must have hurt so terribly to write. I think about having to do the same thing.

What would I write in such a missive? To someone I saw last before I even knew I was a witch? That whole part of my identity is missing for him. He must think of Saba and I as four-year-old twins in pinafores and pigtails. I don't know what I'd write if Mum had just died. *If you're still alive, I'm writing to let you know that the woman you once loved is dead. The children you left are now women. Witches. I learned how to shoot your gun, Daddy. I learned to look after myself. You don't need to do anything, but I thought you should know.*

'I'll give it to Omar. He'll know,' I say, and he nods.

'OK. Thanks.'

I squeeze his hand awkwardly. 'You'll learn. All of it. Zia learned. You will too.'

'But I'm not as good as her,' he says, a tear rolling down his cheek, and I know we're not talking about gardening any more. 'She was in charge, you know? Powerful. People listened to her. She understood them. I'm . . . I'm just a kid. How am I supposed to take charge? How am I going to make them listen to me?'

He chokes back his tears, biting his lip, but it's an effort.

'It'll be all right. It's your destiny to be in charge here. You know that deep down,' I say.

He looks at me strangely. 'I didn't think you were all that keen on me being a witch in the first place. Didn't think you were that keen on me altogether really,' he says.

'I'm not *keen* on you at all. Don't be big-headed.'

'That's not what I meant, Melz.'

'I know,' I say. I feel a smile unfurling slowly round my lips. It's nice to smile. 'I s'pose you're not all bad.'

'Bad enough,' he says glumly. His eyes flicker uncertainly over my shoulder for a second. He clears his throat. 'Look, there's something I should tell you. About

Tom. The battle. The curse you set on Bali and Skye. I—'

I interrupt him. 'Don't start thinking about all of that now, Danny. It won't help anything. It's all in the past.'

I don't want to think about Tom. It's too hard, too painful. There's too much death, and it's hard enough waking up every day in the house of a dead witch, wearing her clothes and making bread in her kitchen, without us rehashing what happened in Tintagel.

'But I need to tell you. It was my fault. Tom dying.'

I look away from him and down at the dough. 'Danny. Please. I really can't talk about Tom now. Please. I know you think it was your fault that the battle happened – Roach wanting your power and everything – but that's not your fault. You're not responsible for Roach. OK?' I sigh and look at the wall. 'I know I said it should have been you that died. That night in my room. But I was upset, OK? I didn't mean it.'

'But . . .' He looks desperately sad then, and tears well up in his eyes again. 'I'm sorry, Melz. I'm just so sorry.' Tears roll down his cheeks.

'Oh Goddess. You don't need to be sorry.'

I reach out for his hand, but I accidentally pull him towards me, half slipping off the stool.

'Sorry, I . . .' I start to stumble over words and feel the blush rising up my cheek. Reflexively I go to kiss him on the cheek fraternally, like I would Ennor, like I have to Biba to quell her tears. And then . . . I don't know what happens, but he turns his head and we kiss — a real kiss: deep and sudden and desperate.

Daniel Prentice, of all people. The boy I hated. The boy that disrespected magic and witches, who only got initiated because he fancied my sister, the boy I thought should have died instead of Tom. But, as it happens, he's a boy who isn't that different to me. An outsider. A witch. A branded one.

I pull away in surprise as soon as I realize what we're doing and he looks away in embarrassment.

'Oh. I'm sorry,' he says.

He looks mortified. Was kissing me really that bad?

I stiffen my posture. 'Oh. No, no that's fine, don't worry,' I say, and, without knowing what to do, I go back to my bread. I stare down into it like it's the most fascinating thing in the Greenworld.

I'm going to pretend that kiss never happened. It was just the grief. He's unhappy. We're both confused and sad. I was here. That's all.

I don't want anything to happen with Danny. He's my friend now, and I'm too messed up over Tom and Bran to have another boy in my life. And . . . whatever it is, that fire, that buzzing in your hands and feet, the adrenalin that hits your heart when you like someone, really like them — it's not there with him. Not for me.

I can feel him looking at me for a long time but I refuse to catch his eye.

'Errr . . . OK. Yes. I need to gather the village. I need to talk to them. I . . . I'd really appreciate it if you were there,' he says; he sounds unsure and nervous, so I look up and give him a tight smile. I'll be distantly friendly and helpful. I won't embarrass him any more than necessary.

'Of course,' I say smoothly, wiping my hands on a cloth and putting a cleaner one over the top of the dough. It'll rise while we're out. 'I'm happy to be of service. That's what witches do.'

'Look, Melz, I . . .'

He's trying to make me feel better but it's too embarrassing. There's no point in mentioning it. I just want it to go away. I shake my head. 'There's no need. OK? Let's just forget about it. It was nothing.'

He looks sad again, and I feel bad for making a bad time worse for him.

'Go and get Biba. I'll get my cardigan, then we'll go,' I say.

He smiles a small not-very-Danny smile and walks out, and just for a minute, while his back is to me, I feel the kiss on my mouth again and trace it with my fingertip. It just feels wrong. Like kissing your brother.

Chapter Thirty-seven

> The first warp-spasm seized Cúchulain, and made
> him into a monstrous thing, hideous and shapeless,
> unheard of. His shanks and his joints, every knuckle
> and angle and organ from head to foot, shook like a
> tree in the flood or a reed in the stream.
>
> From *The Táin*

The villagers gather slowly on the village green, and a huge red-and-white striped maypole spears the grass in an appropriately phallic way. I imagine Beltane, when all the villagers here probably danced round it, wrapping their long ribbons, symbolizing union, and wonder if that kind of life will ever be for me – carefree, sensual, someone wanting me, me wanting them. Love. Passion. Or whether I'll always be on the edge looking in, the one people fear, the severe, forbidding priestess. I was Melz the Red Witch for a while, but that didn't make me any happier. Now I don't know who I am any more.

I receive a lot of sideways looks. The villagers don't really know who I am, what I'm about. They know I'm a witch, but they're suspicious. I watch Danny. I don't know what he's going to do or say.

It takes about an hour for everyone to turn up — when you want to organize an impromptu village meeting it depends on people going around and knocking on each other's doors — usually everything's timetabled into an annual schedule so people know what's on when. So when people get called away from their work and families all of a sudden, it's unusual and they're unsettled. I think enviously of Demi's phone in the Redworld — so easy to reach people, to talk to anyone at any time.

Danny stands up and waits for quiet.

'Thanks to you all for coming today. I'm sorry it's been a couple of weeks since—' I see him start to choke up, but he gets a handle on it — 'since . . . Mum passed away. I know I should have come to talk to you all sooner. I just couldn't, that's all. Not until now. I didn't have the strength.'

I look around at the mothers and fathers, the elders and the children that have grown up here. All of these people have known Danny for a long time. I look for their reaction to him admitting weakness. It's something Mum would never do; she'd see it as dangerous. But the faces here soften when they see the emotion in Danny. They understand.

'So, first of all, I want to tell you that I'm going to

take over as witch here. But I'm younger than Mum, and not as experienced, so you're going to have to bear with me.'

There's a kind of general murmur. Is that it? I wonder. It seems a bit informal. But I haven't witnessed a new witch taking over before. I don't really know what the procedure is.

'Who's that with you?' someone shouts out. They mean me.

Danny turns round. 'This is Demelza Hawthorne. She's one of the Five Hands, the witches in Tintagel. She helped train me and she rescued me, with Omar's help, in the Redworld. We all owe Demelza a debt of thanks.'

I look around, but the empathy that was there for Danny doesn't extend to me. I'm an outsider. They're suspicious. There's a bit of muttering. I don't catch all of it but I recognize that they don't trust me, because I'm not from round here.

I exchange looks with Danny.

'All right, well, you can thank her later I suppose. She's staying with us a bit longer, I think? I hope?' He raises his eyebrows at me. I nod noncommittally.

A grey-haired man stands up; he's stocky, with a belly and wide shoulders. Spade-like hands.

'Danny, it's a bloody shame what 'appened to your mum. Great woman, she was. Great witch. She looked after us really well, din't she?' he says. His West Country accent is as thick as I've ever heard. He turns to the others who are sitting cross-legged around him, or on chairs if they aren't as limber any more. There's lots of nodding and 'Aye, she was that' and 'Good woman'.

'Still,' he says, 'you're right, she was more experienced in running a village. So, in view of how there's a lot of work needs to be done, an' you might need some help, we 'ere decided that we'd form a committee. Help you out, like. You can still be the witch. Do the magic 'n' all that. We'd just do the rest.'

I look quickly at Danny. This is unheard of. They're taking advantage of his grief and his age to – what, launch some kind of coup to take over the village? It's hard to know how effective Linda's whisperings have been, how many of these people have been talked into hating witches, or at least distrusting them? I can see what they're thinking: the gangs made war on Tintagel. How's this kid going to protect us? They're thinking maybe witches aren't the way forward. Maybe they've had their go at things, by Brighid, and now it's time for something different. And Zia dying suddenly – being murdered – well, that's quite convenient really. From a certain point of view.

'Ummm . . . No. I don't think so,' Danny says. 'You can't just change the constitution like that. The witch is in charge of the village, and the witch reports to the other covensteads. That's how it works.'

'Well, with all respect, Danny, that might be 'ow it used to work until your mum passed, but we've all talked about it, and—'

'You've all talked about it? You held a village meeting? Without me?'

'Yeah. You weren't up for it we din't think. We decided we wanted to try it a bit different 'ere, now that things are changing outside. The gangs. The Redworld. The war, 'n' all that. You understand, don't you?'

'No. No, I don't! You can't do this!' Danny shouts.

He's losing control and that won't do him any good. He's not in the right frame of mind for this and they know that.

'If you reject the rulership of the witch, the matter will be referred to the covensteads,' I say, as calmly and clearly as I can. 'You can elect another witch, but a witch has to be in charge of the village.'

'Or what, love?' The stocky man points at me. 'You going to curse us all, are you?'

There's an unsteady laugh from the crowd. I glare at them.

'Don't joke about it,' I say, warning in my voice.

'I'm not, my lover,' he says, meeting my eyes, and there's a murmur of agreement from the crowd. 'Danny's too young to be in charge here. Fair enough, Zia was a grown woman; she knew her stuff, she looked after us. But now . . .'

'Now?'

'Now there's 'undreds of armed gang members out there. We know what 'appened in Tintagel. We know 'ow many people died. Seems like the witches can't protect us any more. So maybe we protect ourselves.

380

Or, even, maybe we make a deal with the gangs so they leave us alone. They wanted some energy 'ole or something, I 'eard. Well, as far as I'm concerned, they can bloody 'ave it. If it means my kids are safe. It means nothing to us. It's a witch thing—' he looks around him, at the crowd, then back at me – 'an' we're not witches.'

'You don't understand. This *hole* – the portal – it's vital we maintain control of it. For everyone's sake,' I say, knowing that this is a difficult sell. Because we've always kept the portals a secret, so why should the villagers rally to save them? Nobody cares about something they don't know is there, far less understand and value. It's the same everywhere. Why bother to stop polluting, fracking, drilling, when you don't know what those things are damaging? When you don't understand the thing that keeps life and death separate, in their respective realms? This is why keeping the portals a secret is no longer viable. Secrets are the bars on a cage you build around yourself.

'What you're proposing is breaking the Greenworld constitution. Witch rule is what you all signed up to; it's what separates us from the gangs and the Redworld. If you've got a problem with it, talk to Lowenna Hawthorne in Tintagel,' I add trying to make my voice authoritative.

'Yeah. Well, I imagine there's a lot we don't understand, my lover, being so dim and everythin', us country people. But 'ere's what we do understand. We know that we don't want to be ruled by a seventeen-year-old kid that's always been more interested in drinkin' in the woods and chasin' girls instead of protecting us. That's what we know. So, you two are welcome to stay. And Biba, someone'll take care of 'er, a' course. But you're not in charge any more,' he finishes, pointing at Danny.

'You can't do this!' Danny shouts. 'Melz! Do something! Show them the portal!' he says. 'Bloody hell, I'll show you all the portal. Maybe that'll make you see you can't give it away. It would be the end of us if you did, don't you understand? The end of the Greenworld. Of everything!'

I look at the crowd, but their minds are made up. I could show them ten dancing elephants and they wouldn't be impressed. They've had enough of magic. Even though magic, ultimately, was the thing that protected Tintagel. If they've heard about the battle, then they've heard about Danny making the tarot figures come alive as warriors, but they're not thinking about that. Maybe they don't believe it happened. Magic in Gidleigh died at the same moment Zia did.

Danny looks at me, desperation in his eyes. 'Melz! Tell them!'

'What he says is true. If you let Roach in here, or if you do a deal with him, you're going to come off the worse. Sooner or later,' I say, but they ignore me.

'But what about Mum?' Biba shouts suddenly. A small sharp voice in the village green. 'She was murdered. She deserves justice.'

There has never been a murder in the Greenworld. Not an internal one: a Greenworld citizen killing another Greenworld citizen. Some have been killed by the gangs, but those were outsiders. Wrongdoers. This is unprecedented. I look across at the man who's been the spokesperson for them so far; he looks uncomfortable.

'Yeah, well, that's the first thing on the sheet for the new committee to discuss. Of course we can't let your mum's death go uninvestigated. But—'

'Her murder. She was stabbed,' Biba interjects.

'Well, now, that's for the committee to decide,' he says.

'No, it's not,' Danny spits. 'I know it was Linda Morgan. She killed Mum. Biba saw it happen. So it's up to us to punish her. Up to me.'

Two older women step forward. 'We can't let you do that, Danny,' one says, not unkindly.

'You don't have the right to kill another Greenworlder. That's not in the covenstead constitution, by Brighid,' the other one says. 'Only outside threats, if absolutely necessary. You know that.'

'Oh. You're going to quote the Greenworld constitution back at me now, are you? D'you know how hypocritical that is?' he roars. 'I don't care. I'm doing it and you can't stop me,' he says, fire in his eyes. 'No witch is going to disagree with me either.'

'Maybe,' says the first woman – older than Zia, grandmotherly. 'But we've told you that we aren't accepting witch rule any more, Danny. So if you continue along this road, well . . .' She looks down at her leather boots.

'What?' he fires back, and I feel the energy coming off him. Tight, compressed anger. Different to the swirling hopelessness of grief. For a second I feel pleased for him. Anger feels better. It gives you purpose.

'We'll have to restrain you. We must have a fair trial, and we'll decide a punishment if one is to be given. Not you. You're hardly impartial.' She reaches out for his hand kindly, but he snatches it away. She looks sad. Perhaps she taught him at school or led the community singalongs.

'You can't stop me,' he says, his eyes darting to me.

No, don't do anything stupid to these people, I think. Be sensible. If you hurt them now, you'll lose them forever.

But he can't hear me, or won't.

Two burly-looking men appear just behind him, one at each shoulder.

'Come on, Dan. Don't do anything stupid now,' one says, and lays a steady hand on Danny's arm. 'Come on. Let's go home, shall we?'

Danny looks down at the hand on his arm. 'Where is she? Linda? You're hiding her. From me. Where is she? I know you know.' His voice is steady, but I can feel the fire under his words.

'Let's just go home, shall we?' the man repeats, and tries to steer Danny away from the crowd.

Danny pulls his arm away. 'Leave me alone,' he says

in a low voice that nevertheless carries across the village green. Everyone stops talking.

The other man smiles at Danny ingratiatingly. Our dads' age. Sandy-haired, a little balding. Slight paunch. Maybe this is what they look like now, our dads. If they're still alive.

'It's all OK, Dan. Everything's fine. Let's just go back to yours, OK? Have a drink and a chat. See what we can sort out,' he says, and places his hand in the space between Danny's shoulder blades. He gives Danny a small but definite push. 'Let's go.'

'No. It's not OK. Everything . . . is not . . . FINE!' Danny screams, and pushes the paunchy man away with surprising strength. He stumbles and reaches out to steady himself on a young woman standing nearby, who is watching us warily.

The two men lunge at Danny; in the same second, I shout out to him. 'Danny! No!'

But it's too late.

There's a kind of crackle in the air like electricity, and I see Danny's lips move, though I don't hear what he says.

The crowd parts as if the psychic wave that we sent through the gangs in the battle for Tintagel has surged a second time. As the villagers step instinctively away from the energy Danny has flung out from himself, a path opens, and Sadie and Linda stand at the end of it. Sadie's eyes are dull and she's pale, exhausted. She wears the look of penitence.

She meets my eyes briefly with recognition, but stares at Danny. And I can feel the power streaming out of him as he looks her and then Linda full in the face, like an ocean of hate. But it's unfocused.

Sadie holds up her hands as if to protect herself from his gaze, his palpable bad energy.

Danny doesn't know that it's my job to get her to Tintagel. He'll think I'm betraying him. Him and Biba. But I'm not. I'm obeying Zia's orders as my fellow priestess of the Morrigan. Nothing good comes of resisting the will of the Morrigan. I ignored Her when I set the curse on Bali and Skye; they're dead because I refused to listen to Her. This time I *will* obey Her. I'll take Sadie to Tintagel to be trained.

'If you won't allow me the decency of a fair trial, then you give me no choice than to do it here and now,' Danny cries, piercing the unnatural silence that has settled over the crowd, as if we are covered in a blanket of black feathers. He points at Sadie. 'Stand aside, Sadie,' he orders, and she cowers, as if whipped by an invisible lasso. He advances on Linda, who is half wary, half defiant.

'Leave me alone, Daniel. I've known you since you were a baby. You can't intimidate me with your magic. Roach is Sadie's dad, remember? I've seen much worse than you.'

'Shut up, bitch.' His voice is flat and controlled. Only I know he cried for Zia this morning. That boy has been pushed aside for the moment.

386

Despair leaks out of every pore in Sadie's skin. The dark rings under her eyes are deeper and her clothes look slept in and unwashed. I remember what it was like, the first few weeks after getting your brand. Everything's heightened. Your power, but your perception too. Danny had it, though he didn't realize at the time. It was partly how he managed to pull that stunt with all the tarot cards – making them come alive in battle and defeat the gangs. His considerable natural talent was amplified.

He and Sadie have both had the shitty end of the stick as far as training is concerned. What's supposed to happen is that it's all very gradual. Gentle yoga and meditation only for a few weeks, and, over time, more complicated tasks. Astral travel, protection spheres, journeying in vision, prophecy. The psychic protection of the village.

But Danny – well, for him, it was crazy. We went straight into battle right after he got his brand. And Roach too – he left the original Five Hands, disillusioned, soon after getting his. Swept up in a maelstrom of his own power and grandiose emotions and visions, that's what I think. And Sadie – for Sadie it's the worst of us all. A few weeks after getting her brand and finally being accepted as a witch by Zia, Linda killed her mentor, leaving her alone with no guide at the most vulnerable time in a witch's life.

I don't know how she must feel. Because Linda is her mum, her blood, her only parent – the same as all of us whose dads aren't around. But Zia – Zia was her connection to her true self. Zia was her high priestess, her path to true self-discovery.

My heart goes out to her and Danny. Neither of them can see a way out of the hell they're in.

Danny circles Linda. The crowd are temporarily confused; they stand watching dumbly. Then I realize Danny's sent out some kind of hush, a dampening energy, which is, for the moment, keeping them from intervening.

'You don't understand, Danny. I . . .' she whispers, her tone softer – maybe she realizes he can harm her after all. But he doesn't want to hear it.

'Damn right I don't understand! You murdered her, my mum. HOW COULD YOU?' The last part he screams, returning to the start of the circle he traced out. The force of his scream shatters all the windows of the houses facing on to the village green. The impact breaks the hush and the villagers panic, running to their houses, running away from us. He lets them go.

He crouches down at the edge of the circle – I can see it energetically, the power pulsing a bruised purple in the air around Linda, caressing her lasciviously with blunt fingers, cutting through the grass in a rough gash. He bows his head and puts his palms on the grass, then stands up, widening his arms until they are above his head, straining at the sky. Linda cowers, but is unable to move. I rush to Sadie and pull her away.

The purple-brown light covers Linda like a bubble;

it's brackish and dirty, not the light of healing or love. This is pure hate energy, heavy and strong, pulled here through the ether from anywhere there is hate, greed and negativity. It's like he's calling it here, knitting it into his own grief, and casting it in a sticky net over Linda.

I run towards him, but he pushes me away.

'Leave me alone, Melz.' His voice isn't his; it's as if he has been taken over by something else. The longer he lets this rough, heavy energy work through him, the more he will change. It will take him over. You can't channel hatred and not have it touch you, change you, cloud your vision too. I know that.

He turns back to her. 'Murderer. *Murderer.* I'll sentence you if they won't. I call upon every dark spirit in the astral realm to possess you. May you be tortured and judged for what you've done. You took her. My mother! My mum . . .' He sobs.

I can see it forming around Linda, getting more definite: what despair and grief and hate would look like if it had a body – a gaping mouth, grasping hands. I remember the energy of the curse when I burned my locket: black, crawling, malevolent, ignorant.

'Leave her alone, Danny!' I scream, but he ignores me and circles Linda, sobbing and watching the shadow take her over. She crumples to the ground. Some remaining villagers stand in clumps, watching. 'Help me, by Brighid!' I scream at them, but they stay well back and refuse to meet my eye.

'Leave her alone, Danny,' I call, holding Sadie's hand. She's shaking and cold; I don't want her to get any closer to Danny than she is. In the state he's in, he could do anything. And I have to protect her. He looks at me, breaking his gaze from Linda, who he is still circling, keeping the dark energy inside the circle focused on her. Tears are streaming down his cheeks. 'You have to let her go,' I say as calmly as I can, but he shakes his head.

'I can't, Melz. She killed Mum.' His voice trembles.

'I know. But this isn't the answer.'

Mentally I pull a dark cloak round myself and shut all my energy centres down. It means the darkness can't get me.

'Protect yourself,' I whisper to Sadie, hoping that she knows how.

If nobody is going to help me, I need my goddess.

I call out to the Morrigan, trying to make my voice as loud and commanding as I can. 'Help me, Morrigan, Phantom Queen, Warrior. I need your strength. I need your courage. Help me against the darkness, O Goddess. Help me.' And I also call to Brighid, patron goddess of the Greenworld, and Sadie's deity. 'Blessed Brighid, Light of Truth, bring your cleansing fire; help us. In the name of the Five Hands!'

Almost as soon as I say their names I feel a rush of power in me and all around. It's like the beating of vast wings behind me, then I feel the Morrigan step forward, then Brighid.

The Morrigan is in Her garb as Warrior, and Her

silver armour is embossed with skulls and crow heads. She holds a shield and a long silver sword, and Her red hair is knotted in elaborate braids. Brighid's hair dances like flames and She wears the blue tartan robes, the same as in my dream. But they are not alone. Another figure is there too: tall, bright, muscular, holding a long spear.

It's Lugh, Danny's god, the third in the Greenworld trinity. I have only ever seen Him a couple of times, but I know who He is, and I watch as He strides into the circle.

Danny's eyes widen as he sees them all. They are the scales and he is the raw heart waiting for judgement.

The Morrigan cleaves the light bubble with Her sword and erases the blood-like gash in the ground with Her red leather boots. I feel the bad magic explode out of the circle towards us and instinctively I pull Sadie to the ground and cover her with my body. The silver light of cleansing streams from the Morrigan's hands, Her heart, the whole centre of Her, and flashes across the village green in a series of lightning strikes. I know the villagers see those, because they look up at the sky, pointing in confusion. She pushes the dark energy Danny called in away, back into nature for it to be breathed in and out by the earth and made clean.

Brighid embraces Linda, and Her touch cleanses the dark energy from her. But, still, Linda lies inert on the ground.

'My son. My son. Come to me.' I hear Lugh's deep rumble and look up to see Him holding out His hands to

Danny. His golden light is blinding, like the midsummer sun, and I can feel His vitality passing through the air to me.

'I'm not anyone's son. Not now,' Danny spits back petulantly. Lugh reaches out for Danny's heart, as if to purify it, but Danny turns away. Lugh takes him by the shoulders and shakes him.

'Accept healing, my son. Accept your mother's death. Accept this is your path, the oath of the witch. You must not harm. You must not!' He booms, but Danny shakes his head.

'No. I can't. This isn't my path. This is too hard. If I can't use my power for justice, what use is it?'

'This is not justice. You are here to heal, not harm,' Lugh thunders back. Danny is mad to argue with Him. 'You have many gifts, Daniel Prentice. Don't waste them.' Lugh towers over us now, a beacon of light, but light can be harsh, and I sense His spear glittering in the golden light refracting across the green. 'Hear my warning. You are my priest. You have much work to do for me. You cannot allow yourself to be tainted by hate and resentment.'

'I don't care. I don't want to be a witch. I don't want to be anyone. Anything. I want to die,' Danny cries, and my heart breaks for him, even though he might have killed Linda. Because I know, right now, he means it. His heart has been eaten, bitten clean away.

'Then you dishonour me and yourself,' Lugh says. 'Let me help heal your heart.' He holds out a huge arm to Danny, but Danny recoils.

'No. I don't want it.'

'As you wish,' Lugh says, and bows His head. He turns away and walks away from us, into the trees, growing fainter as He walks.

The Morrigan glares at Danny; I can feel Her displeasure at his actions, but She turns to me.

'Protect your fellow priestess,' She orders, sheathing Her sword. She leans in and touches me on the forehead. 'My strength is always with you, my warrior. I will be near if you need me.'

'Thank you, Great Morrigan,' I breathe, bowing my head.

Brighid stands next to the Morrigan, concern furrowing Her brow.

'Thank you, crow priestess,' She says to me. 'You must care for Sadie. She is very important for your future. For everyone's future, and for mine most of all.' She smiles kindly, and I feel Her healing energy around us both, suddenly as warm and comforting as being a small child in a mother's arms.

'I will, Great Brighid. Blessed Be.'

Both goddesses nod, and fade away, returning to their realms of pure energy, leaving me with Sadie in my arms and Danny at my feet.

I look back over my shoulder and shout at the crowd. 'Help! Someone. Please. I need help over here!' I call, and thankfully a burly man and a couple of the older women tread over carefully, as if the ground might still be enchanted and swallow them up.

I put my hand on Sadie's arm protectively. 'I'll look after Sadie. You take Linda,' I say to them.

Danny opens his eyes and looks at me blankly. They're his eyes again; it's Danny that looks at me and not a half-wild demon.

'Melz. Help me,' he says pleadingly, as the villagers yank him to his feet and hold him firmly by the wrists. I want to tell them to stop, tell them that I'll take him home with me, but he has to make amends here.

'You could have killed Linda just now. You have to stay here and take the consequences, Danny.'

'But she killed my mum; she killed a head witch!' He tries to pull his hands free, but the villagers hold him tight.

'I know,' I say, helping Sadie up. Poor Sadie – scared, guilty and full of an untrained raw power. Huge reserves that she doesn't realize herself.

Just like Danny. And just like me.

My eyes follow the line of the crowd to Biba, standing alone at the edge of the onlookers; her eyes are wide and full of grief and shock. My heart tugs. Biba. The crows caw from the trees. I have to leave her.

'I thought you were my friend. I thought you understood,' he says, and my heart turns in on itself.

'I am. I really am your friend, Danny. But you can't kill her. You won't.'

'Why do you care so much? You don't even know her.'

'She's a human being,' I plead with him. 'You can't hurt her. That's not what being a witch is.'

394

I see Biba in the crowd, watching, and try to catch her eye, but she looks at the ground and shakes her head.

Danny tries to pull away from the villagers again but they stand firm. He goes limp. 'Don't leave, Melz. Don't leave me,' he begs.

'I have to.'

'Then you're like all of them. Betrayer!' he shouts, and I feel Sadie's hand grip mine in fear.

The villagers encircle Danny. He tries to pull away from them again. 'Leave me alone!'

'You can't be trusted. We're locking you up till this gets sorted.' The same middle-aged man grabs Danny roughly. 'I won't tell you again.'

'Take your hands off me!' Danny twists away, but there are too many of them. He lashes out and catches one of the women; his fist smacks into her face, the crack of it echoing across the village green. He tries to apologize. 'Oh – Dawn – I'm sorry, I . . .'

There is a moment of silence as the woman holds a hand up to her face. When she takes it away, it's covered in blood.

'You little bastard. You wouldn't bloody listen, would you? That's it!'

One of the men, heavier than Danny, pushes him to the ground and kicks him. 'Don't you dare touch my wife! Witch! I've had enough of witches!' He kicks Danny again.

'Leave him alone! By Brighid I order you to . . .' I

run at the group of villagers but they surround Danny and push me away. There are too many of them.

'Get out of here! Witches aren't welcome here any more. Go while you still can,' an older man snarls at me and Sadie.

'But you can't . . .'

'Go. We don't want you here!' he shouts. There's a kind of unhealthy fervour in his eyes I don't like; the mood has turned quickly.

I pull Sadie away. 'Come on. We have to go. Now,' I say.

'But – Danny, they're hurting him . . .' she says, looking up at me, eyes wide.

'No. We have to go,' my voice repeats, echoing in my ears. 'We have to go now.'

Biba's screams echo in my heart all the way back to Tintagel: *Danny. Danny. Danny. Don't hurt him, please don't hurt him.*

Chapter Thirty-eight

Brighid, Morrigan, Powers of the Earth,
Magic of the waters and the secret of rebirth,
Elemental fire and water,
Air and earth, we are your daughters.
Brighid, Morrigan, Powers of the Earth,
Magic of the waters and the secret of rebirth,
Streams and rivers and springs into the sea,
In my blood your blessing, and my body Blessed Be.

From *Greenworld Prayers and Songs*

I knock heavily on Mum's door and listen to the echo reverberate down the empty street. Tintagel's a lot quieter than it used to be. Less bustling. Less people. So many died in the battle.

'Isn't this your house? Don't you have a key?' Sadie asks tiredly. I look at her, at her pale skin, drawn and grey under the eyes, at her pronounced cheekbones made sharper by hunger.

'No,' I lie. I left once and came back unwelcome; twice is really pushing it. I don't have the energy or the inclination to take her through the intricacies of why letting myself in and calling *Mum, I'm home!* cheerily up the stairs doesn't feel right any more. We stand and wait for someone to come, exhausted.

I knock again, but the house seems still, and I can sense that no one's home. Only it doesn't feel like home any more.

But we need rest. It's taken nearly two days for us to get here. I walk back up the path. 'Come on. We'll go somewhere else,' I say, thinking of Maya. She'll look after us.

But as we walk wearily up the high street, a swell of noise rolls towards us like a wave, getting louder and louder. Voices, raised voices. Lots of them.

Sadie looks quizzically at me and I shrug. It's not a festival. Maybe a village meeting. We turn the corner towards the village hall, but we can't even get near it because of the queues of people streaming out on to the street: a long, uneven, shaky line of maybe a hundred people, none of whom I've ever seen before. And I grew up here. I know everyone.

'Come on,' I say, and we push through the queue. Thin children hold on to their parents' legs and old men sit on the pavement, too tired to get up. These people are not from the Greenworld. Their clothes aren't handmade, not vegetable-dyed cotton or wool. And they're not all white; some are brown like Danny or black like Omar. There are other faces, other features, I've never seen here before. But I know where I have seen them.

'Who are they?' Sadie holds on to my arm to stay close as we push through. There are some indignant cries and frowns, but not much. Like us, these people are too tired to argue.

'Redworld refugees,' I murmur back to her, stepping over a girl about our age who is hugging her screaming baby hopelessly, pressing an empty plastic bottle tinged with milk to its lips.

I pull Sadie through the crammed doorway and we come into the village hall, which is also packed full of people. It's sweltering hot and I start to feel dizzy. Not having slept or eaten for a couple of days doesn't really help either. I see Saba and we push towards her.

I shout to get her attention and she looks up, surprised.

'Melz! You're back. Good timing. Here, take these and give them out.' She points to rows of earthenware cups filled with water on the table behind her. 'Get people's names too. Pin a circle on them when you've done it and tell them to go back outside.' She hands me a notebook and a pen and ink, and a handful of green paper circles cut crudely out of thick handmade paper. Then she looks back at the person in front of her, a greying woman wearing what I recognize as a sweatshirt and jeans.

'What's going on?' I raise my voice to get above the hubbub in the hall. 'Where did they all come from?'

'The Redworld.' Saba pins a green circle to the woman's shirt and writes down her name in her notebook. I watch her careful handwriting, her fingers making the childish cursives. She hands the woman a cup of water and takes it back after she drains it immediately. 'If you go back outside and sit down in the shade, someone will come and help you. We've got food on its way,' she tells the woman briskly, who nods and starts to push her way back through the crowd.

'I guessed that. I mean, how come so many all at once?' I shout back as a bearded black man carrying a little girl on his shoulders and holding one by the hand steps forward. Saba hands him a cup, and one to the little girl standing, who gulps it thirstily.

'Can my other daughter have one? She's burning up,' the man says, and Saba frowns, about to say no, I can tell, so I reach behind her and hand it to him. 'Thanks,' he says, and squats so that she can climb off his shoulders, only she's not very steady and tumbles on to the hard wooden floor. 'Oh God,' the dad says, and picks her up, hugging her to him.

'There isn't enough for everyone as it is,' Saba mutters to me, watching the father comfort his little girl, while the other daughter looks on blankly, holding her empty cup.

'Goddess, Saba. Don't be such a bitch. She's a kid.'

'We haven't got enough food, enough water or enough places for them all to sleep. Try standing here for hours dealing with these people and then come and tell me I'm a bitch,' she spits back. 'Where've you been anyway? Back seeing your boyfriend? Nice of you to turn up.'

I flinch, but don't respond. 'Where's Mum? I need to speak to her,' I demand, and Saba points to the opposite corner of the room where Mum is doing the same as her – handing out water, pinning circles on people.

'Over there,' Saba says. She looks for a brief second at Sadie, who is standing behind me. I feel Sadie's hand slip into mine and it reminds me of Biba.

'She with you?'

'She doesn't need a pin,' I say.

'Is she staying?'

'I guess so. But I need to see Mum. It's complicated.'

'If she's new, and she wants to stay, I have to put her in the book. What's your name?' she asks Sadie, and Sadie looks questioningly at me. I pull her away, but the crowd doesn't let me through. They're surging forward, desperate to get at the water. I feel a shove in the small of my back.

'You pushed in. We've been waiting for hours. I'm about to pass out here, so get your feckin' water and move on.'

I look round at a girl about my age. Her hair is tucked into a cotton cap and her clothes are splotched with mud, but I know the sneer in her voice.

'Demi?'

Surprise flickers across her features for a moment,

401

and in that half a moment I read her decision to act like she and I have always been friends.

'Melz! Thank God!' She gives me a huge hug that I don't return.

'What are you doing here?' I ask. I don't smile. I feel Sadie's eyes on my back.

'I . . . I had to leave.'

'Why?'

'Bran . . . Bran's gone. No one knows where. Things are . . . bad. The looting . . . Our flat was trashed. They broke through the security gate.' She's afraid. Fear brought her here, just like it brought all of them. Not even the thought that we might be terrorists or religious extremists, stopped them.

'What about Ceri and Catie?'

'I don't know. There was a riot. I got out,' she says, and looks away, evasive. 'Without Bran no one's in control of Glastonbury. The proles—' she lowers her voice, looking around warily at the people surrounding her, and leans in towards me – 'the . . . poor, they're attacking us. Taking food, clothes, stuff from our houses. I couldn't stay there,' she whispers. 'I'm hoping your mother will train me. I'm a witch already. I belong here.' She smiles ingratiatingly at me, but I stare at her until she looks away.

'You're not a witch. You never were. You don't belong here any more than I belonged in the Redworld, Demi,' I hiss at her. 'Don't expect any special treatment. You'll get none. You're not special. You'll get treated exactly the same as everyone else.'

I take hold of her collar roughly. She pulls away, but holding her gaze I pin a green circle to her coat and hand her a cup of water. I lean in and whisper in her ear. 'There aren't any armoured vans here. There's nothing to protect you against them now. So if I hear about you doing anything other than helping these people, anything other than being really bloody exemplary, I'll tell them who you are and where you're from. I'll tell them that you stepped over the bare feet of their starving children to buy yourself a new handbag, Demi. I'll tell them that you threw away more food in a day than they had to eat in a week. Get me?'

I turn round, dismissing her.

'Someone you know?' Saba asks, looking past me at Demi, but I shake my head.

'No one important.'

Saba frowns at me, but people are pushing and shoving and the babble is bouncing off the stone walls of the old village hall.

'Aren't you the popular one today? All these new Redworld friends.'

'Shut up, Saba,' I snap.

'What's her name, then?' she repeats, looking at Sadie suspiciously. 'I have to put it in the book.'

'Why are you so bothered? I told you, she's with me.'

'Mum said I have to write everyone's names down. That's what I'm doing,' Saba replies.

'You're the least bureaucratic person I've ever known. Why a stickler for rules now?'

'Why are you being so mysterious? Just tell me her name. I don't care who she is.'

'It's all right, Melz. I'm Sadie Morgan,' Sadie says, breaking into our argument, and Saba looks at her clothes. Tatty but recognizably Greenworld.

'You're not from the Redworld,' Saba says.

'No. Gidleigh,' Sadie says, taking a cup of water and gulping it down.

'Gidleigh?'

'Yeah.'

'So you know Danny Prentice?'

'You could say that,' Sadie replies sullenly.

'Sadie Morgan,' Saba repeats, and writes it down, her eyes never leaving Sadie's.

I pull Sadie away from the queue and head towards Mum. We have to wait in line for a bit and I manage to deal with a few of the refugees, taking their names and pinning green circles to them.

Eventually I get through to Mum, who is sweating profusely; damp circles show under the sleeves of her faded yellow sundress.

'Demelza! You're back! Oh, I'm so pleased to see you!' she cries, and hugs me – a warmer welcome than I expected. 'I was so worried about you. Are you all right?'

I disentangle myself. 'I'm OK. But I brought someone back with me, from Gidleigh. This is Sadie.'

Mum knows who Sadie is.

'Sadie Morgan,' she says, looking at Sadie's ragged

hair and the circles under her eyes. 'And to what do we owe the pleasure?'

Sadie looks at me.

'It's complicated,' I say.

'Is it?' Mum looks at me like she doubts it.

'Show her your brand,' I say, and Sadie blushes. It's all so new to her.

'Here?' she says, looking around.

'Her brand?' Mum stares at Sadie and leans in to me. 'A *witch-brand*?'

I nod.

'Is this true?' Mum demands, and Sadie pulls down the neck of her shirt so that Mum can see the triple moon that traces its blue outline into her white, white skin over her heart. The same as Mum. Same symbol, same place. Just like my triskele, at the base of my neck, was the same as Zia's. Just like Danny's brand is on his arm, the same as Roach.

Mum forgets where she is and leans in, staring at the brand, at Sadie's chest.

'Hey, what's going on? What's the hold-up?' someone calls out.

'Oh Goddess. Blessed Brighid. The triple moon,' Mum breathes, floored. She wasn't expecting this, especially not on Sadie, Roach's daughter. Not today. Maybe not ever. Her hand traces her own brand. 'When did this happen?'

'A couple of months ago. I initiated myself in Scorhill circle,' Sadie says, buttoning up her shirt again.

'Initiated *yourself*?' Mum looks at me. 'Demelza. Take over here. I need . . . I need to talk to Sadie. Alone.' She shoves another notebook and a box of pins at me.

'Mum, I . . .'

'You'll be fine. Just take their names and give them a circle. Food's on its way,' she says over her shoulder, then she takes Sadie's hand and propels her out of the hall. And just like that I'm alone, faced with the hot, hungry, exhausted refugees. I watch Sadie's back retreating through the crowd and feel a pang of jealousy. I look across and see Saba watching them too. Her eyes meet mine. She doesn't smile.

Chapter Thirty-nine

> Three to bind, to open, to see,
> The power in them as within thee,
> From life to death and death to life,
> You bring the moon, and she, the knife,
> He brings the sun and the song, the key –
> The power in them as within thee.

It takes us all day to sort out the Redworlders, and as we sit down finally to dinner at home we know there are still days and days of graft ahead of us, getting places for the people to stay, food for them to eat. We've managed to get some villagers to take people in if they have room, but there are lots left that are staying in tents tonight out on the village green and wherever we can fit them. We know some villagers have room, but they don't want to take refugees in.

'And I can't say I blame them,' Mum says, ladling out vegetable soup into bowls and passing them round.

There's me, Saba, Sadie, Merryn, Rhiannon and Beryan round the table. The Hands are reunited, with Merryn's new partner, but without Danny – and with Sadie.

'There's a lot of anti-Redworld feeling. I'm not going to start making them take them in if they don't want to,' Mum adds.

'I'm not sure we should take them in at all,' Saba says. 'It's up to them if they don't want to stay in the Redworld any more, but they should join the gangs in that case. They're only here because they can't get food at home. They thought we were criminals or worse before their food ran out. Now they want some of the Greenworld. They're not here for ideological reasons.'

I take a piece of bread from a plate in the middle of the table, marvelling at Saba's lack of compassion.

'They're hungry and desperate, by Brighid. Ideology's for full stomachs,' I say. 'You'd do the same if you knew you could get food for your children here. I think people should have to take them in. You shouldn't leave it up to the villagers, Mum. You're in charge,' I say, thinking about Gidleigh's villagers and how they turned on Danny. The Greenworld doesn't like outsiders. 'We're supposed to be a caring society. It's our job to enforce that.'

I look round the table but nobody meets my eyes.

'We're feeding and housing them for now, Melz. I'd say that was caring enough,' Mum snaps. 'Who knows how many more we can expect? I mean, there's only so many we can take.'

'Then the other villages have to take their share,' I say. 'Times are changing, like it or not. We can't stay as this closed-off community any more.'

'Why are they coming though?' Sadie asks me shyly. 'What's changed in the Redworld?' I think of Bran immediately and my heart clenches when I see his face in my mind. His broken body. His hair, burning. He must be dead.

'I don't know,' I lie. 'The riots were getting out of control when I left.'

Sadie reaches for my hand, and I look up. Her face has that same look as when we met – a kind of raw open intensity I don't know what to make of. I pull my hand away.

'It's been getting worse and worse there. The poverty. Rich getting richer, poor getting poorer. They were just about coping for a long while. I suppose it got bad enough that they'd risk coming here. Still, it's just one thing after another. First Roach attacking us, then Melz disappearing, Zia dying, now this. At least you're back though,' Mum says, and sighs. 'How's Danny? I haven't had time to check in with him and see how he's getting on. How's he coping without Zia?'

Maybe it's Zia dying that's making her be this nice to me. But I know she's still angry: about the curse, about me leaving, about me and Bran – Saba will have told her, I know.

'He's not doing too well,' I say, and tell them everything. How Danny tried to take over as witch and the villagers refused. How they've decided to rule themselves and negotiate with the gangs. And how I had to leave him and bring Sadie here.

'By Brighid!' Beryan spills her soup down her top. 'That's terrible! What happened to him?' Her fingers reach immediately for the little purse that hangs round her neck, a healing bag containing feathers and stones.

'I don't know. They beat him. I tried to stop them but I had to get Sadie away. I didn't think we were safe there. As witches. As outsiders.'

'Couldn't you have used magic?' she demands, and I don't know how to explain it to her. That it wouldn't have been the right thing to do.

'They don't want magic. They . . . they don't want it any more,' I say weakly. 'It all happened so quickly.'

'We can help him, even from here,' Mum says. 'They can't honestly think that they can take over with some kind of committee. What do they know about running a village? Nothing. They have to have a witch. I'll go over there myself and sort it out if I have to.'

'Danny doesn't know much about running a village either,' I say, playing devil's advocate. 'He's just a kid.'

'But he's one of us. It's his job,' Mum insists doggedly. 'The whole of the Greenworld is based on witches ruling the covensteads, the villages. If one of them denies that basic element, then essentially they aren't of the Greenworld any more. It goes against the constitution.'

'And what about her?' Saba points her spoon at

Sadie. 'She's got the brand. Even though no one initiated her.' There's a sneer in her voice. 'But her mum killed Zia. What do we do with her?'

'She's got a name, Bersaba. Sadie will train with us.'

Merryn looks around at us. 'We can't have the daughter of a witch killer among us. People won't like it,' she says, quiet but firm. 'I don't like it.' She fixes Sadie with a hard stare.

Rhiannon takes her hand. 'I agree. It doesn't feel right,' she says.

I wonder why Rhiannon is here, at a meeting of the Hands. Is Mum training her too?

Saba raises her eyebrows, then says, 'I agree too. She's not one of us. She plotted against us with Roach. She conspired to bring the Greenworld down. Anyway, how do we know that's really a witch-brand? She could have done it herself.' Her amber eyes narrow at Sadie. I'm not sure what I feel for Sadie either but, like it or not, I'm her protector.

'I am a witch. I've always had abilities. That's why I was attracted to Danny, and I wanted to be around Zia. I wanted her to teach me, but she always said no. So I made it up, found it out myself, taught myself what I could, and when I got the brand I knew. It's real. I saw the Goddess. She spoke to me.' Sadie speaks to her knees. Her destiny has brought her here but she's as uncomfortable with it as we are.

Saba snorts, but I know that she knows Sadie's telling the truth. She's enough of a witch to know

411

another, to know that Sadie might be untutored but, like Danny, she's a natural.

'Really. What did she say, then?'

'She told me I had great work to do. That I needed to train here, and that I had a divine purpose. She sang me a song.'

'Oh, how lovely. A song.'

Saba gets up to go in apparent disgust, but Mum grabs her wrist.

'Sit back down, Bersaba. This is happening whether you like it or not. I'm going to train Sadie. I have to.'

She smiles over at Sadie. A difficult, halting smile, but a smile nonetheless. She's made her decision.

'Don't take any notice, dear. Can you remember the song?'

Sadie wrinkles her forehead, remembering.

Three to bind, to open, to see,
The power in them as within thee,
From life to death and death to life,
You bring the moon, and she, the knife,
He brings the sun and the song, the key –
The power in them as within thee.

She sings it in a low dirge, like we do in ritual. The words flow through the darkening kitchen and the candlelight flutters as if in response, the song meandering into the corners, enveloping us. I feel as if it has started something running inside my brain, unlocked a box, a dynamism, a mechanism wound and set on the floor to dance. I know Sadie is telling the truth. We all do. Not because of a simple rhyme – anyone could make that up. But because of the genuine truth of the rhyme, of the message in it that we all intuit. That somehow the three branded ones have a task together. Sadie, Danny and me.

'Big deal. So she heard a song. Goddess be praised.' We can all hear the bitterness in Saba's voice – bitter that she hasn't got the brand. That the Goddess has never connected with her in that way. That she hasn't been chosen. Maybe for the first time I realize that Saba is jealous of me for being branded, just as much as I have always been jealous of her – of her looks, of Tom, of the way that everyone noticed her and never me. 'You can't just make this decision on your own, Mum. We don't want her here.'

Saba takes a sharp knife from the pot of cutlery in the middle of the table and stabs it into the table in front of Sadie, who jumps.

'And none of us will ever know if she's going to gut us in our beds at night. Like mother, like daughter. We've got enough to deal with, Mum – the refugees, Gidleigh rejecting witch power. The people are on a knife edge.' She smiles caustically at Sadie, who is staring at her plate and obviously wishing to be anywhere but at this table right now. 'Excuse the pun, *love*.' Her words are dripping with sarcasm.

And I used to be the bitch, I think. It's like Saba and me have turned into each other.

'It wasn't my fault,' Sadie says to her plate. Then she looks at me. 'Melz. You know I didn't have anything to do with it, don't you?'

'I know,' I say quietly and take her hand.

Sadie then appeals to Mum. 'Lowenna. You know, don't you? I would never have hurt her. You have to know that. She was my mentor. I owe her everything.'

Mum looks over Sadie's shoulder rather than meet her eye; either seeing something spiritually or just not wanting to look at her directly. 'Zia was my best friend. We grew up together. She created the Greenworld with me, with all of us. If I thought you were involved in her death? No. We wouldn't be having this conversation. You wouldn't be in my house,' she says, but she's looking away from all of us as she says it.

Saba stands up. 'I'm not staying here if you train her. I'll go to the Archive with Tressa. The covensteads aren't going to like it, Mum. You know that. If you train Sadie you're going to have a mutiny on your hands.' Saba's hands are on her hips, and I know what's at the root of her anger. It isn't Zia. It's the idea that she's been usurped by Sadie, replaced. Sadie has the brand and she doesn't. At least with me she could always fool herself that Mum still loved her more, like everyone did, because she was prettier, easier, more popular. 'You don't need a mutiny now. Believe me.'

Mum stands up, countering Saba's stare. 'Don't threaten me, Bersaba,' she warns. Merryn, Rhiannon and Beryan look uncomfortable.

'I mean it,' Saba says. 'I'll go.'

'Go, then. I've told you: Sadie's staying. If you want to break up the Hands, it's on your head. But remember that you're sworn to us. You were initiated. I have your measure, just like I have everyone's,' Mum says. Because she's not just our mum. She's our high priestess, the head witch. Saba and I are her daughters but also her witches.

'Cut it, then.' Saba rummages in a drawer for scissors. 'Burn it. Whatever you have to do. I won't stay here if she stays.'

'You don't know what you're saying.' Mum watches her as she pushes ladles and forks aside, looking for the long-handled silver scissors we use to cut herbs in the moonlight.

'I know I don't want to stay under this roof if she's here.' She finds the scissors and pulls them out. 'Cut me off, then. Do what you have to do.' She stands there, the scissors held out with the blades facing Mum.

'Don't make me choose between you, Saba,' Mum warns. Her daughter and a branded witch. Blood or utopia. Family or the Greenworld.

Saba says nothing but holds the scissors out.

'I won't let you go,' Mum says. 'You can't make me. I'm not going to cut your measure up so you may as well stop the performance.'

I watch, knowing my sister, my twin, knowing what she'll do. In this way we are alike. We both follow through with our threats.

Saba looks Mum in the eye for a long moment, and

then walks past her, up the stairs, holding the scissors. I know what she's going to do; Mum watches her go until she hears Saba's footsteps creak on the floorboards in her bedroom.

Too late Mum runs after her.

I see Saba in my mind, opening the wooden box that contains all the lengths of wool from all our initiations, the wool that measures our height when we become witches, which represents us, our bodies and minds, and is kept by the high priestess as a kind of security, a token of commitment to the work.

I run upstairs behind Mum and hear Merryn and Beryan follow me, their breath catching in their throats.

I follow Mum's broad back into her room, but Saba is quick. I look at the floor by her feet, the scissors still in her hand. I don't understand it at first, because there's not one strand of wool but a few, braided together, but now cut and ripped apart.

'What have you done, Sab?' I kneel down and pick up the matted strands. Hair was woven through the plait; I can see that it was stained, too. I know that dark red. Blood. Mum's probably, binding the coven together.

So not only did she keep our measures – standard practice for the high priestess of a coven – she bound them together. Bound us together as a cohesive unit. I count the threads carefully. Six, including Danny. And hairs from all of us, to amplify the bond. Keep us together.

But now the bond has been ripped apart. And I feel it. The coven is unravelling.

'Go!' Mum roars, and points ferociously at Saba. Without thinking about it, she's adopted the Morrigan cursing stance: left hand pointing, right foot raised, left eye closed. 'Leave. You are no longer welcome here. I curse you in the name of Brighid, the Morrigan and Lugh; may their righteous fire cleanse you of your wrongdoing. May you regret this moment forever, and repeat the wounding of this coven in your heart every day for the rest of your life. May your magic fall foul and your spirit be blighted, Bersaba Hawthorne. You are a child of mine no longer, and a witch no longer too. BE GONE!!!!!' she screams at Saba, and the full force of the curse shudders from out of her body and envelops Saba in an almost visible cloud of sound, of resonance. I feel it, and I know Merryn and Beryan do because I hear them gasp.

Saba storms out and Mum sinks to the floor, scrabbling around for all the pieces of wool and hair and flaking blood she can find. But it's too late. They can never be repaired.

I kneel down and take her hands in mine. She pulls her hands away and snatches up the frayed pieces.

Beryan kneels beside me and takes Mum's hands in hers. 'Lowenna. Listen. Leave it. You can't repair it now. It's gone.'

Mum looks up into her eyes. 'But it's everything. The Greenworld is run by witches. I'm the head of the covensteads. My coven can't fall apart. What will that mean for everyone else? My own daughter deserting us, destroying us from the inside out . . .'

'You cursed her. Did you mean to do that?' I ask.

'No. No, it . . . just came. I can't believe she'd do that, that she'd . . . ruin such a holy thing. She knows what it means, the measure . . .'

'Go after her, then. Take it back while you still can.' I try to pull her up but she refuses, instead sitting heavily on the wood floor, despair making her more solid. I don't like Saba much sometimes but she's still my sister.

'It's too late. I can't change her, Demelza. You know that. She won't tolerate Sadie being here and I have to train her. I just know I have to.'

'I know,' I say. But we need all the witches we can get, because there's an emerging new Greenworld out there; the old rule is wavering. Gidleigh wants to rule itself, and it won't be the only village to do so. The people don't like refugees coming in. And I've heard the whispers. That we won the battle with the gangs, but only just. The Greenworld is changing, and not for the good.

Mum looks at me and for the first time I see real fear in her face. 'Oh, Demelza. What have I done?' she cries.

'You've made your choice,' I say, and I feel Sadie's hand slip into mine. I meet her startling blue eyes with mine and feel her power radiating through me, and mine in her. The end of everything is the beginning too. 'Now you have to live with it.'

Epilogue

Excerpt from Demelza Hawthorne's Greenworld Journal

Date – Lughnasadh, 1 August 2047
Moon phase – last quarter, waning in Sagittarius
Menstruation cycle – menstruating
Sun phase – Leo
Card drawn – The Eight of Cups
Dreams – I'm sitting on the boulder-filled small beach under Tintagel Head, watching the sea in my hand-mirror like Mum taught us when we were little. *Watch the water reflected for long enough, girls, and you'll see the lines between land, sea and sky merge, and the sea spirits dance at the edge of the glass.*

As I watch, knowing I'm dreaming, the undines and the sirens reach out their cold fingers for my heart. *Join us, priestess. Merge with us in the deep; forget the world. Forget everything but our song*, they call, and their song is full of the sweet disintegration of death, just like being inside the portal. I sense the unquiet spirits of Skye and Bali here, drifting and lost among the caves and the rocks. I close my eyes and see them holding their drowned arms out to me. *We are still linked, Demelza. The curse is still alive. It has broken your heart and is destroying your home. We linger by the sea, waiting for you,* they whisper. *The curse only dies with you.*

~~Chosen tenet~~

~~Reflection on the chosen tenet~~

Sources

I have imagined Bran's dwelling to be in the ex-Victorian bathhouse that contains the White Spring in Glastonbury, which is one of two holy springs at the foot of the tor, with the Red Spring being in Chalice Well Gardens just a little way away. The real setting of the White Spring, though fabulously atmospheric and deeply mystical, is smaller than I have represented it here. More information about the White Spring can be found at *www.whitespring.org.uk* and for the wonderful Chalice Well at *www.chalicewell.org.uk*

There is a Grand Hotel in York but my version is purely fictional. The Twelve Apostles stone circle can be found on Burley Moor in Ilkley.

The chants for the Morrigan in Chapters seventeen and twenty-nine were written by Laura Daligan and I thank her for her permission to use them here.

The Greenworld tenet *For what we do for good or for ill, shall be returned to us threefold* is an existing concept within paganism, meaning that our own behaviour and actions will be reflected back to us from others in this life.

Melz's sea-mirror meditation is taken from Levannah Morgan's wonderful book of traditional West Country magic methods *A Witch's Mirror: The Art of Making Magic* (Capall Bann Publishing, 2013).

The reference to the Fire of Azrael in chapter twenty-three comes from Dion Fortune's *The Sea Priestess* (Star Books, 1976).

Omar sings the chorus from the traditional Cornish folk song 'The White Rose'.

Chapter headings in *Red Witch* follow the pattern of those in *Crow Moon* in that they include a number of references from Greenworld texts, but also from a wider range of others, including the poetry of (in the eyes of the Greenworld) proto-eco-pagans W. B. Yeats, Lord Byron, Algernon Swinburne and John Donne, as well as excerpts from Redworld public records and a selection of classic Celtic mythic texts, such as the *Saltair na Rann* and *The Táin* wherein the Greenworld derives its own historical context and cultural currency.

Acknowledgements

Big thank-yous as ever go to my family and friends for their support, love, encouragement and babysitting.

Thank you to my wonderful team at Quercus – Rachel Faulkner, Niamh Mulvey, Roisin Heycock, Jennie Roman and Lauren Woosey – for all their hard work and inspiration, and to my continuingly wonderful and unflaggingly energetic agent Ben Illis.

Thanks to Laura Daligan, the original Red Witch, for inspiration, adventuring and magic; to the most excellent Lucy Powrie, for #ukyachats and her vocal love for *Crow Moon*; to my writing buddies Katherine Woodfine and Katie Webber for motivation; and to Team BIA for all your support and being an awesome gang (especially in the event of a future zombie apocalypse). Much love too goes to the UKYA community of writers, readers, bloggers and librarians that provided so much support for *Crow Moon*.

A big '*Ey up, lass*' goes to gorgeous Liz Flanagan for the Yorkshire accent advice for Bran.

Alex Cherry provided the artwork for the *Red Witch* cover – alexcherry.com

Thanks to Kate Large at Pagan Dawn, Cherry Collard, Lu Hersey, Amanda Harris, Waterstones Truro, Tereze at Tales on Moon Lane, Katie and Carolyn at Storytellers, Inc., and Surrey Libraries for being awesome and helping me publicize the Greenworld, and to everyone who was nice about *Crow Moon*. I hope you like *Red Witch* as much.

Like *Crow Moon*, I couldn't have written *Red Witch* without having been raised by an awesome, spiritual and incredibly hard-working single mum, who never let poverty stand in the way of encouraging me to read. She knew that access to books at home (and at the library, where we went every week) is the most important factor in improving your child's life chances, irrespective of income.

Mum always hated being quoted stats about single parents raising low-achieving kids and I like to think she's happy that we've proved hater-of-single-mums-and-the-poor-in-general Mrs Thatcher (and all of her ilk) wrong.

Can Sadie, Danny and Melz
make the Redworld see
that magic is real?

Or is love the only magic that matters?

Don't miss the thrilling conclusion to the

CROW **MOON**

trilogy

Coming March 2017